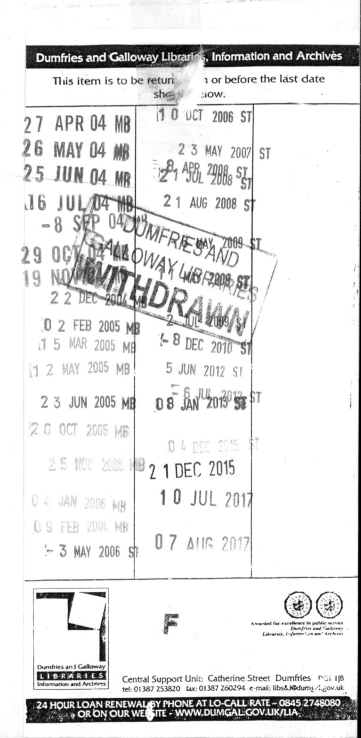

Domino's Effect

DOMINO'S EFFECT

Paul Heiney

Hodder & Stoughton

First published in Great Britain in 1998
by Hodder and Stoughton
A division of Hodder Headline PLC

A CIP catalogue record for this title
is available from the British Library.

ISBN 0 340 69547 1

Typeset by Hewer Text Ltd, Edinburgh
Printed and bound in Great Britain by
Clays Ltd, St Ives plc

Hodder and Stoughton
A division of Hodder Headline PLC
338 Euston Road
London NW1 3BH

To the memory of Prudence,
the kindest cow I ever knew

1

With one carefully aimed kick of a polished military boot, he smashed open the heavy oak door of The Peacock as if he were about to storm it, paratroop fashion. The door crashed back on to its black, wrought-iron hinges with a crack like a bolt of lightning, and the pub shook. Carrying with him a blast of chilly, damp March air, he strode into the public bar like the soldier he was, all senses on full alert, defences ready.

'Freeze!' he shouted in a parade-ground bellow. 'Nobody move!' This was pointless for he could see the pub was empty, except for the innocent landlord who had his broad backside to the door. It all added to the joke.

'Do nothing stupid,' he shouted to the portly host, trying hard to stifle a laugh. The landlord dropped the glass he was polishing and turned to stare at the soldier.

'My God,' he gasped. 'If it isn't Archie Biddell. My dear boy, how very good to see you. For one minute I thought my number was up. Nearly finished me off, you did. Stupid young bugger!' The fear on the landlord's face dissolved into a welcoming smile.

'Good t'see you, Eric,' said Archie, beaming as they embraced like brothers. 'Sorry to disturb the peace.'

'Nothing to disturb, not tonight. Very quiet. Well, till you arrived. But then, there was never much peace when Archie Biddell was around. Mind you, we're talking best part of ten years since you were a regular here.'

'And I've got no better since,' warned Archie.

Eric Thwaite pulled him an invigorating pint of Bullocks Best Bitter.

'Do I call you *sir*, now?' he asked. 'Since they made you captain?'

'Yes, you can,' said Archie. 'A bit of respect from you would be a novelty.'

Thwaite took the beer over to him, now perched on a stool in front of the bar.

'Not quite got rid of that uniform, then?' asked the landlord, spotting the military sweater and polished boots.

'I thought I'd give it one last outing. Then sling it.'

'Army days behind you then, are they? Home for good?' asked Thwaite.

'For good or for bad, I suppose I am.'

'You'll miss it.'

'I *know* I'll miss it. Let's just say this wasn't my first choice of career move, coming back to Woodham Ford and bloody farming,' said Archie.

'It's been the talk of the village, ever since word got round you were returning to your roots.'

'You think I've got roots here?'

'Biddells have their roots in Woodham Ford like the Royal Family has roots in Windsor, my boy. You know that as well as I do,' said the landlord. 'It may not suit you, but you're a Biddell.'

'And once a Biddell, always a bloody Biddell,' muttered Archie, downing the last half pint in a single draught, slamming the empty beer mug on the bar, and rubbing his hands to warm them.

'So what's changed in the village? How has Woodham Ford reshaped itself in the year 2001? They keep telling us it's the new millennium now. New hope, new future.'

'There's a new factory, bigger than the last. They've built a new housing estate up near the church, there's a new pig unit . . .' Eric Thwaite rambled on.

'I didn't mean that,' said Archie. 'I meant, how has *life* changed? Or is there still no life here *to* change?'

'I don't know what you're on about.'

'You wouldn't, Eric, unless you'd seen another life, and then you'd realise what you'd been missing in this one.'

'Most folk seem happy here.'

'And I can remember being content here, once,' said Archie. 'There was a time when I could have seen myself in Woodham Ford – happy, married, all that sort of thing.'

'There's no reason you still couldn't be.'

'Too many memories.' Archie changed the subject, quickly. 'I'm starving, haven't eaten for ages,' he said, shuddering as he felt a cold draught creep through the bar.

'There's always the house special, best for miles around, famed for it we are – spit-roast beef from the Biddell Estate! None better, m'lad,' boasted Thwaite. 'Look.' He pointed towards the wide, open fireplace in which logs were smouldering, embers glowing brightly where they were fanned by the draught. 'The baron of beef still cooks on the spit above the old oak fire, just as it always has. Years may pass but the beef still turns on the spit, every day bar Christmas day.' His voice tailed off, enthusiasm suddenly evaporating. As the words left his lips, he'd regretted them. 'I'm very sorry, lad,' he said, 'I should have remembered.'

Archie smiled at him.

'Forget it. History now. All the same, I'll skip the beef.' He tried to ease his old friend's embarrassment. 'But if you've got one of those mammoth ham and pickle sandwiches . . .?'

'The biggest and best ham and pickle for you, sir. Or "Captain" I should say.' And Eric Thwaite went ambling down the bar and into the kitchen. 'Hot soup? You look starved.'

Archie shook his head, then glanced around. It was ten years ago but so vivid was it in his memory, so lasting the pain, that it could have been only moments since he had last sat by that open fire and Emily had told him she did not have long to live. Archie, who loved her as he had loved no girl before or since, had held her hand as she tried to control her slurred and hesitant speech to break the news.

'The thoughts he'd had then had never left him. He still believed she was too young, too pretty, too perfect to die so young. At nineteen, she was owed a full life but was robbed of it by evil, poisoned proteins called prions; infectious little agents of mutation which burrowed deep into their victim's brain, made a sponge of it, robbed it of its sparkle and coherence, stole personality and replaced it with madness before, mercifully, death.

Seen through a powerful microscope, the doctors later explained to Archie, the malevolent prions looked like fine, silvery threads that might have been spun by a spider. Once Emily's brain had been caught in this pernicious web, there was no escape which medical science was able to provide, no drug which could penetrate the lethal mesh or stop its advance. The threads, unhindered, entwined themselves around her brain until it succumbed to their will. She had been the first of many victims, although at the time neither the true nature of the disease, nor its origins, was appreciated. At least she was spared the news headlines: *Mad Cow Killer Claims First Human Victim.*

The first day of her illness was all too deceptive; a headache, blurred vision in her left eye, a little uncertainty in her speech. The village doctor thought it the worst case of hay fever he had seen and prescribed pills to ease Emily's allergic reaction to the clouds of pollen which hung over Woodham Ford that hot and glorious summer. He might as well have prescribed ice cream. Within three months her memory had gone, her beloved Archie being unrecognisable to her – the hardest of her many demeaning symptoms he'd had to come to terms with.

And when she was gone, and some of his grief had been eclipsed by the thought that she was now at peace, only one unresolved hurt remained. He could not help but feel that the sympathy expressed by his father, Sir Thomas Biddell, held a certain shallowness. And this Archie found unforgivable. Emily had never been a popular choice of future wife for him, from his father's point of view. Like many landowning families, the older generations regarded themselves as aristocracy whose offspring must marry only one of their own kind. Emily, though pretty, educated and charming, did not quite measure up to Archie's father's requirements for a consort to the man who would eventually inherit the crown and lord it over the Biddell Estate. She was, after all, only a student teacher. He never said a word to suggest that these thoughts were running through his head, but Archie knew that his father's sympathy, though eloquently expressed, only thinly masked a real sense of relief.

Joining the army provided a good excuse for Archie to escape. It was a respectable career, 'appropriate' as his father had said, and, best of all, would take him away from home for long periods of time. He made routine visits at Christmas, for birthdays and to lay flowers on Emily's grave, breezed in and blew out again quickly, never staying long, just enough to feel he had done his duty as a son. For ten years he had been on the run, and now he cursed the inborn sense of duty which had forced him home for good to support his aged father.

His thoughts were broken by the slam of the kitchen door as Eric Thwaite emerged with a plate piled high with food.

'Lovely ham, it is. Extra pickle. And what's more, no charge.' He grinned broadly over the heaped plateful he was carrying.

'Then this *is* a first, Mr Thwaite,' said Archie, restored to good humour by the sight of the beaming landlord.

'And it will *not* be the first of many.'

Eric pulled Archie another pint.

'They say your father will be glad to see you back. He's getting on, to be running a big business. It's a job for a young man.'

'But is it a job for *this* young man?'

'You must think it is or you wouldn't be throwing in a good army career to come back here.'

'Not so good, these days. You can go through a whole career in the army and never see active service,' Archie pointed out.

'You won't get through a day on the Biddell Estate without major battles, I can tell you,' said Eric. 'People come in here and tell me things, and what they tell me is that that farm runs more like a factory than anything else. It's not like it was. Things have changed.'

'Ah,' said Archie, 'so they have changed after all?'

'I suppose they have,' the landlord replied, 'and it's not up to me to spoil your homecoming but I'd not say they'd changed for the better. For a start, beef's not what it was . . .'. He opened his mouth to apologise again for raising the subject, but Archie stopped him.

'Don't. It's all a long time ago. Eyes front, like a trooper. Forward-looking now.'

'How is your dad?' asked Eric, changing the subject. 'Haven't seen him in a while.'

'Haven't been up the house myself yet.'

'It's nearly nine o'clock,' said Eric, shocked.

'I know. But once I close the front door of the Manor behind me, there's no going back, is there? And speaking as an old soldier, I don't like cutting off my lines of retreat.'

'Then don't go.'

'No choice,' said Archie, finishing the last of his beer. 'It's called duty. They talk about that a lot in the army. It's like a nasty disease, and once it gets hold of you, it never lets go.' He bit deep into the sandwich

The barmaid appeared. Unruly red hair tumbling across her shoulders, black skirt a few inches too tight – and enticingly short, thought Archie as he saw her bend to put more cans of Coke in the cooler.

'If it gets any glummer in here we can think of letting it out for funerals,' she remarked.

'Watch your lip, Polly,' said Eric, sharply, anxious not to return to the subject of death. 'We've got a customer. They come here for a drink, not to hear your views on life.'

She straightened up and turned towards Archie. 'Oh, sorry, sir. Didn't see you there.'

'But I couldn't help but spot you,' he said, grinning. The girl before him was no beauty; her cheeks a little too round to be perfect, her frame a fraction too broad. But there was something about the pert look on her face, surrounded by its wild cascade of red hair, that told Archie this was a girl with spirit.

'Hey, now watch it, young Polly. This lad has a reputation. At least he did have. And I don't suppose the army knocked any of it out of him.'

'Oh,' she said, 'local lad then, are you?'

'Could say,' said Archie.

'This,' said Eric firmly, 'is Mr Archie Biddell. The prodigal son is back. So show a bit of respect.'

'I've had enough of false respect.'

'I did hear word you were coming back,' said Polly, 'to take over the farm.' She straightened her skirt as she faced him. 'There's been lots of rumours.'

'And I bet all of them were wrong.'

Polly looked him up and down. Tight, muscular body, kind smile.

'Not all of them.'

She started to dust the packets of peanuts and devise other pointless jobs so as to remain in the bar.

'I'd love to have a farm,' she said.

'Have ours,' joked Archie.

'No, seriously,' she said, 'I love animals, love being with them. I'd be great on a farm, really happy. They tell me they've got calves and everything up at the estate.'

'I dare say they – I mean we – have,' he said. 'Shall we find out?'

'When?'

'Now. Why not? If this is my life from now on I might as well face up to it.'

'But your father,' said Eric. 'If you leave it any later he'll be in bed by the time you get up to the Manor.'

'Yes, but there's always breakfast,' Archie replied in tones of resignation. 'I'll finish this sandwich first, and then we'll have a look at the livestock.'

'You'll need a coat, girl,' Eric intervened.

'At some stage,' continued Archie, 'I have to look a herd of cows in the eye again. It might as well be now.'

2

When the phone rings at 9 o'clock at night, even young vets know it is never good news. Michael Pember, tired after a day which had started unnecessarily early at six that morning with a desperate call from the distraught owner of a coughing cat, picked up the receiver, instantly recognised the voice on the other end, stifled a groan, then listened.

'The cow, is she still standing or has she gone down?' he asked. The reply made him groan out loud this time. He had been a qualified vet for only three years, his ears having hardly yet shaped themselves into a comfortable fit round his stethoscope. But he had already learned to recognise the customers who could be relied upon to stretch his newly acquired skills to the limit.

'I shouldn't be more than ten minutes. I'm sure we can do something,' he reassured the caller, trying to hide his own uncertainty. He grabbed a pair of green surgical overalls, his black leather bag of instruments, and headed for the door. After opening it and smelling the cold dampness of the night, he leaped back into the house and grabbed a heavy waxed jacket, struggled into it and slammed the door behind him. There was no one to tell that he was leaving.

He dug deep into pockets stuffed with scribbled notes and discarded syringe caps, searching for keys. Then he had a second thought. The humane killer? It was a hand-held gun which fired a captive bolt instead of a bullet. Held with precision against the skull of a sick animal, one shot could bring a swift end to a creature's suffering. That was why it was called 'humane', if killing ever can be so described. Michael Pember was new enough to veterinary practice still to believe that curing was more humane than killing, and prevention even better. He hated the humane killer; it was the last resort when everything else had failed. When *he* had failed. He opened the rear door of the car, lifted the locked wooden box in which the killer was stored and judged by its weight that it was in there. Finding the car key, which had somehow wrapped itself in an old surgical glove, he sped off towards the Biddell Estate.

It always seemed to work out that whenever a cow went sick at Biddell's, Michael was on duty. His senior partners seemed to know instinctively when trouble was in the offing and always managed to be otherwise engaged. 'It will broaden your experience,' they told him.

The humane killer rattled in the leather-bound box as the car hit a pothole.

On a summer's evening, rather than one which clung to the coat-tails of winter, this would have been a pleasant drive. For generations Biddells had owned land, farms and villages in this part of East Anglia; they could claim that the landscape was as much of their making as it was the Lord's. The village of Woodham Ford was certainly of the Biddells', and not divine, creation. The cottages with their diamond-paned windows, thatched roofs and white picket fencing surrounding tidy gardens were typical of those built by estate owners in the early nineteenth century to house their workers. Whereas in similar villages the cost of the upkeep had become too much for any landlord to bear, Sir Thomas Biddell lived up to his responsibilities, at no small expense to himself, and Woodham Ford still looked a picture – even if the gilt was beginning to flake a little from the frame.

Pember turned the corner, skirting the bare willow trees which stood guard round the village pond. It was beginning to drizzle and not being a tall chap – his pig-farming clients jokingly called him the runt of the Woodham Ford litter of vets – he had to stretch forward to reach the wiper switch. He then resumed his peering position over the top of the wheel.

A few yards further on The Peacock came into view: a village pub with enough brasses to decorate an army of cart-horses, stout black oak beams said to have come from sixteenth-century ships wrecked on the shore five miles away, a vast log fire which roared up the chimney with enough energy to reach the sky and melt the frost from the roof . . . All in all, enough old world charm to satisfy a coachload of American tourists. If anyone made artificial spit they would have mixed it with fake sawdust and spread it on the floor of this pub. It was all make-believe, of course. Twenty years ago, the Biddells had increased their workforce substantially and the expanding village needed a pub. So the Biddells had one built to match the rest of the place. Even the stout wooden beams were fake. It was a local joke.

But the food was for real; the pub was known the county wide for its Roast Beef Specials – vast joints of beef roasted on a wrought-iron spit over a log fire, dripping juices sizzling in a hot pan beneath and tourists salivating for a slice as the landlord carved at the joint. Biddell's beef, of course. The combination of rich, cereal-growing land and verdant grazing meadows made animal-fattening a highly profitable business. Biddell's put meat on animals like The Peacock's customers put on weight after eating it. This was real meat-eating country, where carnivores felt at home.

Michael slowed down a little, placed both hands higher on the steering wheel, and lifted himself off the seat to scan the cars parked outside. Yes, Polly was working that night; her rusty Ford was carefully tucked away so as not to spoil the crafted and crafty façade of this English country pub. How bloody stupid, how predictable, how like something out of one of those blasted James Herriot books for the local vet to fall for the barmaid, he thought. Not that she knew it. Michael was far too shy. His entire life since leaving school had been spent getting his qualifications, which left little time to practise the gentle art of picking up barmaids in pubs. But although she had given him not so much as a second glance, he thought that given the right opportunity they would really hit it off. He was not going to rush it, however. This was no mad infatuation; it was the real thing.

An observer might have said he had been so slow and guarded in his pursuit of this girl that he had made no discernible move at all. Which was indeed the truth. He had sat for hours in the corner by the log fire, hoping something might happen which would bring them together. But he never found the words that might form the basis of that first contact, and it was doubtful that she even noticed him other than as just another regular. His mind wandered briefly from the full-time task of keeping the rattling car on the road and he remembered how her long, red hair framed the most compassionate face he had ever seen . . .

Suddenly, out of the corner of his eye, he saw a dark shape and swerved wildly into the middle of the road.

'Daft old sod,' he spat, glancing in his mirror to see the flickering front light of Arthur Friend's bicycle, wobbling but mercifully upright. Retired and living alone, Arthur pedalled his way down to The Peacock every night for a pint or two and a game of dominoes. And then, despite the advice of everyone who saw him attempt it, he wobbled his way back home in the darkness. It was a standing joke in the village how 'avoiding old Arthur' had become the local pastime. A rear light on the bike might have helped.

Looking once again in his mirror to satisfy himself that Arthur had still not used up all his nine lives, Michael took a quick glance at the cars parked outside The Peacock. There was a Jaguar which probably belonged to a weekender, a couple of cars he did not recognise, and a Land Rover, different from all the others, painted a dark military green. He looked hard in the mirror, saw the lights of the pub's car park begin to disappear and raised himself again from the driving seat just in time to take a final look at that dark green Land Rover. It seemed out of place.

'Must concentrate,' he said to himself as he swung through the galvanised iron gate of Home Farm. 'Must think hard about this cow.'

*   *   *

It is worth considering why it should be that young Michael Pember took so seriously any call to a sick cow, and why his more senior partners were happy to rid themselves of the responsibility.

Although it was now fifteen years since the first confirmed case of 'mad cow disease', the memory of the grief caused to farmers, stockmen, countrymen and vets was still vivid in all parts of the countryside, as deeply felt as any wounds left in a previous generation by a world war. It *had* been a war, really. But instead of men being sent to the front line, it was cows. Within the space of a few years, herds were decimated, farmers bankrupted, stockmen reduced to tears of despair; fine, disease-free cattle were put to the torch in an unselective and unnecessary mass-extermination programme. Another holocaust.

It was never proved beyond doubt what had caused mad cow disease, who started it, or more importantly how it ended; but the mad cow scare and the obliteration of it by incineration was seen by consumers as a satisfactory way of dealing with the threat, and that was what had mattered most to the government of the day. Michael was still at school when the mass burnings took place, his memories of them drawn from the television news which portrayed them as some kind of triumph.

From his earliest years, he had always been at ease in the company of animals; more comfortable with a cat than a cricket bat. And if any one thing finally pushed him in the direction of veterinary medicine, it was his youthful anger at the sight of the jaws of excavators loading rigid bovine corpses into incinerators. The naïve blamed the farmers; the farmers blamed the feed manufacturers for allowing infected material into the animal food chain; the feed dealers kept their heads down while battle raged about responsibility, compensation, blame, solution, consumer-confidence, political need. Michael watched the argument, screaming at the television screen: 'But what about the cows? The cows!'

His newly formed perceptions cut through the political fog that surrounded all these arguments and saw only the betrayal of the cow; this tender, giving creature which, by her willingness to

13

succumb to domestication had contributed greatly to civilisation by providing food, pulling carts, drawing ploughs. Such was the universal respect for her once that she had been called 'the foster mother of the Human race'. But what happened to the cow when the milk of human kindness ran out? They consigned her to the flames – Michael Pember watched it all on the television.

While he was at home fuelling his anger, doing his homework, getting his GCSEs, Arthur Friend, head stockman of the Biddell Estate, was witnessing at first hand the slow destruction of his beloved herd of black and white Friesian cows. It is difficult to understand the bond between a stockman of the old school and his cows. 'Stockmen have changed,' Arthur complained to anyone who would listen. 'You can't learn cows from a computer screen. And all this mucking about with embryos . . . I don't think nothing of it. You can trust a bull to do the job right.'

He had a point. The production of meat and milk had, by his retirement in the mid-nineties, been transformed into a mechanised, industrialised process where cows were milked by remote control, rubber cups guided by computer to udders, with no touch of the stockman's hand. They didn't teach stockmen what Arthur would have called 'cow sense' either, by which he meant an instinctive understanding of a beast's needs.

But instinct was what Arthur Friend had. It was in his blood, and it was what set him above all the others who had managed the Biddell herd since his departure. With that, an unbroken line of four generations of family service was finally brought to an end. As Sir Thomas Biddell had joked at Arthur's retirement party, 'the Biddell herd has no Friends any longer'. Those words carried more truth in them than Sir Thomas had ever realised.

Modern agricultural science had made little impact on Arthur Friend. He had his own instinctive ways of curing cattle of all manner of diseases, helped by an old leather-bound book, kept in a drawer in the kitchen dresser; records of remedies, potions, mixtures, ointments, herbs, anything with which he might be able

14

to cure a sick cow. It was his first port of call in any crisis, the vets were the second.

Pember's senior partners in the veterinary practice also grew up in a different age. The crisis may only have been fifteen years ago, but it marked a watershed in attitudes to farm animals and the period before mad cow disease was already being looked back upon as some golden age of animal understanding and husbandry. Now the cow was under permanent suspicion, devalued as a food-provider in the public perception. There was no affection for it any more and so matters of farm animal welfare no longer inflamed public consciousness as once they had. And running just beneath the surface was a deeply held fear that at any time mad cow disease could return and once again start to steal entire herds away from farmers who had spent the intervening years rebuilding them. Most disturbing of all was the undeniable fact that no one knew quite why the disease had started, so no one could be certain why it had stopped. Self-congratulation on the efficiency of the culling process was one thing, certainty that it was a lasting solution another.

So vets who remembered those days of the early nineties preferred to distance themselves from cows; too many memories, too many fears. That was why Michael Pember was always sent out to sick cows, if there was any choice.

As for Arthur Friend, his life since the outbreak of the disease had been a slow decline and although he went through the motions of rebuilding the Biddell herd and achieved some success, his heart was never in it. He had said too many unnecessary goodbyes. To the government vets who supervised the cull, the cows were numbers; to Arthur they were names, habits, manners, colours, shapes, personalities. He said goodbye to every one, individually. These were his friends and each had to be bidden a proper farewell. The cows had no fear of him, no apprehension when he approached. Even when he raised his arm and slapped his hand firmly on each cow's neck, they did not flinch. He ran that trusted hand down the length of their body, feeling every muscle, till he got to their

15

rumps. Then he slapped the cow again, said, 'Good old girl,' and that was it. Within the hour they were dead.

Home Farm, to which Pember had been called, was no rural idyll. It was, in reality, a factory. It had the façade of a fine, traditional farm with its architecturally perfect nineteenth-century dairies, cow sheds, stables and barns. But this was just a front, as fake as a Disney theme park, as bogus as The Peacock. Immediately behind it was a maze of asbestos-clad buildings housing thousands of pigs which never saw the light of day. There was the constant hum of fans pumping fresh air in at one end and extracting unbelievably foul air at the other. Occasionally the automatic feeders burst into life and huge electric motors would drive conveyors that carried precise portions of feed to every animal. So powerful were these motors that the voltage for miles around dropped momentarily when they started. It was a standing joke in The Peacock that every time the lights flickered, someone would shout out, 'Feeding time, piggies!'

Pigs, over two thousand of them, lived their entire lives in dim light, confined in stalls to prevent them ever exercising their own wills. Sometimes, the pigmen switched the lights off entirely so that any pig with cannibal intent – which was common – would not get any destructive ideas. So frustrated by boredom did they become that sows gnawed at the ironwork for something to do. Teeth were broken, mouths became infected. Biddell's pigs, having lived a miserable life, then went to Biddell's bacon factory to be turned into dreary fodder for the supermarkets. Anything that could be injected, infused or otherwise pumped into the bacon was done so as to increase the profit margins even further. Even the tired old bones of the sows could expect no peace, for they were high-pressure hosed to remove every last trace of meat, fat and gristle and the resulting slurry dried till it was of a consistency that could be incorporated into *Biddell's Butcher's Choice Prime Sausages*. They even had the cheek to market the bacon as *Farmhouse Fresh – Biddell's Best Rashers*, and stamp on the packet a picture of the more acceptable façade of the Home Farm.

The turkeys lived in darkened sheds too, also designed to dissuade them from cannibalism. The desire to eat their fellow turkeys was the inevitable result of both boredom and overcrowding. Having also suffered the indignity of having their natural mating habits curbed by the insistence of consumers on birds with huge, meaty breasts – an agricultural pornography that brought with it the problem of the plump birds no longer being able to rise to the occasion – they suffered further as their spindly legs, undeveloped due to having too little room in which to exercise, crumpled beneath them as those customer-pleasing breasts grew heavier. Cannibalism must have seemed the only sport left for them to pursue.

The cows appeared to lead better lives, but that too was a sham. Admittedly they saw the green fields, but only long enough for machinery to remove the dung and slurry from the covered yards in which they spent most of their lives. Then, like pit ponies for whom a brief holiday in the sunshine was over, the cows were herded back into their covered quarters till their next fleeting release. Fed by machine, milked by machine, treated like machines. Repeated breakdowns were not tolerated, and sick cows were quickly scrapped. There was no room for them to pull over, take a rest, cool down or refuel on this long, productive road which they were expected to travel at maximum speed.

It was from this herd that the Biddells supplied their massive dairy and beef operation. From a herd of three hundred subjugated Friesian cows, they pumped the milk which they boxed and bottled and labelled with poetic images of contented cows smiling in the sun. None of the Biddell cows had in fact seen it for more than half an hour at a time.

The breeding policy was ruthless. Any hint that a cow's yield of milk was dropping, and it was slaughtered and sold to the pet food processors to be consigned to a speedy, ignominious death. Bullocks – young male beasts – were allowed only so much costly veterinary attention, and as soon as the expense outweighed the value of the animal they were hastily dispatched to Biddell's food-processing plant from where the *Ploughman's Choice Beef Pies* were produced. It was not cruel farming, just the modern way. It was how things were and vets who wanted to earn a living kept their mouths shut and made the best of a poor job.

Michael Pember parked alongside a low asbestos building, got out, and with a heave slid the barn door back. The smell of a hundred tightly confined cows poured out; a mixture of sharp urine, pungent droppings, sweet silage and warm bovine breath cascaded over Pember, welcoming him to their fetid world. This barn represented comparative luxury by the standards of the farm, for this was where the pregnant cows were kept while waiting to give birth, and calves born within the last twenty-four hours were allowed to remain briefly to suck from their mothers. The barn gave the cows a little more room in which to move, but not enough to satisfy their natural instincts to find themselves a quiet place, away from the main herd, in which to have their calf. What little freedom they did enjoy was swiftly curbed for at forty-eight hours old the calf was taken away to be fed by bottle, the cow clamped to the milking machine twice daily for seven days to remove the antibody-rich colostrum (which was then poured down the drain), before another nine-month milking season began for her. No rest, not even a kind word.

Even in the dimly lit shed, Michael Pember had little difficulty spotting the cow that was in need of his attention. She was the only one lying on the floor, exhausted, dripping in sweat, face radiating pain, eyes bulging and afraid. She moaned like the cold east wind creeping through the crack in the door.

'It's that *little* vet. Shall I get you a pair o' stepladders?' sneered the stockman, Tomlinson.

'Good evening, Tomlinson,' said Michael. 'Another of your fine examples of stockmanship?'

'I do what the guvn'r says, no more and no less. And it's *Mr* Tomlinson to bloody vets.'

Tomlinson would have been better off working as a mechanic for all the sympathy he had for animals. To him they were items of farm equipment which were either working or broken down. If they were in working order, every ounce of what they had to give was extracted from them. If they were in any way malfunctioning, they were kicked to teach them a lesson.

The cow looked half dead and as Michael went round to her rear end he could see that the breech presentation calf also had the unmistakable look of death about it. The cow moaned. Tomlinson ignored her and lit a cigarette. Michael considered his best approach and was thankful for having brought the humane killer.

'What have you tried?' he asked.

'Every bloody thing under the sun. I've had more ropes up that cow's arse than I would care to mention and done more pulling than a bus-load of horny rugby players on a night out. Best just shoot the bloody thing. There's a chance the knacker will be here by ten and I can be in that pub before closing time.'

'I'm going to have one more go,' insisted Michael, and started to remove his jacket.

'Shoot the bugger!' said Tomlinson.

Michael, angry with him and despairing at the state of the cow, opened his bag of instruments and took out a length of strong white rope with a loop in one end. He lubricated his hand liberally with jelly and forced it deep into the cow and past the neck of the calf to try and feel the obstruction.

'Same as before,' he sighed. 'Same bloody problem as last time, and the time before that.'

'You were saying?' asked Tomlinson in his unsympathetic way. Michael was now in some pain as the cervix of the cow contracted round his arm, trapping it against the neck of the calf.

'If you didn't use such massive bulls on these smaller cows, you wouldn't have this trouble. The calf's shoulders are so bloody broad . . .' he winced as the cow contracted again '. . . they'll never be born naturally.' Tomlinson was not there to hear. Michael heard the trickle of urine coming from behind a bale of straw.

19

The cow contracted again and he screwed up his face with pain, but as he withdrew his bloody hand in response to the tightening, the calf's shoulder slipped forward with it. That was a good sign. If they pulled now it might just work . . .

'Get yourself round here, Tomlinson,' he shouted. 'If you'd called me earlier it would have been better. I might have been able to push the calf back inside and get it into a better position.'

'I was, er, busy with the bullocks,' replied Tomlinson, in a half-hearted way, stifling a hiccup.

Michael slipped the white rope around the two protruding front legs of the calf, placed it above the knee so there was no danger of pulling its legs from its body, and then hauled.

Blood poured from the cow and for a moment it looked as though her entire internal organs were about to spew out; she groaned and rolled her huge eyes till there was nothing but the whites of them to be seen. Inch by inch, the calf emerged. Minute by minute the cow became weaker and less able to help. Suddenly, with a splutter and a splash of warm amniotic fluid on Michael's strained face, the calf slithered into the world. Not that it knew. It was dead.

Never for one minute had Polly taken Archie Biddell's invitation seriously. So when he had finished his sandwich and asked her if she was ready to see the calves, she was not only surprised but excited too. She loved animals and had once longed to be a veterinary nurse, or run a home for stray cats and homeless dogs. But jobs behind public bars were easier for village girls to come by.

'Smells of oil,' she said, climbing into Archie's Land Rover.

'Ammunition oil,' he replied.

'God, is it safe?' squealed Polly.

'Oil's very safe. It's the ammunition that's dangerous.'

'Clever dick,' she answered, cheekily. 'Oh, I'm very sorry, sir. I didn't mean to be rude.'

'You don't have to call me sir.'

''Course I do.' Polly looked shocked at his words.

'Why?' asked Archie, genuinely not understanding. 'I'm not in the pub now, not a customer.'

'But you're a Biddell. It's like being royalty round here. You must know that.'

'I suppose I've never thought about it. I was eighteen when I left. No one paid me any respect then.'

'Well they will now, you'll see. It'll be like being back in the army, although I don't suppose too many people will salute. Although I will, if you like?' And she grinned.

Archie started the engine, and was shocked to find he had to ask the way.

'Cows is up near the pig factory,' said Polly. 'It *must* be some time since you were here if you can't remember where your own cows are.'

'*Own* cows? I've never thought of them as mine before.'

Polly fastened her seat belt, stroked the leather seat with her finger. Archie noticed.

'Get to keep this, do you?' she said, looking around the Land Rover.

'They said I could have it for a short while, till I got sorted out. I don't formally leave the army for another five days.' He gave her a smile and said, 'You could say I'm on manoeuvres.'

Polly did not respond.

'Of course, it will have to go back the day I finally leave. Queen's property and all that. I'll miss it.'

'Miss what? Being one of the Queen's men, or the Land Rover?' asked Polly.

'Both.'

'But think what life will be like here, living in that grand house, with all them fields as far as the eye can see. And all yours!' she said. 'People dream of having somewhere like that.'

'Well, my dreams take me elsewhere,' he said, 'let's just put it that way.'

*   *   *

21

The Land Rover came to a halt outside the cow shed. Through the asbestos walls, Archie could hear a man's voice, raised and angry, possibly slurred. He asked Polly to wait in the Land Rover while he found out what was going on.

'Just shoot the old bitch! Calf's dead, and that bloody old cow will be good for nothing now. Shoot her and get on with it.'

Archie Biddell leaned against the heavy door and with a push of his shoulder slid it back. He took one step forward and although he may not have realised it at the time, by doing so finally accepted his destiny. With one stride forward he had muck on his boots, was a farmer reclaimed, a Biddell back to assume the crown. No matter where in the world the army had taken him in the last ten years, the lure of this estate had finally reached out, grasped him, and hugged him to its bosom.

The cows stopped chewing their cud and glanced in his direction. For a brief moment it was quiet, apart from the rasping breathing of the beasts. Archie walked towards the two men kneeling by the fallen cow. He looked down at a truly bloody sight. Steaming but lifeless, the calf was lying in a tangled heap in the straw, the semi-conscious cow resignedly bleeding to death beside it, rivers of her blood slowly engulfing Archie's army boots.

'What the bloody hell . . .'

'Who the fuck are you?' asked Tomlinson, brusquely.

Archie instinctively straightened, army style. 'Speak to me like that again and you'll get this boot so far up your arse, you'll be able to lick it clean. Now, *answer* my question!'

'I don't take no speaking to like that from any bugger,' said Tomlinson through his mean little mouth. 'I don't know who you are, but I want you out of my cowshed – now!' His eyes were fixed and wide, staring into Archie's like a mad dog's, daring its prey to blink first.

Archie did not bat an eyelid.

'*My* cowshed, actually. These are *my* cows. You, I imagine are *my* stockman. Though possibly for only a short while longer,' he said, making his meaning perfectly clear.

22

'You must be Mr Biddell,' said Tomlinson, subdued now. 'Heard you were coming back, but didn't know it was you. Sorry about the row,' he said, trying to retrieve the situation, 'but I'm afraid the old cow's had a bit o' trouble. 'Course, vet got here eventually, but half an hour earlier might have saved both of 'em.'

Michael Pember, who had been concentrating on the cow and only paying half attention to the interchange between Biddell and Tomlinson, swiftly removed his bloodied hand from the rear of the cow where he was trying to ascertain the extent of her injuries, and made straight for Tomlinson.

'You lying bastard! I was here within ten minutes of your phone call – which, I have to say, had the sound of a fruit machine in the background. I don't know of many cowsheds with fruit machines fitted. You were supping ale in some pub, getting stewed, while this calf was dying and this cow was killing herself trying to give birth to it. As a stockman you're a fucking disgrace!'

'Enough!' called Archie Biddell. 'Who are you?'

'Sorry, I'm the vet. The name's Michael Pember.'

'Some bloody vet,' sneered Tomlinson.

Michael heard the remark and his tight control on his temper gave way. He swung round to face Archie.

'I'm sorry, Mr Biddell, but it is my duty as a vet to warn you, sir, that if you pursue the farm's breeding policy further along these lines, you will only kill more cows. This is the third I have been to in a fortnight.'

'I wouldn't say I had a breeding policy yet,' said Archie, 'but clearly someone has.' He turned to Tomlinson. 'Who decides the breeding programme here? Because at first glance it would appear to be a disaster. And if what this vet is telling me is true, not only a disaster but a downright bloody disgrace.'

'*Your* father,' said Tomlinson, with a smug look on his face, 'said it were more profitable – the way forward and all that.' Archie turned to Michael who was trying to remove lumps of clotted cow's blood from his fingers with a bit of mucky rag.

'You don't agree?'

23

'I know nothing about profitability, only cows,' replied the vet. 'But in my professional judgement, this policy of breeding massive calves from smaller cows is wrong. Wicked.' He bent down again to check the animal's heartbeat with his stethoscope.

The barn door started to slide open.

'For God's sake, don't come in here, Polly!' Archie shouted, and strode across to the door to prevent her coming any closer to the distressing sight of the bleeding cow. He grasped her arm and ushered her back towards the Land Rover.

'Is that blood?' she squealed, turning her head quickly away.

'Just a little,' he lied, 'but she's in good hands.' He took Polly by the arm again and led her away.

'We'll talk again, Mr Pember,' he shouted. 'I want to hear more of what you have to say.' And unseen by Michael, he led Polly back to the Land Rover.

She fell into the passenger seat, tearful and trembling.

'Suddenly feel chilly,' she sobbed.

'I'm very sorry,' said Archie. 'I had no idea what was going on up here. It's not quite the contented scene I imagined.'

'But that cow,' sobbed Polly, 'did you see her? She was in dreadful pain, I could see it in her eyes. And that little scrap of a calf . . . was it dead? That was a calf, lying in the blood, wasn't it? Tell me, will it live?'

'At least one pair of hands in there seems to know what they're doing,' replied Archie, evasively.

Polly took a tissue from her pocket and blew her nose. 'All that blood, and that pitiful mooing from the cow . . . Oh my God, it was dreadful! I never want to see anything like that again.'

'Neither do I,' replied Archie, and started the Land Rover. He looked at her. 'I'm very sorry. The last thing I wanted to do was upset you.' She sniffed deeply, and stared blankly at the road ahead as he pulled away from the barn.

Back inside the barn, Michael Pember's thoughts had shifted briefly from the cow. Something nagged at him; he was certain he had heard the name 'Polly', even though his ears were plugged with the stethoscope at the time Archie had shouted it. Now he was curious. Which Polly might that be? There might be other Pollys. Let it not be *that* one. He threw the rest of his instruments into his bag and made for the door, heading for his car.

'I haven't finished yet,' he turned and called to Tomlinson.

'And I haven't finished with you,' muttered the stockman in reply.

Michael came into the open air, took a refreshing breath and opened the locked leather-bound box which housed the humane killer. The dark green Land Rover was speeding away, back towards the village. Archie Biddell was in the driver's seat, a red-headed girl next to him.

Michael slammed a cartridge into the gun, strode back into the barn and looked the sickly cow in the eye. Without missing a beat he placed the gun, as he had been taught, in the very centre of her forehead and fired. The deadly sound of the explosive shot echoed through the building but the cows did not panic – they had heard it all too often. The blast happened at the precise moment that the Land Rover had come to a halt at the bottom of the drive before turning on to the main road.

'Sounded like a shot,' said Polly, face tense, eyes fearful.

'Afraid so,' said Archie. 'And I thought I'd put shooting behind me.'

3

Supper was always at 9 in Toby Hopscotch's household, except at weekends when they were in the country and ate at 7; in London they kept metropolitan hours and dined later. It gave his wife, Tiggy, more time to make sure that little Georgie was fast asleep. Toby liked nothing to interrupt the serious business of eating. For him it was business, his livelihood depended on it. For you do not rise to management heights in the nationwide chain of Applewhite's Superstores without taking your food seriously.

Sadly for Tiggy his taking his work with due seriousness meant bringing it home with him. Every Wednesday night for supper they would test a product that was in development and give it marks on a score card which was sent back to Research. Every Monday they tested a cook-chill which had just been launched to check it was coming up to expectations. And on Friday they would test a ready-meal that had been on sale for at least a year to check standards were being maintained. On Tuesdays and Thursdays, Tiggy could cook what she liked but if it did not come from Applewhite's, Toby would quiz her: why, what was wrong, was it the packet that did not appeal, were the instructions not user-friendly? So, instead of making up a load of spurious guff to try and convince him that making beans on toast using Tesco's brand was not an insult to his manhood or his employer (difficult to distinguish between the two), she served up more trash from Applewhite's.

Toby's manhood . . . She had that to deal with as well. Although not quite thirty, he was convinced that middle age was about to overtake him and that the youth to which he so dearly clung could only be perpetuated by a careful reading of the columns of *Men's*

Health magazine. Tiggy always checked the cover lines of each issue so she could be one step ahead when it came to reassurance.

This month, for example, she'd noticed the cover emblazoned with 'The Bald Truth about Hair Loss'. That was sure to have him spending ten more minutes in front of the bathroom mirror; 'Mystery Symptoms Explained' would put ideas into his mind about symptoms he had never had. And then she saw 'Seduce Anyone! Ten Guaranteed Tactics!' This was no real worry to her for it took someone as self-centred as him all his time to share his precious body with his wife, let alone anyone else. Tiggy always thought that if Toby were to be discovered having an affair, it would be behind the cold-store with a bar-code reader, kissing it, cuddling it, and telling it he thought it was the most beautiful and mysterious thing in the world.

Being Wednesday, it was New Product night. That afternoon a dispatch rider had brought round a small package from the development laboratory pretending to be a kitchen, and the fax had spat out the cooking instructions fresh from the fertile mind of the package design department. Tiggy never understood why it took an entire design team of grown-ups to tell people that to cook food you must bung it in the oven. It was cottage pie. What could be *new* about cottage pie? Why did the world need yet another? Why the hell couldn't people make their own?

That afternoon she had tidied the already scrupulously clean kitchen to create the surgical atmosphere Toby deemed necessary when tasting. Even at home, he liked to be reminded of his beloved supermarket; if he'd had his way, he would have designed the entire house so that you could push a wire trolley round it whenever you needed something. Tiggy fully expected that one day she would find herself on the doorstep in a basket of items which had passed their sell-by-date. Whenever there was a little love and affection between them she thought it must be because they were on special offer that week.

In the seven years they had been married, she had seen her position gradually eroded from the 'most beautiful creature in the world' down through 'magnificent mother' to the total support system and emergency twenty-four-hour service required to ensure the smooth running of Toby Hopscotch's life and career. These days she did her best to make herself presentable, but was the first to admit that she did not have very promising material with which to start. She had black hair that was never quite straight enough to look tidy, and had to keep it long to cover the rather broad neck about which she was self-conscious. Since Georgie had been born, her clothes had moved well down the league table of things demanding her attention and so she usually wore a faded denim dress, dark tights and flat shoes. It had not always been this way; she had been a bright girl, something of a student activist, always the first to join a march for whatever cause. Now, although she would dearly love to take a cottage pie and, in protest, sling it through the boardroom window at Applewhite's, there was Georgie to think about. And Toby. And the pie.

'Mmm,' said Toby, sitting at the head of the table with a fork in one hand and a pencil in the other, looking like a schoolchild so slow at his sums he had been kept in at dinnertime.

'Mmm,' he moaned again, doing the irritating impression of a Bisto kid which he performed every time he sat down to a meal. 'They've got those scents just right. Can't you smell that old world cottage cooking smell in that packet?' And he thrust his nose into the carton from which Tiggy had just removed the two unprepossessing specimens. She longed to tell him that they stank of chemicals, artificiality, deception and second-rate food purveyed by second-rate people, but instead said, 'Yes, they do smell rather tasty,' and slammed the oven door shut. Then she set the timer to ensure they had no more than the stipulated fifteen minutes.

For some years now she had been trying to find a way of telling him that she thought manufactured food was lousy, and processed meat in particular. She was not, strictly speaking, a vegetarian and would have enjoyed meat if she could ever have eaten any that she honestly thought had led a decent life before being humanely killed and all that sort of thing. How she was going to put on a convincing show of delight when faced with the cooked cottage pie she did not know. The timer pinged.

'No!' cried Toby manically, grabbing her hand as it reached for the oven door. 'Don't open it till I've looked through the glass. I want to see if it says "eat me!"' Tiggy gave it a quick glance and thought she saw the words 'Chuck me up' written all over it. Reassured that Applewhite's cottage pie creations looked as enticing as whores to Foreign Legionnaires, Toby allowed her to bring them to the table. He picked up a knife and with a reverential movement that would have done justice to a concert cellist taking his bow to his instrument (perhaps, thought Tiggy, a pathologist raising a scalpel to a corpse), he slid it across the crust till reeking steam started to escape and the muddy, brown contents oozed on to the plate.

'I think it's a winner. Look!' he cried, stabbing his knife into the gravy. 'It looks like meat to me.'

'It *is* meat, isn't it?' asked Tiggy nervously, unable to get cat food out of her mind.

'Strictly speaking,' he replied cautiously, 'let's say there is *some* meat in there. Anyway, let's tuck in, darling. Did you do those frozen deep-fry courgette slices to go with this? My God, the trouble we've had with those, getting enough water to stay in them. Ah, well, here goes.' And he took the first mouthful.

She looked at him, watching the sensual way he closed his eyes and rolled every bite around his mouth so his tongue could play on it and his taste buds be teased. Yes, it was like sex to him. Here was a man so deeply in love with his work, so driven by lust for everything his supermarket produced, that mealtimes had become an orgy, which Tiggy could confirm as being little fun for a spectator.

'I think I heard Georgie,' she said before she could be urged to take a mouthful herself. 'He's had a bad day at school. I think I'll go and tell him a story. Do you mind, dear, if I take my supper upstairs?' He didn't, of course, being perfectly happy in the company of his cottage pie. This was an old trick, and a very useful one. There never was anything wrong with Georgie, but he provided her with the perfect excuse to slide upstairs with her plate and deposit the filth down the lavatory pan without having to insult her gut by asking it to deal with it first. To explain the flushing of the lavatory, she usually said she thought Georgie had caught a bit of a tummy bug. She had used that excuse so many times now that the kid would have been a walking intestinal disaster had it been true.

'What did you think, darling?' Toby shouted up the stairs a few minutes later.

'Bit more seasoning, I think,' said Tiggy. She usually said that. 'Have you thought of a hint of anchovy sauce? That usually spices up a pie,' she shouted back, making the words last as long as possible to cover the sound of the flush.

'Darling, you're brilliant! Anchovy sauce. I'll make a note of that.' And he scribbled it on the back of a mock-up of the packet which had been sent for his approval. 'Of course, real anchovies would be out of the frame, costs and all that. But I bet our people can come up with something pretty close. Like they did for that kipper-style pâté. Remember?'

Tiggy was back in the kitchen but did not reply. Instead, she thought back over the full horror of the last five years ever since Toby Hopscotch had risen sufficiently high on the management ladder to have some actual say over what went into the food. She had lived through the horror of the satay sauce development programme which had employed food scientists full-time for eight months trying to develop a satay that did not require any real, expensive, peanuts. Some of the early efforts would have made good carpet tile glue, but Tiggy had to eat them, quietly and supportively, every Wednesday night till The Team had got it right. After that they moved on to chicken stock cubes, the thought of which still made her stomach rebel. When they got on to bread, things became more interesting. Applewhite's sent teams of researchers into Romania. There, they had ripped off every traditional recipe they could find, brought them back to Swindon (food development HQ), and spent countless man-hours removing the natural goodness from them and overdosing them with productivity and profit. Tiggy remembered asking Toby if he thought perhaps the supermarket ought to make some kind of charitable contribution to those poor Romanians, as a gesture of thanks for these recipes. He hadn't understood the question.

'The weekend, darling,' she said, grateful that at last she could slide the plates into the dishwasher, 'any plans?' Meaning orders.

'Oh, I need to get away from that damned supermarket,' sighed Toby. Lies. 'A bit of country air. Let's get down to the cottage, shall we, darling?'

Bugger, thought Tiggy. Another lousy weekend in Woodham Ford.

On the opposite side of London, in every sense, lived Amanda Frater. No suburban preoccupations ever filtered through the elegant windows of her bijou Kensington flat; no children trod toffees into her Persian carpets, no sticky little fingers played with the expensive cosmetics which she kept in the fridge, no husband demanded feeding or left grubby towels on her marble bathroom floor. No reason for this young woman to rise each morning from the deep luxury of her bespoke mattress or unwrap herself from the linen sheets. With a father willing to fund her single-girl-about-town lifestyle, she did not have to work if she did not wish. It was an idle, self-indulgent life, lived only for the personal pleasure and satisfaction which, because of her disability, she believed the world owed her.

There were few mornings when Amanda Frater did not wake without some kind of pain. Although the occasional severity of it was not to be denied, it was no more than most determined people would be able to accommodate in a normal working life; but with the financial support of her father, she had chosen to allow her handicap to rule out any activity connected with earning a living.

On good days it would be a mere ache which ran up from her left ankle to just below her scarred knee. She could easily cope without the painkillers on all but the worst mornings.

On the mornings the pain was most severe, she knew she would have to walk with the aid of the stick which she always kept within reach. She hated that stick. There can never be anything stylish, she thought, about walking with a stick. It may add dignity to a dowager duchess, but to a young woman like Amanda it was yet another hateful reminder of her own shortcoming. It was a black cane, silver-topped, which had been her grandfather's: having failed to find anything with a designer label that could be remotely described as an aid to walking, she had settled for a classy antique.

Each morning, as the sun rose above the row of genteel townhouses on the other side of her tree-lined Kensington avenue, Amanda's blue eyes would open and her head be shaken from side to side, allowing her mane of honey-blonde hair to fall neatly into a carefully sculpted bob, as expensive hair cuts should. Then she would instinctively reach down the length of her disfigured left leg, ready to massage it back into life, glancing to see if the stick was in reach in case she needed it.

But this particular morning the pain did not come and she had no need of the stick. The strange thing was that when her mind was fully occupied, she was able to relegate the pain to no more than a minor inconvenience; if she had nothing else to think about, it became a preoccupation. With a sense of relief she threw back the covers and felt she could glide across the bedroom. Eager to greet this particular day, she leaped to her feet in one balletic movement and would have waltzed across the room towards the bathroom if there had been anyone to take her in their arms.

Then the pain hit her, as it always did sooner or later, spoiling every morning as it had for the last ten years. She reached for the cane but it slid from her grasp as the sleeve of her white nightdress caught it and it fell out of her reach. She dropped to her knees to relieve the weight on her leg, and shuffled over to where the stick had fallen. Then she got back on her feet and completed the hardest journey of the day.

But even through the pain, she could not forget that this day was different from most others. It held a purpose and contained a promise that a deeper, more destructive pain might at last be exorcised. For the pain that she felt was not just the physical manifestation of an old injury, but also the profound hurt that comes only from the loss of a lover. Something no painkiller invented can ever relieve.

In some discomfort, she made it to the kitchen where she brewed coffee using an expensive Italian machine, and pressed fresh oranges to make juice. By now, the pain was subsiding. She saw the newspaper lying on the doormat and wondered if it was worth the effort of picking it up. Perhaps the mail had been delivered and might be lying beneath it – the monthly cheque from her father was due. She ignored the newspaper, knowing she would find it difficult to concentrate. Instead she grasped the cane and moved slowly across to the walnut writing desk on which lay her letters. She picked up one which she had read many times in the five days since it arrived. It began, '*Dear Amanda . . .*' The first time she had read this she'd chuckled, for when she'd glanced at the signature she'd seen it was from someone who had never shown anything other than the deepest dislike for her. '*Long time no see,*' the letter continued. Amanda had no problems with that. It certainly had been a long time and she was perfectly happy for it to be even longer.

'*I am sure you know that it is now ten years since my best mate Freddie died.*' That was the phrase that caught her attention. '*I know how much he meant to you and I have an idea to ensure that the anniversary of his death does not go unmarked. Could be interesting, if you still believe in the cause and want to fight for it.*' There followed an invitation to a meeting, and a reminder to her of the need for total secrecy. It was signed, '*Your old mate, Conrad*'.

How *dare* he sign himself in such a chummy way? Conrad of all people!

She looked at the letter again, to check that this was the day he had invited her to meet him. The pain stabbed again at her leg. A warm shower usually helped.

She leaned her body against the cold tiles in the corner of the cubicle to keep the weight off the grumbling leg, avoiding the jet of water which needed to be unbearably hot if it was to soothe her pain. It took only a few moments of drenching in hot spray for it to lessen its grip, then she could lower the temperature and put her whole body under the water. But for the short time it was too hot for her to bear all over, she had to balance with her weak leg stretched out and hope she did not slip. It was a manoeuvre in which she had to overcome her deepest fear of falling.

The simple and accidental act of slipping to the ground was how her beloved Freddie had been taken from her. And although Conrad was not directly to blame, she could not rid her mind of the thought that he bore some guilt in the matter. Conrad, she believed, had killed her lover even if he had not himself delivered the fatal blow.

Freddie and Amanda had been students together at Oxford. She was reading philosophy, he a Latin scholar with ambitions to be an academic. They had met at a concert, Vivaldi, and had fallen into conversation when they both stood by the noticeboard in the foyer of the theatre, reading the same notice urging action against the excesses of factory farming.

'Animal welfare one of your things, is it?' he asked. The moment she had turned to answer, she'd known there was something special about this man, more than his looks; it was his attitude and obvious intelligence too. Distracted, she said, 'Yes, very much so,' never having given animal welfare a single thought before that moment. Suddenly she found herself persuaded, committed, and accepting Freddie's invitation to an Animal Welfare Society meeting – which was where the murky figure of Conrad had come into Freddie's life.

It was difficult to imagine two more contrasting types than smooth, cultured Freddie and rough-hewn Conrad who came to Society meetings by invitation. He was not a student, would never have got through the front door uninvited, but that only made him all the more attractive to the young and impressionable who saw glamour in his street wisdom and degenerate demeanour. He was a good counter-balance too, for there was more than sufficient intellectualising but not enough people willing to get their hands dirty, which was Conrad's speciality. A scruffy specimen, he spent his life ducking and diving to avoid the arm of the law which reached out and tried to grab him from every direction. He indulged in petty theft mostly: shoplifting, nicking stereos from cars, raiding cigarette machines. But Freddie, always able to find something of merit in even the most hopeless people, became increasingly fond of him and thought that involvement in animal rights would help to prevent Conrad from turning to a life of more serious crime.

Conrad disapproved deeply of Amanda's closeness to Freddie, seeing her as a rival for his brotherly affections. She kept Freddie from joining Conrad's more colourful protests, safely on the straight and narrow and far enough away from the temptation of extremism, which Conrad was always urging.

It was he who initiated a mass picket at Dover docks – one of his few ideas which did not directly involve breaking the law. Freddie wasn't keen at first, thought that the animal rights war would be won on an intellectual rather than confrontational front. Amanda had been against it too. But Conrad had insisted that the cause needed to grab the headlines, and that Freddie was the only one amongst them with the leadership to bring together an army of protesters. So, one cold February morning ten years ago, Freddie and Amanda found themselves on Dover docks, bellowing at lorries transporting blameless calves on gruelling journeys to casual slaughter at the far side of Europe. The Oxford Welfare Society had been one of the most vocal and active of the groups trying to disrupt an increasingly disreputable trade. Amanda had been so proud of the way Freddie could harness public opinion, get people on his side, go on to a platform and make a rousing speech while looking desperately gorgeous doing it. She was proud to be standing by him on that cold March morning, a light shower of snow falling, the docks a sheet of ice, the mounted police trying to control the crowd.

Freddie was at their head, like a general leading his army. His trailing college scarf became a banner behind which the crowd marched towards the police lines, insisting that the lorries would not pass. The Chief Inspector had informed him that he was within his rights to protest, but not to block the road. Freddie disagreed and said he would stand his ground. The officer signalled to the first lorry in the convoy to move forward, judging there was enough room between where Freddie was standing, restrained firmly by the Chief Inspector, and the steel framework of the ramp which led down into the ship. Amanda clearly remembered that lorry. It was splattered with salt from the gritted roads, the driver peering through the small area of frosty windscreen which his wipers had managed to clear. He could see ahead well enough, but not clearly to either side. The policeman's signal to move forward he took at face value.

As the lorry revved its engine, the booing of the increasingly hostile crowd grew louder and a handful of angry protesters broke through the police lines and ran towards the ramp down which the lorry was just starting to move. They sprinted down the nearside, putting themselves between the lorry and the iron girders of the dock. The driver caught sight of them in the corner of his eye and swerved to the right to avoid them. Then he saw Freddie and the policeman holding him. The driver braked, but the icy ramp allowed the wheels no purchase and forty-five tons of articulated lorry rolled steadily over the flailing body of Freddie who, in his efforts to get out of the way, had slipped on the ice as the policeman released his grip.

Amanda ran forward, screaming, 'Get help! I love you, darling Freddie. Help him, somebody!' She caught sight of Conrad. 'You bastard! You did this. You!' And in her rage failed to see that the rear half of the articulated truck was starting to jack-knife towards her. The crowd shrieked and fled from the path of the uncontrollable lorry but Amanda, overwhelmed by her need to be with Freddie, heard none of their warnings and pressed forward.

She had just reached him and was bending to support his broken body when the sharp edge of the fuel tank caught her left leg as the two halves of the lorry closed together. Skin broke, arteries punctured, muscles ripped, nerves were torn. 'She's lost the leg. Oh my God, she's lost the fucking leg,' she had heard Conrad shriek before the pain became too much and she lapsed into unconsciousness. Then the final indignity; the sudden braking and haphazard sliding of the lorry provoked terror amongst the calves in the truck which rocked violently as they skittered and stamped, inflicting even more damage on Amanda's trapped leg. Then, in panic, the animals urinated and a scalding, salty cascade fell through drainage holes in the side of the lorry and poured into Freddie and Amanda's open wounds. Only she groaned. He was dead.

Now, ten years on, here was a letter from the man who had killed her lover, inviting her to mark the anniversary of the bleakest day in her life. She scanned it again, trying to read between the few lines, struggling to guess what might be meant by '*if you are still committed to the cause*' and the '*need for total secrecy*'. Probably fantasy, she had thought at first, childish stuff, just Conrad's style. But something did not quite add up and made her curious. It was the juxtaposition of the name Conrad – which she associated with the loutish, scruffy character of her student days – and the quality of the paper on which the note was written, the clarity of the hand, and that address. She remembered nothing about Conrad that would lead her to expect that one day he would be writing letters on expensive paper from a decent Docklands address.

It was a cold March morning; frosty as it had been ten years before on Dover docks. She had to decide how to dress. Every outfit started with trousers to hide the scars on her leg. Not being certain whether to be city smart or casual, she struck a

38

balance between the two and wore tailored black trousers with a white, polo neck sweater. To keep out the cold, a canvas donkey jacket modelled on those worn by council workmen but bought in Bond Street. She wore flat shoes, finding balancing on heels too difficult. It was only when she walked, and her limp became obvious, that there was anything about her to suggest she was a less than completely desirable specimen of womanhood.

She reached for a leather briefcase from the table beside the door and winced as she felt another twinge in her leg. She had no intention of displaying any weakness before Conrad, so delved into the bag and popped two painkillers. She looked once again at the letter to check the address to which she was bidden. A strangely inappropriate place for such a meeting, she thought.

She took one final look in the mirror, smoothed her hair, and turned back towards the sitting room. On the marble fireplace, beneath the gilt-framed mirror, stood a photograph. It was of a young man, hair long and tousled, a heavy coat wrapped round him, a placard in one hand and a winsome smile on his boyish face. His long college scarf was blowing behind him in the wind. In the background was a crowd, behind them the blurred outline of ships – Dover docks. Amanda went across to the fireplace, lifted the photograph, stared at it for a moment and then, as she had done every morning for the last ten years, kissed it lightly. 'See you later, darling,' she whispered.

Tiggy Hopscotch had a secret, and if ever her husband were to find out it would be the end of her marriage – she was being unfaithful to him. Every morning, after suffering a grumpy breakfast during which Toby would earnestly scan the fine print on the cereal packet, looking for printing errors in the hope that he could arrive at Applewhite's corporate headquarters having spotted something the others hadn't, she would take little Georgie to school. But on Tuesdays free from the burdens of family life for just one blissful morning a week, she caught a bus from the north London suburb where they lived and headed into town. Leaving behind the tedious suburbs, if only for the morning, gave her more pleasure than anything else in life. Street after street of Victorian semi-detached houses, people crammed together like survivors in a lifeboat, paddling like hell in different directions in futile attempts to do better than the next-door neighbours. Double glazing and patios, barbecues and Barbie-doll wives. She hated it all.

The bus took her down to Camden, past Kings Cross and on through Bloomsbury until it arrived at the fringes of the City of London. Here she got off and followed the signs to Smithfield meat market. This great market was the last of the inner London markets where meat was still traded at dawn in a glass-roofed cavern not unlike a Victorian railway station. But the passengers here were animal carcasses travelling on one-way tickets from slaughter house to butcher's slab. As Tiggy walked briskly past the gates she always held her breath, certain that she could taste in the back of her mouth the taint of the debris which drained from the haulage lorries.

After Smithfield market, she turned left and went down a narrow alley. In the days when the handling of meat was a more labour-intensive business, this area was once littered with cafes – the haunts of meat porters and dealers. In white overalls stained with blood, they drank tea, ate bacon sandwiches, smoked, grumbled. Many cafes had closed, but it was to one of the survivors that Tiggy headed every Tuesday morning.

It was its reputation that brought her here. Once called the Express Cafe, when meat porters formed the majority of its customers, it had recently been renamed The Social Chapter, and had been written about in the *Guardian* as a 'meeting place for individual thinkers', although Tiggy was not sure what conclusion to draw from that. One thing it meant for sure was that there were no longer labourers to be seen slouched across the tables – meat porters were not much into cappuccino or croissants.

It was the words 'meeting' and 'individual thinkers' that had reached out from that newspaper, grabbed Tiggy's attention, and convinced her this place might provide all the things that were missing from her dreary life. She wanted to meet people and feed off the intellect of others; she craved the company of individuals, not corporate clones like her husband. The closest he ever got to anything individual were those mean, one-mouthful apple pies he'd helped to launch.

Although now fashionable, it was still a mucky cafe, floored with cracked tiles on which the foul boots of generations of porters had trodden heavily every morning. On the walls were reminders of the old days; posters showing the hundred parts of a pig, a sheep diagrammatically exploded to demonstrate its constituent joints of meat. These were hung not for the education of the porters who'd known their joints of meat as well as a surgeon did a torso, but to cover gaping cracks in the walls.

Although the decor had not changed, the clientele had. Paradoxically the cafe's very shabbiness and lack of correctness made it chic to some. The majority of the customers came from the nearby banks and finance houses, motivated by nothing other than the making of money. To be seen in such surroundings as provided by the grubby Social Chapter was a stylish joke at their own expense. These two diametrically opposed elements – new rich in the surroundings of the old poor – formed a reaction, and the resulting chemistry had put The Chapter firmly on the map.

It was here that Tiggy had her affair; not of the physical kind, but an affair of the mind. Toby would have divorced her if he'd found out she preferred this sort of shady establishment to the pink-tiled, surgically clean and atmospherically manipulated Applewhite's Coffee Shop.

Tiggy stood outside The Chapter for a moment and peered through the steamy windows. She saw the cafe was fairly quiet, then pushed against the peeling brown paint on the door. Since it was a cold morning, no one had bothered to open a ventilator to let the mingled vapours of steam, frying, cigarettes and other revitalising substances drift out into the street and be replaced by something fresher. Perhaps the occasional heady, incriminating

41

scents precluded the doors or windows from ever being opened. Not that Tiggy was after any of that.

'Hello, Tig,' mumbled stout and bedraggled Marge from behind the counter, wiping the cream-painted work top with a slightly grubby cloth. Marge was a museum piece, the only remnant of the old Smithfield days and much prized by the new clientele who treated her like a curiosity.

'Decaffeinated, please, Marge,' said Tiggy. 'Busy?'

'Busy?' shouted Marge. 'Gawd help me if there's a lot in at dinner time. That daft lad we had on the washing up got picked up again yesterday. Pilfering! Silly bugger. That's why there's none of them chocolate pains.' Pronounced as in 'pane of glass'.

'*Pain au chocolat*. It's French,' explained Tiggy.

'Sooner toasted teacake comes back into fashion, the happier I shall be.'

Marge grappled with the steam controls of the espresso machine like an uncertain engine driver. It had been put in specifically at the request of the boys from the Foreign Exchange. She still couldn't fathom it.

'It was all Camp coffee when I started here,' she grumbled.

Tiggy picked up the mug of coffee, turned it so she did not have to look at the crack down the side, and took it over to a wooden seat by the window. This was her favourite spot. From here she could see every table and, if she was lucky, on busy days anyone needing the knives and forks kept in an old wooden box in the corner had to squeeze past her, and perhaps say hello.

Tiggy looked round the room. She didn't, of course, approve of all the people she met here. For example, in the far corner beneath the menu, which was scribbled in chalk on the wall, a young girl with two impatient toddlers was alternately handing each grumpy child a sugar cube to keep them quiet. Unmarried, Tiggy assumed. She didn't approve of sugar lumps, not for toddlers. Nor did she approve of gym-slip mothers. But their uninhibited lifestyle she did crave. She had never in her life been drunk, out of work, high on drugs, low on money, in bed with a man to whom she wasn't engaged, pissed at a rock concert or down on her luck. Coming to The Social Chapter without her husband's knowledge or approval was the most unbuttoned thing she had ever done in her adult life.

'Teething, is he?' said Tiggy, looking at one of the filthy children.

'No,' grunted the woman in reply, ''e's bein' a little bugger. That's what 'e's bein'.'

Above the nagging wail of the child, Tiggy heard the front door of The Chapter open and turned to see if it was anyone she knew. It was not. It was a smart young woman dressed in a donkey jacket, black trousers, white polo neck, and carrying an expensive briefcase.

'Am I in the right place?' she asked vaguely, before closing the door behind her.

'Depends where you want,' replied Marge, indifferently.

'Well, I've been invited to a meeting, with two – er – friends. I know it sounds silly but they said it was here.'

'Two blokes?' asked Marge.

'I think so,' said the woman.

'Door's over there, love. Up to the top and turn left. They're there already.'

'Thanks.'

The woman made her way towards the door. Tiggy watched her, noticed her limp. She put down her cup and drifted towards Marge, trying to be casual.

'Meeting on, is there?' she asked.

'Yeah.'

'Anything interesting?'

'Ain't got a bleedin' clue, and don't give a bleedin' stuff.'

'Oh,' said Tiggy, shocked.

'The thing about The Chapter is, we don't ask no questions and that way we don't get told no lies,' explained Marge, leaning across the counter. 'As long as they pays for their tea and coffee and leaves the room clean 'n' tidy they can do what they bleedin' well like. No questions asked. As long as it's nothing mucky.'

'I understand,' Tiggy said in a hushed voice, now feeling part of the larger conspiracy.

Marge ripped open a slimy packet of bacon – *Farmhouse Fresh Biddell's Best Rashers* – and slammed it into the pan. Bacon sandwiches had become smart.

Amanda Frater walked towards the door, opened it, felt the ache in her leg worsen at the sight of the tall flight of bare, wooden stairs she would have to climb. She took a deep breath and wished she had brought the walking stick. She was not halfway up when the door at the top opened and a man appeared, dressed in a smart suit – blue with the faintest stripe, expensively cut – a perfect, flattering fit. His black shoes shone, his pale blue shirt showed off a healthy tan. He grinned as he flicked his long black hair across his brow.

'It still works then, that leg? Miracle of modern medicine, the way they stitched it back. Hi. Good to see you again.'

He came down the stairs towards her, hand outstretched ready to assist. As he reached out, she refused his offer.

'It's not you, Conrad? It can't be,' she said in disbelief.

'Sure is. Ten years is a long time. People change,' said the man.

'Not that much,' replied Amanda. 'Why the suit? Look at you!'

'I'm still your old mate Conrad, deep down. The wrapping might be different, but if you open up the parcel you won't find much changed.'

She was worried that might be the case.

'You didn't even come to the funeral. You never came to say goodbye to him,' she said, still furious after ten years.

'A mistake. I'm sorry,' he admitted.

'Not your biggest, though. Your worst blunder was to exist in the first place. And my biggest mistake was to come here today. I think I'll go now.' She started to turn and the twisting of her body caused her leg to throb viciously. Conrad extended his hand again.

'I want to say sorry. I need to hear you accept that apology,' he said.

'Fat bloody chance!' spat Amanda.

'If you'll come upstairs and listen to what I have to say, you might change your mind. Come and listen. Freddie would approve, believe me. He would want you at least to *listen*.'

He put out his hand again, and against her better judgement she accepted his help.

'There's someone I want you to meet,' he explained as they arrived at the top of the stairs. He was about to reach for the handle of the door when she stopped him.

'*You* can explain a few things first. What's with the suit, the look? All false, like the rest of you?'

'Wonderful place, the City of London,' explained Conrad, brushing his collar. 'Just like the Fulham market my old dad used to work. Sellin' bananas. No different from steel futures, equities, stocks, shares . . . It's all the same. Sell one thing, you can sell the lot. Once a barrow boy, always a barrow boy. City's no different. I've made a bob or two. Done well for myself. Not exactly Ferrari class, but getting there.'

'All legal and above board?'

'Well, there's a thin line,' replied Conrad, grinning, 'between what you might call breaking the law and doing a good deal. I prefer to think of the City as being full of minor criminals. The knack lies in keeping up with them.'

Amanda got her breath back. 'You should be good at that.' Conrad opened the door and she stepped inside. It was a seedy prospect of boards covered with a dreary lino the colour of brown sauce; the wood which remained uncovered had fallen victim to upset tea and spilt greasy meals. There was one small, uncurtained window left slightly ajar to allow the concentrated scents of Marge's cooking some escape, and a table in the middle of the room, pine-topped and grubby; an overflowing ashtray stood in the middle and three plastic bucket chairs has been set out ready. Conrad pulled one chair away from the table and invited her to sit down.

'This is where all the young bloods hang out, is it?' she said, sarcastically. He pushed the chair under her and she sighed with relief as the weight came off her leg. It was not usually as bad as this, she thought, reaching down and rubbing her knee.

'This is Ernest,' announced Conrad. She was startled, having thought they were alone.

'Charmed, I'm sure,' said Ernest, emerging from the shadows. He was taller and older than Conrad, his hair turning grey. His suit was even better cut.

'Please, don't get up, my dear girl,' he said, smiling in an avuncular way. 'Just relax. You look tired. Can I get you anything? Coffee? Something stronger?'

Ernest was a gentleman, distinguished, his manners perfect, thought Amanda. A proper gent, not a fake like Conrad.

He nodded towards the open window. 'Not what you'd call air-conditioned is it? Are you sure I can't get you something? A glass of mineral water perhaps? My handkerchief to mop your brow?'

As he wafted past her, she smelled expensive after-shave and compared it briefly with the laddish scent that Conrad exuded. There was an embarrassing pause while the two men took seats opposite her.

'I'll start,' said Conrad.

Ernest nodded without saying a word, and took a slim, gold pen from his pocket to make notes.

'It's ten years since . . .' started Conrad

'You think I haven't counted the days?' replied Amanda, aggressively.

'He was my mate too,' Conrad insisted. 'And a lot of what I believed then, I still believe now. All right?' He spoke more slowly. 'It's hell out there for those animals: on farms, on lorries, being

46

terrorised, having the shit scared out of them for most of their short, miserable lives.' Ernest raised an eyebrow at the language. 'In memory of Freddie, I want to do something, now that I've got the money.' He glanced across at his companion. 'Or should I say, *we've* got the money.' Ernest nodded.

'What money?' enquired Amanda. 'And what exactly do you want to do? Not another bloody dockside protest? I'm through with all that. Too old. It's for kids, public protest: waving banners, shouting abuse, spending a night in the nick and being proud of it. A kid's game. Not one you play in a smart suit.'

'I think I've invented a new game,' said Conrad, grinning. He turned to Ernest. 'Shall I tell her?'

The other man leaned across the table and gave her a solemn look. 'You must understand that everything we say from now on is highly confidential.' She nodded. Ernest's expression eased into a smile. 'Then I think Conrad can explain further.'

'There's an organisation I've been building up over the last few years called the CFFA – the Campaign for the Freedom of Farm Animals. Right? It's massive – world-wide support, all Internet-linked, activists in every part of Europe. It's really big, Amanda. The sort of set up Freddie would have killed for. He was the inspiration for it all. We organise propaganda, marches, literature . . . that sort of thing.'

'And I pay for it,' interrupted Ernest. 'Or I should say my client does. I am merely an agent for an extremely wealthy individual whose identity must be protected. I am here on his behalf. Personally, I think it's all a waste of time, but it's his money and there *is* lots of it.'

'And I'm spending it for him,' enthused Conrad.

'With my permission and under my control,' added Ernest.

'I want your help, Amanda,' Conrad continued. 'Not for my sake, but for Freddie's. We can achieve what he was only able to attempt. We've got the resources, the money. All the things he never had. I see it as a memorial to him, and I hope you'll see it the same way.'

She had said nothing for some time. Both men sat staring at her, waiting for a reply.

'I don't see what I can do,' she replied eventually. 'I've been out of it for years.'

'And what have you done in those intervening years?' said Conrad. 'Sat in the smart flat your daddy bought for you, pining for Freddie. What has that achieved? Not a lot. If you want to make a mark where Freddie was unable to make his, you'll join us. Here and now.'

'You have the most infernal bloody cheek!' she spat.

'I agree,' said Ernest, leaping to Amanda's defence. 'This must have all come as a great shock to you, my dear, and I hope you don't feel under any pressure. That is the last thing we want, isn't it?' He glanced towards Conrad. 'But things are getting a little urgent.'

'I've never heard of your Campaign for whatever you call it. And I've lived through your fantasies before, Conrad.'

He reached down into a bag and pulled out three glossy magazines, throwing them on the table.

'That's our newsletter. Smart, eh? Don't read it now, look at it later. Do you want me to get out my laptop and show you our Web page? Do you want a list of the direct hits we've made?'

'What kind of hits?'

'Let us just say strikes against the enemy,' Ernest interrupted before Conrad had time to describe them any other way.

'Look at me, Amanda,' he grabbed her by the wrist. 'This is not for you, or me, or whoever Ernest represents. It's for Freddie. It's his bleedin' memorial. And you can help us build it. Say no and we'll forget all about it. But if you say no, you'll walk away from here with nothing achieved to mark his time on this earth other than that bleedin' scar on your leg. Say yes and his death will *not* have been a waste of time. Remember what Freddie always used to do when we got into a bit of trouble? He quoted Henry David Thoreau.'

'I'm sorry?' interrupted Ernest raising one eyebrow.

'A campaigner against slavery,' replied Conrad, 'but a crusader first and foremost.'

Amanda remembered the words well, even though she had not heard them for a decade. She found herself mouthing them now.

'"If I repent anything it is likely to be my good behaviour."'

'Amanda,' pleaded Conrad, 'we *need* you.'

4

Ten years in the army had not allowed Archie many breakfasts at home and he was grateful for that small mercy. Now, a week and seven breakfasts after he'd first arrived back in Woodham Ford, he was forced to admit to himself that the oppressive atmosphere of mornings with his father was never going to improve. He feared this one might be the worst yet. As he came into the dining room, late, Sir Thomas looked up from behind the newspaper, alerted by the heavy clump of Archie's army boots on the oak staircase.

'No slippers?'

'Lost in action,' he replied, smiling.

Breakfast was always taken in the dark dining room of the twelve-bedroomed Manor, at the polished oak table. Although there was only Archie and his father (his mother having died more than five years ago), the old man insisted that standards were kept up, and so Mrs Wilson came in from the village every morning to go through the ritual of making the bacon and eggs, placing them on a domed silver server and setting them on the sideboard where they stood till the fat had congealed and the eggs turned rubbery. But Sir Thomas Biddell was satisfied to see that life went on as he felt it should be conducted. It was perhaps a sign of his insecurity that the ageing man had to surround himself with the trappings of minor aristocracy. Like so many landowning families, the Biddells had built their fortune over several generations and felt they deserved some kind of respect for it. The feudalism of centuries past still lingered in villages like Woodham Ford, lorded over by families like Biddells, where land still meant power.

Clearly, Archie decided, the morning ritual had not been varied since the day he'd left home. His father sat, as usual, with his back

51

to the elegant Georgian window which allowed enough light to fall across his copy of *The Times* to assist his failing sight. Archie always thought he used his eyes as if they were run by a battery which was about to go flat, and concentrated on the most important things first like the price of wheat. Breakfast always began with father's brief resumé of the corn market, the forward prices, the estimated North American yield, the price of Canadian milling wheat, European support prices. Wheat, and more wheat! Then Mrs Wilson would say that she'd heard the weather was going to turn out fine, irrespective of whether it was fine already, before she put the silver coffee pot by Sir Thomas's right hand so that he did not have to stretch to reach it.

Archie shook out the white, laundered napkin and placed it on his lap as he sat down. It was the first time starched linen had ever been in such close proximity to a woollen army sweater at the Biddell breakfast table.

'You'll have to get some ordinary clothes, you know,' said his father, icily. 'You can't play at soldiers now. Looks as though the whole house is at war, or something.'

Archie pushed back his sleeves.

'Archibald, we have something to discuss,' his father said, urgently. 'There's no point mincing words. I'm going to die one day, and probably in the not too distant future.'

'Mrs Wilson's bacon got to you, did it?' joked Archie, then wished he hadn't. There was still a coolness between the two of them, Archie having forgotten that he had promised to turn up for dinner on his first night home.

'Less funny stuff and bit of seriousness, eh?' continued the old man. 'I want to know what your plans are for the estate now you're home for good, eh?'

'At this stage, I'm not certain I could find my way to most of the estate, let alone make plans for it,' Archie replied.

His father was not impressed.

'But I suspect we've got it wrong with the dairy herd, or that's my initial impression,' continued Archie. 'Apparently they're dropping like flies. Those continental bulls leave too large a calf. We'll have no cows within the year if we go on like this. Or that's what I've been told.'

'By whom? Learned all this across the bar of The Peacock, did you? Anyway, what do you know about cows?' said Sir Thomas tartly. 'How can you possibly make a judgement on the basis of what you were told over a pint of beer. Unless, of course, you were lying in bed this morning thinking about it.' He looked at his watch and scowled.

'I've seen enough to know things aren't right, and I intend to put it top of the list of things to sort out.'

'Don't meddle,' said his father. 'There're cleverer people than you working out how to make a profit from our cows. Let them get on with it. Your job is to keep looking at the figures and make sure they're heading in the right direction. No need to meddle further. Quite frankly, I haven't seen a cow for years. No need.'

'I think there's every need,' insisted Archie.

'You'll learn,' replied his father.

'I saw a cow die a terrible death on my first night home,' he replied, irritated.

'When you should have been here for dinner,' his father grumbled.

'I learned more in a few minutes with that cow than I would have done sitting at any dinner table. If you want me to run this estate, then I'll not be responsible for the unnecessary deaths of any more animals.'

Sir Thomas flung the newspaper to the table.

'This family's fortunes are based on good solid farming practices carried out for the last three generations. Are you saying that in my time I have been somehow negligent, and in a couple of minutes in the cowshed you have discovered a better way to do it? Is that what you're telling me? A few minutes of observation is worth more than a lifetime's experience, eh? No, listen first, then act, my boy.'

'I listened to that cow and now I am going to act,' said Archie, flinging his napkin on to the table.

'And put something quieter on your feet!' shouted the old man, as his son clumped out of the room.

And now Archie must go to work. But where? And to do what? Although the last ten years had not been without discipline, none of his army experiences had prepared Archie for the real world of work, or the unreal world of running the Biddell estate. As he clumped around the house, feeling rather lost, Mrs Wilson reappeared, having cleared the breakfast things.

'We shall hear you coming a mile off, sir,' she said, looking grumpily at his heavy boots, and then at the scarred polish on the wooden floor. She was carrying the morning's mail and pointlessly started to fan it out on a small mahogany table in the hall. Archie first opened the hand-written envelopes, of which he noticed there was quite a pile.

'Is there always this much mail?' he asked.

'I expect they'll be replies, won't they?'

'To what?'

'Not my place to say, sir,' she said.

Archie opened the first. It was from someone of whom he had never heard, but who addressed him like a long-lost brother:

Dear Archie,
A great pleasure to welcome you back to the estate, and greatly look forward to seeing you at The Peacock next Saturday evening. It should be a great night.
Yours ever,
Peter Franklin

Archie looked at Mrs Wilson.

'Heard of a Peter Franklin?'

'Land agent, I do believe,' she replied.

Archie opened the next, and the next, and collected for himself a clutch of acceptances for a party to which he appeared to have invited every prime mover on the estate; accountants, agents, managers, feed merchants, contractors – all of whom Archie had no knowledge of whatsoever.

'What a prize collection of pains in the arse, Mrs Wilson,' he said. She blushed.

'If I may say, sir – although it's not my place, but I've worked for your father for so long now that I know his ways – he thought you'd want to get to know everyone on the estate, now you're home. And I'm sure he thought he was doing the right thing.'

'He seems to think that everything he does is the right thing,' Archie remarked.

'That's Sir Thomas for you,' she replied.

Archie grumpily threw on his corduroy jacket, opened the heavy oak door of the house, and strode down the mossy flagstones that led to the imposing wrought-iron gates. Once through these, his feet hit the gravel drive and not being able to rid himself of the habit, he marched across to Home Farm.

On sunny spring mornings like this one, the estate shimmered like a jewel. Although set in the flatter part of East Anglia, the land had a gentle roll to it so beautiful that Archie was always reminded of the contours of a woman's naked back. As the sun moved across the sky, the clouds shadowed different parts of the land, as though she had moved a little. Archie had once been told, when he was a boy, that from the highest part of the farm you could see all the way to the sea, but he never had. He did once smell salt in the air when the wind was in the south-east and brought the saline breeze with it. Now fields of corn, growing in the first warm sunshine of the year, filled the foreground, giving way to meadows of deep green where rivers kept the grass permanently bursting with vigour. Then, after the water meadows, came woods and forests, all the way to the horizon. Trees were beginning to show the slightest tinge of green heralding leaves. Whichever direction Archie turned, it was Biddell land as far as the eye could see. Men earned livings here, crops made profits. So perhaps he should not be so concerned over one dead cow. As he drew closer to the farm, he noticed, parked outside the cowshed, a car he thought belonged to Michael Pember.

It was a week since Archie had first slid back the door of the cowshed that stood at the heart of Home Farm, and now here he was again, sliding back the same door, being faced with an identical sight. Like a horror movie which had been made into a loop and was being played over and over again, he was confronted with the same sickening spectacle of a dead cow sprawled across a bloody mound of straw, her black and white calf lying in a pool of afterbirth, steaming but lifeless.

'Tomlinson!' shouted Archie, suddenly brimming with anger and disbelief. 'Why another?'

The grubby stockman staggered to his feet as quickly as his hangover would allow and mumbled something about bad luck.

'Bad luck or bad management?' replied Archie. 'If you cannot successfully calve these cows, I shall find someone who can. Do you understand?' The Sandhurst influence was beginning to surface. 'And clean your bloody self up a bit, and don't walk around this farm looking like a tramp. Is that *clear*?'

'Yes, *sir*,' said Tomlinson, giving a little too much emphasis to the 'sir'.

Archie was about to leave when he spotted Michael Pember sitting in a dark corner of the shed, slowly wiping blood from his arms before replacing his shirt.

'We seem to be having a run of bad luck lately,' said Archie, feeling that some excuse had to be made for the repeated fatalities. 'That's two cows we've lost in a week.'

'You could call it bad luck, Mr Biddell,' said Michael Pember, tired and a little less careful with his words than usual.

'And how would you describe it, Mr Pember?' he enquired.

'Yes, bad luck it is,' said the young vet, swallowing his words.

Michael stuffed the final tucks of his shirt into his blood-stained trousers and gathered together his instruments, checking the safety catch on the humane killer before replacing it in its heavy wooden box. Archie stood over him, watching silently.

Tired and dispirited, Michael had no intention of letting cows occupy his mind again unless it was absolutely essential. So, although he could have given Archie Biddell a long and passionate speech about how they deserved respect and should not be treated as milk 'n' meat machines, he had no desire to do so now. Anyway it was not his style. He had his own thoughts and kept them to himself. It was simpler that way. He tried also to keep from his mind the question he really wanted to ask Archie Biddell, about Polly.

'Is there any way out of this mess?' enquired Archie, rather more gently, having realised that Michael was in a delicate state.

His mind was elsewhere, far from farm animals. You could just tell me what's going on between you and Polly – that's all I want to know, he thought. But the idea had no sooner crossed his mind than he realised where he was, and why he was there, and so said nothing.

'Let's have coffee,' said Archie, offering his hand. 'The Peacock will be open, we'll grab one there. And since I'm afraid we're likely to see plenty of each other, call me Archie.'

The vet was taken aback. 'Fine, fine,' he spluttered, 'Michael's the name. Coffee would be fine.'

There was now so little profit in selling beer across the bar of a rural pub that The Peacock was more of a restaurant than an ale house. Polly liked it that way. She did not wish to spend every night developing barmaid's biceps by hand-pulling pints of frothy brown ale from deep in the pub's cellars. She had seen good-looking girls go that way before: it starts off as muscle, then it turns to fat, and by the time you've had a drink or two with the locals you're fifteen stone and lumbering round like a jelly mountain, she had warned herself. That was why she always kept herself presentable. Always skirts and never jeans, jewellery if she could manage it. Perfume too, bought on the advice of women's magazines and possibly used a little too liberally. This potent aroma that surrounded her, coupled with the long red hair that fell over her generous bust, made men think she was an easy catch. Nothing could be further from the truth.

'Bloody coffee bags,' she cursed, pulling at a packet of Kenco with her teeth. 'Oh, bugger, look at the mess,' she cried as the contents spilt down the front of her tight yellow sweater.

'Two coffees, please!' shouted a man's voice. She turned and saw it was Archie. 'Can we come and help brush it off?' he said, with a broad grin.

'If you dare,' she replied, sternly.

'Polly, have you met Michael?' asked Archie. 'He's the local vet, you know. Good chap too.'

'Pleased to meet you,' she replied politely. Too politely for Michael who noticed she gave only a nod in his direction and a beaming smile in Archie's.

'Can we help with the coffee?' offered Archie.

'No, thanks,' replied Polly, flashing him a smile. 'You're the first customers today so you'll have to wait. I'll bring it over.' She turned to Michael.

'Sugar?' she asked. He nodded.

Archie fumbled with a newspaper which was lying on the table, Michael sat silent, tracking Polly like radar.

'You're besotted with that girl, aren't you?' said Archie, distracted from the paper by the way Michael's eyes were fixed unblinking on Polly. 'You haven't taken your eyes off her since we came in. Even though she's gone out to the kitchen you're like an old dog, sitting here watching for her to return. You have the look of a man who is well and truly smitten.'

Michael thought he had been cool and collected, shown no emotion.

'I think, sir,' he said, still not feeling comfortable about calling Biddell by his first name, 'that I'm in love with her. Daft, isn't it?'

Archie punched him in the shoulder. 'Good on yer. She looks a great girl. Jolly attractive too. Have you asked her out yet?'

This all took Michael by surprise as he had managed to convince himself that Polly and Archie were floating, hand in hand, through the greatest romance of their lives. But here was Biddell urging him on.

'Get stuck in,' said Archie. 'Do you want me to disappear? Now? I don't mind.'

Confused by the conversation, exhausted by his veterinary efforts and generally knackered, Michael Pember forgot his natural reserve and modesty.

'I really do think she's a wonderful girl, terrific, yes,' he said.

'And so what have you done about it?' pressed Archie.

'Not much really. It's not something I'm too good at. But I thought that, you know, you and she were . . .'

Archie looked confused. 'You thought Polly and I were what?'

'Well, er, she came with you the other night to the farm, didn't she? Wasn't that her in your Land Rover?' Michael asked.

'It was. But don't think for a minute she's got eyes for me. It's the calves she wants to coo over. She adores the livestock.'

'But you brought her up to the farm?' the vet persisted.

'You really do take some convincing, don't you? She told me she never has a chance to get time off for a walk. I merely said I'd show her the cows and calves on her way home. I didn't know that when I opened the barn door, the place was going to be overflowing with blood and guts!'

Polly came through the swing door from the kitchen carrying two cups and a pot of coffee.

'Thanks for the other night, Mr Biddell,' she said, flashing him a smile. She looked straight at Michael.

'Did you save that cow?' she asked, anxiously.

'No, I didn't. Sorry.' He wanted to tell her that he had bravely slaved throughout the night, fought for the cow's life and brought her back from the brink of death, but . . .

'And I'm afraid we lost another this morning,' he added.

He could have kicked himself. He could have lied, or at least glossed over the true facts.

'That shot we heard while we were driving away,' she said to

Archie, 'was that *him* . . .' she gave a dismissive nod in Michael's direction '. . . shooting that poor cow?'

'Yes, it was,' said Archie. 'It was the best thing to do.'

'The cow may have thought differently,' said Polly, face hardening as she looked at Michael. 'There's a lot of cruelty in the world, isn't there? That's one pound twenty for two coffees.' And she slammed the bill on the table and returned to the kitchen.

'Does she mean me?' asked the vet. 'Does she think shooting the cow was cruel? Is *that* what she thinks?'

'Calm down,' said Archie, grabbing his arm.

'I want to go and explain to her how it was,' said Michael, frustrated. 'That cow would have died an even worse death if I hadn't shot her. I need to tell Polly that. She doesn't understand.'

'And she never will,' explained Archie, 'because all she ever sees are the big brown eyes, the wet nose, and the swishing tail. She loves them, like you do. You've *got* to love animals to be a vet, haven't you?'

Michael nodded. 'But it's a different kind of love,' Archie continued. 'With you it's a love born out of respect and deep caring – true love. With her, it's just romance.'

'Possibly,' the other man agreed.

'But don't worry. I think she rather likes you.'

'Do you really?'

'I do,' said Archie. 'Call it instinct. And she'll get over the cow, I bet. So maybe a little drink to help us celebrate?'

'I can't drink at this time of the morning.'

'It's your own time. It's not as though you've got to go back to that surgery and risk breathing whisky fumes over some old woman's poodle. Have a whisky.' He shouted across to the bar, 'Polly, two whiskies!'

She poured two whiskies, avoiding eye contact with Michael and putting them in front of Archie, not him.

'She thinks I'm the biggest bastard that walked God's earth, for shooting that cow,' he said, slugging back the Scotch.

'Probably. Most people would. But they don't always understand what's best. With time it will get easier, it really will, Michael.'

'Not for the cows it won't.'

'You need some sleep. I'll give you a lift home.' And Archie took hold of his arm like a brother and led him to the door.

Michael glanced back, hoping to see the grim look on Polly's face replaced by a smile. But she was in the public bar, pulling a pint for a black-haired youth in a leather jacket who was sitting alone at the bar, slumped on the stool, emitting an odour that could easily have been cured by the application of soap and water.

'I can't make out that young vet at all,' muttered Polly to the unkempt youth who was not listening. His mind was fixed on rolling a thinly filled cigarette and searching the bottoms of his filthy pockets for a match.

'Yer what?' he asked.

'That Michael Pember. The young vet. I don't know what to make of him,' she replied, gazing out of the window and watching Michael and Archie climb into the Land Rover.

'Bloody vets. Same as bloody farmers. Shit! They're all shit!' said the youth angrily.

Half an hour later the pub was empty, except for the youth, and Eric Thwaite now had a clean canvas on which to create his daily masterpiece – roast beef. Woodham Ford and no beef lunch was about as likely as Bakewell and no puddings, or Hogmanay and no Scotch. That was why every day, be it hot, cold or just typically middling Woodham Ford weather, landlord Eric Thwaite began to stoke a large log fire in the main bar at 10 o'clock so that it would be hot enough by 11 to roast a joint of beef on the hanging spit, and start serving perfectly cooked slices from it at 1 o'clock sharp.

Thwaite *knew* beef, bought the best, and to his mind there was none better than Biddell's. Not that he had much choice in the matter of beef; Biddell's owned the freehold of the pub and if Eric Thwaite dared look elsewhere for supplies he would be out of Woodham Ford before you could say sirloin. But he had no problems with the feudal way of life in this village and was happy to stab a great Biddell sirloin every morning, place it on the cast iron spit, and carve every slice himself with the satisfaction of a magician pulling rabbits out of a hat.

This was Eric Thwaite's party trick; he was known across the county for the flourish with which he sharpened his bone-handled knife with a steel, and guided the honed blade through the luscious eye of the meat like a razor through pink silk. Then, once his customers were satisfied, he would remove what was left into the back kitchen, cut himself a slice, slam it between two pieces of bread making a sandwich as thick as a phone directory, close his eyes in satisfaction, and sink his teeth into it. He did this every day. Sometimes twice if there was any left over after the evening service.

As Eric replaced the poker, having stabbed at the logs to liven the blaze a little, he heard a knock at the back door. He glanced up at the clock. It was 11.30. He straightened himself with a groan and shuffled behind the bar, into the kitchen, to open the door, knowing who would be on the other side of it. She was never late.

'Come in, Freda, my old love,' he said, fondly, and a middle-aged woman dressed in clothes which smelled of dead poultry, her hair matted with sweat, headed for the chair by the kitchen table and sat down, exhausted.

'I've never felt so buggered in m'life,' said Freda.

'You'll kill yourself if you keep working nights up at the turkey factory,' replied Eric.

'I wouldn't if there was any choice. But they pays extra, see? It's t'only way t'make ends meet. There's no other money coming in t'house.'

Eric was looking round for his carving knife.

'If you'd done the sensible thing and married me when I asked you thirty years ago, you wouldn't be in this mess now. You'd be behind the bar with me, mistress of all you survey.'

He took the carving knife through to the larder and returned a short while later with a plate laden with cold beef cut from the remains of yesterday's joint.

'Bloody fool, I am,' he said. 'But I can't see you go without a dinner, not after all these years. And don't waste any on that useless lad of yours. If he were mine, I'd kick him up the arse.'

'Thanks, Eric love,' said Freda, who then took a piece of grubby greaseproof paper out of her bag and wrapped the beef in it. 'Old Nellie at the shop usually saves me yesterday's bread, half price. That'll do for m'tea.'

'Get on with yer,' said Eric. 'You'll 'ave me in tears soon.'

The bar was still empty, apart from the youth who was leaning against the bar, his beer glass empty and his thinly filled cigarette smouldering.

'I'm tidying up, and you're the first thing I'm chucking out, Chuff. Do you hear? Your mother's in the kitchen. Remember her, do you?' Eric shouted across the bar.

'Bollocks,' muttered the lad in return, 'the old cow should be at work.'

'You've heard the word then, 'ave you – work? I'm going to get a spoon to baste that beef and if you're not gone when I'm back, you'll feel a boot up your arse. Do you understand?'

'You'll get some of *my* spit on yer beef if you're not bloody careful, landlord,' replied the lad, unmoved by anything Eric had said to him. He had heard it all before.

He waited till Eric had disappeared, spat heavily into an ashtray, and shuffled out.

Chuff's employment record was patchy. He had tried working on the bins, labouring for a bricklayer, and attempted a job involving security where he was given charge of a car park and told to ensure that unauthorised parking was 'discouraged'. He liked that job. They gave him a uniform, and a peaked cap with a badge on it. Chuff had never walked so tall in the world. Had he not decided to punish a driver who had made a genuine mistake by running a sharpened screwdriver several times along the side of the offending car's paintwork, he might still have been there. He enjoyed having authority. Got a taste for it; hungered for more.

Recently, he had managed to find work at Biddell's turkey factory, separating the livers from the rest of the giblets that came cascading from the turkey-killing lines. The livers were used to make exotic pâtés to be sold in smart shops of which Chuff was never likely to be a customer. The other offal was destined for the canned soup factory.

So his day was spent in a silly white apron, a hair net on his head as health regulations demanded, ripping apart the still warm innards of turkeys and placing the only decent bits into stainless steel containers for careful transport to the quality end of the factory. The rest was thrown into plastic dustbins which, when full to overflowing, were dragged across the floor and tipped into hoppers marked 'Turkey Soup'. Chuff hated and resented all people he perceived as being 'pâté eaters', because they were better off than he would ever be. And he became even more embittered when he came face to face with the undeniable fact that even the miserable turkey soup was only just within his financial grasp. But his discontent ran deeper than envy. It dawned upon him, having twice in one day slipped on discarded turkey heads on his way to the lavatory, that he and turkeys had much in common – they were both being robbed of their lives for someone else's profit.

Like the turkeys, he felt owned by the Biddells – slaving in their factory, living on their estate. One day he might very well be strung up by the Biddells, stunned, have his throat slashed and his body drained of blood before he was fully unconscious, like the turkeys. Then he too would be made into pâté if he was lucky – or cheap soup more likely.

For that reason, he had become fond of the turkeys and talked to them as they huddled together in panic, waiting for the electric shock. Once, he had thought of taking a turkey home, hiding it, keeping it as a pet, but had feared the cat might bully it or it might try and savage his tabby cat – the only creature of which he was deeply fond – and the last thing he wanted to do was create any more anguish in the animal world. One day, in a fit of rage after finding a forgotten crate of suffocated turkeys in the back of an airless lorry, he pointed his butcher's knife at the supervisor who had callously told him they would 'end up dead either way, so what's the difference?' And that was the end of another glorious career. Chuff had not worked since.

He lived on the Barnyard Estate. This collection of twenty mean little houses was the Biddells' proudest boast. To encourage village rejuvenation, which was all the fashion at the time, the Biddells had, much against their instincts, given at no charge five acres of land for the development of starter-homes. These were to be made available at modest rents to encourage villagers to remain in the community and not take the all too obvious and attractive option of fleeing to the towns in search of luxuries such as shops, cinemas and public transport. The Biddells had been held up as a national example of caring landowners, considerate farmers, benefactors, saviours of village life. In truth Sir Thomas, whose solicitor, mentor and closest business ally, Marcus Hastings, sat on the transport committee of the county council, had heard that the already infrequent train service to the village was due to be axed and the council was unlikely to subsidise any expansion of the bus service. This left the estate and its food factories vulnerable. So he donated the scrap of land, which was of no other use, and became something of a hero, which he liked.

Of course, he ensured that those who lived in the resulting houses were the families of most use to him on the estate. Then it was pointed out to him that this looked like too much of a fix, and Hastings suggested a deprived family might add credibility. As Hastings was then defending Chuff on a charge of possessing an offensive weapon (he had been caught carving his name with a stolen butcher's knife on an old oak kissing gate), he'd suggested the boy and his mother might be just the people.

'Very good for the community and all that. I'll see there's a clause in the tenancy so you can get them out, if they're any trouble.'

It was 1 o'clock when Chuff opened the door of number six Barnyard Close. Slices of beef would be falling on to plates at The Peacock, but nothing much was cooking here. Hungry, he shambled to the kitchen.

'Mum,' he shouted, 'what's for my bloody dinner?'

There was no reply. Chuff looked at the clock. He'd just missed her. After a brief nap, she was grabbing much needed overtime on the afternoon shift at the turkey factory.

He opened the fridge door and found nothing in it except two already opened cans of Diet Coke and a saucer of leftover meatballs in tomato sauce. Next to it was a plate of meaty cat food. He slammed the fridge door and dragged himself upstairs to his bedroom.

Not another soul, not even his mother, had been in here since they'd first moved into the house. It smelled slightly, probably due to some festering socks which had worked their way under the bed, or possibly because of the window being open and the faint whiff of the turkey factory drifting on the breeze. The bed was unmade, as usual. It was cold and damp. The duvet cover had vivid, violent patterns on it in black and red. Only the gently snoring tabby cat, curled into a placid, tight ball in the midst of the angry design of the fabric, gave any sense of homeliness.

Chuff sat on the bed and gently stroked the cat till it woke, yawned and stretched its limbs.

'You don't know how bloody lucky you are, old cat,' said Chuff, running his hands the length of the cat's swishing tail. 'If you went gobble, gobble instead of miaouw, they'd have had you skinned and minced years ago.' He picked up the cat and cuddled it. 'So watch your step, all right?'

Although he knew he was alone in the house, he checked the door was tightly shut before putting the cat back on to the bed, and opening his desk drawer. It contained magazines. They had started arriving by accident, when he had ordered a t-shirt by mail which carried a cartoon of a rabbit pointing through the bars of a cage at a scientist; the rabbit was saying 'Needle *Them*. Don't Needle Us! Stop Experimenting with our Lives'. There was something about the pleading look on the rabbit's face that reminded Chuff of turkeys waiting for the kill. That was why he'd bought it. But once they had his address, then came the magazines, one with a feature headed *Beat the Security – What Every Sab Needs to Know*, including a description on the sharpening of bicycle chains to provide lethal weapons, and mail order contacts who could supply balaclavas. Much of the activity they were describing, or the methods they were demonstrating, were against the law, even Chuff could spot that. So he kept it all tightly under wraps and took it out only when he was alone and needed his heart hardening even more against the Biddells. He'd only ever received three issues, and wished there had been more.

He had one luxury, paid for by his overworked mother who had sacrificed her annual holiday to earn the cash for it – a computer. It was better than friends, thought Chuff, for it did not answer back nor treat him like filth, and could introduce him in an anonymous way to people who would not otherwise give him the time of day. No one on the Internet knew that he lived in a mean little house, a stone's throw from a stinking turkey factory. Here he was as good as anyone else.

He picked up the phone to check for the dialling tone which he feared might not be there because he had seen a red final demand on the kitchen table the other morning. It was for £300 – a huge sum for a house with just two people in it. His mother had gone crazy. It was a large chunk of her month's wage. Chuff said it must have been a mistake. His mother had gone to work weeping.

The computer went through its log-in processes and Chuff was connected. In an on-screen file, he kept a hundred Internet sites which he had laboriously trawled for during hours connected to the Net. They were all on the same theme. He clicked on the first on the list, his favourite.

Arguments in favour of action

appeared on the screen. Then it posed the question

Isn't extreme activism involving breaking the law wrong?

Chuff got the answer he needed.

Great men and women have demonstrated throughout history that laws can be immoral, and that we can be justified in breaking them. Those who object to law-breaking under all circumstances would have to condemn: the Tiananmen Square demonstrators, World War 2 resistance fighters, the Polish Solidarity movement.

Chuff banged his fist on the table, and muttered forcefully 'Yes!' God, he wanted to be a hero, lie down in front of a tank, inspire a workers' revolution. Anything to get a bit of attention. Anarchy was the only solution, he was convinced. He scrolled down the screen.

'Certainly one of the highest duties of the citizen is a scrupulous obedience to the laws of the nation. But it is not the highest duty' – Thomas Jefferson.

He punched more keys. What he had read so far was merely a warm up to get him into a superheated frame of mind. Then he could focus his attention more closely on animal rights.

Question: Isn't animal rights activism terrorism because it harasses people, destroys property, and threatens humans with injury or death?
Answer: The real terrorists are the people and industries that inflict pain and suffering on millions of innocent animals for trivial purposes each and every day.

Then it gave another couple of quotations for Chuff to study,

'If I repent anything it is likely to be my good behaviour' – Henry David Thoreau

And:

**'I am in earnest – I will not equivocate – I will not excuse – I will not retreat
a single inch and I will be heard' – William Lloyd Garrison**

Chuff understood neither of these. Rather than give them more
thought, he decided to scour the fridge once again. Forgetting to
disconnect himself from the Internet and thereby running up an
even greater bill, he left his screen and went downstairs.

Having found nothing to tempt him, he gloomily stomped back
upstairs and started another journey into the only world from which
he derived any inspiration. He tapped into the Net news groups,
the bar-room chat of the superhighway, the uncensored speaker's
corner where all manner of extremists, fanatics and purveyors of
good sense are given a global platform.

He tapped keys to check any recent postings in this global
letter-box.

From: j.speed @ newslink.dircon.co.uk
**The animal-eating censorship scum can close all our accounts, they can shut
down our Web pages, they can complain to our postmasters, they can force
us on to anonymous remailers, they can force us underground, but they
can't defeat us because we are the future and they are the past.**

Chuff clenched his fist, shouted 'Yes!' again, and the tabby cat
opened its eyes.

'Don't look at me like that,' he said to the cat. 'I'm doing this
for you and your mates, geddit?' He scrolled down to see if there
was a reply. There was:

**One wonders just who this person is referring to. Anyhow the only thing I
can say is that the animal rights organisations seem to have their future
behind them. That's why they're cowardly craven chickenshit nonentities who
hide behind masks, disguises, and anonymous publications. Stand up and be
counted, you cowards.**

Chuff opened his e-mail programme and sent a short, crisp response.

What do any of you bastards know about chicken shit? I've worked in chicken shit, pulled shit out of chickens!

'Don't lecture me on fucking chickens,' he shouted at the screen. The cat dived under the bed. Chuff groped for the power switch. The screen went blank. He went downstairs to the fridge and decided to finish off the meatballs.

5

Tiggy had been at The Social Chapter for at least an hour longer than she could usually afford to stay. Having lingered over her coffee, and even tried one of Marge's heavy macaroons in order to give her an excuse to dawdle, she was about to give up her vigil and leave when the door to the upstairs room opened. This was what she had been waiting for. Five minutes earlier she had seen two well-dressed men come downstairs, shake hands, and smile broadly at each other before leaving. Now, curiosity demanded she waited for the woman.

As she came through the door she stumbled and her face creased briefly in pain. Tiggy leaped up.

'Do you need a doctor?' she asked, overreacting. 'Is it serious?'

'Not at all,' the woman said, dismissively. 'Just bad cramp in my leg. Sitting too long, that's all.'

As Tiggy helped her to a chair by a table, she caught the scent of an expensive perfume she remembered from a scratch 'n' sniff page in a copy of *Vogue* she'd read at the dentist's, and spotted the designer Italian label on the leather case.

'I'll get you some coffee,' said Tiggy, flapping, anxiously trying to remember the First Aid course she'd done before she became a playgroup helper.

'Thanks,' said the woman, 'but please, I'll be all right. It'll pass.'

There was a pause while she rubbed life back into her leg. The watchful Marge sensed something was up and waddled over with two mugs of coffee, returning to the counter without saying a word.

'I love the way they make the coffee here,' said Tiggy eventually, regretting the words as soon as they left her mouth because they sounded so stupid, and anyway the coffee was no different from anywhere else and, worse, it did not sound like the sort of thing that should be said in The Social Chapter; there was no political point to it, nor was it smart. She'd fluffed it.

'Yup, terrific coffee. Absolutely terrific,' replied the woman, managing a smile. She had a dazzling set of teeth, Tiggy noticed, with the slightest touch of lipstick to give the mouth a near perfect shape and colour. Tiggy had tried lipstick once but Toby had mocked her.

'By the way, the name's Tiggy. Tiggy Hopscotch.'

The woman, more composed now, raised an eyebrow.

'I know, it's a daft name, isn't it?' she said, bashfully. 'Can't help it.'

'It does sound a bit like a playground game from the 1950s,' the woman said with a smile. 'I can almost hear kids shouting "Let's play Tiggy Hopscotch!"' Then, realising she might have gone too far, apologised.

'The pain's passing,' she said. 'Thanks for your help. It was those blasted stairs. And the name's Frater. Amanda Frater. Thanks again.'

'Better name than daft old Hopscotch,' said Tiggy. She searched for a way to fill another awkward silence. 'It's a great place here,' she eventually said. 'Lots of life. Really interesting people come and go all the time.'

'Do they really?' asked Amanda, surprised.

'*Do* they?' replied Tiggy, taken aback in turn at Amanda's ignorance of The Social Chapter. 'Haven't you read the *Guardian*?' Amanda shook her head. 'This, they say, is *the* smart place to be. There's nowhere else like it, you see. There's all the young bucks from the City who come down here to show what lads they still are by eating chips and bacon sandwiches every lunchtime, while over in the corner there might be real lads, out of work, hardly able to afford a cup of tea. Every bit as bright as the lads who've made themselves a pile, but just unlucky. You see, some of the City types who've done well started off with next to nothing and they haven't forgotten. So they come here to keep in touch with their roots.'

'How patronising of them,' said Amanda. 'But it would explain why *he* thought this might be a good place to meet,' she added, absentmindedly.

'You can't be talking about those two nice gentlemen you were with earlier? Very smart they looked. And charming too,' replied Tiggy.

'*Too* smart, one of them,' muttered Amanda.

'Sorry, none of my business,' murmured Tiggy, looking down into her coffee.

'Why do you come here, anyway? You don't look like something in the City?' asked Amanda, changing the subject.

'Oh, don't I?'

'Sorry. Didn't mean to be rude or anything.'

'You're right. I'm just a mum up from the suburbs for a day out. This is where I come when I want to get away from the four blinking walls of the house.'

'Why here?'

'Because it's like a zoo,' replied Tiggy. 'I can get in for the price of a cup of coffee, and come here and look at all the wild animals. Like those two lads over there . . .' She nodded towards two men who had just come in; early-twenties, boasting of having made a financial killing that morning and not caring if they spilt Marge's coffee down their black linen trousers. 'I suppose, deep down, I wish I was a bit wilder,' she sighed, 'but I made my own choices and ended up on the wrong side of the bars.' She looked around the room again. 'I've got the sort of husband who wouldn't approve of a place like this. It's too confusing for him. He's been taught to separate the As and Bs from the Cs and Ds so he can sell olive oil to the first lot, and boil-in-the-bag cod chunks to the second. Mix them all up, like they do at The Social Chapter, and he couldn't handle it.'

'Funny,' said Amanda, 'one of the men I was with is a mixture; City smart on top, lout deep down.'

'You've met him before today, then?'

'Yeah,' replied Amanda casually. 'He killed my boyfriend.'

'Oh my God!' squeaked Tiggy. 'He's a *murderer*?'

'No,' said Amanda, with a smile. 'He'd never hurt a fly, directly. I suppose he was more of a spider, gathering people into his web. Once they had become well and truly tangled, it was their bad luck if they couldn't get out. It was their own choice to become involved in the first place. Some escaped, some didn't. My boyfriend Freddie didn't.'

'And it was that man's fault?' asked Tiggy, open-mouthed. Amanda nodded.

'It's a long story. Sorry, I won't go on.'

'So why are you seeing this man, if he did that to you?'

'A question I have not yet been able to answer.'

Marge shambled across the room, a dirty rag in hand with which she was about to threaten their table.

'Are you all right, luv?' she asked, looking at Amanda. 'Saw you take a tumble. We get a lot collapsing in here. Most of 'em drunk, or worse.'

'It's not drink,' put in Tiggy defensively, 'she's got very nasty cramp.'

'They all have some excuse.'

Tiggy's face reddened.

'Leave it,' said Amanda. 'I'm fine, really.'

'You owe me fifteen quid, by the way,' said Marge, looking at her.

'I do?' she said in surprise. 'For two coffees?'

'Use of room for one hour. We'll ignore the extra fifteen minutes. Fifteen quid,' insisted Marge.

'I thought the others would pay,' explained Amanda. 'I'm only here because I was invited.'

'In too much of a hurry to get out of the place, they was,' replied Marge. 'Didn't have time to dig out those fat wallets they looks as though they carry. It's still fifteen quid.'

Amanda started to delve in her bag.

'And what's your game then? You lot are new here. Never seen any of you before,' Marge asked, peering into her bag as she searched it for cash. Amanda, increasingly concerned that she might not have the fifteen pounds and Marge not looking as though she could handle American Express, was caught off guard by the question.

'Animal rights,' she replied. 'I mean, that's *their* game. Not mine. I haven't got a *game*, as you call it.'

'And it don't look as though you've got the fifteen quid either. I can't wait here all day. If you can't find it, you'll have to put it in the post. Although I expect I can wave bye bye to that. I'd better 'ave something for the coffees before you bugger off without paying for *them*.'

'Here,' said Tiggy, pulling bank notes from her purse. 'Here's fifteen pounds. I'll pay. Anything to help.'

'Thanks,' grumbled Marge, and stuffed the notes into a pocket on her apron. Back behind the counter, she muttered, 'Bloody customers . . .'

'I can't let you pay,' Amanda objected.

'Anything to help animals. I've done it before. Animal rights are one of my things,' enthused Tiggy.

'How much do you know about animal rights?' asked Amanda. 'What have you done so far?'

'Well,' said Tiggy, proudly, 'I did a day with the RSPCA, counting money they'd collected from the tins they have in all the dry cleaners. I did that. I've never actually done a flag day; it's a bit risky, a woman on the street with all that money, you know. And I did picket the burger chain when they were prosecuted for mistreatment of beef cattle. I kept the children away for a whole week. Oh, yes, animal rights is nothing new to me.'

'Not quite the same league as my friends are batting in.'

'You mean bigger animals, do you? They're interested in elephants and rhinos and things, are they? Gosh, I love whales. And dolphins. Adore them. They're gorgeous!'

Amanda chuckled.

'What did you say your name was?'

'Tiggy.'

'Then, Tiggy, I should stick to tin-rattling and leave my friends to their end of the game.'

'Why do you say *their* game? Aren't you involved too?'

'They want me to be. Very much.'

'Wow!' gasped Tiggy. 'If I was offered a chance to do some animal rights work, I'd jump at it.'

'Yeah, but it's complicated,' said Amanda, wistfully.

'Because of your boyfriend?'

With some reluctance, but at the same time relief at being able to share it, she told Tiggy the whole story, from first meeting, through love affair, to Freddie's death. When she had finished they sat in silence for a moment. Tiggy spoke first.

'You've *got* to do it. You've got to help them. Whatever it is they want to do. You owe it to . . .'

'Freddie?' added Amanda, enjoying the sound of his name.

'Yes, you owe it to Freddie.'

'But can't you see why I might not be able to trust Conrad? Can't you see why I would want to keep him at arm's length, or even further?'

'I can,' replied Tiggy. 'But love's always stronger than hate. Wonderful things are built on foundations of love. Nothing grows out of malice. What will your boyfriend's death have been *for* if it doesn't in some way further the cause he believed in? You owe it to him to keep that cause alive, and you owe it to the animals too. People just walk away from it all. I know I do. I would love to be in your position, being offered a chance to do something. I would, I really would.'

Amanda smiled.

'I'll think it over. But not now. I've got to go down to East Anglia for a few days. Duty visit to my dad.'

'Funny, I'm off east next weekend too. We've got a cottage in a little place called Woodham Ford,' said Tiggy, gathering her things together.

'No kidding!' said Amanda.

*　　*　　*

Brian Frater was nearly sixty, and the head of a shaky one-man band of a business on the outskirts of Woodham Ford. Frater dealt in animal feed; supplying the Biddell Estate, trying to make a living, struggling to keep his head above quickly rising water. It was the middle of the afternoon and he was at his desk, shifting to one side a pile of increasingly insistent letters from the bank, in search of his diary. The phone rang.

'Frater's Feeds,' he snapped.

He continued to move papers around whilst giving only half an ear to the caller.

'Ten tons. Pig nuts. Medicated? . . . Yeah . . . Tuesday? No chance! Thursday at the earliest. And cash on delivery. Or no bloody delivery, this Thursday or next. Understand?'

He banged down the phone. He had to make some money soon. The profit on ten tons of pig nuts was not going to pay for the diesel to get them from his mill to the customer's farm. Everything in agriculture these days was calculated so tightly that the difference between profit and loss was a hair's breadth. He'd bought two hundred tons of soya at £180 a ton last week, only to see the market dive to £168 in three days with no certainty that it would rise. Running a feed mill used to be a steady if unspectacular way to make a living; now it was more nerve-wracking than running a City dealing desk.

So he would have to buy protein at fantastically cheap prices to mix with his now expensive soya, in order to be able to ship out compounded feed at a competitive price. Or he could hang on and hope soya prices went up, then sell straight at a good profit. But he'd recently tried that with three hundred tons of barley only to find the price creeping down from £294 to £289. And the bank was on the phone every day, asking questions.

He rang a contact at Harwich docks. There was usually someone around who might do a deal on a cargo that had yet to be unloaded, part of which might, accidentally, be loaded on to the wrong lorry. The sweepings left in the hold after the bulk of the cargo had been unloaded was another option. It was often lousy stuff, damp and grubby, having travelled halfway round the world in close contact with the unpalatable mix of seawater and heavy diesel oil slopping around the bilges of bulk carriers. But there was always someone who would buy it if the price was right, and if the price was low enough it was right for Frater. It was an innocent enough fraud; the ship owners were glad to have the holds cleaned out, importers allowed for it in their calculations of natural wastage, so dealers like him took advantage, hired a few men from the Job Centre for a day and armed them with sacks, brushes and shovels. Out of their sweepings up, he made himself a nice little profit. But he could not rely on his ship coming in every week.

He phoned the docks office but his contact was not there. There was one other option but it was not one he wanted to consider. Yet.

He flicked through his diary, glanced at the next few days and groaned when he realised that the Biddell dinner to which he was invited was only a few days away. He *had* to show his face – the Biddell's contract was the core of his business. He needed them, and they knew it.

He drummed his fingers on the desk, pleased at least that Amanda would be coming down for the weekend. With no one else to accompany him, it would be father and daughter attending.

Brian Frater was a besotted father, and Amanda was the only joy in his life. Widowed twelve years ago, his last remaining ambition had been to see his daughter grow into a fine woman and be given all the opportunities her mother had wished for her – he had promised his wife that. So he paid for the best private education, then Oxford. After the accident, he paid for the months spent in hospital while a shattered leg mended, then the plastic surgery needed to rebuild her into the picture of perfection Brian Frater wanted her to be. He gave her a generous clothing allowance, and all the other bullets a smart-girl-about-London needed if she was going to be able to shoot from the hip. He bought the Kensington flat, footed the bill for frequent travel, and hoped that one day she would come good. She told him she 'did charity work'. Her mother would have been proud of that.

He read again the last line of the letter from the bank: '. . . return to normal borrowing limits within 28 days to ensure our continued support'. They had been mild letters until that one.

He moved the bank's letter to one side. Underneath was a scribbled note, a reminder to call Orion Shipping. This could be the answer to all his problems. Orion Shipping ran a fleet of second-class ships which bummed around the world picking up the jobs no one else wanted, moving cargoes no one else would touch, or which broke some kind of international regulation. Unlicensed arms shipment was their sort of game.

Frater fingered the note. He hoped Amanda would arrive and then he could put it to one side, postpone a decision. But he had no real choice and he knew it. He *had* to ring them if he was to stay in business. Not only was the bank nagging on a daily basis, but every post brought a bill for the upkeep of Amanda's London flat or travel expenses which he thought, given her charity work, he should help with. He paid for her car insurance and maintenance too. And gave her a monthly allowance. She was an expensive daughter to run.

Orion Shipping had a thousand tons of imported Far East 'protein' for sale and it could be Frater's for what appeared to be a ridiculously low asking price. If he were to blend it with his now expensive soya, and drop his price to match those of his multinational competitors, he might just scrape a profit. But what mattered more was cash. He needed a cheque from Biddell's, and quickly. He would do a deal: offer them feed at a ridiculously low price in exchange for fast payment. Biddell's had done that before, to secure a bargain. He did his sums again, tapping nervously at the calculator, looking up to see if Amanda had arrived yet.

The problem was that Frater knew nothing about this 'protein'. Although he had a certificate of analysis which detailed protein, minerals, energy and additive levels, there was, and could be, no indication of the source of that protein, or what treatments it might have undergone. For all he knew it could be dehydrated elephant skin, or someone's recycled grandmother – both would give the same sort of analysis.

No reputable feed manufacturer now dealt in cargoes like these. Since the eighties and nineties when poisoned protein, legally traded, had panicked the world into understanding the devastation that could be caused by contaminated feed, regulations had banned the importing of feeds from countries with no controlling legislation in place – meaning most of the Far East. Reimporting through a less than vigilant country was the way round this, and Orion Shipping were masters at it. On paper, it would appear that this cargo was shipped from an 'approved country of origin', but it had never been out of the hold of one of Orion's rusty tubs since it was loaded from a stinking quayside somewhere on the coast of Thailand. Lousy stuff, but cheap.

What its contents were was anybody's guess. The word 'protein' covered more things than Frater wanted to contemplate. It had always been assumed that processing at high temperatures destroyed all things toxic while preserving all things nutritious; but the infected sheep's brains which led to the plague of BSE proved that such generalisation was dangerous. There could be any kind of unknown bug in Orion's 'special offer' and Frater knew the risks. But it *was* cheap.

Glancing through the window, he saw Amanda's car swing into the drive, soft top rolled back. As she got out of the car, his eyes instinctively went to her leg to see how she was walking. He loved her so much that he too winced with pain as she walked. He could deny his little girl nothing and needed money not for himself but for her. So while she went round to the boot of the car to extract a Harvey Nichols carrier bag – her new trouser suit for the Biddell dinner – he quickly picked up the phone and dialled Orion Shipping. They were closed. He left a message saying he'd called.

6

The grandfather clock in the lobby of the The Peacock struck 5.30 and on cue the door of the saloon bar opened. 'I think you buggers work it by the speaking clock,' said Eric Thwaite, his head in the fireplace, blowing on the embers of the fire, trying to raise a flame. His lips showed the slightest smear of gravy. He had just come from the larder where he had been picking the last of the beef off the remains of the rib devoured by the Saturday lunchtime trade. It was the night of Biddell's party, and he had specially chosen a vast hind-quarter which needed all the heat his fire could give it. It had already had two hours on the spit, and if Eric had not dozed off for half an hour in mid-afternoon, it would have been well on its way to perfection. The Biddells had booked their dinner for 8.30. But the fire had gone out, and Eric saw the cool embers as an omen of the reception he would get from Sir Thomas if the beef was not right.

'What can I get you?' he shouted impatiently over his shoulder to whoever it was in the bar.

He heard a quick intake of breath; a sort of 'chuffing' sound which had given the lad his nickname.

'Oh, hell, it's you,' Eric muttered. 'Just you lift those arms of yours off that bar. There's enough zips on that leather jacket to keep a Marks and Sparks trouser factory going and I'm not having you scratching them along my varnish. Do you understand?'

Chuff didn't bat an eyelid. He was used to being spoken to like a child. So he pressed the cuff of his jacket as hard as he could on the bar, waited till Eric was concentrating on poking the fire once again, then swept his arm in a wide arc, leaving scratches all the way from the Heineken lager pump to the lemonade dispenser. 'Pint!' he insisted.

'I'll just see that the dog has what it needs,' came the reply. It was Polly, not Eric. 'And then I'll check the upstairs room. But dogs first, then Biddells,' she said firmly, thinking it was Eric's voice she had heard shouting. She peered round the door.

'Oh, it's only you. You'll have to wait too. I've got the dog to see to, then the upstairs room to prepare. Anyway, it's only just opening time.'

Chuff didn't much mind taking second place to a dog, but he did not take kindly to being pushed into third position by the Biddells. So he slammed his other heavily zipped arm onto the bar and dragged it all the way from the cashew nut machine to the Bullocks Best Bitter pump. That would teach them.

'I want a pint o' Bullocks,' he bellowed, which brought Eric back into the bar.

'Where's that girl? Polly! Oh, do everything yourself round here, why don't you? What was it? Pint of Bullocks?' He put the glass under the tap and pulled on the pump.

'Mother all right?' he asked Chuff.

'Not too bad.'

'I saw her in the Post Office the other day. Didn't think she looked too good. And she didn't seem much better this morning,' remarked Eric as he waited for the head to rise and settle again before he filled the glass to the brim. 'How a nice woman like that ended up with a lad like you defeats me. I don't suppose working in that turkey factory is doing her any good, at her age,' he added.

'When did that lousy place do anybody any good?' grumbled Chuff, reaching for his pint.

'Money, please.'

He'd scraped together just enough change for one pint. It would have to last him all night.

'Polly!' cried Eric again. 'We must get that upstairs room sorted!' But he was wasting his breath. There was nothing that Eric Thwaite could say which would persuade her to change her priorities. It

82

would not have mattered if the Queen of England herself were dropping in for a pint of bitter; the pregnant golden Labrador, Floss, would have to be petted, patted, cooed over and fed first. Then, and only then, would the rest of her tasks receive some attention.

It was nearly 6 when the bar door opened again. Two lads staggered through the door, late for work. One wore a white chef's jacket that buttoned up to his neck, but was still wearing jeans. The other was wearing the regulation blue-and-white check trousers, but over them a grubby grey sweater and a scarf. They were the kitchen staff and looked far from on the ball.

'You lads had better get yourselves straightened out,' shouted Eric. 'This is no ordinary Saturday night. It's supposed to be a special occasion we're laying on for these people. If they see the kitchen staff dressed like that they'll die of the shock and we shall have a funeral on our hands.'

'And then you'd charge 'em for that, you fat bastard,' muttered Chuff.

The lads scurried to the kitchen. Chuff shouted after them, 'Hey. What's the Biddells 'avin for their tea tonight then, eh?'

'What's it to you?' replied one of the lads. 'You couldn't tell a fish finger from a salmon terrine, you couldn't.' The other lad stifled a snigger.

'No, come on, tell us what they're 'avin. I want to know how the other 'alf live.'

'Not the other *half*,' interrupted Eric. 'Don't think for one minute you're in anything but a very small minority.'

'Yeah,' shouted one of the chefs, 'a minority of one!'

Chuff banged his fist on the bar.

'I want to know what them bloody Biddells are 'avin to eat.'

'For Christ's sake,' said Eric, 'they're having the very best roast beef of Old England, straight from that spit over there.'

'Spit over there? Is that an order?' said Chuff, hawking in his throat.

'Mucky bastard!' shouted one of the lads before diving through the door into the kitchen, worried by the direction in which the spit might fly.

'Piss off!' muttered Chuff under his breath, swallowing. He raised his arms, intending to inflict more damage on the bar, but just as he was about to do so, a hand came from behind him and gripped him.

'I shall break this arm if you do any more damage to my pub,' said Eric, eyes fixed on Chuff's. 'Get in that corner, out of sight, and drink your beer. Else bugger off home!'

Eric relaxed his grip and went back to poking the feeble fire. 'Bollocks,' muttered Chuff.

The upstairs dining room of The Peacock had never looked so stately. With its heavily beamed walls and ceilings, its tapestries and shields hanging from the walls, there was no escaping the mediaeval atmosphere – providing you did not inspect the joints in the glass-fibre beams too closely. The fireplace was possibly the only authentic bit of architecture in the room: a carved sandstone surround, a large black grate in which lay seasoned logs, and an heraldic fire-back which looked like something from centuries ago but had in fact been cast by the local iron-foundry to capitalise on the heritage business.

The furniture too had an Elizabethan look to it. Black oak, caned seats, very Olde Englande – made just outside Birmingham in the mid 1980s. The chairs and the heavy black refectory table looked like a Hollywood set of English life in the sixteenth century. There was even a tapestry which depicted the hunting of a unicorn, copied from an original in some dowdy stately home and available through the National Trust Christmas catalogue. But despite the deep and cheap nature of the fraud, it was a welcoming room, comfortable, an easy place in which to enjoy a meal. It would be even more inviting when Polly had lit the fire.

She shivered a little as she came in – the cool of the day having given way to an even chillier evening – and went across to draw the heavy red curtains. She shivered again as she looked around for the box of matches. It was next to the envelope which contained the place-names she had yet to distribute. She went over to the fire, struck one match and lit a corner of the newspaper on which the fire was built, then waited to make sure it had caught. She eased herself into the chair while she watched it blaze. All she needed now was someone to cuddle up to before that blaze, and to hug till the last of the embers died. The room was quite dark now, and she watched for a while as the gathering flames cast flickering patterns across the beams. She relaxed, fell back slowly into the chair and, seduced by the warmth starting to come from the fireplace, closed her eyes.

But only for a second. The door slid open, a wedge of light from the landing spread across the starched table linen.

'Is that you, Eric?' said Polly.

She heard a sharp intake of breath and jumped up to reach the light switch.

'Chuff! You frightened me to death. What are you doing here? If Mr Thwaite finds that you've been up here . . .'

'He won't know unless you tell him. And if you don't tell him, I won't tell him you've been slipping me the odd pint and not charging. Is that a deal?' he said, moving towards her.

Why she had ever taken pity on him she could not imagine. But it was true; she had slipped him the occasional pint when Eric's back was turned, and the odd packet of fags. Crazy, especially as it had all started because of a cat. When Chuff's tabby fell sick he had brought it to her, cradled in his leather jacket, and asked her to do anything she could to help it. She'd told him to go to the vet, but he'd said he had no money. And as the sickly tabby cat lay in Chuff's arms, she saw the slightest hint of a tear in his eye. With a tremor in his normally aggressive voice, he had asked if the cat was going to die. That was when the thin veneer of bravado cracked to reveal the frightened child beneath, desperate not to lose his only pal. She had said to him not to get so upset, there probably wasn't much wrong with the cat. He had brushed the tear away, claiming it was something in his eye.

Since then, she'd thought of him as just another of the sad mongrels she had helped while working at The Peacock. Like Chuff, they came to her baring their teeth, itching to bite, ears back, barking. But show them a little kindness and affection, Polly found, and soon they'd curl up at your feet, quite content. Sometimes when Chuff was at his most drunken and abusive, she thought he was one mongrel too many; a crazy mixture of resentment and aggression she might never be able to bring to gentleness. Then she remembered the cat cradled in his arms and persisted.

'What's taken your fancy?' she asked, spotting the smile on his face.

'This room,' he said, 'I've never been up here before. Never been anywhere as smart as this. Is this where the Biddells will be having their tea?'

'Dinner, actually,' said Polly. 'Yeah. This is it. Nice room. Comfortable.'

Chuff grabbed one of the black oak chairs and placed himself at the head of the table.

'Is this where the old man will sit? Is this the bastard's seat? Is my arse where his arse will be tonight? Eh? Is this Sir Thomas's chair?'

'Get up,' urged Polly. 'If Mr Thwaite hears you, we'll both be out.'

Chuff wouldn't budge. 'And who sits here?' He looked to his left and then his right.

'I haven't a clue till I put the place-names out. Pass me the envelope,' Polly insisted. 'You're right,' she said, studying the names and the seating plan which showed where the guests were to sit, 'the old man's sitting exactly where you are. On his right is young Mr Biddell.'

'Oh,' said Chuff, 'is that what you call him? *Mr* Biddell, is it, even when you're off up to the farm with him after dark, eh? You were seen, you know.'

'I went to see the cows and calves. He offered to show me. Nothing more than that. You've got a mucky mind!'

86

'And those Biddells 'ave got mucky habits too. Fancy him takin' off with you on his first night home instead of getting back to see his old dad. Fancy that. Those Biddells think girls like you are just there for their pleasure, you know.'

'You're crazy. This is the twenty-first century, not the sixteenth,' protested Polly. 'I wanted to see the cows. No more, no less. I like cows – lovely they are, all milky and cuddly.'

'And were they then?' asked Chuff.

'No, they weren't as it happens.' Her voice dropped. 'It wasn't very pleasant at all.'

'Go on. Tell me more,' said Chuff, spinning her along.

'Well,' said Polly, sitting in a chair beside him, 'to be honest, I've never been so shocked in my life by the state that poor cow was in, the one that died.' Her eyes started to fill with tears. 'It just lay there, in terrible pain, looking at its dead calf and . . .' she paused to blow her nose '. . . and that vet, Michael whatever his name is, shot her dead.'

She looked up. Chuff was grinning.

'Are you laughing at me?' she asked, quickly composing herself.

'No,' he said, 'just enjoying the moment which will surely come when the Biddells pay the price. I am in earnest, Polly. I will not equivocate. I will not excuse. I will not retreat a single inch and I will be heard.'

'You'll be heard by Mr Thwaite if you're not careful. Talking such rubbish.' Polly wiped her eyes and started to read out the list of guests.

There were Sir Thomas and Archie Biddell. Marcus Hastings was coming too, with his wife. There was a senior partner from a local firm of land agents, Peter Franklin; there was another couple who had something to do with a large firm of agricultural contractors, she knew that. Then came Amanda Frater. Polly looked again at this name.

'Hey, Chuff. Have you heard of an Amanda Frater?'

He had risen from the head of the table and moved towards the window where he was drawing back the curtain, waiting for Eric Thwaite to pay a visit to the bottle store in the back yard. That was when he hoped to slip back down to the bar unobserved.

'Frater? Yeah, there's that chap at the mill. Makes the animal grub. He's called Frater. Funny bugger, he is. Don't see much of him around. Never heard of an Amanda Frater, though.'

'No, neither have I,' said Polly.

'She'll be his sister, 'cos his wife's dead, I know that. She'll be one of those dried up old tarts off the Parish Council, I suppose,' said Chuff. 'The sort of old bag that gets a job as a magistrate and then tries to 'ave me banged up just for 'avin a piss in a bus shelter.'

'Chuff!' hissed Polly. 'It's time you disappeared. It's quarter to seven.'

He heard the back door of The Peacock open. It was Eric, bound for the bottle store. 'Bye,' he said, and sprinted down the stairs back to his dark corner of the bar, to skulk like a disgraced dog.

'It's a quarter to seven,' Archie's father shouted from the bottom of the polished staircase of the Manor. The grandfather clock, in the Biddell family for four generations, chimed in agreement.

'We must not be late,' Sir Thomas shouted. 'I've asked for the car to collect us at seven sharp. Do you hear me, Archie? Archie!'

Archie heard him fine. With a sigh, he swung his feet off the bed and tiptoed carefully across the floor in his bare feet, wincing slightly as his warm toes touched the coldness of polished wood. He opened the door.

'I – heard – you!' he shouted, and swiftly closed the door before his father had a chance to bark any more orders at him, stubbing his toe on the skirting board and cursing on his way back to the bed where he lay down again, stretched out in his underwear. His dinner suit, he noticed, was still covered in bloody war wounds – splashes of red wine, or possibly pink champagne. He had last worn it when he went over the top and defeated the enemy called sobriety at the dinner to mark his last night in the army.

He could hear his father pacing the wooden floor in the hall. Archie should have been up, getting dressed, but instead he covered his eyes with his hands, pressed them tightly to his skull till he saw patterns in his head, and wondered if there was any way he could get out of it all. Landowning, farming . . . none of it was his game; and had he not been the only and deeply loyal son nothing would have brought him back to Woodham Ford. Tonight he was to be crowned, declared heir to the estate, paraded before the populace. The reluctant prince was to meet his people.

'Christ!' He pulled his hand away from his eyes and looked at his watch. It was 6.55. Father would be shouting again, the car would be arriving. He pulled on his trousers, pushed the cufflinks uncertainly through his shirt cuffs, cursing when they did not emerge at the other side, clumsily tied his bow tie and threw on his jacket. He came running down the stairs, only remembering he had forgotten his socks and shoes when his feet hit the bristly door mat. He sprinted back upstairs. His father was standing by the door, tapping his foot, watching Archie's every move with increasing anger. It was a blessing that he had forgotten his shoes for when he opened the bedroom door, there, lying on the bed, were the notes for his speech. Downstairs, his father fumed silently.

'Look,' Sir Thomas finally said, 'tonight will be one of the milestones of your life. As we have agreed, I shall announce my intention to stand down as chairman and managing director of the Biddell Estate. We shall also announce that you are to take my place. Had you forgotten already? Does it mean so little to you that you cannot even be ready at the required time?' He glanced at Archie's untidy cuffs. 'And properly dressed?' He felt like a ten year old.

'I've invited Marcus Hastings, of course,' said his father.

Hastings was one of the few people Archie remembered. What an arse-ache that man is, he thought.

'You can always turn to him,' his father went on, 'for sound advice. And I mean *sound*. Good man is Marcus.'

Balls-achingly tedious man, thought Archie.

'The land agents are coming too. I recommend you get to know them well. I've also asked the manager of our agricultural contracting division and his wife. Plus one or two key people from manufacturing and marketing. Feed supplier, that sort of person. All important to you in your future career.'

Archie checked that his speech was in his pocket and looked at him as if to say 'ready'.

'It is by service and loyalty down the generations that we are in the position of heading the finest estate in the eastern counties,' pontificated his father. 'Loyalty, service, devotion.'

'Devotion to making loot?' Archie laughed, then swiftly apologised.

'Don't waste it all. Don't chuck it away,' the old man pleaded.

The heavy front door of the Manor closed behind them, then the door of the Jaguar. Archie counted all the doors that were closing behind him, as they headed for The Peacock.

'Do I *have* to make this speech?' he said as the Jaguar headed out through the wrought-iron gates and turned left into the village. 'I mean, what's the point? I shall see all these people in due course. I don't see why we have to have a dinner, and I certainly don't see why I have to make a speech.'

'Because,' said Sir Thomas, irritated, 'how many times do I have to tell you – this is a milestone. From this moment on the estate takes a new turn.'

Does it bloody hell as like, thought Archie, remembering the politburo of his father's advisers.

'Anyway, we want to hear of your plans and ideas,' Sir Thomas continued. 'You do have some ideas, don't you?'

Oh, yes, Archie had ideas. Like a one-way plane ticket to Alaska!

'You do have some plans?' his father urged.

Archie's thoughts were elsewhere. 'Oh, yes, Father. Great plans. Of course, I can only give a brief outline of them tonight, but I think it only fair to let everyone know what I see as my vision for the estate.'

90

'I like the use of the word vision,' said his father, pleased now that his son seemed at last to be taking his responsibility seriously.

'It's hell when we're as busy as this,' sighed Polly as she pulled Chuff another surreptitious pint for which once again she did not bother to charge. He sipped a mouthful without waiting for the head to settle. The white froth coated his lips and made his black stubble even more noticeable.

'Was it really sick-making, that cow you saw?' he asked in the way that a child seeks pleasure from the gory details of an accident. 'Would you say it was real suffering, Polly? Eh?' he asked.

'For God's sake, I want to forget all about it,' she said. 'It really upset me. I didn't sleep that night. It was the look on that cow's face . . . There was pain, sure. But there was pleading too. I'm sure I saw that cow asking why it had to go through all that. I've seen that look before, when those stray cats appear in the back yard. They just want someone to love them. If I could have hugged that cow, I'd . . .'

She shrieked, feeling a pair of man's hands come from behind and grab her by the waist. She smelled drink on the breath that was burning her ear and cried out again as the hands closed for a squeeze.

'Huggin' nice girls like you is better than huggin' cows. I can tell you that from personal experience.'

She struggled a little and turned round to find it was the intoxicated Tomlinson, herdsman at Home Farm.

'Get *off* me,' she told him firmly, and elbowed him under the ribs. She had learned that trick early on in her career as a barmaid.

'Sorry, girl. Only Tomlinson's little joke,' he said, winded.

'Not funny at all,' said Polly. 'I stink of your filthy cigarettes now.' She put her nose down to her blouse. 'And what's that other stuff I can smell? Phew, it's strong! What is it?'

'Probably the disinfectant we use up at the farm. Had another bit of a mishap, we did, this afternoon.'

'Another poor cow?' asked Polly, screwing up her eyes.

'Another lousy cow, yes,' said Tomlinson. 'Pint of Bullocks!'

'She not dead, is she?'

'As stiff as that beer mat, my dear,' said the leering Tomlinson.

Polly sniffed. 'I'm just going to see if the cats have finished their tea.'

Standing by the huge slab of beef, which was skewered by the spit slowly rotating above the open wood fire in the other half of the bar, was old Arthur Friend. Above the noise of the crackling logs and sizzling beef, he had heard Tomlinson's dismissal of another dead cow and the thought tormented him although it was five years since the herd had been his to run. There were very few cows left alive from Arthur's time. A milking cow, these days, could expect to last for four years at the most; it had been six or seven when he was running things, ten or twelve in his father's day. But the demands on the cow were ever greater and if her body failed in any way to measure up to the pressures, that was the end of her. Farming, he thought, was as simple, commercial and heartless as that.

Arthur still tried to see the cows as often as he could, and not entirely for sentimental reasons. For he had become convinced that only he knew how to care for them properly and that they were gravely at risk from another catastrophe on the scale of the one which had marred the latter days of his working life. So, every day, he got on his bicycle and pedalled up to Home Farm, usually waiting till he spotted Tomlinson's car parked outside The Peacock. Then he could wander amongst the cows, chat to them, tell them his troubles, listen to theirs and perform his secret daily task . . .

Arthur Friend had channels of communication with cows which were not open to many men, and certainly very few modern stockmen. It was probably no more than a stockman's instinct which told him when a cow had a sore teat, lame foot, or aching back; but to an outsider it would appear as though he could walk along a row of cows and have each of them tell him her troubles. It was no master/servant relationship; cows and Arthur Friend lived and thought on the same level. Which was why he felt such bitterness towards the methods and philosophies which had brought cows into low public esteem today. The 'mad cow business', as he called it, the slaughtering of his beloved herd, he considered the final betrayal of the animals who were his closest friends. He had spent many hours, alone in retirement, trying to fathom the reasons for what had happened, attempting to make sense of the biggest catastrophe in his life.

There had been no such thing as 'mad cows' in his father's day, or his grandfather's, he concluded. So it made sense to Arthur's simple way of thinking that the way they treated their cows then, both in sickness and in health, was fundamentally better than the methods modern farming prescribed. He remembered his father's old notes, written in a flowing hand in the leather-bound notebook and kept carefully in a brown paper envelope at the back of the kitchen dresser in his cottage. He read those notes over and over again; the prescriptions for every ailment from coughs to colic. Many used ingredients Arthur could still get hold of, like gentian powder, capsicum powder, camphor and castor oil. Others he had no clue about, like oil of rhodian, oil of vitriol, or black antimony, copper and mercury something, and various lead compounds.

Then, one wet afternoon, sitting by his cottage fire thumbing through the pages of his father's notebook, trying to fathom some of the words which had become smudged by damp, a distant but dazzling memory burst to the surface of his mind. It was like a gift from God to Arthur; a divine sign. It was the recollection of his mother's words, spoken forty years before, when she had packed his late father's Sunday suit and sent it to be sold. In the bottom of the cupboard where the suit had been hanging was a padlocked wooden case, the size of a shoe box. She had picked it up, Arthur recalled, and rattled it. 'It's your dad's damned cow pills and potions. Might as well burn 'em,' she had said. He had grabbed it from her, not because he knew what was in it or the

93

value of it, but because it was his dad's and therefore precious to him. He remembered taking it to the attic. One day, he'd thought, he would get round to opening it.

Forty years later he did. Having hunted through the kitchen drawers for a torch, he got out the stepladders and heaved himself into the dark and dusty attic. Arthur looked round, trying to remember the day he had hauled the heavy box up through the trapdoor and thought he must have either hidden it behind the old feather mattress, now robbed of its stuffing by mice, or beneath the tin trunk which had kept the family Bible out of the jaws of hungry rats. He decided the trunk was more likely and pulled it away from the wall, causing fat spiders to scurry to new, safer homes. He kicked with his foot and scattered the shreds of newspaper and twig which birds had brought under the eaves to build nests. And, by the feeble glow of the torch, he saw the wooden box.

The hinges had rusted and so although the padlock was still in place, the lid came away in his hands to reveal pill boxes and medicine bottles, just as his father had left them. Dampness had eroded some of the words on the labels.

That night, Arthur sat in front of his fire with the box at his feet, removing each bottle and carefully brushing off the dust with his fingers. Then he sat in silence, gazing at the fluted, green bottles glinting in the glow from the coal fire.

They seemed to be talking to him, he thought; trying to send him a message from a simpler age. After an hour of staring at them, deep in thought, Arthur decided what that message was. It was his duty to see such a dreadful thing as a 'mad cow' never appeared again in the Biddell herd. He felt his father asking him to do that, pleading with him. He could clearly hear his father's voice reciting the names of the cows: 'Blossom, Amy, Marigold . . .', begging his son to save their lives. And here, he thought, at his feet, was his means of doing just that – the old way, his father's way, with traditional remedies. No cow need ever go mad again.

*　　*　　*

When Tomlinson shuffled his way through from the public bar towards the fire, Arthur was standing close to the beef. He had not heard Tomlinson approach and turned quickly when he heard him, stuffing his hand hastily into his pocket like a child that had been caught with a bag of forbidden sweets.

'What yer creeping up on people like that for?' asked Friend, nervously.

'What are you so jumpy about, you silly old bugger?' said Tomlinson. 'You've been up to see them bloody cows again, haven't you? I can see the cowshit on your boots. I'm going to have a word with Sir Thomas. See if I can't get you banned from that place.'

'I don't see I do any harm,' said Arthur.

'You get in my way,' replied Tomlinson. 'Interrupting my routines and disrupting my work.'

'You haven't got any routines except getting down to this pub as fast as you can. If you call *that* a routine.'

'Cheeky old bastard! All that crap you used to go in for, that's all out of the window now. We've got a computer, it monitors the lot. I don't need to do all that bloody touching and feeling stuff you wasted your time on.'

'Your clever computer didn't save that cow that died this morning, did it? I could have told you she was going to calve when I saw her day before yesterday. She had that look.'

'What bloody look?'

'Not a look you'll ever learn to spot,' sighed Arthur. 'And I'll tell you another thing . . .' Tomlinson was rolling a cigarette and hardly listening '. . . that cow with the kind eye and good length of leg . . .'

'Kind eye? What bloody use is that to me?' asked Tomlinson, irritated. 'They've got microchip implants. That's how we identify 'em these days. What's her ID number? I don't give a stuff how long the bloody cow's legs are.'

'Well, anyway,' said Arthur, 'she'll be calving before the night's out. I'd put money on it.'

'No,' said Tomlinson, firmly. 'If it's the cow I think you mean, BDL 294 is her number actually, she's due next Tuesday morning and not a minute before. Anyway, it's my night off, and the relief man's sick, and I'm not sitting in the shed all night just because some bloody old fool in the pub thinks he knows better than the computerised Cattle Care system which was invented in this very village.'

'If you're not there tonight, you'll miss it,' muttered Arthur, and stared fixedly at the hunk of beef.

'Bollocks,' grumbled Tomlinson, slinking back into the bar.

With the stockman gone, Arthur thought he had this bit of the bar to himself and went towards the chunk of beef, putting his hand deep in his pocket as if looking for something.

'Blast,' he muttered, hearing another voice.

'You reckon tonight, do you, Arthur?' It was Michael Pember who had crept into the pub unnoticed and had been leaning against the bar, hoping for a word with Polly. 'You sounded confident about that cow. I wish I knew your diagnostic secrets.'

'Oh, it's you, Mr Pember. Waste of bloody time, that man Tomlinson. Cows are better off dead than in his care,' Arthur declared.

'It's not that bad,' said Michael, pulling Arthur's empty pint glass away from him and taking it over to the bar.

'How many cows dead this month?' asked the old man.

'That I know of – er – six. Could be more because I had a couple of nights off. But certainly six. Two pints of Bullocks, please,' he called to Eric Thwaite.

'Well, in my day, if we lost six a year, let alone in the last month, old Sir Hubert Biddell would have been down to the dairy, wanting to know why this and that, and what were we going to do about it?'

Michael grasped the pints of ale and brought them over to the table.

'*I* want to know,' he insisted, 'how *you* know that cow's going to calve tonight and not next Tuesday? I tell you, there's a lot of evidence to suggest it will be next week. There's no displacement of the pelvic bones, no visible mucus-like discharge. The records tell me exactly the date she was served and, given the usual gestation, it is reasonable to assume it will be next week. I know it can vary by a day either way, but not much more. I must say, if I were Tomlinson – and thank God I'm not – I'd feel fairly confident about having the night off.'

'That, with the greatest respect,' said Arthur, choosing his words carefully, 'is because you are a vet and not a stockman. And Tomlinson is neither. I know you understand all these medical things, but I understand cows. And I say tonight.'

Michael was enjoying the sport.

'Give me a clue. Tell me one thing you've spotted that I haven't, to prove it will be tonight?'

Arthur smiled, opened his jacket pocket and took out a small pocketbook, bound in leather, dog-eared and obviously older than its owner. Tape held together the spine, a rubber band tight around the book prevented pages from dropping out. Some had crept from between the leather covers though, and Michael could see that whatever was written on them had been inscribed in ink, by hand, in a beautiful flowing style.

'It's all in here,' said Arthur Friend, 'in my old dad's book. Everything you need to know about cows. But it's not like an instruction book. You couldn't just pick it up and know as much as I know. There's more to cows than that. But this book would be a good start.'

'I would love to see it some time, if you would allow that?'

'I might. Or I might not.' And Arthur pushed the notebook back into his inside pocket and took a long, slow draught of the beer.

Then he said, 'Do you play dominoes, Mr Pember?'

'Sort of.'

'Well, looking after cows is a bit like dominoes. You put two and two together and there you are. Get my meaning?'

Michael Pember did not, but instead reached across to the next table where the box of dominoes lay and said, 'I haven't a clue what you're on about, Arthur, but I'll give you a game.'

*　　*　　*

Archie and his father were the first of the party to arrive. Eric Thwaite met them at the front door and would happily have thrown himself down for Sir Thomas to use as a doormat had his knees not been so stiff.

'A sherry, sir? With my compliments.' The servile landlord was laying it on thick. The old man refused the sherry. Archie asked for a half of Bullocks but his father told him it was not a dignified sort of drink for him to be seen holding. Against all his natural instincts, he took up the offer of sherry and prayed none of his army chums would appear to see him drink it.

He and his father stood by the fire in the upstairs room, uncomfortably silent, waiting for the first guest to arrive. Hearing footsteps and muttering on the stairs, the old man drew himself up. Archie played a game with himself, awarding each of the guests he knew a dreariness factor. Marcus Hastings, the solicitor of whom he had the most vivid memory, got a massive ten points – top of the house. The thought of Hastings brought to mind *Mrs* Hastings! He had not forgotten *her* either. Was he going to have to sit next to the overperfumed, overweight, overbearing and over-sexed Priscilla Hastings? He sighed out loud.

'Problem?' said his father.

'As a matter of interest, who am I sitting next to at dinner?' he asked.

'Well, I shall be on one side,' said his father, 'and I thought you might enjoy Priscilla's company. I've put her on the other.'

It was Priscilla Hastings who had accosted Archie at a garden party when he was only fifteen and tried to make a man of him. Being an innocent, he had honestly believed she was frightened of taking a short-cut back to the house alone. She'd told him that woodland always made her nervous and would he walk with her? She had been drinking. Archie was taken completely by surprise when she pinned him to an oak tree and started to explore the deeper recesses of his grey flannel trousers.

'Do you know anything at all about women?' she'd asked,

choking Archie with her pungent perfume. He did not, and certainly had no intention of doing any homework on Mrs Hastings. So he screamed. It was loud enough to be heard by the people in the tent on the lawn who hurried to investigate. When they found him and Mrs Hastings sitting in the grass together, she told them that she thought poor Archie had twisted his ankle and the scream they had heard was him crying out in pain. That was many years ago now but Priscilla Hastings's appetite for teasing had not diminished. Archie still did not feel safe sitting next to the woman. The door opened.

'Marcus! How very good to see you,' growled Sir Thomas as the solicitor came through the door.

Marcus Hastings had aged. Doing sums quickly in his head, Archie reckoned he must be turned seventy. He now walked with a stick, head held with more of a droop than Archie remembered, his words showing the first hint of a slur. Archie made a mental note never to marry a woman twenty years younger – obviously too knackering.

Hastings put out a trembling hand and Archie clasped it.

'A significant day in your life,' said the lawyer, 'probably one of the most important. I remember the day your father took over the estate from his father,' he turned and looked at Sir Thomas, 'and we wondered then what he'd make of it.'

'And now you're wondering what I'll make of it,' said Archie.

'I'm curious as to why you want to make anything of it at all,' said Hastings.

'So am I,' said Archie.

'In that case,' Hastings moved closer so Sir Thomas could not hear, 'you'd be best not meddling at all. Between us, your father and I have built something here that is unique, a model to others. I don't want to see it wasted. It has been my life's work as well, do you understand? Destroy this, and you break your father's heart.'

'And dent your bank balance?' replied Archie, cheekily.

'Is Priscilla downstairs?' asked Sir Thomas, rejoining the conversation.

'I fear,' said Hastings, 'that much as she wanted to be here, she is simply washed out by a terrible cold. She had a bath before we came out, got dressed, and then more or less collapsed on the bed saying it was no use, she didn't have the strength. There did not seem any point trying to persuade her, Thomas. Does it muck things up terribly?'

'So sorry not to be seeing her again, after all these years,' said Archie, trying not to punch the air in joy.

The door of the upstairs room opened again. It was Polly with a fresh tray of sherry, closely followed by the agricultural contractor and his wife, and the managing director of the artificial insemination centre (Biddell's were major shareholders), who seemed to have brought his secretary, and then came a miserable-looking individual in a blazer two sizes too small whom Archie guessed from his pinched face might be an accountant.

'Excuse me, my dear,' said Sir Thomas, spotting Polly, 'we've had a slight change of plan. Mrs Hastings is ill so the place-names will need moving. Err . . . we . . .' The old man was lost. These were the moments when he missed his wife most.

'I suppose that if we put . . . er . . .'

Archie selfishly took charge. 'Who's this Miss Frater? I'll risk it and sit next to her,' he said, wondering if he had made the right choice. He imagined Miss Frater was some old biddy from the village. The name Frater meant nothing to him; in fact very few of the names meant anything in the slightest. Archie glumly imagined Miss Frater was another of his father's dear friends; a pillar of the church, polisher of the pulpit, arranger of flowers, tea-maker extraordinary to the Mothers' Guild, and general do-gooder. But still a safer bet than Mrs Hastings.

'Good evening,' came a quiet voice from behind Archie. It was Brian Frater, duty-bound to attend on account of his contract and feeling miserable as sin.

'We are honoured to be asked, Mr Biddell. The name's Frater, Brian Frater. I mostly do business with your father. Feed supplier.'

Archie said, 'I thought you were a woman. Sorry, no offence meant. But the card distinctly said *Miss* Frater, and now you turn out to be a bloke. Hard luck. It looks as though you're sitting next to me.'

'Oh, there *is* a Miss Frater, my daughter Amanda. She's here somewhere. This is something of a rare appearance for her, in the village. She has a busy London life. Charity work, you know.'

Brian Frater turned his back and started to scan the room. Amanda materialised beside him.

'I'm sorry, Mr Biddell.' She fixed Archie with a pair of deeply intelligent eyes, eased her body slightly so that her weight fell on her stronger leg, and dropped her voice till it was the same pitch as the purr of a satisfied cat. 'You've got me this evening. How do you do? Amanda Frater.'

Rumbling down the motorway, bound for Woodham Ford, disgruntled, bad-tempered – and, most importantly, late – was the Hopscotch family, packed into Toby's company Merc, piled to the roof with duvets and toys stuffed into Applewhite's carrier bags. There would usually have been room in the boot for all this clutter but prime position had to be given to six boxes of Turkey and Cranberry Ready-to-Cook Pasties which were 'in development' but smelled as if they were in the final stages of decay. As if to add to the cheery atmosphere, Georgie was feeling sick, and Tiggy was a touch queasy at the thought that Toby's department was spearheading a new drive on slimy, ready-made Japanese food which she knew she would also have to taste that weekend. Toby was sick to the pit of his stomach at the thought of being late for the Biddells' party. All in all, it was a typical jolly down-to-the-country journey for the Hopscotch family.

'If you'd said I would have been ready earlier,' pleaded Tiggy, half closing her eyes as Toby impatiently swerved to overtake. 'I had no idea. I thought it was just a normal Saturday night. We know so few people in Woodham Ford I never guessed anyone would ask us out for the evening.'

'This isn't *anyone*. Anyway, there are things going on in my world, dear,' said Toby with a smug grin, 'that you can't always be the first to know about. The element of surprise is vital in stealing a march on the enemy.' He narrowed his eyes and gripped the wheel.

'What enemy?' pleaded Tiggy.

'Business talk. I don't expect you to understand.'

But a depressingly familiar scenario was beginning to unfold as she remembered the string of country cottages they had owned previously and how they had been forced to leave each in turn on account of 'business'.

'We haven't got any business in Woodham Ford,' Tiggy reminded him. 'You promised. No more, you said. This was going to be where we have our weekends, put our feet up in front of log fires, have country walks. There wasn't going to be any *business* in Woodham Ford. You swore.'

Toby glanced into the rear mirror and chided Georgie for picking his nose, and then, as if about to deliver the killer line in a movie, said, 'I meant it at the time. But promises, like pie crust, are made to be broken, darling.'

How bloody typical of him, thought Tiggy, to have ready a cheap reply with food in it.

'Is there something going on that I don't know about?'

'Might be.'

'What, in Woodham Ford?'

'Might be. There again, might not.'

'You mean, we didn't buy this cottage because, as you said at the time, it would be a lovely place for the kids to grow up: walk through fields of cows, get a taste of fresh air, recharge batteries. And no more *business*!'

'That was all true. Well, mostly true,' he replied.

Tiggy knew that the only way to glean any further information was to show no interest and let his own bloated ego become his Achilles heel. So she chatted to Georgie, passed him Applewhite's Liquorice All Sorts, promised chips for Sunday lunch if he had finished throwing up by then. It was fifteen minutes before her silent offensive bore fruit.

'Oh, all right then,' Toby finally cracked. 'Woodham Ford's not far from St Edwich. It's a major centre, and under-exploited we think. Still lots of those little town-centre shops. Nothing as big, or as cheap, as us. The plan is this . . . Are you listening?'

Tiggy nodded, depressed by what she feared was coming.

'I want this to be the biggest and best that Applewhite's has ever opened. The rest of the board think it's just another development but I've got this dream . . .'

'Have you?' said Tiggy, wearily. She had been here before.

'. . . I've got this dream that this site can make the rest of the Applewhite's chain look like non-starters. They've never had anything like us to shop at so they're deprived, understand?'

Deprived? she thought. Not being able to shop at Applewhite's was some kind of handicap in life? 'Yes, understood,' she sighed.

'But what I've spotted and the others haven't is the Biddell Estate and its factories.'

'The Biddell Estate?' asked Tiggy. 'It's just one big farm. What has the farm got to do with it?'

'It is *not* just a farm. It's a bloody great food factory. They spend a fortune carting that food round the country. If we offer to buy their entire weekly output to stock our new supermarket, not only can we buy from them at the cheapest possible price because there's no transport costs, but we've got captive customers who work in their factories. We're talking big numbers here, darling. And not just for Applewhite's but for us too.'

'Where do *we* come into all this? Why are there big numbers for us?' Tiggy dreaded it would mean more 'product development', soya-packed sausage rolls and genetically engineered macaroons.

Toby grinned. 'The board. A seat on the board for me if I pull this one off. Shares, stock options . . .'

'So what has tonight got to do with that?' asked Tiggy, who had quickly extrapolated Archie's vision far enough forward to see the For Sale sign over Woodham Ford's village shop, as there had been over all the others. Kiss of Death Hopscotch, she thought wearily.

'Tonight is the key,' said Archie. 'Tonight, not only can I make social contact with the Biddells, but everyone who makes any kind of decision – planning and that sort of thing – will be there too. There's this chap called Hastings, chairs all the committees round there. Met him for lunch last week. He thought it might be good for me to be seen around the village so he swung me an invite to this do of the Biddells. It's supposed to be some kind of family thing, but Hastings said it was really business. Everything the Biddells do is business.'

'But you're seen around the village anyway, when we go for walks,' said Tiggy

'Not just seen, but *be seen*. With the Biddells. Get them on side, make myself a blip on their radar screens, make Hopscotch the name of a man with whom they want to do business. Then we're halfway there. But this chap Hastings is the real key. If you get introduced, you'd better give him all you've got.'

Tiggy thought through all that she was about to be party to: the building of an Applewhite's superstore less than ten miles from Woodham Ford. She remembered the others, the five previous villages in which they'd owned a weekend cottage till Toby's commercial instincts overtook his slender desire for relaxation and a weekend family life. In went the planning application, up went the superstore, out of the village moved the Hopscotches under a cloud. There were protests from village shopkeepers and nearby town councils who saw the hearts of their towns vacuumed clean of customers. Objections as futile as the squealing of cornered rabbits.

Then she thought of The Social Chapter, of people like Marge running small businesses against all the odds. These were the people that Applewhite's trampled over while gorging their corporate guts to bursting points. And it was her husband who put the boots on the corporate giants and showed them which way to march. Then she remembered Amanda Frater and how she, Tiggy, had promised to help her. Her body began to tingle with both nervousness and anger. Perhaps this was going to be the one occasion on which she did not sit on the sidelines while Applewhite's imposed its will on yet another reluctant community.

'I'm looking forward to it, I really am,' said Tiggy. 'Hastings, did you say, and Biddell? Mmm. They're the ones to work on.'

'Good to have you on side,' said Toby, smiling, as he dropped down a gear to take the left-hand turn signposted 'Woodham Ford'.

7

Ten minutes sitting next to Amanda Frater and Archie forgot
that this was one of the least eagerly anticipated nights of his
life, and found it was turning into one of the best. Amanda
had sparkle, wit, a sharp intellect, and the most kissable lips
he had ever seen. His mind should have been on his speech,
thinking about putting on a good show for the honour of
the family and the estate. But he could hardly keep his eyes
off her.

'It's beef. We get through a lot of beef here. It's basically our
business.'

'I had heard,' said Amanda. 'It's not exactly my favourite,
though.'

'Mine neither. Haven't touched it since . . . Well, I haven't eaten
beef for ages. But round here it's part of life. Beef.'

'And how much beef do you produce a year, Mr Biddell?'

'Please, Archie.'

'So, how much beef a year, Archie?'

'Pass. Several thousand tons, I guess.'

'You don't sound exactly on top of this business,' said Amanda.
'Most manufacturers know exactly how much they produce at any
given moment. It's the sort of number that comes to their head
before their phone number or their wife's birthday. But clearly
not with you. The wife's birthday comes first.'

'If there were one – a wife – yes, I suppose it would . . .' So
Amanda had cleared up that little detail '. . . but the sort of
chaps who have those numbers in their heads are committed,
aren't they?'

'And you're not?'

'Give me a chance! I'm only just into my third week here, running things. Or trying to.'

'My father supplies most of your feed, right?'

'Does he? If you say so.'

'And he says that what this gathering is all about is . . .'

Archie was anxious to hear how it was being described by those on the outside looking in.

'. . . if your eyebrows go any higher, Mr Biddell, they'll be through the ceiling,' Amanda remarked looking him full in the face, her glance lingering. He did not miss the slightest hint of a smile in her eyes.

'What this is all about, according to Dad,' she continued, 'is a coronation. Tonight this entire food and farming operation – which produces so much beef you don't even know how much it is – passes into your hands. The soldier returns home in triumph to be crowned king of all he surveys. Sort of romantic, isn't it?'

'No,' replied Archie. 'Tonight this estate, in the shape of a bloated agricultural ball and chain, is firmly shackled to my ankle to prevent me from ever escaping. Like a prisoner of war, except there was no war. I gave myself up, came home of my own accord, waved the white flag, surrendered to Father, did the decent thing.'

'There are worse kinds of incarceration,' she said.

'You think so? You should see some of what goes on here,' Archie replied darkly.

'Meaning?'

'Meaning just that. Then you'll see why it's difficult to envisage being proud of it. Or at least of the bits I've had time to see.'

'I'd like to take a look.'

'Great. I'll take you up to the farm, show you the cows. Later, when this is all over. And let's hope it's a more enjoyable trip than the last time I took a young lady up to the barn late at night.'

'This is some kind of habit of yours, taking girls into the cowshed late at night?' asked Amanda, surprised.

'Only when they ask nicely,' he replied. 'How about tonight, then?'

'Tonight?'

'A soldier should never flinch from battle. Got to face up to it. No use putting it off till tomorrow.'

'Why do you call it a battle?' asked Amanda, confused. 'A bit overdramatic, isn't it?'

'Because I sense that if anything round here is to change, it's going to be a fight all the way.'

'And who is the enemy?'

'Just look around.' Archie's eyes scanned the room. 'These are the first ones that have to be faced up to.'

'Hey, my dad's sitting over there! He's not a baddie, is he?'

'Let's give him the benefit of the doubt,' replied Archie. 'But I saw a cow die the first night I came home. It was a terrible death. A death devised, managed and implemented by these same kind, decent people around this table. An agreeable conspiracy to make money out of cows, whatever the cost to the animals.'

'I think we might have a lot in common,' said Amanda.

'Oh? Like what?' he asked.

'Like a mutual dislike of beef. Do you think we'll be able to hide it under the peas?' she said, giggling.

Eric Thwaite had been fussing over two seats that were still unoccupied. Both carried the place-name Hopscotch. No one could quite remember who they were and no one could offer any explanation as to why they might be late. The only person who really knew was Marcus Hastings whose idea it had been to invite them. Eric bent over and took advantage of a pause in the close conversation taking place between Archie and Amanda.

'I don't want to disturb Sir Thomas, but do you think I might serve the first course? The beef's done to a turn and if we wait any longer it will be overcooked. It's the best part of the hind-quarter of that prize-winning Aberdeen Angus cross. Criminal to overdo it.'

Overcooking was probably the least of the crimes inflicted on it, thought Amanda.

'Yes, anything you like, Eric,' said Archie. 'Who are we waiting for? Anyone I know?'

'Name of Hopscotch, I believe.'

'I'm sorry,' said Amanda, suddenly alert, 'but who did you say?'

'Hopscotch,' said Eric Thwaite.

'Sounds like a game kids play,' said Archie. Amanda thought that phrase had a familiar ring to it. The landlord went to find Polly to tell her to start serving the soup – mushroom made with a thick beef stock.

Amanda felt uneasy. If she was recognised and the damned Hopscotch woman started to twitter on about animal rights it would be a disaster.

'And what are your hobbies?' asked Archie.

'What a bloody boring question! That's the sort of thing the Queen asks you. Let's talk about something more interesting.' She leaned closer to him. 'Like *your* hobbies.'

In the downstairs bar, pints were put down and all eyes turned as the dishevelled Hopscotches burst through the door, panting slightly, looking lost.

'Er, Biddell's party. We're expected,' said Toby to Eric Thwaite, as if addressing a pile of dog dirt in the street. 'We're a little late. Would you show us up straight away?'

He pulled the next pint as slowly as he could short of no beer emerging from the pump, then wiped his hands very carefully on a cloth, straightened his tie and said, 'And can I say who it is?'

'Mr and Mrs Hopscotch. Guests of Marcus Hastings. We're invited. If we could just sneak in quietly . . .'

'Of course,' said Eric, and led them up the stairs. As the door opened, the warm air, heavy with the scents of gravy, beef and roast potatoes, fell across them as if poured from a ladle. Eric Thwaite opened his mouth and bellowed as loudly as he could, 'Mr and Mrs . . . er . . .' He looked around.

'Hopscotch, the name's Hopscotch,' said Toby, through gritted

110

teeth, flapping his hands, trying to persuade Eric to moderate his voice a little. Too late. The scrape of Sheffield steel on bone china halted, the roar of conversation became a murmur, the jaws which were chewing the fore-quarter of the prime Aberdeen Angus cross were stilled. All heads turned towards the door. Suddenly conspicuous, Tiggy glanced at the other women to see how they were dressed, but saw only high street clothing and felt easier. Then her head quickly flicked back to the top of the table, drawn by an image her mind had captured in another place. She saw those eyes, that hair. She began to stare, certain now that this was Amanda from The Social Chapter. Here? Why? As Tiggy stared, Amanda stared back. She raised the index finger of her right hand and placed it lightly across her lips.

'Er, very sorry we're a little late,' said Toby, trying to be cool.

'Over here, Hopscotch,' cried Marcus Hastings, spitting a little gravy as he shouted. 'If you don't get sat down, Thwaite will have you on the spit and roasted. Get a move on, lad.' The room chuckled and Toby and Tiggy pushed their way forward with an excess of excuse mes and I beg your pardons.

'Nice to see you, *my dear*,' said Hastings in the way he patronised all women whether he knew them or not. 'I've been *so* looking forward to meeting you.' He rose from his seat in a gentlemanly way as Tiggy took the empty chair next to him. The old boy shuffled his chair a little closer to her till his arthritic old knee was touching hers. Tiggy shuddered.

'Who are they? That oaf and that weedy little woman?' asked Archie, his eyes drawn to Amanda's face.

'Which woman?' she asked, casually.

'The one you clearly know. The one who just came in. I've never seen eyes widen so quickly as yours did. Beautiful eyes, if I may say so. Or perhaps it was the man you recognised. Old flame?'

'Don't be daft,' scoffed Amanda.

'So it was the woman you recognised?'

'And what if I did?'

'Nothing, nothing at all. Except I'm curious as to what the big secret might be.'

'Secret?'

'When people put a finger to their lips, it's usually a sign for others to keep their mouth shut.'

Amanda raised her right hand, slowly extended her arm, looked Archie straight in the eye and brought her warm index finger slowly to rest on his moist lips.

'Later,' she purred.

She held her finger in place, teasing him, then removed it quickly when she saw his father watching, wide-eyed at their behaviour.

'Anyway, how do you know I was staring at anybody?' she asked playfully now she was feeling safer.

'Because I was staring at you,' he said.

'Well, don't.'

'Why not?'

'Because if you stare long enough you'll notice that I hate bloody gravy as much as I hate beef and this plate is swimming in it.'

'Shhh,' said Archie. 'If Eric hears you he'll take it personally. He might throw himself off the roof if he finds someone isn't enjoying his beef.'

She had diverted the conversation, taken his mind off the arrival of the Hopscotches.

'You're a brave woman, to come here and say out loud you don't like beef. It's more than I dare. I'd mark you down as a gutsy sort of lady,' Archie continued.

'I will not be marked down as anything by anybody,' she replied, haughtily.

'Too late, you're marked. You've got guts. I just ticked the box. Alongside guts I've given you eight out of ten.'

She turned to him indignantly.

'A lousy eight? Why not a full house? Where did I lose the two marks?'

'By not telling me how you come to know that strange little

Hopscotch woman. I'm curious. It was the way your eyes went as wide as a frightened cow's the minute she walked in the room. I thought that was odd. So, want to earn those extra couple of points?'

'More gravy, Mr Biddell?' replied Amanda. 'Or do you have enough sauce already?'

The Hopscotches skipped the mushroom soup and got stuck into the beef. Toby made his peace with Eric Thwaite by asking for a second helping. Not entirely forgiving him for being late and risking the beef, Eric used the leftover gravy that was slightly too cool to be appetising. Tiggy did not make such a good impression, only nibbling at the roast potatoes and the peas. She occasionally glanced at the top of the table, looking hard at Amanda. Their eyes met once more but the intensity of Amanda's reaction warned off Tiggy who, for the rest of the evening, played the humble wife and tried to forget about Amanda Frater.

Toby started to play big business, but soon found that with Marcus Hastings he was batting in a higher league.

'Do you understand country ways, Hopscotch?' asked Hastings.

'Pheasants and things. Deer stalking. That sort of country way?' Toby replied.

Hastings put down his knife and fork and glanced from side to side to ensure that those within earshot were deep in conversations of their own.

'What I mean is, do you know how business is done round here? Because if you want your superstore in St Edwich you had better start finding out. That's why I asked you here tonight.'

'I'm grateful,' fawned Toby.

'I need not tell you any of this,' said Hastings, 'but it will save time. You'd find out for yourself in the end but it's quicker this way. Tonight you will see Archie Biddell formally take over the running of this estate from his father. But that changes nothing. His father never really ran it, and neither will Archie. *I* made this estate what it is. That is the first thing to understand, and never to forget. You and I do the deal. Forget that silly boy soldier at the top of the table.'

Toby nodded deferentially.

'All this stuff about the great Biddell family having the Midas touch is rubbish,' said Hastings. 'I have the touch round here. And this is the last time I intend to wave the magic wand. When you get to seventy, it's time to draw back a little. And let us say that I want a few comforts around me when I do.'

'A few comforts?' asked Hopscotch.

'It goes without saying,' said Hastings, 'that this conversation never took place.' He lowered his voice. 'I own a little land on the outskirts of St Edwich which is ideal for your plans. All I ask is a good price for it. A *very* good price. In return, you will get a good business deal with the Biddell Estate, rock bottom prices that will have you undercutting every other supplier. That blasted boy Archie has no clue what goes on, and never will have. Whatever deal you want, I can get. If the price you pay for my piece of land is right.'

'There's no planning permission,' said Toby. 'The council would have to approve it.'

'And, of course, as the owner of the land I would have no part in that decision, being also the chairman of the planning committee.' Hastings smiled. 'That's why I transferred ownership five years ago to an offshore holding company. I have been waiting some time for a chap like you to come along, Mr Hopscotch.'

'It's corrupt,' said Toby, never before having dabbled in any deception greater than the ambiguous labelling of Cornish pasties.

'Delightfully so. But everything is corrupt round here. Has been for generations. You don't get the Biddells to where they are now by playing it by the book. I've effectively run that estate for them for thirty years, seen the way the profits have soared, and now it's time for my final commission. Look at that boy sitting next to his father.' Hastings looked at Archie with disdain. 'He'll ruin

114

the estate, drive it under, make it into a has-been of a place. No future here now, whatever he might say. So I might as well grab what I can. A little bonus is what I'm after, and I'm looking to you for it.' He licked his lips as much in anticipation of a neat deal with Hopscotch as to remove an excess of horseradish sauce from his chin.

Having said all he intended to say to Toby Hopscotch, he turned to Tiggy whose knee had felt the pressure of his all night.

'My dear, you've hardly touched your beef. Your husband and I have been getting what you might call a slice of the action. Are you sure you wouldn't like a slice of fresh, hot beef to go with it?' He chortled at his own humour. 'More claret over here, Thwaite,' he bellowed, 'and more beef for Mrs Hopscotch.'

Tiggy's stomach churned. She looked at the top table and saw Archie Biddell whispering in Amanda Frater's ear.

Through his open bedroom window, Chuff could hear the roar of the party drifting in the still March air all the way from The Peacock to the Barnyard Estate. It made him angry, for he knew the sounds of merriment made by the owners, the managers and the executives would not penetrate the thick walls which enclosed their pigs and cows. They would not share the fun, he thought. And neither would his mum, locked in that turkey factory for the night, sweating over vile cauldrons of turkey waste, straining to hear any conversation over the mechanical rattle of the production line. He pulled off his boots and slung them, in a rage, against the door. Then he went over to his computer and stabbed his finger on the keyboard to bring it to life. He dialled the Internet. Once logged on, he clicked his way to the CFFA Home Page, the regular starting point for his evening travels of inspiration into the veiled world of animal rights.

When he saw the words, **Welcome to the CFFA Home Page** he felt he was home. First he clicked on **Animal Rights Literature File.** Here were collections of articles from newspapers, magazines, discussion documents, philosophical texts, fictional works; a mishmash of unordered ideas. He read as much of it as he could understand, taking each word very slowly, making sure he had grasped fully the connection with the previous one. He read his screen several times (still running up connection charges to be paid eventually by his hard-pressed mother):

Any system of rights must define who must qualify and who should not. The accepted view is that all people qualify for rights.

Chuff had no problem with that, although even he recognised that within Woodham Ford, having rights and having any right to make use of them was a different matter. He read on.

It is not enough for just people to have rights. Take severely handicapped babies; they have rights without any doubt, even though they may have less mental capacity and intellect than many farm animals. So shouldn't animals have equal rights?

Chuff roared his approval with the enthusiasm of a football crowd greeting a goal. Spot on, direct hit! He loved every word. His bellow woke the tabby cat which until then had been soundly asleep on his bed and now skulked downstairs in search of peace and quiet. Chuff read on;

The most important attribute is the capacity to suffer, which is self-evidently present in both humans and animals. Therefore the animal's suffering must be taken into account whenever a decision about their treatment is to be made. Some experiments might justify the suffering caused to animals in the laboratory – finding of a cure for, say, AIDS – and might use that to excuse the death of a monkey. But, if so, it could equally justify experiments on a severely mentally handicapped person; anything else would be speciesism.

Chuff laboured with 'speciesism'; repeating it out loud till he thought he had got it right. The tabby cat reappeared round the door, confusing his attempts at pronunciation with the call to food.

In order not to be speciesist, all creatures must qualify as individuals and enjoy strong rights. The accidental death of a young man is regarded as sadder than the death of an old one, because he is being deprived of his future. In order not to display speciesism we must extend the same idea to farm animals. Even if the animal killing is painless, it is wrong, because the animal is being deprived of its future.

'Yes! Yes!' roared Chuff, banging his fist on the table, remembering the turkeys. The tabby cat fled.

Exhausted by the mental effort of reading and understanding, Chuff wanted something easier, such as pictures, to look at. He clicked back to the CFFA Home Page to see if less demanding avenues of exploration were on offer. He looked at a box marked '**QUIZ**' and wondered if he should have a go? He'd been tempted before, but feared making a fool of himself. Exams and suchlike had never been his thing. This time, he was tempted.

Only take part in this quiz if you seriously wish to win a major prize
Click OK or ESCAPE

Chuff clicked the positive option. Then came another warning.

You will be asked to enter your name and address and a telephone number where you can be contacted if you win a major prize. If you do not wish us to contact you, you should not proceed any further.
Click OK or ESCAPE.

OK

Questions will appear on the screen. If you can give answers to all the questions then you may be selected for a major prize. If you are one of our lucky winners you will be hearing from us within the next few days. We regret that those not lucky enough to win one of our prizes cannot be informed individually.
WARNING
Some of the questions require you to make difficult personal decisions. You are free to reply honestly. This game makes only irregular and brief appearances on our Home Page and so it is unlikely that your entry can be observed by third parties. So feel free to be honest. Click OK or ESCAPE.

Chuff shivered, sensed this game was getting serious. He clicked **OK**.

QUESTION 1
Do you believe that farm animals have the same rights as human beings, and if so why?

Difficult starter. It was lucky that Chuff had been diverted into a little animal rights literature, and had been forced to repeat over and over again the word 'speciesism'. He composed his reply in his head before tapping it out in the screen space provided.

Yes, farm animals have the same rights as humans. More rights in some ways because they cannot defend themselves. I am against speeshesism.

ENTER

QUESTION 2
If you discover that animal husbandry practices in your area do not add up to a fair deal for the animals, would you be prepared to take direct action? Answer Yes or No.

Chuff answered **Yes**.

QUESTION 3
You have answered yes. In that case, how far are you prepared to go?

Chuff thought about this. How far *was* he prepared to go?

As I do not have any transport of my own, I can not get very far at all.

The screen blinked back at him.

You have misunderstood. How much are you prepared to do to stop these improper animal husbandry practices?
Answer now.

* * *

Sorry. See what you mean now. I live next door to farming bastards who ruin the lives of all the animals on their farm, and the lives of everybody round here. I would do ANYTHING to fuck them up good and proper.

A final message appeared:

Thank you for answering the questions. You will be hearing from us if you have won a major prize. In order to win, it is important that you leave your name and address within the next thirty seconds or this window will close and you will not be able to reconnect. Give your name and address now.

Chuff typed as quickly as he could but the pressure of completing the entry within the thirty seconds did not help. When he thought he had got it right, he pressed **ENTER**.

It was now 4 o'clock in the morning and all this added up to several hours of connection time, more pounds on the phone bill, more hours his mother would have to spend, slaving over the contemptible vats in the turkey factory.

Roast beef gave way to sherry trifle, and claret to port. The Queen had been duly toasted, and Archie noticed Amanda stumbled as she got to her feet to drink the loyal toast. He had offered his hand but she refused it. Cigars appeared around the room. Archie made small talk with his father to his left, but the real centre of attention was to his right.

'You have the most fabulous eyes,' he said in an offhand way, although he had been working towards this moment all night.

'And you have a speech to make,' she said, coolly. 'You'd do better to dwell on that.'

'And why should I not dwell on you?'

'Because it's not worth giving too much thought to things you know nothing about. And you know nothing at all about me. What I do, where I come from, why I am here.'

'Wrong,' said Archie. 'You are Amanda Frater, a charity worker, you have a flat in London, your dad's our feed supplier and you love him so much that when he asks you to a balls-aching event like this, you come. But I admit, there is one area of knowledge in which I am lacking . . .'

She raised her eyebrows.

'. . . and that is who you *really* are.'

'What you see is what you get,' she replied.

'I doubt it,' said Archie.

'What's the burden of your speech? Want to give me a flavour?' asked Amanda, trying to change the subject.

'I'd rather get a flavour of you!'

'A word of advice, Mr Biddell,' she said, 'don't waste your time with cheap remarks. You don't strike me as a cheap sort of bloke. Now, your speech.' Archie looked serious for the first time that evening.

'If I had the guts, I'd tell it to them like it is. But I'm not quite ready yet. It's too soon. I've got to be clear in my own mind what's going on here. I think I've got a picture of the lousy way the cows are run. But there's pigs and turkeys too.'

'You'll be man enough one day,' she said.

'Planning on sticking around to see?' he said, with a broad smile.

'I rate him very highly,' said Hastings to Hopscotch, 'Thomas is one of the finest farmers of his generation. I suspect the son, Archie, is hopeless. Been out of it too long, marching up and down, playing soldiers. Farming is a vocation and you have to give all your life to it, not drop in and out as you fancy. As soon as I heard the boy was coming home, I realised I'd seen the best of it. Everything I'd worked for would be down the pan, every bloody bit of it. Terrible waste of a good business, to see it go to a boy like Archie with no idea at all.'

Toby was pushing the remains of the sherry trifle around his plate, wondering if he completely understood what Marcus had told him. The site for the supermarket, currently owned by Hastings but under a different name, could be his in return for £2.5 million, planning permission guaranteed. Hastings would ensure a tight deal between the Biddell Estate and Applewhite's, which meant the supermarket could buy at prices lower than any retailer in Britain. Hopscotch turned this around in his mind, like claret in a wine-taster's mouth, enjoying every subtlety.

'I shall leave as soon as the speech is over. I doubt we shall ever meet again,' said Hastings. 'No one here will remember seeing us talk together – they're very loyal like that. Just pursue the purchase of the land in the normal way, you won't meet any obstacles. Nice to do business with you. Now, I must say good evening to your dear wife with whom I've hardly had a chance to exchange a word.' He turned his head towards her. 'Oh, my dear!' he exclaimed. 'You've hardly touched your trifle. If I can give you one word of advice: it is best to be seen to enjoy beef if you want your husband to do well in business round here.'

'But it's the cream on the trifle that I've left,' said Tiggy, confused.

'Cream, beef . . . It's all cows, my dear. All profit for the estate. Eat up, there's a good girl.'

'Do as Marcus – sorry – Mr Hastings says,' muttered Toby.

Tiggy, feeling like a child told to clean her plate, could take no more. She looked towards the top of the table again, caught Amanda's eye and transmitted a message of her own: 'Yes, I'm with you all the way. Whatever you do, whoever you are, whatever plan you have, I want to be with you. I want to be anywhere other than here, with these disgusting people, with my selfish, blinkered bloody husband!'

Amanda felt the stare and although she had avoided eye contact all evening, Tiggy's focused eyes became so insistent that she could not withstand them. Amanda nodded her head slightly, which was enough of a signal for Tiggy to read into it 'message received and understood'.

Archie's mood changed in the few moments before he was due to get to his feet. His playfulness and boyishness had gone. He stared at the empty plate in front of him, fiddled with the cork from the claret bottle and nervously broke it into pieces, checked a dozen times that the bits of paper on which he had written his notes were still in his pocket, and even forgot for a time that Amanda Frater was sitting next to him.

It was she who broke the silence when she leaned closer, put her hand on his and said, 'Tell them what they want to hear. It is as much your duty to do that as anything else, to keep the peace for your father's sake. Then, afterwards, you can tell *me* how you really feel.'

Eric Thwaite nodded from across the room to Archie, who nodded back. It was the signal for Eric to bang a silver spoon on the table and call for silence. Archie got to his feet, swallowed hard, took a deep breath and launched into his speech.

'Friends and guests, I have dreamed all my life of the day when the Biddell Estate would become my responsibility, and now it has happened I am overwhelmed. It is safe in my hands. I only hope that in the years to come I can maintain it to the high standards set by my family and in particular my father.' He rambled on for five more minutes, along those entirely predictable lines.

A ripple of 'Hear, hear' went around the room. Marcus Hastings had closed his eyes. None of what Archie thought mattered to him.

'I had it in mind to make changes to the way we run things, particularly our hugely successful livestock enterprise . . .'

That caused Hastings to open his eyes.

'. . . but then I thought, well, how could we do it better than the way we do it now?'

There was a huge cheer.

Sir Thomas leaned over to Amanda Frater. 'That was my line. I fed him that one. Good, wasn't it?'

Archie worked his way through the entire estate, thanking each branch of the operation for its continued support and profitability. Then he came to Brian Frater who, up till now, had not been enjoying the evening, thinking more about where the cash was to come from to pay for the next delivery of wholesale feed, and in particular the reply to his phone call to Orion Shipping.

'And to our feed supplier, Brian Frater, whose excellent products make all the livestock on our farms burst with health.'

There was a modest round of applause, but confusion too for Frater was a minor player compared with the others. Those who were perplexed did not have to wait long to find out why Archie had spoken as he had.

'We always thought those pig nuts were the best thing you ever produced, Mr Frater, but now we realise your finest creation is your daughter, Amanda.'

There were whoops of laughter at the joke. But Archie wasn't joking.

Archie had made a promise, and Amanda was going to keep him to it. Still in his dinner suit, he walked her up the hill to the barn to see the cows.

'You did well tonight. I believed you. Everybody believed you,' she said.

'It was an act. Nothing to be proud of,' he replied.

A light shone out of the giant cow shed, unusual for the time of night. Archie slid back the heavy door which grated on its rusty bearings and sent piercing squeals through the cathedral of a shed, causing every cow's eyes to look in their direction.

Amanda gasped. She had never seen so many cows together in one place, staring at her, eyes fixed and unblinking. She did not know whether to be afraid.

'Will they charge?' she asked.

'Charge? For looking at them? No, I don't think they'll make a charge. Very generous are cows.'

'Don't be stupid, you know what I mean. Is it safe in here, with all these animals? They're looking at us. That one over there is snorting.'

'That's not snorting,' said Archie. 'If I remember correctly she's just blowing down her nose. It's what cows do to make friends. Instead of swapping kisses they exchange breath. If you went and breathed back at her you'd both be friends for life. We used to

123

do it when we were kids, in the days when the cows went out to the meadows all day. We used to lean on the gates and blow down their noses.' Archie smiled and said, 'Lean towards me and I'll show you.'

'Keep your heavy breathing for your cow friends, thank you,' said Amanda. She was trying to guess how many cows were staring at her. At least a hundred, she thought. She tried taking a deep breath so she could snort back at them but the ammonia in the air caught her in the back of the throat and made her cough.

Archie's eye was caught by the flicker of a torch in a darker corner of the barn.

'Tomlinson!' he shouted, expecting it to be the stockman. 'Is that you over there?'

A wavering voice replied but it was not Tomlinson's.

'I could do with a little help, if you don't mind.'

'Who the bloody hell?' cried Archie, taking Amanda by the hand. 'Come on.'

'What, through the cows?' she said, still nervous of the herd.

'How else?' Archie briefly lost patience. He grabbed her hand. It had been a long climb up the hill from The Peacock to the barn and Amanda's leg was beginning to feel the strain. As the pace quickened, she stumbled.

'Are you OK?' he asked.

'Fell into a patch of straw, nothing worse than that.' She clenched her teeth and hoped the pain would pass, then hurried as fast as she could through the deep, heady and adhesive mush of trampled straw and droppings.

In the far corner of the barn, away from the lights, an elderly man was kneeling beside a prostrate cow, caressing her neck with long, firm strokes from behind her ears all the way down to her shoulder. He was talking to her in a low whisper.

'Soon, old girl, you'll be all right. Very soon you'll be fine. You'll do all right.'

Archie looked first at the cow, and then at the old man.

'I think I know you, don't I?'

'You should,' replied the old man. 'It was me who taught you that trick of blowing down a cow's nose. Sorry to eavesdrop and all that, couldn't help it.'

'Arthur, isn't it? Arthur Friend. Good to see you. I thought they'd retired you years ago.'

'I did retire years ago, Mr Archie. But I still get these odd feelings about the cows, and if I think something's wrong I just can't leave them be. It's none of my business, and I apologise for trespassing among your cows, Mr Archie. But, you see, I was certain this one was going to calve tonight and no one would listen, so I just had to come up and see to her. Good job I did. Hell of a struggle she's had.'

'Don't apologise, Arthur. We've all got a responsibility, if we think things aren't right with the cows. Just because we pay a stockman doesn't mean our bit's done. Though where the bloody hell is he, anyway? Shouldn't he be here?'

'Not my place to say, sir,' replied Arthur, 'but a good man would do extra hours round about calving time. Nearly lived with 'em, we did, in my day.'

Amanda was staring down at the semi-conscious cow, her head in a pool of blood, rear end resting in the debris from when her calf had been born. She wanted to be sick. Arthur caught the look on her face.

'There's nothing unpleasant about it, miss, nothing at all. It's a miracle, I always think. Another little calf coming into the world. I always thought it was special, except the first time I saw it when I admit I was sick for the rest of day. Your first time, is it?'

Amanda nodded.

'You'll feel better if you see the calf, then you'll think it's all worthwhile,' said Arthur.

'Is she going to die?' asked Amanda, unable to take her eyes off the cow whose eyes were staring, as if in pain. She slowly dropped to her knees, for once forgetting the discomfort she always felt when kneeling, and unaware that her expensive clothes were being soiled by the noxious mash of straw and droppings. She reached out and stroked the cow gently between her eyes and down the length of her nose till she felt its warm breath on her fingertips.

'She'll be fine. Between you and me,' said Arthur, 'I've just given her a little something that I always used to give them in the old days when I was stockman here. Perks 'em up no end. Knocks 'em out to start with but they feel all the better for it.'

'You mean a drug?'

'Drugs! I don't muck around with no drugs. Don't need 'em. Never have. It's all in the book, you see, all written down by my old father who I reckon copied it from *his* father as soon as he learned to write.'

Archie knelt next to the cow, the soiled straw imprinting itself on his dinner suit, and stroked her and tried to imitate Arthur's hypnotic lilt as he calmed the creature with his voice.

'With the greatest of respect to your old dad,' he said after a while, getting up and brushing the filth from his knees, 'I think we'll have the vet check her over. I'll be back in a minute.' And he strode across to a small office in the corner.

'Did you say there was a calf?' Archie shouted across the barn as he picked up the phone.

'Yes,' replied Arthur, 'a fine little heifer calf. I just moved her over here so she's out of the draught. Didn't want her to get a chill. Soon as her mother's on her feet she'll come over and sort her out. Lick her into shape, see what I mean? Lovely little calf she is.'

Amanda gathered her strength, defied the pain, and got to her feet. Dazed by the intensity of the life and near-death around her, she stumbled through the straw towards where the calf was lying.

'Not too fast,' warned Arthur, 'you'll put the wind up her if you move too fast. Little thing's only been in the world ten minutes. Never seen a great big human before, begging your pardon, miss. Look, this is how you say hello . . .' He crept slowly towards what appeared to be no more than a pile of straw, Amanda following precisely in his footsteps. Just by the wall, in a corner where the wind could not blow nor the rain penetrate, he knelt down and parted the straw. Amanda gasped at the beauty of what she saw.

126

Lying there was the tiniest black and white calf, a creature still glistening with the amniotic fluid which had protected it while it grew inside its mother for almost a year. And now it was in the world, flickering its eyes as they became used to the light, feeling its legs, learning the position of every extremity of its body until it had sufficient mastery of them to be able to stand, find its mother, and suck the life-sustaining milk from her udder.

Arthur placed his index finger deep into its mouth, and after a moment, he smiled. Yes, it sucked hard. It would feed well when it was able, which would not be long.

'Try it. Feel it for yourself,' said Arthur, taking hold of Amanda's hand. 'I think it's the most wonderful thing, to feel that suck a calf gives your finger, telling you it knows what it's doing. Miracle, ain't it?'

She looked at him, nervously. He nodded back in encouragement. 'Go on. Little creature can't hurt you.'

She felt the lips of the calf part as she pressed the tip of her finger against its mouth. She was surprised to find teeth already formed. Inside, it was warm, almost hot, and she was startled by the tongue which had the feel of coarse sandpaper. She looked up at Arthur.

'Rough, ain't it, that tongue?' he said, guessing correctly what was going through her mind. 'Needs to be, you see, to get a good hold of the mother's teat. Some of those cows don't always make it easy for the little ones. I've seen calves have to hang on for grim death while mother gallops round the field. That's why their tongue feels like that. Got to get a good grip, see?'

The wide eyes of the calf were looking at Amanda, expecting to see its mother but confronting a human instead. Nevertheless, the instinct was too great for the calf to ignore, and it wrapped its rasp-like tongue round her finger and sucked hard.

'She sucked! I felt it. She really sucked.'

Amanda turned, but Arthur was no longer there. He was back with the cow who was now struggling to her feet. By some amazing telepathy, the calf started to flex its legs too; it tried first to raise

127

itself up using the back pair, and failed. Then it tried the front, and ended up in a hopeless heap. Finally, after trying every combination of legs possible, it hit on a winning formula and rose, astounded by what it had done, swaying for a moment to gather strength for the next move.

Arthur saved it from further effort by gently placing his hands under its belly and lifting, then carried it across to its mother who suddenly remembered what all the fuss was about, and made straight for the little animal. Then she stood perfectly still while Arthur gently put the calf to the ground by her flank, standing on its own four trembling legs, and guided the teat into its mouth. The cow closed her eyes in a way that could be taken for bliss as loud sucking noises came from the calf's mouth. It was not long before thick, yellow, creamy milk was dribbling down the calf's chin, reminding Amanda of a greedy child eating vanilla ice cream too quickly.

She heard Archie's footsteps returning. Even so, she could not take her eyes off the miracle that was being enacted before her.

'Vet's on his way,' said Archie. 'He thinks the cow might need some antibiotic. And the calf will need inoculating; minerals and vitamins and all that sort of thing.'

'She don't need nothing. Neither of 'em do,' said Arthur. 'Fine pair they make. Healthy as they come.'

'All the same,' said Archie, whose instinct was to believe Arthur but whose business sense told him that a jab was good insurance, necessary or not.

'I've given them a little something of my own,' said Arthur. 'It's what my old dad called a pick-me-up. Just something to get a bit of life into her. Calf don't need anything. Fine little thing, she is.'

He fumbled in the straw till he found the old canvas bag, a relic from the Second World War and designed for carrying gas masks. He opened the flap and placed in it a small, brown medicine bottle. It was not of the modern kind with a child-proof cap and waterproof label, but fluted and stoppered with an old cork. Then, out of his inside pocket, he pulled the old leather-bound notebook and put that in the canvas bag as well. He slung it over his shoulder.

'Well, goodnight, miss. Lovely to have met you. I'd say you had a real feel for farm animals, way you took to that calf. I wouldn't be afraid if I was you. They seem to take to you too.' And with that Arthur was gone, and there was the sound of his bicycle making its way across the concrete yard and then down the lane.

'I didn't plan on the evening ending up like this. Sorry if I've spoiled it,' said Archie.

The calf was now exhausted from its sucking and bloated with milk. It lay flat out on the straw. Amanda took a deep breath and, entranced by the calf, absentmindedly hitched up the left leg of her trousers to make it easier for her to kneel.

'It has been the most wonderful evening. Thanks,' she said, kneeling next to the calf. And where Archie might have hoped she would reach out to touch him, instead she gave the calf one more gentle caress on its damp neck and wished it goodnight.

'There's something funny about this little calf,' she said, staring hard at it. 'It's her markings. She's very spotty. It's as if she's got white dots all over her. Look.'

It was just another calf to Archie.

'Dominoes! That's what she looks like, doesn't she?' Amanda sounded excited now. 'She's so spotty she looks like a domino. Will you call her Domino?'

Archie was distracted. He had just caught a glimpse of Amanda's bare leg, scarred and dappled where surgeons had clearly been at work.

'Call her?' he said, surprised. 'I'm afraid the nearest she'll get to a name is BDL814, or whatever the next number might be. I don't suppose cows here have had names since old Arthur left. Too confusing. I remember when I was a kid, at one time we had four cows called Sunshine and no one knew which was which. Except Arthur, of course.'

'Well, it's time for names again. So it's Domino, OK?' said Amanda.

It seemed a small thing so Archie nodded his agreement.

'Shall I help you to your feet,' he asked, reaching out a hand. She glanced down and realised he had seen her leg.

'I'm not a cripple. It's not pretty, but it works,' she insisted. 'No sympathy, no help needed.'

8

Because Chuff had spent the entire evening on line, the turkey factory had been unable to get through to tell him of the accident. The police woke him at 6 o'clock to tell him that his mother had been killed. Details were still sketchy, but she was the only person involved. The young WPC who broke the news did not stay long. She offered to make him a cup of tea, but he refused. His mum would make him one when she got back from work, like she always did. No, she wasn't coming back, she was dead. Oh, Christ! She was dead. He'd make his own cup of tea, thanks. He looked around for a clean mug, and couldn't find one. His mum usually washed up, as soon as she got in. Oh God, his mother was dead, wasn't coming back, never, ever. Killed, in a bloody turkey factory!

'I knew something was going on,' said Eric Thwaite with a tremor in his voice, hands covering his face, elbows resting on the bar. 'I heard the sirens, you know. Middle of the night. After the party I slept like a log so you can imagine what sort of row they made to wake me up.'

'You look as pale as a sheet,' replied Polly. 'I think you ought to sit down.' She saw the redness around his eyes.

'Poor Chuff. What's going to happen to him?' she asked.

'Well, when I was a lad,' said Eric, 'Chuff was the sort they'd have put in a home – and the best place for him. Pity they can't do that with him now. He killed her, if you ask me. Ground her down. Grind any bugger down that boy would. Still, he's lost his mother so I suppose he deserves some sympathy.' Eric picked up a cloth and started to polish glasses.

'All looks a bit odd, as far as I can make out,' said a voice from the far end of the bar. It was the stockman, Tomlinson, who had crept into the pub unnoticed. He came over and leaned on the bar.

'Do you want to know what they're saying?' he whispered.

'I don't want no bloody gossip. Not over Freda's dead body. She's dead . . .' Eric swallowed hard '. . . and we've all got to come to terms with it.'

'They say it was suicide,' Tomlinson persisted. 'They found her leaning over one of those big vats they use to boil the turkey carcasses. The lid was right down, resting on her neck.'

'I don't want to hear no more,' insisted Eric, drawing away. Tomlinson raised his voice. 'They reckon she'd have choked in the steam and fumes. Heavy, you see, them lids are. Couldn't have dropped on its own because she didn't have any marks. No, she must have pulled it down on herself. You know, to do herself in.'

'Have you finished? Enjoying this, aren't you?'

'You're not, Eric, I can see that. Sweet on her once, weren't yer? I remember.'

'Its all in the past now.'

'You can say that again,' remarked Tomlinson.

'Has anyone said anything about, you know, murder?'

'Nah,' said Tomlinson. 'Money troubles. Or bloody lousy useless son troubles, more like.'

They heard the latch of the door open behind them and looked round to see Chuff, head bowed, hands in pockets, hair uncombed, shirt hardly tucked into his trousers.

'We're all very, very sorry to hear about your mother. I've no doubt she was good to you, and she was good to me in the past. So, as I say, I'm sorry.' Eric stumbled over the words, not finding it easy to show any compassion towards Chuff. 'Sit down by the fire and I'll get you a drink, on the house, lad.'

'Aye,' said Tomlinson in a low voice, 'very sorry. She were a grand girl. Used to go to school with old Freda, I did. Nicer woman you couldn't wish to meet.'

Chuff stared into the middle of the room at nothing in particular.

'She's dead, did you know?' he mumbled, sounding bewildered.

'We do, lad, we were just saying . . .' Eric sat next to him on the long bench alongside the dart board.

'If there's anything we can do to help, you know, just ask,' he said.

Polly came back into the bar. 'Oh, love, I'm so sorry. So, so, sorry. When did you last have something to eat?'

Chuff did not reply. 'Have you had any breakfast?' she asked. He did not reply to that either, and continued to stare into his brimming pint of beer.

'I'll get you some breakfast,' said Polly.

'I'm skint,' Chuff said.

'Don't worry about that. On the house,' sighed Eric.

Chuff played with the egg and bacon, chewed half-heartedly on the toast, but said he felt a little better for the food. After Polly left the bar, conversation came to an end. Both Eric and Tomlinson had spoken all the words of sympathy they knew, and there was little else to say. The silence was uncomfortable and Eric toyed with the idea of inventing an excuse to bring Polly back to the bar, just to cut through the atmosphere. Then the sound of a car coming to a sudden halt followed by hasty footsteps and a swift opening of the door caught his attention.

It was Archie Biddell. As he came through the door, he removed his cap and made straight for the boy.

'I guess you must be Freda's son. Can I introduce myself? I'm Archie Biddell. I'm very sorry to hear about your mother. If there's anything I can do, you need only ask. Of course, there'll be a full investigation.'

Chuff jumped to his feet, slopping his untouched pint of beer as he rose.

'You're all so bloody sorry, aren't you? So fuckin' caring. But none of you gave a bugger when she was alive so don't pretend you give a toss now she's dead! As for you, Tomlinson . . .' he spun round and looked the stockman straight in the eye. 'We know just how soft-hearted a bastard you are. You don't know what sorry means or you'd say sorry to those poor bloody animals being carried out of that stinking farmyard in the back of the knacker's lorry every day. And you . . .' he was now face to face with Archie Biddell '. . . why don't you go and boil your lousy head, like my mother did in your shitty turkey factory?'

Chuff spent the rest of that day alone. The phone rang once or twice; undertakers, police, distant relatives, that sort of thing. He shuffled around the house, attempting for the first time in his life to do something for himself. In the moments when he forgot that his mother would not be coming back, he cursed her for not having got more milk, allowing them to run out of cornflakes, not having done the washing up, not mended his trousers. The oaths passed through his mind and on to his lips some time before the realisation hit him that she was never coming home. That was when he cried.

By the middle of the afternoon, he felt sleepy and stretched out on the plastic-covered sofa and closed his eyes. He had not been asleep for long before a bang on the door brought him to his senses once again. He had already had a bellyful of sympathy and if it was yet another person telling him they were 'so sorry', he was in a mood to tell them to bog off. He flung open the front door, ready to give a frosty reception to the caller.

'Chuff, I thought you'd like a bit of pie for your tea. Steak and kidney.' It was Polly, just the hint of a sympathetic smile on her face and a pie dish in her hand. 'You'll need a bit of looking after, to start with.'

'Now that my mother's dead?' he said.

134

Polly brushed past him and headed for the kitchen.

'Oh, hell. You need a hand to get this place a bit tidy. Just look at that pile of clothes. Haven't you got hooks in your house, then?' she said. 'What kind of bomb hit this place?'

'Well, Mum was on nights, you see. Always too tired to do much around the house when she got home,' he tried to explain.

'So you didn't bother to do anything yourself?'

'I didn't kill her, if that's what you think. It was the bloody Biddells that killed her. Worked her into the ground, put her head in the bloody turkey boiler. THEY DID IT!'

'Sit down, love,' she said, 'I'll warm this pie for you. I didn't mean anything. Just trying to help.'

Polly put the kettle on and lit the gas oven to warm the pie. Then she grabbed a pile of washed but unironed shirts which were lying in a heap on the sofa, and demanded to be shown where they should be put. Chuff led her up the stairs to his room.

She gasped as he opened the bedroom door and saw the computer, hard drives, modems and associated paraphernalia. 'What do you do up here, launch moon rockets or something?'

'It's my computer set up. All I've got really.'

'You might have got a smart computer,' she said, 'but the rest of the room's like a pig sty.' She carefully lifted the lurid red and black duvet off the bed. The tabby cat fled in fear, having for the first time seen someone other than Chuff in the room.

'Ugh! These sheets haven't been washed in weeks. Hey, there's a pair of old socks down here.' And she reached under the pillow and found another.

While Polly busied herself tidying a shower of computer magazines into orderly piles, collecting a dozen encrusted coffee mugs and picking up items of soiled clothing and stuffing them into a plastic bag as quickly as she could, Chuff had started to boot his computer into life. Polly looked over his shoulder.

'What does all this do then? Oh, God!' she wailed in disgust having just spotted under the bed the mouldy crusts and discarded rind of a half-eaten bacon sandwich.

135

As she stooped to pick it up she noticed that Chuff's computer screen had burst into colourful life. 'Better than telly, eh?'

'This isn't a sit and stare machine, this is a get up and do machine,' he replied coldly.

'Well, if you get up for a minute I'll straighten that carpet under your chair,' replied an unimpressed Polly.

As she stooped, she took a closer look at the screen and started to read out loud from it.

'Campaign for Freedom of Farm Animals Home Page. What's that mean then?' she asked.

'Getting a better deal for farm animals. That's what it means. Doing away with intensive systems, unnatural methods, all that sort of shit. Hey, they ran a competition yesterday. Win a major prize. You never know, I might be lucky.'

As he said that, he noticed her hand reach for his cabinet and pull open the drawer. Chuff's voice rose.

'Keep your bloody nose out of there!' he screamed. 'Just keep your nose out of my things, will you? You've no right.'

But the damage had been done. Polly had opened the drawer as far as it would go and seen the newsletter of the CFFA. She sat on the bed and started to thumb through it.

'Hey,' she said, 'are you sure this sort of thing's within the law? I mean there's articles in here on using sprays to blind people, and how to cut off burglar alarms. I thought you said this was all to do with animals? Farm animals, you said.'

'It's a war we're fighting. A bloody war where any kind of tactic is valid. Have you heard of speciesism, eh?'

'I bloomin' well haven't,' replied Polly, 'but I have heard of the law and all this stuff . . .' she picked up another magazine '. . . about sharpening bicycle chains and ten tips on how to resist arrest, doesn't seem to me to have much to do with that. You're going to get into trouble. Seems to me you've got enough problems in your life without getting deep into this sort of thing.'

Chuff clenched his fists, remembered his dead mother.

'Those Biddell bastards have built their fortune on the backs of exploited farm animals. For hundreds of years animals have suffered at the hands of these people. *And* my mother. They killed her!'

He paused for a moment. '"I am in earnest – I will not equivocate – I will not excuse – I will not retreat a single inch and I will be heard!"'

'You do spout a load of old rubbish. Come and have that pie. And if you've got any sense you'll light a fire with those magazines. Do you hear what I say?'

9

The funeral of Chuff's mother, Freda, took place the following Tuesday, the first in April. While a small congregation was assembling in the Church of All Saints, Woodham Ford, in the secular surroundings of The Social Chapter Amanda Frater was being pressed by Conrad and Ernest over whether she was ready to make a commitment to the Campaign for the Freedom of Farm Animals.

Her instincts had told her not to meet them again, and she thought that if she dropped a note care of The Chapter (rather than get too involved and write to Conrad's Docklands address), they were bound to get it eventually. She would just say that although she still felt strongly about animal rights, she had neither the time nor the appetite for the kind of direct action which she'd taken ten years ago. It would be a polite note, but a firm one. A definite ending to an uncomfortable, but thankfully brief, episode.

The evening before, as she was sitting at home, alone, writing the note, she'd turned towards the picture of Freddie, as she always did when tormented by self-doubt. In difficult moments she spoke to him, asked him for advice, told him her troubles, and believed she understood his replies. But this time she did not seek his opinion. She had made up her own mind that she was having nothing to do with Conrad and his CFFA, and that was final. Yet as she tried to turn her head away from his stare, she could only manage to pen a few words before she was drawn back to him. He was talking to her again, and much against her better judgement as it was, the conclusion she drew was that he wanted her to go, if only to find out more. Perhaps he was right, she thought; maybe she *was* being premature, or cowardly. She slept on it, having kissed Freddie's picture goodnight and told him that she loved him.

The following morning was the first day she could remember for many months when she had not woken in pain. Such was her surprise that in her dozy state she reached for her leg to see if it was still there, and took the absence of discomfort to be another sign that she ought to go to the meeting – the final omen to suggest she should at least make the journey. She nodded at Freddie. 'OK, you win, darling.'

She was in the upstairs room of The Chapter at 11 o'clock sharp, as Conrad's pressing invitation, left on her answering machine, had stipulated.

'Glad you came,' he greeted her, fiddling with his gold cufflinks.

Ernest looked up from his papers and peered over the rims of his tortoiseshell reading glasses.

'Very, very good of you to come, Miss Frater. Such a pleasure to see you again.' He clicked his gold ball point pen and replaced it in the inside pocket of his grey suit.

'So you're with us?' asked Conrad, beaming.

'Not sure,' replied Amanda.

The smile vanished from Conrad's face. Ernest removed his glasses, folded them carefully and put them in his top pocket. He leaned forward. Benevolence, she felt, was giving way to something else.

'The fact that you're here says it all,' Conrad urged.

'Yes, I would have thought so too,' agreed Ernest.

'Not quite,' replied Amanda. 'I don't know what you want of me. I don't really know who you are, except for you . . .' she stared coldly at Conrad '. . . I don't know who's paying for this, or what they want out of it. So how can I decide about anything?'

'Information is sparse, I grant you,' agreed Ernest. 'You must understand why we have to keep it that way for the time being. We're working in very sensitive areas.'

'But what areas?' demanded Amanda. Ernest turned his head towards her, and spoke slowly and deliberately. 'If this conversation goes any further, you have to understand that new rules apply. Until now we have been just friends meeting for a chat, for old times' sake. But once we start to bring you into the picture we are putting ourselves, and in particular my client, in a vulnerable position. You understand?'

Amanda nodded. 'I'll listen, but there's no guarantee I will say yes.'

'Understood. What the animal rights movement needs, according to my client,' explained Ernest, 'is some kind of major display of force.'

'Force?'

'Some kind of staged event which will put animal rights, and particularly *farm* animals' rights, back on the agenda. He, or she, feels that other environmental issues have been grabbing the spotlight. They want to see this moved back to the top of the list, become a national issue again. Like it was when mad cow disease first appeared, for example.'

'A rally, a big protest, Trafalgar Square, that sort of thing?' suggested Amanda.

Ernest shook his head. 'No, my dear. They tried that for a decade in the sixties and it didn't achieve anything towards banning the bomb, did it?'

'We need to meet violence with violence. It's the only way,' urged Conrad. 'I want those who exploit farm animals to feel what it is like to be on the receiving end of some of their own medicine. I want to see them suffer.'

'No violence,' insisted Amanda, shaking her head. 'Not for me. You can if you want, but I get the strong feeling you're as mad as you always were – new suit, same daft head. Same Conrad, engineering other people's deaths. I'm out of this. It's not for me.'

'You needn't be directly involved,' said Ernest, quickly intervening. 'We need intelligence on the ground too. Someone who can meet people, get information. Someone above suspicion, just like you. We need you to help us find a target, and then determine how we may best aim our fire at it.'

141

'Freddie would have jumped at the chance,' Conrad murmured, without daring to raise his eyes to hers.

Amanda could not bear to hear Freddie's name on his lips and would have burst into a rage at Conrad's manipulative use of it had there not been a knock on the door. Ernest hastily covered his notes and shouted, 'Come in!' It was Marge, carrying three chipped mugs of coffee.

'You'll pay for the use of the room this time, will yer? Buggerin' off without payin' last time, eh? All dressed up in your fancy suits and can't even be bothered to leave fifteen quid behind yer. Tight bastards!'

Ernest gasped. 'I cannot begin to apologise . . .' He went into his inside pocket and took out a fine leather wallet. He opened it and pulled out a five- and a ten-pound note and handed them to Marge. Then he drew out a crisp, unused fifty-pound note and stuffed that into her hand as well. 'Please, with my apologies, madam.'

'Well, yes, thank you,' spluttered Marge, unusually lost for words.

She was about to close the door behind her when she suddenly remembered that it was not only coffee that had brought her upstairs.

'That girl's downstairs,' she said. 'What's her name – Tiggy? She wants to know if she can come up and join you.'

'Tell her to sod off,' said Conrad.

'You can't do that,' Amanda objected.

'Make your bloody minds up. I've got teacakes toasting down there.'

'I've met her before,' explained Amanda. 'Chatted to her after our meeting here last week. She's a regular, comes for coffee once a week. I'm afraid she caught me unawares, and I did let on that we were discussing animal rights.'

Ernest's eyes widened. 'I hope you didn't tell her anything more?'

'No, nothing. She's into flag days, lost puppies, that sort of soppy stuff.'

'Then what I suggest,' he said, hastily, 'is that we invite her to join us for coffee. It might arouse suspicion if we don't.' He turned to Marge. 'That will be another coffee please.' Ernest waited till she had left the room. 'You say she's into flag days and things? Then we'll pretend we're fund raising – er – to build a dog shelter in Kings Cross. How about that?'

'Sounds like a waste of time to me,' said Conrad.

'Wrong,' said Amanda. She turned to Ernest. 'She could be useful to you.'

'To *us*,' insisted Conrad.

'To *you*, at this stage,' replied Amanda. 'I think she said her husband was some big shot in supermarkets. By chance I bumped into her at the weekend, down at Woodham Ford.'

Ernest seized on her last two words.

'Ah,' he said, 'Woodham Ford. Really! Now there's a place. Do you know it?'

Amanda did not have time to answer before Tiggy came diffidently through the door.

'Hiya, Amanda,' she said, twisting a tissue nervously between her fingers.

'Tiggy, nice to see you again. Enjoy yourself the other night?'

'Well, I did, actually,' she replied, 'when I'd got over the shock of seeing you there. I mean, what a coincidence. Who'd have believed it? Gosh. No, it was quite pleasant, actually. Except I was sitting next to this old man who kept putting his hand near my thigh on purpose. At least, I think it was on purpose. I thought: You dirty old devil. Some big noise he is. Toby's doing business with him. Hastings . . . that was it, Marcus Hastings.'

Ernest dropped his gold ball point pen and it clattered against the mug of coffee. 'Very clumsy of me, sorry,' he said. He took a handkerchief out of his top pocket and mopped up the mess.

'You two seem to know each other quite well, if I may say so.' Conrad sighed, impatiently.

'Well, we were at this dinner, weren't we?' said Tiggy. 'Me and Amanda. There's this big farming estate . . . the Biddells', isn't it?' Amanda nodded. 'Well, we've got a cottage in the village and Toby, that's my husband . . . sorry if I'm prattling on . . .'

'Not at all. Do go on,' Ernest encouraged her. 'I would like to hear more about the Biddells. They're not the people who make *Biddell's Best Bacon Rashers* by any chance?' He chuckled.

'The very same,' replied Tiggy. 'And turkey steaks, chicken burgers, milk, beef, all that sort of thing. That's Toby's interest. He wants to do a deal with them.'

'Big farm would you say?' asked Ernest.

Amanda was following every question and had a growing suspicion of where this line of enquiry might be leading. She tried to change the subject.

'Done many flag days, Tiggy?' she asked.

'I'm sorry,' interrupted Ernest, 'but I would like to know more about Biddell's farm. Did you say there was a food factory there as well?'

This was Tiggy's cue to launch into a long speech in which she described the vastness of the operation, the feudal nature of the community, the dark and restrictive conditions in which she thought the pigs, cows and turkeys were kept, the number of times she had seen the knacker's lorry coming to take dead animals away. And that was only at weekends when she was down there. 'God knows what it's like in the week!'

'I'm sorry, I don't have your surname,' said Ernest, who had been listening carefully and making notes.

'Hopscotch. Tiggy Hopscotch.'

Conrad smiled for the first time that day. 'It sounds like a . . .'

'Like a playground game, I know.'

'Well, we must not keep you. I don't know what Miss Frater has told you . . .' said Ernest.

'Oh, nothing. Nothing at all. Except you care about animals, like I do. Especially the big ones: rhinos, elephants.'

'Almost,' he agreed, confused. 'It's dogs, actually. We want a much better deal for dogs, particularly in Kings Cross. Can we rely on you if we hold a flag day? I know it's a lot to ask.'

'Oh, of course, anything like that. I don't usually care for flag days, standing on streets with all that money. Not these days. But for a cause like this I shall just have to be brave.'

'As brave as some of those poor dogs out there,' replied Ernest, compassionately. 'Thank you for coming to see us.' He rose from his chair and opened the door in a gentlemanly way and saw her down the stairs.

When he returned, Amanda guessed what his first words would be.

'Woodham Ford!' he said with a satisfied grin on his face. 'Now I think of it, it's the obvious place. The Biddells! Big farmers, landowners, famous for the intensive way they farm. Are they not the perfect target for us? Don't you agree, Conrad?'

Amanda did not like this. She watched them both and thought it looked too well rehearsed.

'It's a strong possibility,' Conrad said, nodding. Ernest turned to Amanda.

'It depends on you. You say you know the place?'

'Not well. My father's got a feed mill nearby,' she admitted, reluctantly. 'Supplies Biddell's farm. I go down twice a year at the most. Look, I wouldn't want him involved in any of this.'

Ernest grinned. 'Of course not. It would be the Biddell family we were after. Now, my dear, is there any chance you know any of them, or can get an introduction?'

Conrad leaned forward. 'Unless, of course, you know anyone there already?' He smirked. Amanda's eyes flashed.

'You bloody well know I've met Archie Biddell, don't you?' she said, angrily. 'I can tell from the grins on your faces. This is a set up! What's going on here? I think you both need to explain a thing or two or I am up and out of here, pretty damned quick!'

'Well, as quickly as that bad leg of yours will take you,' said Conrad slyly.

'Look,' said Ernest, avuncular image discarded, 'I warned you, we are a serious operation and my client has serious money to spend on achieving his aims. If you think we'd spend what could be substantial sums on the basis of guesswork, you couldn't be more wrong. Of course we know about Biddell's and we did receive a report that you were sitting next to Archie Biddell at a dinner. That apart, you have to remember that they are just about the biggest factory farm in Britain. Heartless, cruel farming, my client calls it. We needed contacts, so we did research. We came up with the name of your father, and that led us to you. Which was the first stroke of luck because Conrad remembered you. Even better for us that you should once have felt so strongly about animal rights and might well do so again.'

'Devious bastards' said Amanda, under her breath.

'And we had some luck. I wasn't, at this stage, going to put you fully in the picture, but that silly Hopscotch woman has rather forced my hand. I hadn't planned on meeting her. Anyway, the cat's out of the bag now.'

'How many other targets has your so-called CFFA got?' Amanda asked.

The two men looked at each other. Ernest chose to reply.

'We are concentrating all our efforts on Biddell's at the moment.'

'And in the past? And what about the future?' probed Amanda.

'You are indeed an intelligent woman,' he said. Conrad nodded. 'We cannot lie to you. Not if we expect you to work alongside us. There is, and only ever has been, one target. Biddell's.'

'Any problems with that?' asked Conrad, hastily. 'Freddie would have dreamed of such an opportunity.'

'He wasn't into violence,' insisted Amanda. 'He was into debate, politics. Don't taint his memory, Conrad.'

'He would have been into violence by now because that's all that works. Arguments have got us nowhere. A show of strength is all we have left. Freddie would have worked that one out for himself, and then he would have been with *us*, against *them*. As you should be, *if* you really loved him.'

'Don't dare question my love for Freddie!'

'Prove it, then,' replied Conrad, hitting the table with the flat of his hand. 'Prove the worth of his memory by giving him one great posthumous victory.'

Amanda did not reply. Instead, her head spun with questions, and in the mad whirl thoughts of Archie Biddell surfaced.

'Will anyone get hurt?' she asked.

'No promises,' replied Conrad 'There's no bastard anywhere in that Biddell's set-up that cares about the life or death of any animal. You have to admit that,' he urged. 'If someone gets hurt, it will be no more than *they* have been guilty of.'

Ernest leaned forward confidentially. 'I know this might affect your father's business, from what we hear about the set-up there, but my client will see he is compensated, so don't let that hold you back.'

'Are we ever going to know who your client is? It might help me if I had an idea of his identity,' replied Amanda.

'And it might make life a lot more difficult for you too. My client is a man, I can reveal that, of good heart who deplores the cruel methods of modern animal husbandry and wants to, shall we say, help the animals fight back. He is not doing it for his own ends, he is merely the servant of the animals. He believes they have spoken to him and this is what they want. My client is a man of deep convictions, but more importantly from your point of view he is very rich and very impatient. So, what answer do you wish me to convey to him?'

'I *might* help you,' replied Amanda. 'I need more time to think.'

There was silence while she tried not so much to wrestle with the thoughts in her head, as to acknowledge some of them for the first time and try to understand them.

'This is the one, Amanda! This is the one Freddie would have wanted us to do,' insisted Conrad, again daring to bring his name

147

into it. 'He did not die the way he did so we could sit here and fail to make a decision on a plan of action which will go some way to avenge his death. *My* best mate, *your* lover, did not have the luxury of thinking time before he was spread all over that road. He died for what he believed in and all we can do is sit here and "think" about something we "might" do. Fuck you, Amanda! Get off your arse for the first time in your life and let's get on with it.'

Ernest, blinking in embarrassment at this ungentlemanly language, opened a folder lying before him and withdrew from it a computer-printout of names.

'We have not been idle, as you will have gathered by now. And our efforts are paying off.' He pushed his reading glasses higher on to his nose and started to scan the long sheet of paper as he unfolded it.

'Here we are,' he exclaimed, and took up the gold ball point pen to ring one name.

'Lucky, eh?' said Conrad. 'We've had so many lucky breaks that I've got a good feeling about this.'

Ernest passed the printout to Amanda. 'On our little Internet page,' he explained, 'we decided to try and enlist help. Without being specific, we outlined our aims and then asked for volunteers, hoping someone might turn up within fifty miles of Woodham Ford.'

'And?' asked Amanda.

'Look for yourself,' said Conrad, enthusiastically. 'Someone called Chuff. Lives right in the bloody village!'

She looked at the other addresses which, because of the global nature of the Net, included animal rights enthusiasts from California to Alice Springs. But there, in the middle of the list, was clearly written 'Woodham Ford'.

'Lucky,' she remarked.

'An omen,' replied Conrad.

'It hasn't got his precise address,' Amanda noticed.

'That's for you to find out, my dear,' said Ernest.

Silence except for the bubbling of Marge's boiler, audible through the floorboards.

Though Amanda's deepest thoughts should have been focused on the ambitious plan being hatched round that table, they were in fact firmly on Archie Biddell and she was not certain why. She liked him, yes, but nothing more than that surely? She would always love Freddie first and foremost.

'I say, get the Biddells!' roared Conrad.

'Which Biddell?' replied Amanda, hastily.

'Does it matter?'

'Possibly,' she whispered.

'Are you with us, or not?' asked Conrad.

'With you,' she declared, staunchly. Freddie, his aims and ambitions, must always come first after all.

The playing of the church organ had never been the forte of the amateur organist who was drafted in to perform the slow dirge at the beginning of Freda's funeral. It was even more difficult for her, as the dead woman's sister. But that's how things are in villages; small communities are brought close in life and death. So if she was a little more faltering than usual and the notes less than certain, it was because the continuous wiping away of tears made the instrument all but impossible for her to see.

It was a good turnout, for a village funeral. Most of the villagers took an hour out of work to attend and Sir Thomas, stepping briefly out of retirement to enjoy playing Lord of the Manor once again, had let it be known that he was agreeable to the factory's closing for an hour, though no more, as a mark of respect. He had not bothered to tell Archie, whose decision it should properly have been. Chuff, squeezed into a suit bought years before for his father's funeral and not worn since, was in the front row with Polly next to him; she was holding his arm, saying the occasional sympathetic word and wiping tears from her own eyes. He fiddled with the unaccustomed jacket, fastening it, finding it too tight and undoing it, then starting all over again. Behind them sat Eric Thwaite who kept blowing his nose and saying it wasn't emotion but a cold coming on. Even the surly Tomlinson had turned up to bid farewell to a woman to whom he had hardly spoken a civil word in twenty years. But that was the way things were in Woodham Ford – tribal.

Archie Biddell crept into the back row of the church just as the service was about to begin. Sir Thomas did not come. 'Never heard of the woman,' he had said. 'Playing golf with Hastings, anyway.'

Archie did not yet feel able to join the main body of the congregation. It would have been presumptuous, he thought, to have taken a seat in the ostentatious family pew in which generations of Biddells had gazed out over their workers at prayer. He did not have the arrogance for that.

That morning he had made his first visit to the turkey factory and, since the half-hearted attempts by the vicar to explain to the congregation that passing from life to death is some kind of victory did not hold his attention, his mind wandered back to the killing lines, the noxious bubbling vats of 'soup', the vile heaps of entrails piled in a corner awaiting incineration. He had known in principle what went on in the factory but nothing had prepared him for the crudeness of it. Archie knew animals had to be bred, killed and packaged, but had always hoped that somehow a little dignity might creep into the process. But perhaps it doesn't matter, he argued, because they're not humans – just stupid turkeys, devoid of emotion or sensibility.

But cows were different. They were intelligent, sentient, quite possibly capable of love, he thought. But the way in which the cows were kept, he decided, was hardly different from the casual approach to turkey welfare. It just went on longer. The cows were made pregnant artificially, genetically manipulated to produce calves of the required sex, fed beyond their natural appetites either to fatten them as speedily as possible, or to make them give so much milk that the effort of producing it shortened their lives to a fraction of what they should be. And who really cared? Was he the only person on the Biddell Estate who ever allowed these subversive thoughts to cross his mind? He closed his eyes tighter and started to pray, as much for guidance for himself as for a blessing on Chuff's dead mother.

Archie wanted more information. As he idly mouthed the words of the 23rd Psalm, 'The Lord is my shepherd, I shall not want. He leadeth . . .' he decided that if he was to give leadership to this estate now ostensibly under his control, then it would have to be run on his terms; farmed the way he wished, managed to his standards, rid of all its excesses. But he knew little about farm management and all the other skills which had propelled the family business to its now legendary status.

He rose from his knees at the end of the prayers, as smartly as a soldier should. But the prayers had not been a devout moment for him, for he could not get out of the schoolboy habit of opening his eyes to look around the church and spy on others. A silly game, really. But the sight of the entire village, with heads bowed, had sobered him. Each and every one of those people depended now on *him* for their livelihood. He could not fudge decisions, dodge arguments, skip details, pass orders down the line. To guarantee these workers a future, he knew that the only tried and tested course was to follow the policy the estate was already ruthlessly pursuing, every aspect of which he distrusted. But what did his discomfort matter when the lives of these people, gathered here in this church, could be turned upside down if he failed in his duty to them?

'Hymn 499. *Abide with Me*,' intoned the vicar, and the congregation rose to its feet.

And what if the direction in which his conscience was taking him was another one entirely?

> *When other helpers fail, and comforts flee . . .*
> *Help of the helpless, O abide with me.*

Helpless! Bloody helpless was how he felt. He could imagine the reaction from his father, and Hastings, if he suggested a more holistic approach to the estate. Yes, 'holistic' was a good word; an all-embracing philosophy which would allow profit, but not at *any* cost. There should rather be good and decent lives for animals, workers, and even himself, although his own needs came fairly low on his list of priorities.

> *Who like thyself my guide and stay can be?*
> *Through cloud and sunshine, O abide with me.*

The trouble was, Archie thought, that he had no guide whatsoever. No idea where to start, or where precisely he was heading. All he knew was that the pursuit of profit was no excuse for exploitation. And then, in the midst of his gloom, he had the feeling that there was something in his life which transcended all his woes. He could not instantly put his finger on it and flailed around in his mind trying to push the mental button. Eventually he found it. To his surprise, it was labelled 'Amanda Frater'. With greater heart he sang the last line:

> *Heaven's morning breaks, and earth's vain shadows flee;*
> *In life, in death, O lord, abide with me.*

The service came to an end. Tea and beef sandwiches had been laid on in the village hall for those who wanted them. Just as the villagers filed out of the church, the lights along the nave dimmed briefly as the voltage dropped due to sudden demand. It was automatic feeding time again for the pigs on the Biddell Estate.

Most of the congregation returned glumly to their homes or jobs, only a few went down to The Peacock. It was a subdued lunchtime, long silences broken only by the spitting of the fat which dripped off the perpetually revolving joint of beef into the flames below.

'We won't sell much today,' said Eric Thwaite sadly. 'I reckon as I might have a slice or two myself, if I feel up to it. Must say

I don't fancy it much today, and that's sayin' somethin'. Still, outside'll dry up if I don't carve a bit off.'

'You'll soon look like beef, you will, Eric,' said Polly, who was busy polishing glasses.

Chuff did not come back to the pub after the cremation. Michael Pember had passed him in the car park, offered a word or two of sympathy but got not much more than a grunt in return. Now he was in the bar, as keen on a word from Polly as on a pint.

'He didn't look happy, but you couldn't expect it, could you?' Michael said.

'I'm afraid his mother's death is the least of his problems,' said Polly. 'I'm worried – really very worried – about what that lad is up to.'

'Drugs?' said Michael.

'Nah, it's not drugs, unless you call Bullocks Bitter a drug. No, it's more – well, violence, I suppose you would call it. It worries me sick.'

'Robbery . . . guns?'

'No, it's that animal rights caper.'

'There's nothing wrong with that, up to a point,' said Michael. 'You might say *I* was into animal rights.'

'Yeah,' said Polly, 'but I bet you're not into that balaclava and sharpened bicycle chain stuff?'

'Nasty,' he agreed.

'I may be imagining it,' said Polly, 'but something's got hold of Chuff and it worries me. I mean, he's not a bad lad, deep down. I just don't want to see him in any trouble.'

Spotting an opportunity, Michael said, 'A trouble shared is a trouble halved. We could talk about it later?' This could be considered somewhat forward behaviour for a diffident lad like him.

'Oh, could we?' Polly replied. 'That would be great. I've been so worried and I really need someone sensible to talk to about it.'

'Polly!' shouted Eric. 'I want some more plates through here, to warm if you please. Beef's going better than I thought. There's a coachload arrived. Come on, girl!'

Michael Pember reached out and held her lightly by the arm as she brushed past him on her way to the kitchen for plates. It was difficult to say which of them was more surprised.

'Are you working tonight, or have you got the night off?'

'I'm free, as it happens.'

Polly had not expected to find herself in a social situation and so had quickly to calculate whether she wanted to talk through her worries about Chuff in a distant, professional sort of way, or whether she needed a shoulder on which to lean and pour out her troubles. She glanced at Michael, boyish, blushing slightly, shirt tucked untidily into his trousers, stethoscope hanging from his jacket pocket. Why not? she thought. She liked the look of him, he amused her, and he'd listen.

'Seven o'clock?'

'Good,' said Michael. 'I'll collect you from here, and we'll try the Indian restaurant in St Edwich.'

All this was happening faster than he had planned; it was runaway stuff for him. Depending on the next words she spoke he would either have a date or a broken heart.

'All right then,' said Polly, 'but no beef. Is that understood!'

Chuff had forgotten his front door key and so when he stumbled back home from the funeral, he spent five minutes on the front doorstep delving into his grimy pockets. He had never had to worry about keys before; his mother was either there when he got home, or had put a key in his pocket for him. Now he had no key and no mother and for the first time that day cried with utter desolation. Having sobbed for a while and wiped his wet face and nose on his sleeve, he was about to pick up a piece of brick from the garden and break the glass when he thought to try the handle. It had never been locked, because his mother had not been there to lock it.

He had no idea what to do next. Where did he begin when

it came to running his life, now there was no one to kick-start every day for him? All other things failing to grab his attention, he went upstairs and booted the computer. Unusually, the screen greeted him with a message.

There is e-mail. Do you wish to collect? Press ENTER or ESCAPE

Chuff pressed **ENTER**.

Thank you. You must enter your password. Please enter that now, or press ESCAPE.

He couldn't remember it. He had made it up one night when his brain was clouded by Bullocks Bitter. He thumped his head to try and jolt his memory. CHUFFBARN! That was it! His name and his street joined together. He typed it out and pressed the enter button.

Sorry, you have made an incorrect entry. You may have one more attempt

Bugger! One f too many, Chuff remembered. Only allowed eight letters. It was all coming back to him.

CHUFBARN ENTER

There was a pause, the screen changed and revealed a short message.

Hi, Chuff, this is the CFFA. Thank you for entering our quiz. We are pleased to tell you that you have won a major prize and our representative will be calling in the near future. Please do not tell anybody about this win otherwise the prize will be forfeited. We shall be in touch shortly. Thank you for taking part. End.

He pressed the off switch. Well, bugger me, he thought. A prize! I've actually won something. Hey, Mum, I've . . .

10

Tonight, Archie Biddell decided, he would bite the bullet and get to grips with the way this estate was run. The funeral had taken up most of his working day, he must waste no further time. He would spend an evening in the farm office, try and understand more about the estate, and through gaining a better working knowledge, work out how to bring about change.

He was not alone in working late that night. Across the other side of the village, also at his desk, sat Brian Frater who had received a depressing little note from Marcus Hastings and was wondering what to do about it. Also working hard at making himself presentable was Michael Pember who spent the hour between 6 and 7 scrubbing his hands with washing-up liquid and a Brillo pad to rid them of the clinging smell of pig with which they were saturated after a lengthy operation to replace a prolapse in a farrowing sow. Of the three men, it was difficult to say who was in the greatest state of panic.

As Archie sank back into the chair in the farm office – the one from which his father had dictated the affairs of the estate for nearly forty years – he felt no sense of command. The roll top desk had been his grandfather's, he remembered. A pile of letters had been left on one side of it by the farm secretary, mostly for routine signature. On the other side had been placed a heap of files which he had requested. The letters he put to one side, and instead decided to look through the heftiest file of all, marked 'Veterinary'. Archie opened it and discovered an unsigned cheque for £6,500 attached to a bill for a mere three weeks' work. He looked carefully at the itemised bill and noticed there was no single day when a vet had not been called to turkey, cow or pig.

Reading the bill in more detail, it became clear that the cows were the largest consumers of veterinary medicines. Archie could not believe that a herd of cows could supposedly be healthy, and at the same time need intensive care at this level. The list of ailments was depressing – mastitis of the udder was the most common, then lameness, and finally problems due to difficult calvings. Few cows escaped one or other affliction.

Across the office, on the wall, was a poster designed for the county show to proclaim proudly '*Biddell's – Best All Round*' with pictures of contented cows, smiling pigs, and turkeys wandering grassy fields. He felt sick, disgusted at the deceitful nature of it all, and got up from the desk leaving the cheque unsigned, threw his jacket over his shoulder and slammed the office door behind him. He had tried to get to grips, but like a child who could not bring itself to swallow a bitter pill, his body and mind protested.

The red light on Brian Frater's answering machine blinked twice to tell him there were two messages. The first was from the bank, an insistent voice: '. . . urgently call us before signing further cheques. Thank you.' Beep. 'Meester Frater, Orion Shipping here . . .' The voice explained that in the holds of one of their ships was at least a hundred tons of 'protein'. No, they could not specify its origin, date of manufacture, precise contents, or whether it had passed any international inspections. But it was cheap. A decent feed supplier would not touch it, and anyone caught supplying it would never find a customer again, but it was Frater's only way out. It was that or go bust, and with that came the dread of no longer being able to support Amanda. He banged the delete button to rid himself of the messages. Just as he removed his finger, the phone rang, startling him. It was Amanda.

'Daddy, darling.'

'Hello, sweetheart.'

'You sound low,' she said.

'Low-ish. Just business, you know how it is.'

'Yeah. Thanks, by the way.'

'What for?' said Frater.

'For taking me to the Biddell's dinner the other night. Super evening.'

'Are you pulling my leg?'

'No,' said Amanda, 'I really enjoyed it. Archie Biddell is quite hunky, isn't he?'

'Never noticed.'

There was a silence when the small talk dried up. Brian was not in the mood for aimless conversation.

'Much happening in Woodham Ford, is there?' asked Amanda.

'There was that funeral today.'

'What funeral?'

'The woman who fell into the turkey-boiling vat. She died.'

'Oh, sad, really sad. Do I know her?'

'Shouldn't think so,' said Brian. 'What's her name? I can't remember. She's got a stupid lout of a son called Chuff.'

'Again?'

'What again?'

'The name of the son,' she insisted.

'You won't know him. Lives on the estate. Scruffy sort of kid.'

'His name, Dad, please?'

'What's the urgency? I tell you, you won't know him. Chuff, if you must.'

There was a silence while Amanda pulled from her pocket the notebook in which she had scribbled the name of the CFFA contact in Woodham Ford who had replied to the electronic quiz, the one that Ernest and Conrad were keen should be contacted. She dropped the phone while trying to flick over the pages, anxious to see if the names matched.

'Are you still there, darling?'

'Sorry, Daddy. It's just this Chuff . . . he might qualify for help from a charity I'm involved with. Do you know his address?'

'He's not the sort of person in whose whereabouts I would be the slightest bit interested, actually. But the inquest's all over the front page of the *Chronicle*.' Brian reached for the newspaper and read through it till he came across the address. 'Of Barnyard Close. That's all it says. Rough part of the village that is. Funny damned charity if you ask me.'

'It must have been Biddell's turkey factory, where she died?' asked Amanda.

'Who else would own a factory round here?'

'Accident?'

'That's the official line. Although some think it could be negligence. I'm looking at the verdict of the inquest now. Said it was misadventure. The son, of course, is blaming the Biddells. Myself, I blame him.'

'He must be angry with the Biddells, this Chuff person?'

'Livid as far as I understand. Threatened murder, so I heard. Blames them, of course. But most people think it was suicide. Quite frankly, I'd top myself if I had a lad like that.'

'Well, you haven't, Daddy darling. You've got me. Love you.'

'Hey, shall I see you back here?'

'Possibly. Soon, even. Night night, Daddy. Love you.'

'Before you go,' he put in hastily, 'your cheque might be a bit late this month. No problem. Just a few days. Love you too.'

It was a busy night at the Al-Koomah Indian Restaurant in St Edwich, which meant that apart from Polly and Michael, at least one other table was occupied. Polly thought she would stick to prawns or vegetables, and avoid meat. Michael didn't care either way.

'You didn't have to, you know, take me out like this,' she said, tentatively. 'But I'm grateful. I really am.'

Grateful, thought Michael, *she's* grateful! It was he who was counting his blessings.

'Something hot and spicy? That's what I like best,' he decided.

Polly burst into giggles and said rather too loudly, 'I'd never have marked you down as the hot and spicy type, Michael. More a korma than a vindaloo. Long, slow burn.'

The elderly couple at the other table who were attempting the impossible task of trying to be genteel and eat poppadoms without making a crunching noise, looked round at the noise.

'Shhh,' said Michael, catching the hostile glance. 'I'd forgotten we were in church. Let's pray for our safe deliverance from this curry.'

A waiter carrying a stained cloth over his shoulder placed before them dishes of indeterminate mush, one of which he announced as being prawns, the other lamb, and the third rice, which looked to be of the sloppy variety. He got out a box of matches from his pocket with the intention of lighting the candle, but the match would not strike. He said he would be back with a new box, but he never came. Michael stared at the dish before him. 'I could swear I saw this in the surgery half an hour ago.' Polly collapsed into giggles. The people on the next table shuffled in their seats, decided things were getting out of hand, and left.

Michael leaned across the table and whispered, 'They're booked into an all-night rave. She's got a Lycra body-suit tucked away in that handbag. She's going to get changed behind the bus shelter while he piddles in the phone box.' Polly laughed out loud.

'You really are a funny lad. I thought you were the serious type. Whenever I've seen you in The Peacock, you've always sat in the corner, keeping yourself to yourself.'

'Could be that you bring the best out in me,' he said, smiling.

She groped under her chair and out of her bag pulled three magazines. She laid them on the table. 'Sorry to change the subject,' she said. On the cover of the first was a photograph of a pile of still-born piglets being shovelled by a farm worker into a skip, the next had a grainy picture of a turkey acting cannibalistically towards another, and the third cover showed a burnt-out Land Rover – the property, it said, of an intensive poultry farmer.

'Not the sort of thing you get on the front of *Country Life*, is it?' Michael remarked, casually.

'Doesn't it upset you?' asked Polly, surprised at his indifference.

'I see this sort of thing every day,' he explained. 'I'm afraid this is what it's like. Not that I've ever seen a burnt-out car, but the piles of dead piglets and the pecked-to-death turkeys are all part of the modern farming scene. It's vile, but it's my job to treat and not to preach. So I learn to open my eyes only to what I have to see to do my job. Otherwise it would be too depressing.'

'Well, I think that's cowardly,' said Polly, dropping her knife and fork heavily on her plate.

'Sorry, but how else am I supposed to earn a living? What's the point in turning up at a farm to treat a sick cow and spending my time telling the farmer I think he's a bastard? It's the cow that wants the help.'

'I didn't mean you personally. I meant all of us. I found these magazines in Chuff's bedroom.' Michael raised an eyebrow.

'Don't be silly. I was only tidying round.'

He reached out for the first of them and started to thumb through it.

'This is really nasty stuff,' he said as he examined the contents more closely.

'It gets worse. There're some really vile pictures of a puppy farm later on.'

'I didn't mean the pictures, it's all this stuff about "targeting your local farmer – ten ways to disrupt his working life" and how to obtain lists of scientific establishments doing agricultural research work. God, there's even a guide to rendering cars dangerous! Look, it shows you how to put miniature punctures in tyres so they don't burst till the car is up to speed. This is stuff for the police, Polly.'

'That's not really what I wanted to hear,' she said. 'I'd worked that out for myself. The trouble is they'll only make Chuff's life a misery if we do that. The Chief Constable will tell Sir Thomas and Chuff will never get a job for miles around. It will be the end of him.'

'So what?' said Michael.

Polly sighed. 'Michael!' she said, with increasing impatience.

'He's a human being who deserves a chance, not to be put down and condemned by everybody in Woodham Ford. He needs help to get himself out of this sort of thing, not harassing and locking up. Help is what he needs.'

'I decided, when I first became a vet,' explained Michael, 'that the problems of animals I could solve because I could understand them. But the problems of humans were beyond me.' He pushed the magazines back across the table at her. 'I'm not the one to help on this. If I were you I'd shop him. Otherwise he'll hurt himself and other people and achieve nothing in the end.'

'Thanks a million,' said Polly, tight-lipped, pushing her plate away from her and getting up from her chair.

'Don't go,' he pleaded. 'What have I said? I'm sorry but I don't see what I can do. I'm only a vet.'

'I thought you were a human being as well. Can't you see, he needs help? Think of him as a sick mongrel or something.'

'He's a waste of space, Polly. He really is. If he gets his kicks out of this sort of thing,' Michael stabbed his finger at the magazine covers, 'then he's seriously sick.' On hearing his raised voice, an Asian face appeared round the kitchen door.

'You will have dessert, yes?' asked the waiter.

'No, thank you,' replied Polly, huffily, as she gathered the magazines from the table and made for the door. She flicked her red hair back over her shoulders, opened the restaurant door and glanced back.

'I thought you were better than that, Michael, I really did. Thanks for the curry.' And she slammed the door behind her.

'Dessert, yes?' asked the waiter again.

Instead of driving home as he'd intended, Archie Biddell was drawn once again to the barn which housed the pregnant cows. He thought that if he spent time with the animals he might come to understand them better, develop an instinct for what could resolve the conflict between the need for profit and his desire to see all livestock on the estate lead a decent life. He stood once again in

163

the midst of the herd of cows, watching them peering back at him, remembering the last time he had been here with Amanda, and Domino the new-born calf. He hadn't heard from Amanda, and wanted to. But he knew his thoughts must not dwell on her; instead he should take a long look at this herd and decide how he could best engineer a new life for it. It was a leadership challenge of sorts, the sort of thing army officers were trained to do: take command, steer people in new directions, shape events, determine futures. He could recall all those themes from Sandhurst lectures, but not one of them seemed appropriate for the situation in which he now found himself. Somewhere, deep within this estate, was an enemy with which he had no idea how to deal.

He walked through the cows, talking to them in the calm, clear way that old Arthur Friend used. Some stood their ground and let him gently stroke them; others skittered out of the way and sent a ripple of fleeting panic through the herd. But all he had to do was stand still for a moment, and then it was calm again.

While standing, he wondered where Tomlinson might be. His truck was parked outside the barn but he was not to be seen either in his small office or anywhere amongst the livestock.

Archie kicked the straw about with the toe of his boot as he wandered through the herd, and then his foot hit something that did not feel like straw, or even a wet pile of droppings. Whatever it was, his foot bounced a little, made a duller noise as his toe hit it as if it were fleshy. Whatever was under that straw, it was heavy and unyielding and well buried. Archie bent down. Cows gathered round him, equally curious, and bent their heads as he started to part the straw with his hands, like a child scooping up sand on a beach. The friendlier cows came close.

Six inches beneath a thick layer of stinking, urine-soaked straw lay the body of a calf; it could be nothing else. Archie found the foot first and then pulled more straw away so that he was able to follow the leg up to the body. After a few minutes, he uncovered the head; a beautiful soft head, eyes closed, a once shiny muzzle now dry and shrivelled, the hair on its body thick and matted. Its tongue, as stiff as wood, dropped from its open mouth where it had fallen the moment the calf had expired. Archie feared there was something about this calf that was familiar. It had dots, like Domino had done. Could it be her? he wondered. He racked his brain to try and conjure up a detailed image of the animal Amanda had hugged. It was so unusual, so distinctive, that Archie thought this must have been the calf over whose life Friend had struggled, the one Amanda had loved, the one to which she had given the embrace Archie wished had been his. Now it was dead, lying where the herd could foul on it and trample it till it was forgotten. He tried to convince himself it was another calf, a *bit* like Domino. He wasn't convinced. He looked again. Much of its body was smeared in dung and urine and its markings were unclear. With great regret, he decided it probably *was* Domino. What bloody bad luck.

He heard a rustling behind him which did not sound like the steps of one of the cows. He turned, and silhouetted against the light was Tomlinson, swaying slightly and smelling of drink.

'Poor little thing,' he said. 'Hard, ain't it, when you lose 'em?' Archie noticed a slur in his speech.

'Depends if you've done much to try and save them,' he replied.

'No lack of care here, sir,' insisted Tomlinson. 'Nothing but the best for your cows.'

'You call this nothing but the best?' Archie pointed to the dead calf.

'We have accidents. But there aren't any complaints from Sir Thomas,' Tomlinson blustered, stifling a belch.

'I saw no report of this in the herd book, no call to a vet to come and treat it,' said Archie, firmly. 'No request for the knacker to collect the carcass, no evidence of the slightest bloody effort to remove the body. In fact, no reason at all to believe you even noticed it was dead.' His voice broke as he declared, 'You drunken, useless bastard, Tomlinson!'

He got up and marched towards the stockman, finger pointing

towards his chest, jaw set, anger boiling inside him. The cows edged away. As Archie strode forward Tomlinson moved back as best he was able, given the drink.

'You have the skills of an imbecile, and there is more dedication to duty in a lousy dog than in you. I have watched you . . .'

'And I have watched you, *sir*,' said Tomlinson, 'walk around the estate as if you owned the place. Well, not yet you don't. Do you know what they say about you, eh? They say his father's still got his little toy soldier on the end of a string. They're all laughing at you, did you know that? People in the village . . . folk who work on the estate. And *I'm* laughing at you as well. But you can't get rid of me, sir, because only I know how this little lot runs, *and* I know about deals that have been done in the past, and how Marcus Hastings did a little creative paperwork so we could claim twice on BSE cows that went to be burnt . . .'

'Don't threaten me!' cried Archie, still furious. 'Get off the estate, now. Not tonight, not tomorrow. Get in your fucking truck and never come near a cow of mine again!'

Tomlinson stopped moving as his back collided with one of the pillars which supported the hay loft above the shed. His hand grasped one of the many empty beer bottles concealed about the place.

'You can't talk to me like that,' he said, smashing the bottle against the pillar and removing the neck, leaving a wickedly sharp weapon in his hand. 'I don't like people talking to me the way you just have, *sir*. If I were your father I'd put you over my knee, but as you're bigger than that I'll just give you a little something to remember old Tomlinson by.' He edged towards Archie, bottle held at arm's length, eyes wide and staring, sweat pouring from his brow. He stabbed the weapon at Archie's face, but he ducked and it missed him by a hair's breadth.

'Difficult to catch, are we, sir? Tricky little calf, are you? Old Tomlinson's good at dealing with animals that have minds of their own and think they can do what they like.' He looked down. 'Like this one.' He stuck the steel toe of his boot deep into the hardened belly of the dead calf. 'Once they're down, that's when I really get to work on them. I make them say sorry. I kick them – *hard*.' His boot went once again deep into the guts of the rigid corpse. 'And I kick and I kick . . . But I'm a Christian soul, deep down. If they pleaded for mercy, of course I would stop. But, you know, they never do. They never says a word. And so I kicks the troublesome ones till they're dead, and the others seem to get the idea that when Tomlinson's around, they behave.'

'You're mad! Do you really think cows understand?' said Archie, taking deep breaths to steady himself. 'Or is that just an excuse for violence and killing? The methods of a violent man who hasn't the guts to take on one of his own, so beats the shit out of an animal instead.'

'If that adds up to calling me a coward, *sir*,' said Tomlinson, 'then I shall have to defend my good name. I shall have to prove to you that Tomlinson is not afraid to take on one of his own size, even if he *is* a captain.'

'With a broken bottle in one hand? That's really courageous.'

At this further suggestion of cowardice Tomlinson snapped. He screamed with rage as he lunged forward, rushing towards Archie who was backing away as fast as he could. But behind him was a slimy patch of concrete where the straw had parted, and it was on this that he lost his footing. He went backwards, falling into the filth, arms and legs outstretched, lying helpless, with no chance of regaining his feet.

'Oh, dear,' said Tomlinson, as he stood over him, leering. 'We seem to be down now, don't we, sir? Where the calves die. How appropriate.' Archie saw no way out. The jagged edges of the bottle, dripping stale ale, came closer till his eyes crossed trying to keep them in focus. Tomlinson was now so close it was impossible to tell whether the stench of drink was from him or his weapon.

'I'm not going to give you the satisfaction of getting this over quickly. I thought I might grind it nice and slowly, just to see what happens.'

Archie raised his hand to his face, to feel its smoothness perhaps for the last time, but Tomlinson's foot came down heavily and painfully on to his wrist and he could not move at all. Beer from the bottle fell on his lips; sweat from his brow flowed down his face to meet them.

Tomlinson opened his foul mouth, and grinned.

'Do you still want to sack me, eh? I don't bloody well care! I could finish you off here and now, if I wanted. But old Tomlinson's not half as bad as you like to think he is, sir. Maybe we'll call it a day here and now, and say nothing more about this. If anyone asks, we'll just say you tripped in the shit. Just don't muck about with me again, see. 'Cos I know too much.'

Before Archie could respond, the barn vibrated to an angry roar, a bellow sending out a shock wave of sound which instantly drove one hundred cows into a frenzy. Within a fraction of a second, panic sent the herd into mad confusion. They roared, kicked out, scrambled over each other in a desperate attempt to move somewhere, anywhere. The roar continued to rattle the walls. Feet flew, straw was thrown in the air, the walls shook as frenzied cows bounced off the asbestos sheeting walls. And the echoing cow shed amplified every noise till it sounded like the cacophony of Hell in there. Wherever this noise might be coming from, it distracted Tomlinson long enough for Archie to get his wrist out from under the restraining foot, curl himself into a ball and roll away. He was now as close to the wall as he could get. He looked up and briefly saw the look of total fear on Tomlinson's face now that the manic, galloping herd was heading towards him.

He screamed as he fell backwards, having slipped on the same patch of slimy concrete floor which had felled Archie. Drunk, he was too slow to move away as the front hoof of the first cow smashed on to his hand, crushing the broken bottle into his own fist. Hoof after filthy hoof then came down on him, pressing into every organ, some cows stumbling and the full half ton of them falling directly on him. It was a mercy he lost consciousness for the next hoof that came to rest was on his head and punctured his cheek. As the cow struggled to remove it, that side of his face was ripped away.

Above the panic-stricken clamour, Archie thought he heard an elderly but firm voice cry out from the back of the barn. Although strange to Archie, it was one which the herd evidently recognised for as soon as the shout was heard, the cows stopped their mindless careering and slowly came to rest, panting but calm.

Tomlinson lay in a pool of his own blood which was pouring from nose, mouth and ears and mingling repulsively with the cow slurry. Archie scrambled painfully to his feet.

'Who is it? Who's there?' he shouted across the barn, the cows' heads now turning towards him. There was no reply. He staggered through the herd, clutching his wrist which was bleeding from where Tomlinson had ground it with his heel.

'That's me, Mr Biddell. Mr Friend. Arthur Friend. Are you all right, sir, can I help you?'

As Archie got further across the barn, he saw the pale face of Arthur materialise ghost-like out of the gloom. His left hand was in the pocket of his coat, his right hand held a white twisted cord which led through the brass ring in the nose of the most massive of the many black bulls on the Biddell Estate. The beast was broad as a tank, and muscled like an athlete; it was also as hot with frustration as a dog that could see a bitch but whose master would not let go the lead. It scraped its foot along the ground in fury, bent its head to the floor, snorted and roared. The cows stiffened, looking at Arthur as if awaiting an order.

The confused Archie could not take all this in. 'Just get that bloody bull back into the bull pen where he's safe,' he ordered.

'He's safe enough here, as long as I'm with him,' said Arthur, confidently. 'Knew him as a calf, you see. Must be ten years ago. Come on, Nero, old lad. Calm down, game's over. Go steady, old boy.' The bull's rage subsided at Arthur's bidding, and beast and man turned calmly and left the barn.

Archie staggered back to where Tomlinson lay in the straw and slurry. He thought he should try and feel for a pulse, but there was no piece of untorn flesh against which he could press a finger. The man was clearly dead. Archie heard the metallic scrape of the steel bolt on the door of the bull pen and breathed a sigh of relief that the fearsome animal was now safely confined. Relief gave way to a feeling of shock and he leaned against the wall and slid weakly down it till he was resting on the floor. Arthur Friend made his way towards him.

'He'd have killed you, sir, Tomlinson would. Not hesitated. I've seen him fell animals for no reason. They just got in his way. Knocked 'em down he did. I was looking at the cows tonight, like I often do, just having a stroll last thing. Anyway, I heard him come back from the pub so I nipped up into the hay loft. I often does that, 'cos he usually falls asleep when he's just back from the pub and then I nip off home. But I saw you arrive and guessed he'd be in a foul temper when he saw you here. I'm afraid you weren't his favourite person, sir.'

'I think I just found that out.'

'Anyway, I saw he was going to have you as soon as he reached for that bottle. And the only thing to stop him was to get the cows worked up into such a frenzy that with any luck they'd have him over. Well, all I could think of was the bull. Cows go wild if you suddenly put a bull in the middle of them. So I got a halter on old Nero as fast as I could. I only had to bring him to the door and they went crazy just as I'd expected.'

'But they stopped as soon as you called. I heard you.'

'Yes, well, cows will if they know and trust you. They trust me, see, because I visit them most days and talks to them. It's all a matter of trust, really.'

Archie looked at the body of Tomlinson.

'I'm minded to leave him there. Let him be trampled and shat on like God knows how many calves. But we'll have to ring the police.' He glanced at Arthur. 'It was, of course, an accident, Mr Friend. The bull escaped and that was what frightened the cows. Tomlinson was unlucky enough to be in the middle of them when that happened. Understand? In fact, had it not been for your skill in catching him, the bull might have got me as well. That's what I shall say.' Archie winced from the pain of his twisted, bleeding wrist.

'Sit down, Mr Biddell, on that bale of straw. I've something in my bag that will take that swelling away . . .'

'I'll take it to a doctor when I've dealt with the police.'

'Needs no doctor. Just sit down and you'll be right as rain.' Archie surrendered and Arthur Friend fumbled in the bottom of his canvas bag.

'Arnica – tincture of arnica is what that needs.' And he withdrew a tiny, corked medicine bottle. He pulled the stopper and suddenly the air filled with a sharp, medicinal fragrance.

'Are you sure about this stuff?'

'It's tried and tested, sir. Over many generations. More than you can say about some of this modern stuff, eh?'

'And what else might be in that bag of yours?' asked Archie, who had heard the rattle of many bottles while Arthur was looking for the arnica.

'Just my bits and pieces. Now, this will sting . . .'

Archie closed his eyes and winced as the arnica hit the wound, like a hot needle straight through a nerve.

Brian Frater decided he would take up Orion Shipping's offer of the cheap protein, and ask no further questions. A letter from Marcus Hastings had clinched his decision. Brian read it again:

> *. . . cuts will be necessary in estate expenses in order to meet budget forecasts in the forthcoming year and so existing contracts will be put out to tender. The cuts are necessary to be able to meet price commitments we have made to Applewhite Supermarkets PLC. As you no doubt appreciate, the contracts we are negotiating with them will, in the long term, ensure the stability and future of the entire estate and its workforce. We wish to maintain our close and valued working relationship and providing you can meet a price cut of 2 per cent this year, and a further 2 per cent the following year,*

then I see no reason that the contract should not be awarded to you.

It read like a fair letter, but he knew it was typical Biddell blackmail of the highest order. His was not a large business, and Biddell's was far and away his largest customer. Without them there was no hope of survival. But equally he would have trouble keeping going if they insisted on imposing these price cuts. It made the cheap protein even more important now, and in the future. It was a flagrant breach of the law, but others probably did it, he thought. So he faxed Orion Shipping.

Brian Frater assessed the risks of anyone discovering what he had done, but did not see how any suspicion would be aroused. The protein would arrive at Frater's Mill, be sucked into hoppers through pipes and mechanically incorporated into all the feeds. It would never be seen. His decision caused him a few uneasy moments, but not enough to cost him a night's sleep. He thought only of Amanda. He wanted the best for her.

11

The following morning, Toby Hopscotch was prancing bare-chested round his kitchen at breakfast time, waving the news-paper and smirking like the cat that got the Applewhite's Fat-free cream.

'This is going to liven the place up a bit. It will be the making of them *and* us, Tiggy darling.'

'What do you mean exactly?' she asked indifferently from behind the ironing board, becoming increasingly impatient with her smug husband and fantasising about putting razor-sharp creases into his shirts – sharp enough to slice an artery or two.

'Woodham Ford, St Edwich, the Biddells, us! Look, it's front-page news in their local paper – "Council Gives Superstore Go Ahead".'

'Lovely, dear,' muttered Tiggy. 'Hardly the front page of *The Times* though, is it? Will you be at the office if there are any calls?'

But Toby was now in a world of his own, dreaming aloud.

'Everything's in place. I've got the builders on a rapid build contract with massive penalties if they fall behind on the three-month deadline . . .'

'Three months?' she said, astonished. 'You can't throw up – I mean – build a superstore in three months.'

'These boys can. In fact, they'll have started this morning. We've got a contract as tight as a . . .' his eye caught Tiggy's who flashed an urgent message to him that Georgie was within hearing distance '. . . well, a damned good contract anyway. I've set the opening date. It will be the fifteenth of July and *that's* the day our fortunes will be made.' He pranced some more. 'I shall take my seat on the board, have the congratulations of the chairman pressed upon me in the form of share options, and then, when they think I've pulled the best trick of my life, I shall astound them with another!'

Overwhelmed with indifference, Tiggy paused before asking, 'Oh, what's that, dear? More plans?' Toby sensed she was a little less than ecstatic.

'Look,' he said, eyeing her over the ironing board, 'this will make us rich. Very rich. Understand? You seem far from enthusiastic if I may say so.'

'You'd better move away from me,' warned Tiggy.

'What is it about me you don't want near you all of a sudden, eh?' he asked, injured.

'It's just that unless you get your hand off the cable I can't move the iron and it's burning a hole in your shirt.' He rapidly put his hands in his trouser pockets.

'It's not that I'm not as thrilled as you are,' said Tiggy. 'It's just that the fifteenth of July was going to be Georgie's first school sports day. Sorry.'

'Your place on that day will be by my side, Mrs Hopscotch,' he said pompously. 'Anyway, Georgie will be moving on to a better school by then. I have a plan . . .'

'But Mr Huxwell is a wonderful headmaster, and it's such a dear little school. We'll never find another in London like it.'

'I don't have London in mind,' replied Toby, taking the ironed shirt from the board. 'In my new position I think somewhere in the country might be better. Sort of Gloucestershire way, you know. Tetbury seems a nice area.'

'That's where Prince Charles lives.'

'Does he?' said Toby, pretending indifference. 'Then he can open my next superstore, can't he? The one *after* St Edwich. It would be an honour for him. You can get me on my mobile,' he cried cheerily. 'I'm off to Woodham Ford for the morning. They'll all want to meet me, I dare say, now they've read about it in the newspaper. Best show my face. There could be TV crews and media things to be done.'

After he was gone, Tiggy almost smelled the heavy odour of self-importance trailing in his wake.

When she finally heard his car leave the drive, she went over to the calendar and marked the fifteenth of July in bright red by taking the largest indelible marker she could find and swirling it round and round the date till it looked like an open sore. Georgie peered round the door.

'Mummy, Mr Huxwell says it's naughty to write on walls.'

'It is,' she said, 'very naughty. But I'm writing on the calendar.'

'It's a waste of paper, drawing such a big ring. If Mr Huxwell were here he'd say you were being very silly and make you rub it out.' Georgie went across to the calendar and looked up at it, examining it closely. 'That's a big, red ring you've drawn,' he remarked, 'and you usually write in tiny, little squiggly letters that Dad can't read. Mr Huxwell tells us off about that too. He says we've got to be big and bold.'

'Well, Georgie,' said Tiggy, 'there are things that we sometimes feel all little and squiggly about, and things we sometimes feel big and bold about. See?'

'I know why you've put a ring round that date. It's sports day.'

'Yes, darling, that's why I put that big ring round the fifteenth of July.'

'And you'll come, won't you, Mum? Mr Huxwell's going to need some help starting the races.'

'Nothing will stop me, darling, I promise. Nothing at all will get in the way of that.'

There was a huge media presence as Toby Hopscotch drew into the car park of The Peacock later that morning. If he'd known there was going to be as much interest as this he would have got Public Relations on to it, set up a press conference. He went through the tricky questions in his mind, rehearsing his answers.

'Yes, it's true that superstores in rural areas are a great threat to small businesses but customers have to be given the choice. Why should they miss out on the huge range of goods that are on offer to city dwellers?' That dealt with the economic effects. He hoped he looked good, not too city slicker but not yokel either. He had carefully chosen a double-breasted blazer, crisp white shirt and silk tie, but topped all that smooth dressing with a rural, broad-brimmed hat made of moleskin. He strode through the car park where at least two film crews and four photographers were standing around, and two reporters with ears glued to mobile phones.

'I'll see you inside, lads. If you want a quote, or a pint. Pints are on me on a grand day like today.'

They stared back at him, open-mouthed. A police inspector came out of the pub.

'Did I hear you offer yourself for interview, sir?' he asked.

'Well, only if they want it. You know what the press are,' he explained, trying to look bashful.

'And might I know what it is you have to add to this story?' asked the officer.

'Well, I suppose you could say I'm responsible. It will be a great thing for the village. Some will see the black side of it, but I can assure them that in the long term they will come to understand that what I have done is right.'

'Can I make a note of this, sir? "What – I – have – done – is – right".'

'Can't deny it,' added Toby.

'I think you'd better step inside.'

'My pleasure. Please, have a pint on me. Jolly good job your men are doing on crowd control. Never thought there'd be a turnout like this. Very impressive.'

The inside of The Peacock was quiet in contrast to the car park, still buzzing with disgruntled reporters frustrated at the lack of any hard information and perplexed by the arrival of Toby Hopscotch. Eric Thwaite was at the bar, looking less than his usual robust self. Sitting alone in the corner by the fire was Arthur Friend. It was quiet and subdued once the door had closed and the rabble of reporters was excluded.

'You see,' bragged Toby, launching into his prepared patter, 'this place needs a bit of life putting into it.'

'I would suggest,' said the inspector, 'that to talk about putting life into the village might be a little misjudged at the moment. We had the funeral of a much loved villager yesterday, and now this.'

He ignored the policeman. 'We've done this before, many times, though not on this scale. And although there has been initial opposition, the community soon comes to realise it is for the best.'

'I don't suppose *Mrs* Tomlinson will see it that way,' put in Eric Thwaite from behind the bar.

Toby Hopscotch looked blank.

'Are you telling me,' said the inspector to Hopscotch, 'that you know something about the death of the stockman, Tomlinson? Because if you do, you had better let me know before I nick you for wasting my time.'

'Death?'

'If I may remind you, sir, you said only moments ago,' the inspector opened his notebook, '"What I have done is right". We call that a confession in our line of work.'

Toby went white. 'I'm sorry. I thought all the media were here because of me.'

'Oh, some kind of pop star, are we?'

'No. I'm the brains behind the new superstore.'

'There are brains behind it, are there?' muttered Eric, turning over the pages of the local paper.

'I think that the front page of one very local newspaper is the sum total of the media attention, sir,' said the inspector wearily. 'Now, a farm worker died here last night while tending the cows. A bull caused the herd to stampede and he was crushed. I have to check for foul play, and as far as I can see there does not seem to have been any. Mr Biddell was there and says there was nothing he could do to prevent it. In fact, if it hadn't been for Mr Friend over there, bravely stopping the bull, Mr Biddell might have gone as well. Mr Friend is a bit of a hero round here. *That's* who the press want to talk to.'

'I think I'll pop out for a breath of fresh air,' said Toby. As soon as he was out of the front door of The Peacock, he could hear laughter and decided there was urgent business needing his attention back at head office.

'You'll have a pint, George?' said Eric Thwaite to the police officer.

'Just a half, Eric. My God, you do meet some tossers in this game, don't you? What's all this about a supermarket?'

'On the outskirts of St Edwich,' said Eric. 'You've read about it in the paper, haven't you?' he called across to Arthur, sitting quietly in the corner.

'Yeah, just off the roundabout on the new bypass,' he replied.

'Do you know the spot?'

'I do,' declared Arthur. 'It's where they buried six hundred tons of ash from the incinerators after the cow cull in the nineties. There'll be the ashes of the best cows I ever knew under that bloody new supermarket of his. You won't catch me wiping my arse there, let alone buying anything.'

'Best tell him,' chortled the police officer. 'That should make his day! Hey, we can tell him his beloved media want to know how he feels about having the remains of ten thousand old cows under his feet.'

'I'm not worried about no supermarket,' said Eric, 'they'll not serve roast beef, not like we do at The Peacock. People will always come here for the best.' Arthur was peering into his beer glass, his thoughts on the cow cull. Occasionally he glanced at the revolving baron of beef over the spitting flames.

Then there was a crash, and a smashing of glass followed by a groan of despair and frustration. Eric had let the pint glass of beer slip from his hand and it had smashed into wicked fragments on the stone floor.

'Well, bugger me,' he said, dizzily slumping across the bar, his speech a little slurred. 'I've never done that before in my life. Just lost my grip on it.'

'I'll help you to a seat,' said Arthur, moving across to the bar. 'Grab my hand and I'll pull you up.'

The two men clasped hands. 'Get hold of me,' demanded Arthur, 'or I can't help you.'

'Get hold of you! I'm grabbing you as best I can,' shouted Thwaite. 'Can't you feel it?'

'Can't feel a thing, Eric. Your fingers haven't even moved.'

Amanda debated whether or not it was a good idea to seek out Chuff on the day following his mother's funeral. On balance she decided it was, given his reported anger; she did not want him going off the boil. She decided to wear trousers, as usual, a beret, and a long, blue overcoat which was past its best; after all charity workers, she thought, should not flounce around, looking like mannequins. She decided flat heels would be more suitable in case there was a lot of walking. She caught the train to St Edwich and took a taxi to Woodham Ford, asking to be dropped off outside The Peacock. There she paused for a moment and looked at the windows of the upstairs room where she and Archie had met. Then she tried to find Six Barnyard Close, hoping this person called Chuff would be at home.

She could have asked directions but was afraid of drawing attention to herself so wandered aimlessly for a while. This was a mistake, for no one is more conspicuous in a village than someone with only a vague idea of the direction in which they are going. She walked first towards the church as briskly as her bad leg would allow. Arriving at the gate to the graveyard, she saw fresh flowers piled high on a newly filled grave. Directly opposite, she saw the village shop and decided to ask for directions there.

The 'stores', as it was known, had been a shop as long as the eldest resident in the village could remember. Despite all attempts by successive generations of health inspectors, it held on proudly to its hand-wound bacon slicer – Berkel, red and chrome – which took pride of place on the wooden counter.

On a pair of rickety steps, leaning against an enamel sign for a brand of cigarette that had long gone out of production, a rotund woman of advancing years was pressing drawing pins into the window frame to support a large notice which read: '*We're here today, but we'll be gone tomorrow – when Applewhite's opens up!*' It was the first of the village protests. All communities' first reaction was to resent the intrusion of supermarkets into their cosy towns and villages. Predictably, they put up a game little fight for a while, forecast doom and gloom – yet six months later were happily doing their shopping in what had once been the enemy camp while, shop by shop, the local village stores closed. The big superstores used to try and buy off the locals with offers of 'free car parking' or a computer or two for the primary school. They didn't bother now; they knew that all they had to do was sit and wait for the population to come to them.

'Excuse me,' said Amanda, slightly worried that the woman's balance might be disturbed, 'but I'm lost.'

'We're all lost, dear, in our own way. I'll be lost when this place closes, I can tell you. Best part of my life I've spent here.'

'I'm sorry to hear it. Can I hold the steps for you? They don't look too safe.'

'You don't look so good on your feet either, if I may say so,' replied the woman, who had been watching her meanderings. 'But you can hold the steps if you want. Mind you, another death in the family won't make any odds,' she sighed.

'I'm sorry?' asked Amanda.

'Not half as sorry as he is, I expect. I can't say he was the best brother in the world, but he *was* my brother and that's that.'

'Look, I'm sorry to have bothered you. I'll ask elsewhere. You're obviously upset.'

'You'd be upset, if your brother was trampled to death by cows!'

'God, how awful. When? How did it happen?'

'I can tell you've only just arrived, or you'd know. Entire village is talking about it. They're all sayin' there'll be a third. Things goes in threes, especially deaths. Old Freda buried yesterday, m' brother killed last night . . .'

'I'm very sorry,' said Amanda.

'And if they aren't all talking about death, they're discussing Applewhite's bloody supermarket in St Edwich. 'Course, they say it will mean more jobs in the village with the estate supplying this superstore, but I'll believe that when it happens.' She pressed home the last drawing pin and slowly came down the steps.

To make ends meet, the shop was open at 6.30 in the morning so the early shift at the turkey factory could buy a newspaper on the way in, and it was still open at 9 the same night so the night shift could buy a snack or two to see them through the long hours. And all was run by this one ageing woman. To make such a life possible, the shop had effectively become her front room, and to drop in for a loaf of bread was also to share a cup of tea, a gossip, and sometimes a slice of sponge cake. But only when she had time to bake.

'You don't look too happy yourself,' she said to Amanda. 'I think we both need a cup of tea. Come on in, then I'll send you on your way Where was it you wanted?'

'Barnyard Close.'

'What are you, a debt collector or something?'

Amanda followed the woman into the parlour behind the shop. 'It's none of my business what you want on the estate, of course.' She paused. 'But what *do* you want up there? You see, that's where my brother used to live, the one who died last night. Not a bad lad, he wasn't. Had his funny ways.'

'I do charity work, helping bereaved families, that sort of thing,' said Amanda.

'Well, that's fast work. He hasn't been dead twenty-four hours.'

'Oh, it's not your brother I'm here to see. Not unless his name is – I mean, was – Chuff.'

'Chuff! What do you want with that layabout? He's just idle, he is. Never brings his videos back, he doesn't. And he doesn't rewind 'em.'

'Well,' said Amanda, 'his mother died recently, and I thought we may be able to help.'

'So what is this charity then?'

'Oh, connected with the church,' was her rehearsed reply.

'I see,' said the woman, clearly not satisfied. Amanda hoped she would not be pressed further.

'Funny business, old Freda. They said it was an accident, but it couldn't have been, not the way she was found. Unless it was suicide, though I don't believe that either. I knew her well. She came in every day to buy the day before's bread. Nice woman, really.' She looked up, disturbed by the opening of the shop door. 'Customers. Blast 'em,' she muttered, and groaned as she got to her feet and shuffled through to the shop, not closing the door behind her.

Amanda listened to the conversation. The woman was explaining to the customer that she didn't have books of *ten* first-class stamps, only twenties. Did he want twenties?

'Twenties will do fine,' came the man's firm reply.

'Thank you kindly, Mr Biddell.'

Amanda picked up the local paper that was lying on the sofa and quickly put it up in front of her face. Even so, she thought she had caught Archie's eye before she'd had time to hide herself.

'I'm very sorry about your brother,' he was saying. 'I was there when it happened. We did everything we could. It was dreadful. I am most terribly sorry.'

'He was a bad bugger in many ways,' the shopkeeper replied, 'but he didn't deserve to go that way.'

'Nothing . . . I mean, no one does,' said Archie, remembering Domino.

The woman came back into the parlour and Amanda lowered the newspaper from in front of her face and gulped her tea in relief.

'Biddell? Local landowners, aren't they?' she asked, innocently.

182

'Have been for generations.'

'And that was one of them?'

'Young Mr Biddell. Yeah, he's not a bad lad. We haven't seen much of him in recent years. But they say he's back now to run the estate, his father getting on and all that. Army's done him a world of good. Made a man of him. We were very worried about him after poor Emily died. We thought they'd make a lovely couple. Must be ten years since. Tragic. Village loved her, we all loved her. She was the first, you know.'

'First?'

'The first to die of the mad cow business. I don't think there's been anyone in his life since. One-woman man is our Mr Archie. I've never understood that, have you?' asked the woman. 'Seems strange to me, to be so wound up in one person that even when they're dead you can't let go of them.'

'Very strange,' replied Amanda. 'Barnyard Close?' she asked, gently changing the subject.

'Past The Peacock, left at the War Memorial, and you come to what we call the estate. They're all new houses so they built a big wall in front of them, not to spoil the view. It's behind there. I must say you look a bit familiar. Have you been to Woodham Ford before?'

'Only once or twice. Well, thanks for the tea. And best of luck with the fight. Big business doesn't always win.'

'It does round here, love, but thanks anyway.'

Amanda stepped out on to the pavement, took deep breaths of air and turned towards The Peacock. Then she heard the buzz of an electric car window and a voice shouted to her.

'Amanda, hi! It's Archie, Archie Biddell. I'll give you a lift.'

She did not want this sort of complication, not on a day like today.

'I rather hoped I hadn't been spotted.'

'It takes more than a newspaper to hide beauty like yours.'

'Smart arse,' she snapped.

'All right then, I recognised the handbag,' admitted Archie. 'We

183

don't see too many of that quality in Woodham Ford. Or ladies either, for that matter.' He grinned.

'I don't want a chat up, I want a lift.'

'You want a drink.'

'I want a lift, please. I've got a date.'

'In Woodham Ford? I'll fight him to the death. Give me his name?'

She could not help but laugh.

'You're ridiculous,' she said, and as Archie opened the door of the car, stepped happily into it.

'It's good to see you again,' he said.

'Yes, and you.'

There was a pause while he refastened his seat belt, leaned across Amanda to show her how to fasten hers, then started the car.

'Hey,' she said, 'this isn't the way I want to go. The woman in the shop said I had to look for the big wall. I'm sure it's the other way, back there.'

'I know, but The Peacock isn't.'

'Archie, I don't want a drink. I've got work to do.'

'What is this work? I mean, *exactly* what is it? And don't say charity work.'

'We help bereaved families,' she said, repeating the well-rehearsed reply. 'Give them counselling.'

'Ah, so if I came to you with a problem, you would talk it over with me, help me, guide me. Yes?'

'Are you winding me up?'

'I was going to say that I had this major problem finding someone to go to supper with tonight, and thought we might talk it over. Under the strict heading of counselling, of course.'

'Please, no jokes.'

'Sorry.'

'I'm sorry too,' said Amanda, 'but I've got a lot on my mind. These visits aren't always easy.'

'Especially so soon after the death. I can understand that. And you won't find Mrs Tomlinson very easy to talk to either. I don't think she's all that bright.'

'Everyone's talking about Tomlinson. Who is this Tomlinson?'

'Who else might you be going to see in the Close?' asked Archie.

'Tell me about Tomlinson first?'

'He died last night, in the cow shed. I was there. Terrible accident. Trampled by cows.'

'You don't sound very upset, for a man who's just witnessed an unpleasant death,' she remarked.

'On one level I am. On another, not. He had it coming. He was a drunken, idle bastard. His luck had to run out one way or another.'

Archie did not really wish to pursue this conversation any further so changed the subject. 'Who are you going to see if not the Tomlinson family?'

'Someone called Chuff.'

'That idle sod!' exclaimed Archie, unsympathetically.

'I'm sorry,' said Amanda, reproachfully, 'but his mother died in your turkey factory, remember? Or do you have so many people dropping dead in your service that you lose track?'

'I went to the funeral,' he said defensively. Amanda apologised. 'You may think he's a lost cause,' she continued, 'but my charity wants to see him given a proper chance in life.'

'He's had plenty of chances, believe me. Which brings us neatly back to supper tonight,' said Archie. 'Any chance of that?'

She did not reply. Instead, her mind was wandering back to the last time she and Archie had met. 'And how is that dear old man, the one we met who was looking after the cows . . . Arthur, wasn't it?'

'Arthur Friend? He's fine,' replied Archie, cautiously.

'And Domino must really be growing up. Sweet little thing. I shall never forget the way that calf looked at me. No one's looked at me like that before.'

'I can't believe that,' he said.

'I mean, she just trusted me so deeply. Wasn't afraid, just lay there while I hugged her. So pretty with all those tiny spots. She looked so funny. Hey, I'll do you a deal. Take me to see Domino and then we'll have supper, how about that? I'd love to see her again.'

'She's dead,' Archie admitted. There were a hundred ways of softening the news, but he opted for the stark truth.

'She's what?' cried Amanda in disbelief. 'How? She looked so healthy, so ready to get up on those legs and take the world by storm. And you're telling me she's *dead*. Why?'

'I can't answer those questions because I don't know. I found her dead in the straw.' His voice lowered and his head drooped in shame. 'She'd been dead for some time.'

'Just found her, like rubbish or something? You mean you came across a dead calf like you might stumble over a pile of dog crap in the street? Are you serious or what?'

Archie said nothing.

'And if she'd been found earlier, might there have been some-thing someone could have done to help her? Is that what you're telling me?'

'Possibly,' replied Archie, knowing it was a lame reply.

'All you can say is *possibly*! Don't you know? Didn't you take the trouble to find out . . .'

'This isn't fair,' he said, interrupting her increasingly angry flow.

'I dare say that calf didn't think life was very fair either.'

'You can't love each and every one of them. It doesn't work like that. They're not pets, they're farm animals. Otherwise the whole of farming would be one long heartache at sending your friends to be killed. You learn to draw a line between yourself and the animals.'

'A line, yes,' said Amanda, 'but not a curtain, not a blind.'

Archie did not reply.

'You can be distant if you like,' she said, 'but I loved that calf. Don't you understand that? Or have you drawn such a heavy line you can't even see the possibility of *caring* for any of these animals? When I held her, that calf trusted me. Do your cows trust you? I doubt it. Because you let them die and don't bother to find out how, or why, or go to help. It must be wonderful being a farmer, Mr Biddell. I am just about to see a lad who lost his mother in your turkey factory. I have just drunk tea with a woman whose brother was trampled by your cows. I have now been told that a magical creature like Domino is dead and no one bothered to find out why because there was no one who cared enough. I'm getting out of here!'

She unclipped the seat belt, opened the door and bundled herself on to the verge, trembling at the thought of Domino lying dead and undiscovered in the straw. She was sure that if she had been there she could have saved her, like years ago on Dover docks when she and Freddie worked to save weakened calves which had been crammed into lorries bound for a continental death.

She turned and looked at Archie, and despite her hatred of him for the lack of care she believed he had shown towards Domino, she could not ignore the expression on his face. His face was pale, knuckles white as they gripped the steering wheel, eyes filled with the same bewilderment she had seen in that newly born calf's.

Archie watched her in the mirror as she walked away. Probably forever, he thought.

12

Having never visited a house like six Barnyard Close before, Amanda had no idea of the etiquette involved. For example, when asked to take a seat on the sofa, should she choose the small patch that was covered by the remaining imitation leather and look selfish, or opt to sit on the voluminous folds of foam-filling which were escaping like an eruption of hernias? She had never felt so uncomfortable in her life; not only because of the filth and the threatening nature of Chuff, but because of Archie. His final, helpless expression had unsettled her more than she could have thought possible. And Domino was dead.

'How many sugars?' asked Chuff, brusquely, carrying in two mugs, a spoon clanking in each. He put them on the floor beside the sofa. There was no table. 'Not very good at this. My mum used to . . .' His voice tailed off.

'I don't take sugar,' she answered, feeling the reply sounded precious and that she must try harder to knock some of the refined edges off her voice. And all the while she was kicking herself, cursing herself for having made the bloody stupid mistake of telling Chuff her real name when he answered the door. She had invented one, in case he asked, but too much had happened that day for her to be able to remember such details. It had been a great mistake, and she knew it.

'Sure you've never been here before?'

'Not to Barnyard Close, no,' said Amanda.

'No, not Barnyard Close. The only decent-looking women we get round here are from the Probation. Better tits in Probation. Flat-chested bitches are from Social Services, you can bet on it.'

His eyes passed salaciously over Amanda's body. She wrapped her coat even tighter around her.

'I meant the village,' he said. 'Are you sure you haven't been here before? Name rings a bell.'

'I think we should talk business,' she answered.

'I'm all in favour of that.' Chuff leered at her and sat next to her on the sofa when he could just as easily have chosen a chair opposite.

She could not go through with this. This was disgusting, demeaning. The man was a moron and there was no level on which they could communicate. She had not yet learned that armies are made of squaddies as well as of generals.

'So what's this prize I've won? Something tasty, I hope. I haven't had anything tasty for a bit. Know what I mean? Cheer old Chuff up, that would. Buried my old mum yesterday, I did. Nothing much left in life now. Really would be an act of charity.'

'Why did you say charity?' she asked.

''Cos Nellie in the shop tells me everything. She's my mate is Nellie. As soon as you left she rang me to say you was on your way. But you stopped off, didn't you?'

'Did I?'

'With Mr fucking Archie Biddell. Looked ever so cosy, Nellie said.'

'In my work, we have to make contacts at all levels,' she said primly.

'Must be nice,' replied Chuff, 'a bit of contact. I haven't had a bit of contact for some time.'

The only safe course was for Amanda to get to her feet and she used this as an opportunity to make the speech she had been rehearsing.

'The CFFA is a dedicated group of people fighting for animal rights, and in particular the freedom of animals kept on farms. We carry out propaganda work. I notice you are on the mailing list for our newsletter and replied to our Internet questionnaire.'

'Yeah, good stuff is that.'

'I need to assess your commitment to the cause before I ask you

190

to become any further involved. We cannot afford to have people in the organisation who are not entirely committed, or who are likely to open their mouths to the wrong people.'

'Action. That's what I want,' said Chuff. 'I've got scores to settle.'

'It's not about settling scores,' Amanda explained. 'It's about fighting for what we all believe in.'

'Yeah, well, *I* believe in settling scores. Those fucking Biddells murdered my mum, I know it. They kill every bloody thing round here. They killed Tomlinson last night. Did you hear about that? He only lived three doors down. Miserable bugger, but that ain't no reason to kill 'im, is it?'

'It was an accident,' said Amanda, too defensively.

'Oh, did Mr Archie whisper that in your ear, eh? An accident? Bollocks! Tomlinson never got in the way of stupid bloody cows. Too clever. He had the mind of a bull. I reckon *they* killed him.'

'That is no business of the CFFA. We are an animal rights organisation.'

'But in Woodham Ford there's no difference. Don't you under-stand that?' said Chuff. 'It makes no difference if you're a turkey or a factory worker; if you don't perform you're topped, one way or another. With humans they might get away with the sack; with animals it's the gun. Same thing. There's no other employer round here. If you get the sack from Biddell's, you might as well be dead. Look at me.'

She looked at him, noticed his grubby flies were half undone.

'How can you help us?' she asked.

'I can sharpen chains, like you showed us in the magazine. I reckon I could build a bomb if I had to . . .'

'We have all the technical expertise we need. What we desperately need is information.'

'Eh?'

'We need to know every time a consignment of animals leaves the Biddell Estate. How many, where to, sheep, pigs, cows or turkeys.'

'And then what?'

'And then something else,' said Amanda. 'But I'm telling you no more than that at this stage.'

She felt Chuff's puffy red eyes scanning her body again.

'Sit down and have another cup of tea,' he offered. 'Come on. Sit next to me, on the sofa.'

'No, thank you. I'd best be off.'

'Off back to Biddell?' he replied casually.

'No, not back to Biddell.'

'Nellie in the shop said you looked real pleased to see each other.' A broad smile passed across Chuff's face. 'And, do you know, I've just remembered where I've heard your name before. You was at that party the other night, at The Peacock, weren't you? Sat next to young Archie, eh? Went to bed with him afterwards, did you?'

'I did not! Most certainly not.'

'Like to though, wouldn't you?' Chuff was grinning evilly.

She should have denied it instantly, but she didn't.

'I want information from you,' she said, trying to divert the conversation, 'about Biddell's. You can rest assured that however things may appear, I fully intend to use all the force I can muster to teach Biddell's to treat animals with proper respect.'

'I'm not certain about you,' said Chuff. 'Could be you're a plant, put here by the Biddells to get me out of this house. Get some other poor bastard of a factory worker in here. For all I know you're a faker, Miss Frater.' He moved closer to her. 'You could prove otherwise, you know. A little bit of contact with Chuff, as we discussed earlier.' And he pressed his thigh in grubby jeans against her long blue coat. 'We could call it a token of your good faith, just to prove that the freedom of farm animals matters more than anything else to you.'

'Information is what I want from you. *All* I want from you.' She was trembling now, wanting to call for help. 'Give me the facts and you will get your reward.'

'I call that a contract, I do,' shouted Chuff. He moved even closer, face threatening. 'But first I want to know exactly how you feel about Archie Biddell. Because I know how I feel and I need to know if you feel the same.'

Amanda had taken a step backwards and felt the sofa behind her knees. Her aching left leg crumpled beneath her and she involuntarily fell back on to the couch. She gasped at the pain. Chuff moved closer, face next to hers.

'Tell me you hate the Biddells!' he snapped.

'I hate . . . the Biddells.' She was swallowing hard.

'Mean it!' he screamed. 'Say it as though you mean it.'

She shouted as best she could, 'I hate the Biddells! I hate them!'

'Enough to kill them?' insisted Chuff.

'To kill them,' agreed Amanda. This did not satisfy him.

'Say it! Say: I hate them enough to kill them! Say it!' And his hands crept towards her throat. She repeated the words, and felt deeply sick.

'And Archie Biddell. I want to see him dead. Dead! Pay the price for what his family have done for generations! Say it! Say it, Miss lahdi-dah Frater.' He paused. 'He'd look good on a slab, would young Mr Biddell. Wounded, scarred across his pretty face.'

Chuff moved his face even closer to Amanda's till she had no option but to inhale the foul breath he expelled. She could feel her heart pounding and wanted to scream with fear. She wanted someone to rescue her. She realised that someone was Archie.

'You're a faking little bitch, aren't you?' Chuff went on in a low voice. 'Trying to set up old Chuff. Now, if I understand the CFFA, they won't be too pleased to find out one of their top people happens to have fallen for the target, eh? Will they? Going to tell them, are you? Are you fuck!' Amanda froze on the sofa, unable to respond. Chuff took this for agreement.

'Well, I'm going to do a deal with you,' he went on. 'Chuff will help you all he can, get you all the information you need. Because when the day comes to pay the price, I shall be there to ensure that Archie Biddell pays properly for his crimes against animals, against my old mum, even fucking old Tomlinson.'

Amanda nodded, mesmerised by him.

'So if you want a fling with the pretty boy from the big house, I suggest you get on with it real fast. 'Cos there's not much lovin' to be had from a corpse.'

She had never been so close to a dangerous man before and it revolted her. She thought of Freddie, how he would have urged her on, persuaded her with rational arguments that fighting on behalf of animals who could not fight for themselves was justified. She thought of Domino and her heart swung one way, then she remembered the look on Archie's face and it swung the other. She had not realised till now how vile a business this was in which she was mixing. It had none of the spirit which she remembered from student activist days; this was vicious stuff. And she had seen a side to Chuff she had not expected; a deep streak of violence, malice and vengefulness which, she had to admit, made him the ideal recruit.

She got up, wiped the tears from her eyes, straightened her coat.

'It's a deal. Communicate via our Internet page. It's secure. I'll be in touch.'

'And if you're not, then I can safely say you'll be hearing from me,' said Chuff, looking her straight in the eye.

She closed the front door of six Barnyard Close behind her. Inside she could hear Chuff still ranting, his muffled words just discernible through the thickness of the front door.

'I am in earnest, I will not equivocate,' he roared. 'I will not excuse. I will not retreat a single inch, and I will be heard!'

The Peacock was eerily silent. The unthinkable had happened, an event as likely as the hands of Big Ben going backwards or the atomic clocks of the world failing to register accurate time – the baron of beef was *not* on the spit above the fire, the spit was not revolving, there was no sizzle as the fat hit the flames. The fire was out.

'No beef?' asked Archie, stunned by the silence and still dazed from his unexpected encounter with Amanda, and now seeking solace in beer. Eric Thwaite, instead of leaning across the bar reading the racing pages of the *Daily Mirror*, was instead slumped in a chair by the empty grate. He did not reply.

'Are you all right, Eric? You look dreadful.'

'You're looking none too good yourself, if I may say so, Mr Biddell. You look like you've seen a spirit.'

'Actually, I've just said goodbye to someone quite spirited.'

'I'll be fine in a minute,' said Eric. 'Just came over a bit queer. Funny how these turns take you.'

'I'll get you a drink,' offered Archie.

'Well, that's really turning the tables, sir. You getting me a drink. I think I'll have a brandy to steady myself.'

Archie dived behind the bar. 'Do you want a doctor? I'll ring if you like?'

'No, thank you. It will pass. I've had it before. Do you know, I dropped a pint mug the other day. Never done that in thirty years in the licensed trade. I was shocked. It was as if my brain and my hand didn't connect for a moment.'

Archie was just about to reach for the brandy bottle but froze. What Eric had said worried him.

'What do you mean when you say your brain didn't connect?'

'Just that, really. You know how the lights flicker when the voltage drops as the pig feeders start? It's a bit like that really. Like a flicker and everything goes haywire. Funny feeling.'

Archie was curious now.

'Happen often?'

'Three times so far this week.'

'Last week?'

'Once.'

'Before that?'

'Oh, I think I had a bit of a turn four or five weeks back.'

'A doctor would say that means whatever it is is getting worse,' said Archie, who had now pulled the bottle from the shelf and was pouring Eric a stiff measure. He brought it over to the seat by the dead fire. As Archie approached, the landlord extended a shaking arm. Archie pressed the glass into Eric's hand and asked him to grip it, but he might as well have asked a baby.

'Try the other arm,' said Archie.

Its grasp was fine, and Eric sipped his brandy till he felt strong enough to stand. Archie watched him till he was upright, and saw him wobble and grasp the bar for support as he tried to move across the bar towards the stairs.

'I'll lie down for a little,' he said. 'Polly will be here in five minutes, if you don't mind just watching the bar, sir?'

'Could be the start of a whole new career. Sure you don't want a doctor?'

'I'll be fine. But there'll be no beef tonight.' He closed the door behind him.

The back door opened and Polly rushed in, hair tangled after a shower and still uncombed, make-up not yet done.

'What, no beef?' she said as soon as she saw the empty fireplace.

'Not tonight,' answered Archie. Polly turned, expecting to see Eric.

'Oh, dear. Eric's not took bad again, is he?'

'Has this happened before?'

'More times than he'll admit. Four times last week. Always after lunch. He just couldn't grip anything, hold anything, get his words out. The turn he took last Thursday was the worst. He seemed to lose all coordination. He was trembling, sweating, slurring his words. He gets over it in an hour or so, and by the time the doctor got here there was nothing wrong with him. Poor old Eric. I'll let him sleep and then take him a cup of tea.'

Polly went to open the front door to let a breeze through the pub now that the fire was not performing its usual magic of drawing fresh air into the room. On the doorstep stood Michael Pember, behind him Arthur Friend.

'Oh, it's you,' she said curtly.

'Came to say I was sorry,' replied Michael, boldly.

'You can say nothing on the doorstep because you're stopping Mr Friend getting to the bar. Isn't he, Arthur, dear?'

'Damned vets, always in the way,' grumbled Arthur, and shoved his way through to the bar.

'Hell!' he exclaimed. 'No beef!' And sat down with a pint of Bullocks drawn by Polly out of habit.

'I really do want to apologise,' Michael said to her.

'Not necessary,' said Polly, crisply. 'Why should my problems be your problems, eh?'

'But I want to help, if I can.'

'Didn't sound like it the other night.' She took a deep breath. 'Look, I'm sorry. You've got enough on your plate without all my worries, especially about Chuff. I'll sort it. Shouldn't have bothered you in the first place, that was wrong of me, and walking out too. I am sorry, Michael.'

He was lost for words.

'And I never said thanks for the supper,' she added, smiling. 'So thank you. Have a drink on me.' She poured him half a pint of beer, tapped his hand affectionately as she gave it to him, then went to check the kitchen.

Archie, who had been sitting quietly by the bar, came across to Michael whose spirits were higher now he felt his apology had been accepted.

'I'm curious about something,' he said. 'Were you around in the early nineties, mad cow disease time?'

'I was around, but only twelve years old, I'm afraid. Why?'

'Nothing. Just wondered,' replied Archie, turning away. He joined Arthur at the table by the fireplace.

'Game of dominoes?' he said.

'Might as well,' said Arthur. 'You know, it's bloody funny without that lump of beef going round and round. Like the life's gone out the place. Dead, ain't it?' He leaned across to the next table for the box of dominoes, slid the lid back and poured them on to the table.

'You were stockman then, weren't you? Back in the mad cow days?'

Archie shuffled the dominoes and took six.

'It's not likely I shall ever forget them days.'

Arthur took his six and started to stand them upright.

'Did you ever see it in humans?'

'I did, sir,' said Arthur, 'but it was the way my old cows suffered that sticks in *my* mind. I mean, we brought it on ourselves. The cows didn't. They didn't ask to be fed infected grub, did they? No, we did it to them so it's the cows I think of first.'

Arthur placed the first domino on the table.

'A double six,' he said. 'It will be someone's lucky night.'

'Pember's, I would imagine, seeing the way those two are chatting away,' Archie remarked, glancing across at Michael and Polly, now head to head over glasses of beer. 'But the symptoms in humans . . . Do you remember them at all?'

Arthur paused and chose his next words very carefully.

'No, sir, I can't honestly say I can. But I am very surprised that you cannot. You know, with everything you went through. Have you got a six, sir? Can you go?'

Archie shuffled through his dominoes and by luck found a six. Emily had been only six when he'd first met her. They'd been friends from childhood, children who grew up together, never guessing that what was between them would eventually turn to love.

'Blast! I ain't got a five to put next to yours,' said Arthur. 'You'd best have another turn.' He knocked on the table, as the rules stipulated.

Archie put a five on the table, leaving Arthur to find a three. It was three months from the day Emily was diagnosed as suffering from a brain disease to the day she died. Only later was it recognised that she had been suffering from the human form of the disease which had devastated Arthur's beloved herd of cows.

'Ah, I can go now. Thank you very much,' said Arthur, and put Archie in the position of having to find a five. He placed a five, leaving Arthur with a two to find. Arthur did not have one and knocked on the table again, muttering about his bad luck. It was just such a heavy knock on the door of his father's house that had brought Archie the news that Emily had died.

He jumped to his feet and swept the dominoes from the table, pushing past Polly and Michael at the bar, leaving Arthur apologising for something that was not his fault.

'Where's Eric? I need to see him,' Archie demanded. Polly told him to go carefully up the narrow stairs and take the first left.

Eric was still asleep. Archie stood at the foot of his bed. Although he'd never realised till now, every moment of Emily's life, every change in her behaviour in the three months following the diagnosis, every up, every down, was recorded deep in his mind and now he was suffering from playback. It was the way that Eric was completely unable to coordinate any movement of his hands that brought it all back from the depths of his memory. He remembered asking Emily to hold him, when she had broken the news to him that there was no cure, but her pitiful efforts to coordinate the movements of her arms upset her so much that he had felt bad ever after for asking. Like Eric, at first she'd thought it was not much to worry about – just tiredness or a bug. But the inability to grasp became worse, anxiety took over, and then the darkest cloud of depression rolled over her and she lived the rest of her short life in its shadow.

And there was nothing anyone could do. Cell by cell, her vital, imaginative and unique brain had destroyed itself under an influence that was not then fully understood. Now, looking at Eric and remembering the way the glass had slipped and his handshake failed, Archie was filled with a deep fear that the disease which everyone had assumed buried in agricultural and medical history might now have re-emerged on the farm for which he was responsible. The cruellest of spectres had come back to haunt him.

It was well past 6 o'clock when Brian Frater slammed down the phone on Orion Shipping.

'Bastards!' He thumped the desk which was laden with demands for unpaid VAT, the final payment of an overdue tax bill, a request for money for servicing bills on his transport lorries, and countless other scraps of paper – all of which added up to deep shit for Brian. And now Orion Shipping wanted an extra 5 per cent on the price they were charging for the protein since, although they acknowledged it was of dubious quality, they insisted that the handling of it carried with it certain risks to their reputation for which Frater should compensate them. He knew this was fair but it didn't help him when it came to finding the money to satisfy their demands.

He had no choice, which made it worse. Already he was unable to afford all approved proteins and was now making full use of the 'sweepings' bought from Orion Shipping. Every direction he looked it was uphill; it was just a question of picking the least tortuous route. He grabbed the phone again, dialled Orion back.

'Hi, it's Frater. OK, let's do the extra five per cent on two hundred tons. But I don't want you coming back to me next month asking for six because you won't get it. Understand?'

He pressed the phone to his ear, listening carefully.

'Of course I know there's no certificate of origin or approved analysis. I know both those bloody things! Yes, I know I buy it at my own risk. Now will you just ship the bloody stuff over here?' He put the phone down.

'Risk? What kind of risk?' Brian swung round in his chair.

Amanda was still shaken from her meeting with Chuff. And shaken even more by the tone of the conversation she had just overheard.

'Daddy, what are you up to? I heard you use the words "no certificate of origin" and "no analysis". Are you crazy? Do you know what they'll do to you if any of that feed you send out contains unapproved additives? What are you playing at?'

'You suddenly seem to know a lot about the feed business,' said Brian, surprised both by his daughter's appearance and her understanding of his trade.

'I've picked up a thing or two as I've gone around,' she said cautiously.

'It's lovely to see you, darling,' he said, hoping to divert the conversation. And he walked across, arms outstretched in anticipation of a hug. There was none.

'I heard you, Daddy. You said you knew it had no certificate or analysis.'

'So bloody what!' he shouted. 'Let me run my own bloody business the way I choose. Now, I'm going to make some tea and then perhaps we'll both calm down a bit. Anyway, what are you doing here? I didn't expect to see you. You're such a rare sight in the village.'

'Sounds like I ought to be a bit less rare.'

'Truce, eh? And leave the business side of things to me. Now I'll make that tea.'

Brian went across the yard where lorries were working late, reversing between giant hoppers, loading manufactured feedstuffs and carting them off to farms. Alone now, Amanda looked at the mound of paperwork on his desk. She spotted the unpaid bills first and added them up roughly in her head. It came to about £25,000. Shocked, she slid into the chair. Then she turned up a letter from Orion Shipping. It was confirmation of her father's recent order, stressing the lack of certification and inspection of the feed. It was not against the law for Orion to supply it, and so they could be perfectly open about their terms of business. But the regulations stated that such material could never be incorporated into animal feed. The BSE crisis of the nineties had brought that about. And now here was her father, breaking the law, risking lives.

The door opened behind her and Brian appeared carrying two mugs. She swung round in the chair to face him. 'Why are you doing this, Daddy?' She fingered the letter from Orion Shipping as she spoke. 'You know the rules.'

He could have given her the straight answer, told her he needed the money partly to pay the bills which were a consequence of her lifestyle. Instead he said, 'Never been proved, BSE and feedstuffs.

No scientific connection ever shown. My conscience is clear. The protein is clean. It's just not got a certificate. That doesn't make it poisonous, for God's sake.'

'But the risks?' said Amanda. 'To animals, to humans. Why are you taking this risk again?'

Brian put the mugs of tea on the desk and pulled out a letter from Marcus Hastings outlining the need for a four per cent cut in feed prices if the contracts with Biddell's were to continue.

Amanda read the letter and noticed it had not been signed by Archie although dated two days after he assumed control. She wondered if he knew about this. She read the letter again and tried to cheer up her father.

'They do say this supermarket deal will lead to stability and assure the future of the estate.'

'If I can just hang on long enough to see the day,' he replied, gloomily.

'But, Daddy, there have been times like this before. It's a game they all play. In the past you've always been able to get a few per cent off your suppliers to make up for it. What's the problem? Why not do that this time? It would be better to do a deal than take a risk like this.' She looked out of the window. 'You have no idea what those lorries are shipping out of this mill. Disease . . . anything!'

There was the roar of an engine as it revved before a lorry reversed beneath a hopper down which Frater's blended cattle feed was about to be poured.

If Brian had not been interrupted by it, he might have delivered another platitude. Instead, he could conceal the truth no longer. It had been his duty, since his wife died, to see that Amanda had everything she wished for. After the accident, this had seemed doubly important. But sooner or later he knew that her demands would outstrip his resources and he would have to call a halt. He should have done it years ago, ignored her persuasive ways, told her that it was all very well being a charity worker but not when you depended on someone else's charity while you did it. To the best of his knowledge she had never had a job, preferring causes to a career. He could only afford so much of that, and now he had no more to give.

'I'm bust. There's no more money in the pot. That's why I can never do a deal – because I've nothing to do a deal with. They'd agree to a price drop, if I settle the outstanding accounts. But I never can.'

'Where's it all gone?' asked Amanda, genuinely surprised to find that her father was not a bottomless pit of wealth.

'You tell me,' he replied. 'It's all been through your bank account. Whatever you've wanted, you've had. And I am very sorry, but there's no more.'

'How long has this been going on, getting worse and worse like this?'

'The last five years have been tight.'

'And how long have you been buying this cheap muck to put in the feed?'

'Only the last six months, since things got really bad. I had no choice.'

She sat down at the desk again, dazed, shaking her head in disbelief as she looked over the outstanding bills and demands.

'Is there any way out?'

'If Biddell's go back to the original deal, I can get by. Make the books balance within the year. That should keep the bank happy. And there'd be some spare for you.'

'I think I've had enough already, don't you?'

'I've never begrudged you, my sweetheart. You don't know how proud I am of you, trying to make a mark in the world by doing good. Actually, I'd heard you were in the village. Someone spotted you.'

'Nothing much is secret round here, is it?' asked Amanda.

'When I heard you'd come all this way to try and help a lad who'd lost his mother, I could have cried. There's so much selfishness in the world, and here is my daughter, trying to help someone. I wanted to help you, Amanda, and money was the only way I knew how.'

203

He paused and looked her straight in the eye.

'There's one thing you could do for me now,' he said to her. 'I can't appeal to Marcus Hastings. The old bastard never gives an inch, famous for it.' He took a deep breath. 'But *you* could appeal to Archie Biddell.'

Amanda turned her head quickly away from her father towards the open window. She saw a multi-wheeled lorry drawing into the yard, the words '*Orion Shipping*' in bold letters across the protective canvas.

'I hardly know him,' she said, biting her lip.

'But better than I do,' said her father. 'You sat next to him at that party the other night. Seemed to get on all right. Everyone remarked how relaxed you seemed. It's worth a go.'

'You mean, ring him up, out of the blue. And ask him – what?'

'Don't ask him anything. Just tell him. He won't have the slightest idea any of this has happened. It will be all Hastings's little game. The Biddells won't know anything. Just tell him how the suppliers are being squeezed to death. He won't approve of this way of doing business.'

'You want me to go grovelling to him?'

'Not grovel, just tell,' he insisted.

Amanda could see no way she could ever face Archie again. Yet, strangely, she wanted to. And if her father had been driven to abandon his principles and sup with the devil at Orion Shipping, then maybe she should not be too proud to make the same sort of compromise.

'Give me his number,' she said, just managing to speak the words before the Orion lorry tilted its tailgate and allowed the tons of pale green cubes of whatever it might be to slide unchecked into the mill. Cows would be chewing them within the hour.

Some men are immune to the tears of their children, others will crumple before them. Toby Hopscotch stood his ground. With seven weeks to go to his first school sports day, young Georgie had to come to terms with the fact that his parents would not be there.

He was crying his heart out, inconsolable, gasping between deep sobs and asking why, why, why could Mum not come to his first school sports day?

'George, you're looking rather silly. And your nose is running like a tap. Go and clean yourself up,' his father rebuked him. Which were not the words George wanted to hear from Toby. He wanted him to cave in, submit to his son's will and turn up at sports day like all the other dads. And if it took a tantrum to do it little George was going to play this one for all he was worth.

'Look, George,' said Toby, trying to knot his tie, fretful about a meeting with the St Edwich Strategy Group, 'Daddy's got to go to work now, and I hope that by the time I get home you will have stopped crying. All right? Let's say no more about it.'

Tiggy was stacking the dishwasher, interpreting the conversation. Roughly translated, what Toby was saying was: 'Stop this little brat screaming by the time I get home. You can put up with the row during the day, but I do not want to hear it tonight. My job is to do the damage then walk away from it, leaving you to pick up the pieces. Understood?' Up till now, she'd had no problem with this message; she had been receiving it loud and clear for twelve years.

'Mummy, Mummy!' cried her son. '*You'll* come, won't you, to my sports day?'

She wanted to say, 'Yes, YES! I *will* be there. To hell with your father's bloody supermarket.' Instead, she trotted out the parent's last resort of 'We'll see'.

There were more loud sobs. 'Whenever you say "we'll see" it means no,' her son wailed.

Tiggy saw no reason to try and keep this piece of stretched elastic from breaking, so gave it the final tug which caused it to snap and fly back in their faces.

'Oh, all right then, George. No, I'm not coming to sports day and neither is Daddy. It's to do with his work. He's opening a new supermarket. We can't help it. I'll get Granny to come, and we'll give her the video camera so we can watch it afterwards. But no, we won't be there.'

'For Christ's sake, couldn't you handle it a bit more gently than that?' hissed Toby in exasperation, polishing the toes of his shoes on the hand towel.

'And how exactly were *you* going to handle it? By mobile phone from St Edwich?'

Toby was amazed at her response which, mild though it might seem, contained more spirit than she had ever shown before throughout their married years.

'We'd better talk,' he said, and walked across to his wife, dropping the clean towel on the dirty floor. He led her to the kitchen table and sat her down. He poured a cup of tea from the pot, not noticing it was stale and cold.

'You've been like a stranger this last few weeks,' he reproached her.

Tiggy was looking the other way, trying to guess why George's crying had stopped. Perhaps he'd found the start button on the video and it would be peaceful for five minutes.

'Look at me,' said Toby, concerned rather than angry. 'If you need to talk, I'm always here to listen. Not at this moment, of course, because I've got a meeting to get to. Tonight. We can talk tonight. I'll try and make it not too late, rattle through Bar Code Focus Group. Then we'll chat. How about it?'

206

Tiggy nodded. She had one eye on the clock. It was already 8.15 and she had to get George to school, do some photocopying and be at The Social Chapter by 10 o'clock. It was Tuesday.

'I know what the problem is,' said Hopscotch, oozing concern with every word, 'I understand about women, and things, and all their complicated works and bits and pieces.' He was pink with embarrassment. 'And I think I can help. It's biological. I understand, darling, I really do. We've got some marvellous new stuff in the pharmacy for, well, older women. Not that I'm saying you're old,' he added quickly, 'but it's the biological clock, isn't it? We all suffer from it.

'I suppose you haven't noticed because I've been trying to be brave about it, but it's taking *me* a little longer to get up to speed too.' Toby was back on his favourite topic and felt easier now. 'I can sense all those young hounds yapping behind me, drawing closer, trying to overtake. So I know about all this getting older business. But you'll come to terms with it, and a bottle of *ReJuvenal* – get it? – will do the trick. There's a move to put it on special offer, but I'm fighting it; start discounting your basic bestsellers and you're in trouble, that's what I always say. Be a love, could you? Finish polishing these shoes?'

Tiggy said nothing. She bent to pick up the towel from the floor, spat on it and sent her husband on his way to work gleaming round the feet, dull as ever in the head. Georgie came through from the front room, school bag in hand, more composed now.

'Mum?'

'Yes, darling?'

'Are you dead certain you won't come to sports day?'

'You can never be absolutely certain of anything in life, sweetheart.'

'Does that mean yes or no?'

'It means Mummy has to decide which things in life are most important to her.'

'I see,' said George, thinking hard. 'And if you decided sports day was the most important, would you come?'

'You try and stop me,' said Tiggy, hugging him hard, then bundling on her coat and herding him towards the car. She was just about to slam the front door when she remembered the document folder which she had kept safely hidden in Georgie's wardrobe. No danger of Toby ever looking there.

After school, her next stop was the photocopying shop. She could have used the machine in Toby's study but she wasn't allowed in there – it was his private domain, the 'lion's den' as he called it. More like a parrot in a cage spouting Applewhite's cod philosophy all day long, thought Tiggy. Sometimes she longed to throw a blanket over him, shut him up. The other reason she did not want to use his photocopier was because she'd once read a thriller where the villain had been caught because he took the incriminating copies away, but left the original in the machine. It was all too easy to do, and Tiggy wanted no mistakes.

'Oh, Applewhite's!' said the dim girl in the photocopy shop, breaking the rules and reading all the documents as she passed them through the machine. 'I always shop there. Marvellous bargains they have. I always think it's such a good, friendly shop that those who run it must have hearts of gold. Don't you?'

The Social Chapter was deserted except for Marge who was buttering scones as if they were about to be rationed. The air was foul with the remains of last night's menu which had yet to be scraped from the pans. And to make it worse, roadworks further down the street were causing lorries to have to change gear noisily outside The Chapter, their filthy fumes creeping under the tightly shut door. The smell of burned bacon fat usually eclipsed anything, but not today. To make yourself heard over the roar of impatient diesel engines, you had to shout. It had put Marge's nerves on edge.

'You're all back then,' were the words with which she greeted Tiggy. 'Haven't seen any of you lot for the best part of a month. Thought it might be something I said. There again, perhaps I didn't give a bugger. They've asked for you twice. Shouted down,

"Is Tiggy here yet?" I said, "Where the bloody hell do you think I've put her? In the slop bin?" Bloody daft question. I'll bring your coffee up if you like. I wouldn't keep 'em waiting. Lousy mood all three of 'em are in this morning. Traffic don't help. I wish they'd piss off somewhere else with their bloody lorries.' And then, with a change of tack as quick as the wind, she said, 'I reckon that Amanda'd been crying before she came here. I've seen enough tears from behind this counter to recognise the signs. Sugar?'

'Two, thanks.'

'Hey,' called Marge, 'sixty-five pence. It's not a bloody charity!' Tiggy carefully opened the door of the upstairs room. Marge was right: Amanda had been crying, she could see it.

'Shut the bloody door,' said Conrad, waiting for a lull between engine roars. 'Anyone might hear what we're saying.'

'Fat chance,' muttered Ernest.

Tiggy pushed the door to and sat down after carefully straightening her skirt.

'What yer got?' asked Conrad sharply.

'Schedules,' she said, drawing papers from a carrier bag.

'Thanks,' Amanda said.

'Forget the fucking manners. Schedules? What schedules, what of? What use are bloody schedules? Has it taken you four bloody weeks to get *schedules*?'

'I think we should listen. We might learn something,' said Ernest, calmly taking out his gold ball point ready to make notes.

'I've got copies of how the delivery system will work, how they'll get the animals direct from Biddell's to the factory and then to the St Edwich superstore. They're going to sell at prices far below anybody else's. They're calling it a marketing miracle.'

'I don't suppose the turkeys see it that way,' said Conrad.

'I think it is safe to say,' said Ernest, choosing his words with care, 'that my client is already well aware of the trading relationships between Biddell's and the new superstore. What he wants to know, and what I have to take back to him from this meeting, is what the CFFA intends to do about it. At our last meeting, I think I made it clear that his patience only extends so far.' He turned to Amanda. 'It is now a month since you went to Woodham Ford. More than enough time for you all to have made up your mind about our course of action. I have to take something back to him today which will persuade him that further funding is worth his while. And it had better be good.'

'Well, all we've got so far are bloody schedules,' said Conrad morosely.

'May I say something?' asked Tiggy, nervously.

Ernest leaned courteously towards her, deluging her in the scent of his ridiculously expensive after-shave. 'I get the feeling you have more of importance to tell us, my dear?'

'Well,' she said, 'they've decided that the only way to make the transfer of animals efficient is to send them in convoy to the abattoir. If they run fewer lorries throughout the night, they've got to staff the whole abattoir operation all night too.' She shuffled the photocopies in front of her. 'I learned that from this memo from the transport department.' She pushed it across the table. 'So, there'll be a convoy every night of about ten lorries loaded with livestock, leaving Biddell's around ten o'clock and arriving at the abattoir by midnight so that there'll be fresh meat on the Applewhite's meat counter the following morning at eight. And that way they'll only need to run the lorries for a couple of hours.'

'How disgusting,' said Ernest.

'Yeah, vile,' agreed Conrad.

'I was thinking of the beef,' said Ernest, 'killed at midnight, wrapped and sold next day! A good bit of beef hangs for a fortnight, you know. Then it can be called real beef.'

'Can we keep cookery out of this, please, *Mr Meat-eater*?' spat Conrad.

'I'm only here at my client's bidding,' said Ernest, 'to pay the bills. I'm leaving you to look after the principles.'

'Officially the first convoy will run from opening day,' said Tiggy.

'But that's the middle of bloody July!' Conrad objected. 'I'm ready for some action now.'

'They're going to start practice runs six weeks before the superstore opens,' said Tiggy proudly.

'Next week,' deduced Conrad, looking more enthusiastic.

'Look, it's all here, on this next memo from the transport director,' added Tiggy.

'"To fully assess the operational aspects of animal transfer, I propose weekly runs of at least fifty animals starting the first week in June."'

All eyes turned to Amanda who had said nothing so far. Making herself heard above the lorries was even more of an effort for her than for most people. Anything to do with lorries made her nervous for every time she heard the hiss of an air brake, she remembered the driver's frantic pumping of the brakes which failed to stop his truck from sliding over Freddie's helpless body. She associated lorries with pain and death, and the mere proximity of them sent twinges through her leg.

She had nothing to say now. Conrad sniffed deeply and spoke.

'It's got to be a phuffer. I can't see any other way at this sort of short notice.'

'I'm sorry, a what?' said Ernest.

'Phuffers we call 'em,' he said, 'because they go "Phuff!" Bombs, you daft bastard. I'm talking about bombs. Bomb the convoy! Finish the whole business, that would. After that they'd have to lay on such heavy security it would blow the economics of the whole thing right out of the window. Yeah, a bomb. I vote for a bomb.'

'I'm not sure . . .' objected Amanda.

'And I'm not sure about you!' he shouted. 'What's got into you these days? Where's your guts, eh? Died with Freddie, did they?'

'Fuck you,' she shouted, jumping to her feet and screaming to make herself heard over the lorries' roar, which was unsettling her more with every moment that passed.

'Use a bomb if you want, but try explaining to people then how blowing up innocent animals is helping them. I don't see how blasting a cow apart shows how much you care for animals. We're not about bombs, we're about political action, bringing things to people's attention.'

'People will understand actions long after they've forgotten words. It's like a war,' he said. 'Some have to die to make a better world for others. Isn't that what they said in both World Wars?'

A lorry shifted gear, revved its engine till the windows rattled and crowned the crescendo of its racing engine with a piercing hiss as the brakes were released. Amanda reached down to massage her leg and try and ease the pain.

'You can't ask a cow if it minds being blown into a thousand pieces so that all cows that come after it have better lives!' she screamed above the traffic.

'No,' said Conrad, 'but we can speak for them. Through action. By stopping those convoys of farm animals forever. I'll kill a few cows to achieve that, won't you, Amanda? Though I am beginning to think you might not, actually. Strange, isn't it, what the passage of a few years can do? It seems like only five minutes since you and Freddie were prepared to lay down your lives for farm animals. He laid down his. I wonder if he'd think it was worth it, to hear you speak now? You've lost it, haven't you? All that fire, all that commitment. You've pissed it down the pan.'

She looked around the table, waited for the rumble of another blasted lorry to stop before she spoke. She was weary from Conrad's taunting, stressed by the pain, confused by her love of Freddie and the conflicting attraction she felt towards Archie. In one brief moment, she had to weigh these pressures and decide which way the scales would tilt. Freddie won. Not just Freddie, she thought, but Domino as well. Sorry, Archie, she said to herself.

'If it's a bomb, then I'll press the button,' she declared.

'Great!' yelled Conrad. 'I'll hold you to that. Your finger on the button. Good girl.'

Marge banged on the door.

'You've got fifteen minutes before the Yoga people have the room booked. So get a move on! Hot dinner's beef stew if you'll be wanting any.'

Ernest started to pack his briefcase, and turned to Tiggy who was looking rather pale. He tried to comfort her.

'Does any of this upset you? Are you worried by anything you've heard here this morning?'

'I don't think I ever imagined bombs . . .'

'Neither did I till this morning. I trust we still have your support, your full support? And, of course, your complete silence?'

'Yes, you have.'

'Then answer me one question,' he continued. 'Why is it that you are willing to help in an operation which could destroy your husband's business? I take it he is closely involved?'

'Yes, he is. If you really want to know, all of you, why I'm here, it's simply because come the fifteenth of July, when Applewhite's plan to open that lousy superstore, I want to be somewhere else, doing something that is more important to *me*. I don't care how I achieve it, I just want that date rubbed off the calendar. That's all.

'Now, must go, Georgie's got a dentist's appointment. Nothing serious. Well, 'bye,' she gasped as she pushed the remaining photocopies into the middle of the table and trotted off down the stairs.

It was not till Amanda had replaced the papers in her briefcase, said goodbye to Ernest who had a meeting in the City, and tried to calm Conrad who appeared excited at the prospect of bomb-making classes, that she fully realised the commitment she had made. She would press a trigger that fired a bomb.

She went downstairs into the main part of The Social Chapter and sat quietly at a table. She nodded to Marge, which was the understood signal for a mug of coffee, and looked for the small piece of paper on which her father had scribbled Archie Biddell's phone number. She must ring him, offer some kind of apology, see him again, ask if he could help her father. And all the time she would have to look him in the eye, knowing that it would be the pressure of her finger on the button that would bring his world collapsing around him, possibly even cause his death. Her leg pained her as more lorries paused outside The Chapter, revving their engines, hissing their brakes.

A mug of coffee appeared before her, and Marge pulled out a chair and fell wearily into it. She never usually sat with the customers.

'Feller?' she asked sympathetically.

'Sorry?' said Amanda, pulled out of her thoughts.

'There's a look on your face that's got feller trouble written all over it.'

'I don't think . . .'

'There's an artist bloke comes in here,' said Marge, confidentially, 'looking for women to paint. He says the ones who've got man troubles are the ones he wants because they've all got that look . . . like the one you've got.'

'Are you sure he just wants them so he can paint them?' asked Amanda. 'Anyway, what if it is a sort of feller problem, as you call it?'

'Good,' said Marge. 'If it is, and it's none of my business one way or the other, but *if* it is then all I would say is that you're not going to solve it by sitting round that table upstairs. There's a lot to be said for some of what goes on at The Chapter, but there's people who get into deeper trouble than they ever intended, just by sitting with others and getting carried away. Don't get carried away. That's all I'm saying.'

She paused and watched Amanda sip her coffee.

'Is he one of them, part of your upstairs gang, this feller?'

'Not exactly.'

'On the other side then?' asked Marge. Amanda nodded.

'Tricky. Do you love him?'

'Early days, Marge.'

214

'So it's on your mind then, that you might do?'

'As I say, early days.'

'So don't waste your chance! All this mucking around in the upstairs room will keep you going for a year or so. Bit of excitement, plotting to change the world ... But then you'll get fed up with it and you'll look back and realise that while you were wasting your time round that upstairs table, trying to grab the world and shake it till it was the way you wanted it, real life in the real world was slipping out of your grasp. I've seen it happen. I've seen them wake up and realise it was all a silly dream.'

'Possibly,' agreed Amanda, reluctantly.

'What about that blinking tax that Thatcher woman brought in – remember her? Poll tax, was it called? We had a riot at the end of the eighties, Trafalgar Square, thousands of us. We planned it here, round that same mucky table you've been round this morning. That's when I first got to know this place. Mind you, it wasn't called The Social Chapter then. Something to do with wholefoods, I think. Can't remember now. But there's been someone plotting something here for generations. Before you were born, kid.

'Anyway, then we all went to Trafalgar Square, broke a few shop windows, smashed cars, set fire to a police van or two. Then they arrested me. And do you know, the lad who nicked me lived five doors down our street and I'd fancied him like hell for years! He'd just got to the point of asking me out too. Can you imagine worse bloody luck than that?'

'What happened?'

'He nicked me. Had to. Nothing ever happened between us after that. Dropped me like a stone. Still hurts. He did all right, kids and a wife. I ended up here, making coffee, washing up, watching other people bugger up their lives, thinking that if I hadn't been there, chucking stones for no real reason, my life might have turned out a bit different.'

'I see.'

'I hope you do.' A customer opened the door. Marge pressed down hard on the table and heaved herself up, leaving Amanda contemplating Archie's phone number. Sitting at a table in a dark corner was Tiggy, sipping cold coffee. The intensity of the previous hour had been too much for her, her mind was still spinning, and even if it meant she was late for Georgie's dental appointment, she needed one more cup of coffee.

She had heard part of Marge's conversation with Amanda, but not all of it. After a while she crept across to Amanda's table, sat quietly next to her and leaned closer.

'Do you want to tell me all about it?' she asked.

14

Although Archie and Amanda never spoke directly to each other, they made a date via terse messages left on answering machines to meet at The Peacock for an early-evening drink. Amanda intended to fulfil the promise she had made to her father – to make a direct plea to Archie. After hearing nothing from her for a month, and having started the painful process of erasing all memory of her, no one had been more surprised than he to receive her call, and no one more astonished than Amanda to receive his reply. She had played his curt message over and over again, trying to guess from the way he phrased his words whether he was pleased to hear from her, ecstatic that she'd called, or didn't give a damn. She would shortly find out, she realised, as she sipped a glass of chilled white wine after finding herself a seat in The Peacock as far away as possible from the revolving baron of beef, the sight of which made her feel sick. It had once been a calf, maybe just like Domino.

She looked across at the bar where the body language of the barmaid and the chap leaning close to her made her think how much simpler life might be if she could enjoy a simple relationship like those two were having. In fact Michael Pember, less than fresh from a hard day in the surgery, was offering Polly an apology as well as making her an offer. They spoke quietly so as not to be overheard.

'I said I'd help, and I will, but I need to see for myself exactly what it is Chuff's up to. I've given it some thought . . .'

'A month's thought,' she scolded him. 'I thought you'd forgotten all about it.'

'Some of this animal rights stuff is no more than boys' comics with a bit of blood and guts,' he continued. 'But the really nasty stuff – well, something ought to be done. But I've got to see for myself. It's not just magazines, either. He's been boasting about that computer of his. I'd like to get an eyeful of what's on that.'

'I don't see how.'

'Will he be in the pub tonight?'

'The moon will stop rising in the sky before Chuff stops coming in for his pint.'

Michael fiddled in his trouser pockets and found a couple of ten-pound notes. He gave them to Polly.

'Buy him as many drinks as he wants. I need a good couple of hours in his house.'

'You're not going to break in, are you?'

'Not exactly. If anyone sees me I'll say I was called to a sick cat. He's got a cat, hasn't he?'

'Yeah, big tabby,' said Polly.

'Tonight, then,' said Michael. 'No point waiting. If he's in here about seven, as usual, I'll have a pint with him then slip away. Providing you give him enough drink, he'll hardly notice I've gone.'

'Michael,' said Polly in a soft voice, 'I really do appreciate this, honest. Thanks. And I've missed you this last few weeks.'

A woman came over to the bar and glanced at the clock. Polly thought she looked as though she was having difficulty walking.

'There hasn't been a message for me, has there?' asked the woman, crisply. 'I was supposed to be meeting someone here.'

'I didn't see no messages when I came in. Can I ask the name?'

'Yes, Frater. Amanda Frater.'

'I thought I recognised you,' remarked Polly. 'You were at that Biddell's party a while back. Sorry, no messages. You've been visiting Chuff, haven't you? About his old mum, wasn't it? He'll be along in a few minutes. You can see for yourself how he's getting on.'

Amanda could not risk it. Chuff, she sensed, had no self-control.

He could all too easily open his big mouth and bring her plans to a swift end. It was getting too complicated, so she thanked Polly, grabbed her briefcase, and went back to her car.

Eric Thwaite appeared at the bottom of the stairs, still dressed in pyjamas and looking pale and drawn, having been in his bed all afternoon. The phone rang and despite the difficulty of coordinating brain and body and successfully grabbing it, he eventually got it to his ear.

'Oh, hello, Mr Archie,' he said. 'No, no one here. Nobody looking as though they're waiting for anybody that is. But if anyone asks, is there a message? That's fine then, Mr Biddell. I'll explain you've got some sick cows and you'll be along later. Right oh.'

Eric put down the phone with some difficulty and walked into the bar where Michael and Polly were standing out of earshot.

'Polly, be a love and cut me a slice of that beef. A bit of beef might just perk me up a bit.' Then, as Chuff materialised, he muttered, 'Oh, Christ, that's put the mockers on the evening.'

It seemed that every time Archie went to see the cows, Arthur Friend was one step ahead of him. He was like a spirit inhabiting the barn, rising up from behind bales of straw like a guardian angel never far from his herd of cows.

'Ah, Mr Biddell,' Arthur said when he spotted Archie. 'I likes to be regular. It's easier if you do things with cows same time of day, every day. I remember my old dad saying that. Cows like routine.'

'And what *things* do you do to them?' asked Archie, bemused.

'I beg your pardon, sir, but stockmen have their secrets and my father would turn over in that churchyard if I gave any of 'em away. It was all they had, you see. Their secrets. If it weren't for their knowhow, they'd be no better than the next man.'

'I'm worried,' Archie confessed abruptly.

'Good,' responded Arthur, ''cos I'm a bit concerned too.' They both stood in silence for a moment, scanning the herd of cows.

219

'It doesn't look to me as though they're in the best of health,' added Archie, who had sensed all was not well the moment he came through the door.

'Blowed if I know what,' said Arthur, 'but there's something that's not quite right, I agree. And if I may say so, you spotting it suggests you have a stockman's eye.'

They both stood and looked, trying to find a symptom they could describe to a vet, but there wasn't one. Archie felt sure that if you took their pulse and temperature or listened to their hearts, not so much as a beat would be out of place. But they were sick and both Archie and Arthur knew it.

'Whatever it is,' Archie decided, 'I'd say they all had it.'

'Well,' Arthur agreed, 'I couldn't point to one as looks what I'd call one hundred per cent. You see that one over there – I call her Daisy after a lovely old cow we used to have – well, usually there's no way she'd stand against that wall knowing I was here. She'd be over having a chat, like we do most evenings.'

'I can't ring the vet and tell him to come quickly because one of the cows doesn't feel in the mood for conversation!'

'Perhaps they'll look better in the morning. Sometimes it's the weather that does it. They go funny if the wind changes, or it gets a bit thundery.'

'Perhaps whatever it is you're doing to them isn't working,' joked Archie.

Arthur breathed in sharply. 'I think you'd find they'd be a lot worse off if I didn't – shall we say – look after them.'

'They won't look any different for us standing here watching them,' said Archie, reaching for the barn door. Just as his head turned, he thought he caught sight of a cow that was not behaving like the rest. It was no more than a twitch, the slightest oddness about a reflex, but enough to catch his attention. He turned to Arthur and said, 'I'm going up the back, take a proper look at that cow. Coming?'

Arthur followed. The cows parted as they made their way through the herd, though not in the spirited, playful way they usually behaved towards visitors into their world. But one cow did not make the slightest effort to get out of the way. Instead, she held her head low, rocking it from side to side.

'Now that *is* sick,' declared Archie.

'Proper poorly. One for the vet,' agreed Arthur.

'Nothing in your little black book then?'

Arthur did not rise to Archie's taunts. Instead, he asked if he could just rest his legs for a moment.

'You don't look well yourself,' said Archie, grasping his arm and easing him down on to the corner of a water trough. Archie noticed the old man was breathing deeply, face pale and lips trembling. His eyes were fixed on that one particular cow standing alone in the corner of the barn.

'Are you all right, Arthur?' Archie asked.

'There's something about the look of that cow that I don't like at all,' said the stockman. He blinked rapidly, but his eyes did not leave the cow for a second.

'Look at her,' he insisted. 'Watch her try and move those legs. Does she look to you as though she's not certain how to do it?' Arthur bit his bottom lip and thought for a moment before saying, 'Please, let it not be *that* again.'

'You'd better tell me what you think it is. Come on, man! If it's serious I've got to act, and act fast,' said Archie.

Arthur sniffed. 'I daren't say the words, sir.'

'Mad cow?' guessed Archie.

'I don't know,' said Arthur, 'but let me just . . .' And he got up from the water trough on which he had been resting, and crept slowly towards the cow so as not to disturb her. With some effort, he knelt in the straw till he could wave the open palm of his hand across the line of sight of the beast. 'See, she don't blink, don't react, doesn't know I'm here. She can't move that leg. If you push her, the leg doesn't move. Nothing connects.'

'What did you say?' asked Archie, remembering Eric Thwaite's similar words about his own condition.

'I said, it's as if there's a connection missing. She sees my hand but doesn't flinch like a normal cow would.'

'I'll get Michael,' shouted Archie, urgently making for the phone. 'As for you, Arthur, I'll drop you off at The Peacock and you can sit there till you get some colour back in your face. There's nothing more you can do up here. I'll come back and wait for the vet.'

Michael reckoned he was safe for a couple of hours. He had switched off his mobile phone and left the answering machine switched on at the surgery. He had also taken the precaution of putting three pints of the strongest stout down Chuff's gullet and persuaded him into ordering the dish from the menu which took the longest time to cook, especially if Polly told the kitchen to slow it down a bit.

She had lent him her key to Chuff's house – the one he had given her so that she could occasionally leave him a hot meal in the oven – and so Michael had no need to indulge in housebreaking. He carried his bag of veterinary instruments with him so that if he was spotted he could claim he was seeking out the sick cat.

Not having committed trespass before, he was unsure how to tackle the problem of finding his way around the house without drawing attention to himself. If he put on the lights it was bound to be noticed, for everyone in that road knew that Chuff would be in the pub and certainly not moving around his own home in the middle of the evening. But the problem solved itself as soon as Michael turned into the Close – Chuff had left the house lights blazing. As long as Michael remembered not to get himself between the light bulbs and the curtains, and cast shadows, he would be fine. All this plotting unnerved him and as he parked the car and started to walk up to the house, he wondered why the hell he was bothering. But he knew it was a one word answer beginning with P.

He scanned the other houses to check there were no onlookers, then quickly strode up the path to the front door, slipped the key in the lock and was in. The house stank of stale food, cigarette

222

smoke and beer. He looked around the sitting room and in the jumble of magazines, greying t-shirts, worn socks and empty pizza boxes, tried to spot anything which might relate to animal rights, activism, anything at all. There was nothing obvious.

Now he had a problem. The light in the bedroom was out and he did not want to draw attention by switching it on. He decided to make use of the only light he had with him and fished out of his case of instruments a fine, pencil-like torch, the beam of which he used for looking down the throats of sheep and cattle. It was tightly focused, like a laser, and no stray light spilled from it. If he was careful where he shone it, he should be able to scan Chuff's bedroom in safety. The curtains were a problem. The glow from the computer screen was sure to fill the room with light, and so he decided he would have to close them. He crept along the floor, his nose occasionally coming too close to unsavoury clothing for comfort, and took hold of the curtains by the hems, slowly pulling them closed. Then he could stand up in safety. He found the main switch on the computer and booted it into life.

Michael was no ace with a computer, but he fancied he had a brain that would easily match Chuff's. With his face lit only by the stark, electronic glare of the screen – which he adjusted using the brightness control so that he could just barely read it – he started to scan Chuff's stored files.

It made for disappointing reading. Little to condemn the man of having anything more than a squalid fascination. His eyes roamed the screen and the computer's mouse made erratic circles as Michael followed the web of links. He wondered what he was going to say to Polly. It was clear that this was an unhealthy preoccupation, and everyone might well feel safer if Chuff directed his interests towards crosswords. But apart from there being nothing to prompt any further action, there was also Michael's own minor crime of illegal entry to consider. He was about ready to pull the plug on this little episode.

But before doing so, he thought he might check Chuff's mail

223

box. Here were stored messages in and out, as well as any mail as yet unread. Pember found it had not been security-protected and so he needed no password. He started to flick through the e-mails, a few of which came from the CFFA. The first one read:

Vital we now adopt maximum security practices to prevent accidental reading of information by third parties. Please inform us of encoding patterns you prefer.

There was no record of Chuff having done so.

The next message read:

We now believe intelligence services have dealt with network providers to prevent the use of anonymous e-mails. This means that all messages can be traced. It therefore becomes even more important that we adopt encoding practices. Urgently request details of your preferred encoders.

Chuff had replied:

Hang about. I am doing my best. It is real headache stuff. Give us a break.

There followed a gap of five days with no traffic at all. Then, with a hint of exasperation detectable even in an electronic message:

We are still waiting for your encoding. It is therefore with great risk that we confirm the details of the visit by our agent. There will be no further communications from us on this matter and we are relying on you to make the required responses. And get the bloody encoding working before you send any messages!

Then came a series of messages which Michael could not unscramble. Whatever he did, they appeared as a random list of dots, dashes, numerals and letters. He looked around Chuff's desk and found a tatty envelope with a computer disc inside, and a thin, cheaply photocopied instruction booklet. Scribbled on the disc in ball point pen were the words 'Encoding Disc'. The envelope from which it fell had a central London postmark.

Pember put it to his nose and thought it smelled of cooking fat; a smear down the back of it looked as though it might be tomato sauce. A fertile mind would have said blood, but Michael thought ketchup.

He inserted the disc into the computer. Lucky. It had the effect of turning a key and unlocking the encoding designed to camouflage any further messages. There was now nothing that he could not read. He decoded Chuff's reply. It hit him like a thunderbolt.

Am now maintaining constant watch on Biddell Estate and factory and will inform of any major animal movements which are due. This is what you want to hear about – the woman told me you did. I hope you get the bastards and teach the fuckers a lesson they will never forget. I shall also send you any other information that I think might help. I noticed they have a new lorry driver who comes every afternoon about three o'clock but only because he is shagging one of the girls in the office while her husband's away. I shall pass further information as . . .

This was where his eyes became firmly riveted to the screen.

. . . your Amanda Frater requested. She's not a bad girl but her dad is a bit of an arsehole. Chuff.

Michael was just about to kill the screen when he heard the sound of a key being pushed into the lock in the front door. It turned slowly and carefully, which meant it was probably not Chuff who would have entered with no hesitancy whatsoever. Or perhaps it was him drunk out of his mind on the money Michael had left to pay for his drinks. He had no time to shut down the screen, but instead moved across the bedroom so that he was out of the line of sight of the open door. Footsteps moved along the downstairs hall but no lights were switched on. The stairs creaked, and then the slow, measured footfalls became quieter as they hit the carpeted landing that led to Chuff's bedroom.

'Hey, where are you?' came a whispered voice.

225

'Polly, what the hell are you doing here?' he replied, and reached for her arm as she drew nearer. 'I thought I was a gonner.'

'You nearly were. You *had* to pick a night when there's a big football match on which Chuff wanted to get home early to see, didn't you?'

'He's on his way back?'

'No, I gave him another pint and sent him to one of the bedrooms in The Peacock. Eric would go spare if he knew, but he's had one of his turns again and gone to bed.'

She spied the computer screen and started to read.

'Hey, this looks serious, Michael. It says he's spying on the Biddells. I knew that bugger was up to something.'

'Yes, but it doesn't tell us exactly what they're planning to do with this information. We need to know what they want it for.'

'Do you think Chuff knows?' asked Polly.

'I suspect he does. There's clearly been a lot of dialogue. If I had more time I could go through it all.' He pointed at the list of a hundred or more files which appeared on the screen and clicked on one at random. 'This one's telling them the registration numbers of all the lorries.'

'It's not one of them violent things, is it?' she asked, nervously. 'Where people get killed? And animals sometimes. I've read about some of these attacks these people make. People die, you know.'

'Yeah, and animals.'

'I think I can find out what he's up to,' said Polly.

'So could I if I had time to read through all these files.'

'My way will be quicker,' she insisted. Then she glanced again at the screen, reading it more carefully. 'Amanda Frater! That's the name of the woman who was in the bar tonight, asking for Mr Biddell – the one who came to the party.' She turned to Michael, her face pale in the light reflected from the screen. She chewed frantically on her fingernails. 'I'm really frightened by all this.'

'There's nothing to be frightened of until we know what they're planning. That's the time to start worrying.'

226

Polly took a deep breath and pushed her red hair back behind her ears. In control again, she said determinedly, 'Michael, please forgive me for what I have to do tonight. But I must know what that bloody fool is up to and what this Frater woman wants. You've done your bit now, I have to go and do mine. Meet me back at The Peacock about ten, there's a love.'

A love! he thought, overjoyed. Polly called me *a love*!

Polly walked back alone to The Peacock, feeling frightened. The more she thought about Chuff, the more she realised that a gradual change had come over him in the last few weeks, and it was not a pleasant one. He behaved, she thought, like someone with new-found confidence; as though he had at last reached a place in the world which gave him some of the self-respect he'd never had before. She used to think of him as a sad youngster whom nobody loved, a puppy that had been kicked from an early age and knew only how to snap back at its tormentors. That, she thought, was why he sat in the corner of the bar, sneering, grumbling, seeing faults in others, goading authority. It was just Chuff's way of growling at the world, trying to convince all within his reach that this creature could bite. As she walked back towards The Peacock, she pondered the change that had come over him. How his anger at the death of his mother had subsided; how the scruffy boyish looks which she admitted to herself she had once found attractive in a queasy sort of way, had been replaced by a more threatening aspect. He had now grown out of his youthful, disruptive stage, she decided, and into a new mood of cold-blooded hatred.

She reached the back entrance to The Peacock, swept back her hair and strode into the pub, gathering all the courage she could muster. Should she have a stiff drink? No, she decided, she would need to keep her wits about her.

She waited till half-time in the football match. There was no point trying to distract Chuff while soccer was on. She poured him another pint of stout, took it upstairs, knocked on the door of the upstairs bedroom and crept in. He was already draped across the bed, belt undone to relieve the pressure on his beer gut. Judging from the smell in the room, he had broken voluminous quantities of beer-induced wind. His hair looked uncombed and greasy.

'Hello, Polly, my old love,' he said. 'Hey, thanks for the ale. Someone's being generous to old Chuff tonight.'

'Maybe it's me,' she replied, sitting next to him on the bed. She had never felt more scared, or revolted, in her life. 'Perhaps I've not given you enough thought in the past,' she whispered into his greasy ear. 'Funny how you can see people every day and not really notice them.'

'Eh?' Chuff was not getting the message. So Polly stretched out her hand and stroked his leg, reaching a little higher with every stroke till she dared go no further. She looked him in the eyes as she caressed the grubby denim of his jeans, fearing she might have to kiss him. Then the penny dropped and Chuff got the message. He wrapped both his hands round her waist, and in one clumsy, unromantic movement pulled her on top of him. She smelled the odour of sweat rise from his armpits and moved her head to one side to be out of range of it, trying hard to look as though she was a willing partner.

'Well, I didn't think old Chuff was going to get any pudding with his dinner tonight, but it seems I'm in luck.'

'Might be,' said Polly.

His hands were sliding down her body and trying to reach for the hem of her skirt. She could only take short, nervous breaths which he mistook for passion.

'Do you know what people say about you?' she gasped.

'What's that?' whispered Chuff, rough hands now rasping her thighs like sandpaper.

'They say you're a coward, that's what they say. They say you're the sort who'll never make anything of his life because he's got no guts to stand up and fight for anything.'

'Is that what they say?' Chuff subsided beneath the pressure of Polly's body.

'But I tell them I think you're a man of iron,' she said, anticipating the lewd reply she would get.

'Yeah,' he said, leering. 'Hard as iron old Chuff can be.'

'Trouble is,' added Polly, ignoring the remark, 'there's some big noises round here who want teaching a lesson or two. Biddell's for one.'

'Yeah,' he said, grinning, as his hands made a determined movement from the back of her thighs to the front.

'If it's Biddell's you're talking about, I'm your man,' he declared. 'I'm going to make them bastards *pay*!' He tried to kiss her but she pulled her head back a little and in doing so pressed her body tighter to his, feeling the hard manifestation of the desire she had deliberately aroused in him.

'I don't see how you could,' said Polly, her voice very soft by now. 'I mean, what can you do all on your own? A chap like you in this village?'

'That's what they'll think, ain't it? That Chuff's just a sad bastard living all on his own, totally useless. Well, I ain't fucking useless any more. They'll find that out, very soon. *They'll* learn.' He drew back a little from her. 'Can you keep a secret?' he asked. 'And I mean *keep* a secret, not go blabbing it round the fucking bar?' She nodded. 'Well, I'm part of a wider set-up,' he continued, snaking his grimy body so as to rub himself against her, aroused to the point where his mind had no further control over his mouth. 'I'm a sort of spy who provides information for others to work on. Don't look like it, do I? Don't look like a spy. But I am. And do you know what, my little lovely? At the moment I'm spying on the Biddells.' He grinned, blasting her with ale-drenched breath, and forcibly pushed his filthy hands into her underwear. 'Because those fuckers need teaching a lesson!'

Polly felt his heart pounding; beads of sweat appeared on his forehead. 'They'll die – they'll *all* die. Cows, pigs, turkeys . . . and the fucking Biddells if I have my way. All it takes is a word from me . . .' his soiled fingers were beginning to delve '. . . and once the bomb goes off they'll regret the day they tried to walk all over me.'

'Bomb?' said Polly, startled. She quickly drew back just as Chuff's hand was about to score a bullseye. 'Oh my God!' she gasped, frantically searching for an excuse to leave. 'The bar will be full. I'll be back.' And then, in an act of unparalleled courage, she kissed him deeply.

'You'd *better* be back,' he shouted as she closed the door. 'I've got something for you.' And he gave a gloating little snigger.

Polly went straight to the bathroom and brushed her teeth. In the linen cupboard, she kept fresh clothes in case of spillages or other accidents. Not able to live with the thought of Chuff's hands on the clothing she was wearing, nor his fetid scent, she changed hastily and went back down to the bar.

Michael was back in the bar, wondering where she had been.

'You've changed,' he noticed.

'Yes, in more ways than one. Sorry, I'll have to have a drink. I don't usually when I'm working, but I need one tonight. Desperate.'

'Are you all right?' he asked, concerned.

'Not exactly. But we need to talk. Someone's going to be killed. I knew it all spelled trouble, all that stuff in Chuff's head . . .'

As she spoke, the door opened. It was Archie Biddell.

'Here you are. I've been trying to get you all night,' he said crossly, looking at Michael. 'Fine bloody vet who can't be contacted!'

'Sorry, Mr Biddell,' said Michael, suddenly remembering switching off his phone before going to Chuff's. He reached into his pocket and switched it on again.

'I'm not certain what it is but the cows aren't right. You'd better have an urgent look. I have a horrible idea that I know what it is . . . I just hope to God I'm wrong.'

'We'll finish this later,' shouted Michael, disappearing into the yard with Archie. Polly heard the sound of his Land Rover heading hastily for the farm.

The phone rang. She answered it.

230

'The name's Frater, Amanda Frater. I wondered if Mr Biddell had turned up yet? We were supposed to be meeting at the pub tonight.'

'His cows are sick, and he's with them. Lots of sick things around here, aren't there?' said Polly sharply, and put the phone down.

15

Like all vets, the first thing Michael did was to ascertain the animal's temperature. Since it was a herd he was treating, he would check the first cow he could corner. This was no easy task for within the couple of hours since Archie and Arthur had first become concerned about the health of the herd, there had been a marked deterioration. Cows which had stood silently with distant, staring eyes, were now beginning to move in an uncoordinated way, their listless movements like the twitches of a sleeper experiencing nightmares. Because they had lost the power of coordination, their reactions were unpredictable, making them almost impossible to hold or capture.

Archie had taken two stout wooden gates and made them into a V-shape with a gap where the two gates met, just wide enough to allow a single cow through. It was to act like a funnel and drive the cow into a corner where it could be haltered, constrained, then examined. The cow they had caught – BDL 831, it had no other name – was the easiest of all the catches. Risking injury to themselves, they had got several cows as far as the makeshift funnel, only to have them go berserk to the point where it was no longer safe to be near them. They would rear, kick as best they could, and attempt in a random way to fling themselves over the gates and escape. Five cows did this, one pressing Archie against the wall as it fled, the rest of the herd becoming increasingly agitated and posing a greater threat to the two men working in the corner.

'Got you!' gasped Archie as finally he successfully draped the halter over a cow and tied the other end of the rope to the stoutest steel beam supporting the barn. The cow tugged till its eyes bulged and mucus seeped from its nose and between its lips. It released ear-splitting bellows of frustration as its legs ceased to support it and it fell, first on its front knees and then on its back.

'It's crazy,' cried Archie, who was trying to calm the frenzied cow while Michael was trying to insert a thermometer into the animal's rectum. 'It's sick. The whole bloody lot of them are sick. Is it mad cow disease, again? Is it?' But Michael was reluctant to make a diagnosis on the basis solely of observation.

'There are tests we can do, on the brain. But we'll have to shoot it first.'

'Then shoot it!' insisted Archie. 'And do it quick before it gets any crazier and kills us.' He was looking at the knot with which he'd tied the cow to the beam and wondering how much longer it could last.

'I'll have to get the humane killer,' said Pember, 'it's back in the village. I'll run. It's in the back my car, outside The Peacock. I could give it a shot of tranquilliser, I suppose . . .'

'Go and get the gun,' said Archie, 'get it done with. Quick! If this cow gets away from us there's going to be havoc in this bloody place.'

Michael shut the door of the barn behind him to contain the boiling cauldron of sickness. Even through the walls he could hear the animals' painful bellowing, several decibels higher than when he had arrived an hour before. It crossed his mind that he might not be shooting one cow tonight, he might be shooting them all.

As he ran towards the car, he tried to remember the clinical indicators of mad cow disease. It had become legendary throughout the veterinary profession for it was one of those diseases which appeared to strike in a random way amongst herds of both the highest and lowest quality. At first it was just an animal health issue, but when it manifested as a public health matter then the burden of responsibility on the vets attending sick cows became enormous. The eradication of the disease depended upon their swift diagnostic skills.

Pember remembered scenes from the television news of his boyhood – fit disease-free cows being flung into incinerators. He fought to remember all he had been taught at veterinary school: symptom recognition, treatment, autopsy. He thought he should ring his senior partners but was sure they would only confirm that what he was doing was correct. Anyway, he did not know where to find them. He was on duty, and the buck stopped with him.

Just as he arrived at the car park of The Peacock, a woman came towards him.

'Excuse me,' she said, 'it's Mr Biddell I'm looking for. The girl behind the bar said if I found the vet, I might find him.'

'How did you know I was the vet?' asked Michael, trying to get away from her politely.

'Let's just say the barmaid gave me a flattering description.'

He wanted to hear more, but he had a cow to kill.

'You'll have to excuse me,' he said, 'we've got a sick animal. Haven't I seen you somewhere before?'

'Yes,' said the woman, 'I was here an hour or so ago, asking for Mr Biddell.'

'Amanda Frater?' he asked.

'How could you possibly know that?'

'I remember now,' said Michael, his already confused mind spinning out of control. 'You – er – said so in the bar.'

'I don't think I did,' she replied.

'He's in the barn,' said Michael, not wanting to waste any more time and conveniently evading any further questioning.

'I know where that is,' said Amanda. 'I've been there before.'

'I wouldn't go up there now, it's not safe.'

'In what way? How can cows be unsafe?'

Knowing now who she was, he did not want to say any more. An outbreak of disease, especially mad cow disease, amongst the Biddell herd would be ideal ammunition for any group of animal welfare activists – a perfect excuse to show the world how evil were the livestock farmers, how public-spirited the activists in drawing attention to their shortcomings.

'If you take my advice, you'll stay away,' were his final words before he sprinted across the car park to where the humane killer was locked in the boot of his car.

Amanda Frater took no notice. She walked to her car and drove straight to Home Farm.

Amanda had rehearsed the words she wanted to say to Archie until she could recite them in her sleep. She wanted him to understand that she was speaking on behalf of her father, that this request had nothing to do with her. She had to make him understand that the pressures exerted on her father by the estate were greater than he could bear. The only thing she had not decided about was whether she should tell Archie that the strain was forcing her father to cut corners and buy feed from suspect sources. She would see how it went, she decided, and only divulge that last fact if she had to.

The barn door squealed as she rolled it back, as it had done the night she saw Domino born. She blinked in the full dazzle of the lighting, all of which was blazing. When her eyes had adjusted, she sensed immediately that she was not in the placid atmosphere she remembered from the last time she was here. There was no quiet ruminating, no hypnotic chewing of the cud. Instead there was wildness in the air, and as Amanda stood by the open door she wondered if she dared enter.

'Archie!' she shouted. 'Archie Biddell, are you in there?'

'For Christ's sake, get over here as fast as you can. I don't know if I can hold this much longer.' Archie's hands were white where he was gripping the cow's halter, raw where the rope had rubbed against his fingers, chafing the skin till it bled. He hadn't heard her voice over the blaring of the crazed cow, but had heard the squeal of the barn door. He'd assumed it was Michael returning.

'Shoot this poor sod before she kills me, then I think there's another that looks as though it's going the same way . . .'

'Archie. Where are you?' shouted Amanda again.

'Who the bloody hell is it?' he replied. 'Is that you, Michael?'

Amanda was about to take a step forward when Archie

looked up and barked at her, 'Stop! Don't move! Stay where you are!'

Amanda came to a terrified halt as two frenzied cows charged across the barn. Had she taken that step forward she would have been trampled.

'Run when I say. I'm here, in the corner. Can you see me?'

'I can see you.'

'Then wait till I say . . . now. NOW!' And Amanda ran as fast as her aching leg would allow her and maintained her balance till she was almost upon Archie, whereupon she stumbled and fell in a heap at his feet.

'Get up! Fast!' he said, barely in control of his voice. 'If I lose this cow, she'll get you before you've a chance to move.'

'I can't,' cried Amanda. 'It's my leg. My bloody leg!' she wept. 'You'll have to pull me to my feet.'

He slowly released one hand from the halter, and gripped the rope even tighter with the hand that remained. He applied forward pressure, hoping the cow would respond to his urging and take a step to him. Then, with his other hand, he could reach Amanda's outstretched arm and pull her to safety.

'They're mad,' said Archie. 'The whole bloody lot of them. Out of their bloody bovine minds. Ever seen mad cow disease? Seen it for real? Well, this is what it looks like. The disease they'd said they'd eradicated. Pretty sight, isn't it?'

Amanda was lying helplessly in the foul straw, inching forward to meet Archie's hand. She wanted to scream, or weep, or curl up into the tightest of balls as an admission of her mortal fear. But she had the wit to realise that anything she did now, other than stay as still as she possibly could, might provoke the already demented cow into greater insanity.

Archie willed the cow to take a single step. 'Just one step, old girl,' he whispered to her. The cow obliged. He took hold of Amanda's hand and she leaned heavily on it and regained her footing. The left leg of her trousers had ripped from hem to thigh and he saw for the first time the full extent of her scars, hints of which he had spotted the night Domino was born.

Amanda saw the disbelief in his eyes as he gazed at the blemishes on her leg. She tried to wrap the remnants of her trousers round it.

'That looks as though it must have hurt,' said Archie, trying to make light of his shock at the severity of the disfigurement. The cow took advantage of Archie's fleeting distraction and, harnessing the latent energy building in its contorted body and mind, leaped into the air with such force that not only would it have been suicide to try and hold it, it was beyond the strength of any man. The cow was out of control, trailing the rope from the halter around its feet and momentarily strangling itself, then untangling the rope from around its limbs and charging round the barn like a demented bull in a ring.

Amanda screamed. Archie grabbed her arm and dragged her behind a large, circular bale of straw for protection. It was like being in a trench in World War I, she imagined, where the enemy was not only deadly but crazed and advancing. And there was nothing anyone could do to stop it.

'It will have to die,' Archie explained.

'Poor thing.'

'You wouldn't have said that if it had gone over you, like the cows that trampled Tomlinson. Did you hear about that?'

'I heard talk.' Amanda sought for something else to say. How could she bombard Archie with a plea on behalf of her father's business when before her own eyes a lingering, tormented death scene was being acted out by the Biddell herd?

'Where has it come from, this disease?' she asked.

'It's anyone's guess. They never established where it came from in the first place so I doubt they'll have much idea what started this outbreak.'

'But it was supposed to be gone forever, wiped out, eradicated,' said Amanda, confused.

'There were a lot of people as well as cows who paid with their lives because of the mistakes of the last generation,' he told her. 'And I am not going to let anyone pay like that again. I shall shoot the whole bloody herd if I have to. Every cow, calf, bull. And then, to be certain, every bit of livestock on the bloody farm. No one is going to suffer like Emily suffered in the three months it took her to die.'

It had been simpler in the army. You knew the enemy, from which direction it came, and how to aim at and destroy it. There was nothing here that Archie could do, no order he could give which would resolve this conflict one way or the other.

'How can it be?' asked Amanda.

'It could be the feed,' snapped Archie, for the first time making the connection between Amanda, her father, and the animal feed.

'It's *not* the feed,' she insisted. 'Daddy's . . .' And then just as she was about to say '. . . straight as hell, plays by the book' she remembered the conversation with Orion Shipping, the words 'uncertified feed' and all the other nuances of the conversation which had led her to the conclusion that what her father was doing was outside the law.

'You can't say it's not the feed,' said Archie. 'I know it's all come from your father, but no one is above suspicion in this. Not even him.'

'My father *is* above suspicion,' she insisted doggedly.

'I am not having another row with you, Amanda. I am telling you that when I get out of this barn, if I get out alive, the first door I am knocking on will be your father's. And if he does not have some good, solid answers about what exactly my cows have been eating, I shall kick his arse all the way from this village to whatever prison he ends up in. Go and tell him that!' shouted Archie. 'Tell him what he has done. Because I cannot see any other way these cows have ended up in this state if not because of what they have eaten. You were good enough to tell me you didn't think I cared too much for the animals or the people of this farm. But when it comes to signing the death warrant of a complete herd of cows I am just a beginner compared with your father. Now go and tell him that! GO ON!'

239

Amanda, tears streaming now, looked in every direction like a child trying to cross a busy road, seeking a safe gap in the mob of confused cows milling around the barn.

'How Daddy runs his business is up to him,' she retaliated, not revealing any hint of her private doubt. 'But I know what's driving everyone on this estate to the point where they have to cut every corner to make ends meet,' she added. 'It's you and your precious bloody supermarket contracts!'

'That's nothing to do with me,' replied Archie.

'It is *everything* to do with you,' she hissed. 'I've seen the letter. It may have Marcus Hastings's name on the bottom, but I was there when responsibility for this place passed to *you*. And *you* are screwing people in this village. Screwing down profits till there's barely a living wage for any of the people who supply you. If my father has done anything wrong, it will have been because of pressures *you* have put on him.'

She turned and hurried as fast as she was able for the door. Safely outside, she opened the car door, took the key from her pocket and turned the ignition. The light on her mobile phone was flashing, indicating a message on her answering service. But she wanted to get away from Woodham Ford as fast as she could, so decided to wait till she was home to check it out.

Michael Pember was lucky not to be run down by her as she reversed out of the car park without bothering to look in either direction. He was clutching the humane killer and had been delayed by not being able to find the new box of cartridges. Just as he was about to head back towards Home Farm, Polly dashed out of the pub.

'What's wrong up there? You look so white, Michael. Do you want a drink?'

'Polly, this is pretty serious. I'll be some time.'

'Look, there's something you ought to know, something I found out from Chuff . . .'

'Can't it wait?'

'Not really. It's important. He's talking about bombs.'

'Bombs?' said Michael. 'Daft sod! It's all fantasy. He's just a stupid boy playing games in his own daft mind. I'd forget all about it if I were you. Look, I've got some real life and death stuff to deal with up at Home Farm. Sorry, Polly. I've got to go.'

She pleaded with him: 'It's not fantasy. What about Amanda Frater? *She's* not fantasy.'

'I can't waste any more time,' said Michael, becoming impatient.

'And she was here tonight,' Polly pleaded. 'In that little blue car that just roared off.'

'That's the bitch who nearly ran me over,' he remembered.

'I think she's planning far worse than that.'

'I've got these cows to see to. I'll call you later.' And Michael got in his car and drove back to the farm.

It was dark, past 10 o'clock, and as Polly made her way across the car park back towards the pub, she bumped into Chuff, high on the mixture of a win for his team, a gutful of free beer, and the promise of more from Polly. She had hoped the drink might have dulled his mind to the point of forgetting the latter, but a woman was a rare event in Chuff's life – she was possibly the first ever – and he was not going to let her escape from his grasp.

'I've got a little job to do,' he slurred, trying to whisper, 'for those people I told you about . . . Hey, you won't say a word, will you? Old Chuff'll get into terrible trouble.'

'Job?' said Polly. 'At this time of night? What can you do for anybody in the dark at ten o'clock?'

'I could do plenty for *you*, I could,' he insinuated. 'I'll be back soon and I expect to find you waiting for me in that upstairs bedroom. Promise?'

He stumbled out of the car park. Polly stood and watched him. He walked into the middle of the road and stood, turning his head in both directions, looking along the white line in the middle. When he had spotted whatever it was he was looking for, he walked up to it, then looked round to see where he was in relation to the pub and paced forward, counting. He did this three times, then shambled back towards The Peacock.

Polly was behind the bar by then. 'If anyone wants a top up,' she shouted, 'they'd better ask now. I've got to pop out to see to the dogs. I'll be gone five minutes.'

'It'll be more than five minutes,' mumbled Chuff as he made his way back up the stairs.

Polly felt deeply sick as she entered his room. The lights were off, the television silent. She was searching for some kind of strategy which would ensure that she found out more of what he clearly knew, yet enable her to keep his vile hands as far away from her body as possible. She thought of Michael, how brave he had been to go into Chuff's house. She had to be brave too.

'Chuff, sweetheart,' she whispered as she entered the darkened room. Suddenly, the door closed behind her and out of the dark came a pair of rough hands, the foul scent of ale and cigarettes on toxic breath, the stale odour of his naked body. He put his lips firmly to hers and forced the slimy vastness of his alcohol-stewed tongue deep into her mouth. She wanted to be sick.

She felt him edge her back towards the bed, and had no option other than to lie down on it with Chuff on top of her. He smelled slightly of vomit. He cleared his throat and without any kind of invitation shoved his hand down the waistband of her skirt.

'Not so fast,' said Polly, 'a girl likes to talk a bit first.'

'As long as it's quick,' said Chuff, pressing his hand to exactly the same place he had left off at half time.

'Mmm. You're what I call a real man, you are,' said Polly. 'It takes a real man to be brave enough to take part in all this bombing stuff.'

'I'll show you what a real man I am, very soon.'

'You know, when I saw you walking down the middle of the road, I thought to myself: "Yeah, there's a real feller."'

'You saw me? You weren't supposed to be looking. That's top secret all that stuff. Don't you say a word. Those people

... the organisation, the army, you know ... whatever they're called ...'

'Yeah?' said Polly

'Have you got tighter knickers on, or something? They don't feel like they did last time Chuff had his hand in your skirt.'

She had already given so much she decided she'd give this last thing, and splayed her legs a little wider. 'There you are, love. Better? What were you saying about the road? What's so secret about it?'

Chuff explored with new vigour; Polly planned her escape if what she desired – information – did not come before that which he sought with mounting urgency.

'There's a manhole cover,' he said, his hand now as far as it could reach, 'which covers a nice deep hole in the road.' He used his fingers to emphasise the point. Polly flinched in fear. 'My friends plan to put something nice and deep in that hole,' he probed again, 'and when it goes off then we'll all feel better.'

'Not a bomb!' she said.

'Dead right,' said Chuff. 'Something that goes into a hole and makes a nice explosion. When the lorries go over. Biddell's convoy of lorries.'

His hand pressed harder. There was a scream followed by a dull thud. It was not Polly, nor did it come from Chuff. It was Eric Thwaite in the next-door bedroom and he seemed to be in trouble.

Polly said under her breath every kind of thank you prayer she could remember. She would love Eric forever and ever for this.

'I'll have to go, he might be hurt,' she explained, pushing Chuff off her and putting on the bedside light.

'But I haven't finished with you, my little treasure,' said Chuff, clamping his arms around her.

'For the moment you have. But there's always another day. 'Bye, sweetheart. Now get off home as fast as you can. If Eric finds you up here you're as good as dead.'

*   *   *

243

It could have been worse, thought Polly. The commotion from Eric's room was no more than the sound of his hot-water bottle dropping to the floor, and his cursing was over a glass of water he had spilled over his bed while trying to switch on the bedside light. It was 11 o'clock. Polly closed the pub and locked the door, having made sure Chuff was no longer on the premises.

It might just have been fantasy, what he had said about the manhole cover. All silliness, make believe, the product of a lurid imagination, she thought. To check, she reached for the torch which Eric kept by the till in case he had to get into the far corners of the cellar. Polly waited till she could hear no traffic coming in either direction, then walked to the middle of the road where she had seen Chuff standing.

There was a manhole cover, dead in line with the front of the pub.

She wanted to tell Michael immediately: about the bomb, the manhole cover, the danger to the lorries leaving the Biddell Estate. But when she finally arrived at the barn it was locked and sealed with notices forbidding any entry. '*Disease Precautions – Keep Out*' exhorted the vivid red letters. She pressed her ear to the door, but heard only the low rumbling moans of demented cows.

16

The following morning dawned fine in central London. A perfect
June day for an outing to the country. With only a month to go
to the opening of his St Edwich superstore, Toby Hopscotch could
contain his excitement no longer, and felt he must share it with
the press. All plans were on target, builders working to schedule,
dummy runs from Biddell's farm to abattoir about to start.

The day in the country was his own idea, and so enthusiastic
was he that he was the first to arrive, just after dawn, daringly
dressed in white shirt, yellow spotted cravat, and a blue blazer.
He had debated whether to appear in more formal dress which
might establish him firmly as a high-flyer. Or should he set the
tone of what he hoped would be a light-hearted trip by dressing
more casually? He played safe and became, of course, neither one
thing nor the other. The same could not be said of Tiggy who knew
firmly where she stood, which was definitely on the side of loathing
any venture like this. She had been through this before, worn the
dainty garb all servile wives wore on such occasions, making sure
it fell well below the knee – she knew that food writers licked their
lips at more than recipes.

The coach was about to leave and Toby grandly felt he had
to make a short speech of welcome so snatched the microphone
from the driver.

'Good morning, ladies and gentlemen . . .' No one looked his
way. He might as well have spoken into thin air. He noticed that
Charles Danbury (who described himself as a freelance, but was so
generously free with his lancing that no one could ever remember
him writing a word) was fast asleep. Two women representing
the knitting pattern end of the magazine market were gossiping

over who they thought might be the next fiction editor of *Home Life* magazine. The only two journalists who paid the slightest attention to Toby were two women, sharp in mind and appearance, notebooks out, questions pre-formed in their heads.

'Mr Hopscotch' said the first woman, who had a nose like an ant-eater, 'we will need to know your policy on renewable resources.'

'And the balance of employment between jobs created in St Edwich versus work lost in the local community due to shop and other closures,' chimed the other. 'I hope you've got figures for all that?'

'Of course,' said Toby, knowing he was unable to fulfil either of those requests, and felt his pocket to make sure his mobile phone was there and head office could come to his rescue.

'And breakfast,' shouted Charles Danbury, opening one eye as he half-heartedly re-entered the world. 'We'll be stopping for breakfast? We did on the Sainsbury's trip!'

'I thought that with its being only an hour and a half at the very most we might skip . . .' Toby could sense this was not going down well. 'We might skip along as fast as we could now, and stop halfway. We'll book in at a decent hotel for breakfast.'

'I can recommend somewhere if you tell me the route,' said Danbury. 'Been to most of them.'

'Ever paid at any of them, Charlie?' asked the woman with the pointed nose.

The coach pulled away from the bus station and Archie dialled his secretary for a list of all the eating houses between London and St Edwich. He could not stop at a Little Chef, although the food there was at least of a certain standard. But the danger with picking a hotel at random was that there was no guarantee at all, and Toby knew that a well-fed journalist was a happy one. He needed them in the best frame of mind if his new superstore were to get the write-ups he wanted.

'Excuse me,' shouted the woman with the pointed nose. 'Vegan for me, if you're booking.'

'And for me too,' shouted her companion.

'Excuse me, Mr Hopscotch,' cried the elder of the two mature ladies. 'If you want to stop and get some rolls, we'll butter them and all that. We could have a really smashing picnic. A proper day out.' She and her companion giggled like schoolgirls.

'I have visited every hotel from Monte Carlo to Montreal,' intoned the portly Danbury, 'and I am not going to insult my digestion by offering it buttered rolls when what it really needs is a damned good breakfast. I suppose you do sell bloody breakfast food in your shops, Hopscotch?'

'Great idea, Charles. If I may call you that,' said Toby in ingratiating mode. He fell back in his seat and started hammering the mobile phone like a demented woodpecker. His secretary answered.

'Listen,' he said, 'I want you to get hold of the manager of the Chelmsford store, it's about halfway, and tell him to prepare a huge box of everything that could vaguely be called breakfast food. What? No, not baby food as well, stupid. Just grown-up food. All sorts. And get it into a fast car and tell it to rendezvous with our coach on that big roundabout just south of the town. We'll be there within the hour. And booze, plenty of booze. What? How the hell do I know what booze you drink for breakfast? This lot will drink anything.'

He stood up again, taking hold of the microphone.

'Chaps,' – that got a black look from the woman with the pointed nose – 'a superb breakfast will be waiting for you at Chelmsford. We at Applewhite's pride ourselves on the full range of breakfast produce we offer, and so the manager of our local branch will be personally bringing a selection for us to try. Bit of an adventure, eh?'

'Oh, goody. A sort of picnic,' enthused a matronly lady.

'Bloody disaster,' muttered Danbury.

'Excuse me, but our editor expressly forbids us from taking any gifts in kind,' said the woman with the pointed nose.

'Then suck your bloody thumb while I tuck in,' said Danbury.

Within the hour they arrived at Chelmsford. Parked on the slip road to the roundabout, in a car painted in Applewhite's livery, was the beaming manager of the local branch, car packed to the roof with cereals, meats, eggs and bread. The journalists got out of the coach. Charles Danbury excused himself. 'I'm going round the other side of the bus where that hook-nosed woman can't see me to have a piss,' he told Toby. 'Give me a shout if she heads my way and I'll put it away. One look from her and it'll wither and drop off. Did I see a drop of Scotch? Pour me a stiff one, there's a good chap.'

Toby greeted the manager like a saviour.

'Great! Terrific! First-class! Now get the knives and forks out, and the paper plates. Jolly clever of you to keep the stuff warm.'

The manager looked blank.

'It is cooked, isn't it?' said a frenzied Toby. 'We can eat it, can't we?'

The terrified manager shook his head. 'You didn't say you wanted it cooked, or to *eat* any of it.'

'You mean . . . so what's in . . . your mean, not even tea? Everybody back on the bus!' shouted Toby. 'Afraid we have to move on. Er . . . police not happy with us parking here.'

'What?' cried Danbury who had overheard the conversation while stuffing himself back into his splashed trousers. 'No bloody breakfast? I warn you, Hopscotch, you'd better have some excitement laid on for us when we get to St Edwich or there'll be trouble.

'Remember one thing young man, it was the power of my pen that closed the Queen's Hotel in Monte Carlo. One wrong word from me and this could be the end for you.' He climbed the steps of the bus and collapsed into his seat, hungry enough to chew the arm rest if that woman with the sharp nose weren't watching his every move.

They had gone ten miles further north when there was a sudden shout from him.

'Stop the bus! Emergency!' He pulled himself up from his seat and grabbed the driver, almost forcing the steering wheel out of his hands.

'Over there! A Jolly Chef. Head straight for it. Good man!'

'Sorry, Charles,' said Toby, bravely pushing Danbury back

towards his seat, 'but we've got a schedule to keep to. I don't want to be late for the town planners and the landscape architect, who I know want to speak to you all.'

'You can take your town planner and shove him down the deepest drain,' said Danbury aggressively, 'because if I, Charles Danbury, former food editor of a string of European magazines, do not get any breakfast, then you will be having all your meetings with your planners in the sewers because your board will turn you into so much shit. Pull over, driver.'

'I think I'll have a banana,' said the matronly lady.

'Make mine just a coffee,' said the woman with the hooked nose. 'Decaff, if they have it. If not, a mango tea.'

The coach drew up outside the Jolly Chef and parked in front of the large windows. Only Danbury decided to eat there. Meanwhile, the rest of the entourage sat impatiently in the coach, digesting the news that there was no fresh fruit and certainly no mango tea, and watching in astonishment Danbury in full feeding frenzy. It would have out-faced a weight lifter: slices of fried bread, greasy black pudding, chips, and *Biddell's Best Bacon Rashers*.

'Do you think he'll be much longer?' asked Tiggy, who had barely spoken a word all the trip.

'I'm not a bloody mind reader,' snapped Toby.

'But you *can* at least be civil, dear,' she replied.

'Think so?' He got out of his seat and strode across to the cafe to try and speed Danbury down the long, self-indulgent road he was slowly navigating. The woman with the hooked nose leaned forward and whispered to Tiggy.

'You don't have to take any of that sort of shit, you know. I can get phone numbers from our social affairs action desk, support groups and so on.'

'No, thanks,' said Tiggy. 'I already belong to an action group.'

Danbury arrived back in the coach after forty-five minutes of stuffing himself. He belched.

'Fabulous, Toby. Applewhite's pulled it off again. Real treat. I think the magazine will be very much behind you.'

'You haven't seen the new store yet,' shouted the woman with the hooked nose. 'How can you say you're going to like it?'

'I haven't been to bed with you, darling,' replied Danbury, 'but I've got a fair idea of the messy bloody business *that* would be.' And he bellowed coarsely.

'Oh, sorry,' said Toby, 'ought to explain. There's not exactly a *complete* store to see. There's walls, but no roof yet. Mostly foundations.'

'Foundations?' cried the hook-nosed woman, as if about to explode. 'You're taking us all this way to look at *foundations*!'

'We're doing foundation creams in our next issue,' said the matronly lady. 'What a coincidence! We've been testing them.'

'On your arse?' said Danbury, chortling.

Toby felt pressured by the increasingly hostile atmosphere. He had thought of this as something of a warm-up exercise; get a few journos down to the new site, explain about the landscaping, environmental initiatives, talk about the food supply system and the unique tie-in with the Biddell Estate. Then, suddenly, he had an inspired idea. He snatched the microphone.

'You may not think foundations are much worth looking at, but these are the foundations on which we shall build something great. We have a unique supply deal with one of the most famous farms in the country, a farm that produces healthy animals providing first-class food. And you are the first to hear of it. I promise you, this will be a real scoop.'

This did little to lift the atmosphere. So he pushed harder. 'And I am going to take you to see that farm. It will be the jewel in Applewhite's crown.'

'Will that be after lunch?' asked Danbury.

Affected animals show behavioural changes such as aggression and apprehension, lack of coordination of the hind legs leading to a high-stepping gait and eventual weakness and loss of condition, leading to slaughter before the animal succumbs.

Michael was reading a textbook, trying to confirm his diagnosis. He read it again out loud while Archie listened and weighed each word. Neither had had much sleep the night before, both deeply disturbed by lingering images of mad cows. Now, twelve hours after Archie's worst suspicions had been confirmed, both men were sitting on bales of straw, numbed by tiredness, staring at the cows staring blankly back at them.

'Only a brain tissue test will tell us for sure,' Michael explained. 'I spoke to the other partners in the practice and they couldn't believe it. They said it was like being in a war you thought was over long ago, and suddenly hearing another shot.' He glanced down at the humane killer.

'Old Arthur's pretty shook up by the whole business,' said Archie. 'Looked dreadful last night. I told him to stay away, till things were sorted. He's lived through this once. No one should have to suffer it twice.'

'I rang the Ministry. They didn't have any advice other than to put signs on the door. I see you've done that already. They said to keep everyone out for the moment.'

'Well done,' said Archie, pouring himself another cup of coffee from the flask. And there the two men sat, staring dazed with disbelief at the cows, like seafarers watching the ocean for any sign that the storm might be abating.

'There will have to be a first,' said Michael. 'One of them will have to be the first to be shot. Perhaps it would be best to get it over with. One of them has got to be slaughtered tomorrow morning when the Ministry of Agriculture's Disease Surveillance team turn up. They'll want tissue to work on straight away. Till then we can't be sure.'

'It's not possible, is it,' Archie suggested, 'that it might be something else? Something we haven't thought of?'

'Do you think I haven't checked every possibility? I even went over the tropical disease stuff, just in case something had somehow got through. Poisons are a possibility, but there are so many of them and they need tissue samples to check for all of them, and

251

the Ministry said we were to do nothing till their team moved in. I've tried to consider every possibility, but everything leads back to the same thing. Mad cow disease. Sorry.'

'Caught it from the feed?' asked Archie.

'Most likely,' said Michael. 'Although it was never conclusively proved last time, everyone agreed it was infected feed then, and I dare say it will be again.'

'Bloody Frater,' muttered Archie.

'Frater?' said Michael with surprise. 'That's the second time I've heard that name today.'

'Yeah, Brian Frater supplies all the feed here. He's got some bloody questions to answer.'

'I've got a woman in mind,' said Michael, 'not a man. Probably not connected.'

'You're thinking of Amanda,' said Archie, with a sigh.

'That was it,' said Michael. 'Amanda Frater.'

'She was here last night,' said Archie. 'She's odd. A nice girl, attractive certainly. Between you and me, I like her a lot. But there's something about her that doesn't quite add up. She tries to be friendly but can't quite manage it. She seems to go so far then something stops her from going any further. Don't know what's wrong with her.'

'You say she doesn't get on with you?'

'It's difficult. I certainly want to be friends with her, or more than that if I'm honest. And I get the feeling she wants to feel the same. One minute she's all lovey-dovey, but as soon as we get on to talking about the farm . . .'

'Or the animals?' interrupted Michael.

'Yes, now you mention it. As soon as farm animals come into it, she goes all funny. What do you make of that?' Michael shook his head.

'And she's got these terrible scars down her leg . . . Must have been in a really bad smash or something. She's a confusing girl. More to her than meets the eye, I guess.'

The herd was becoming restless again, behaving like a giant lake into which a stick was occasionally thrown, ripples of dementia spreading from wherever the stick fell. The cow in whom they had first observed the symptoms of insanity was now unable to stand, but still had the will to try. With every wild movement of her legs she was not only in danger of damaging herself, but of wounding every other cow that came too close.

'You've got your first victim. Get the gun loaded. I'm not prepared to see animals suffer until the Ministry gets off its arse,' declared Archie. 'Let's catch the bugger. It shouldn't be too much of a fight this time.'

There was hardly any struggle at all. This cow had decided the effort of resisting was not worth it. Her bowels had ceased to be continent and she lay wallowing in a pool of her own liquid droppings, trembling as if with fear, kicking herself free of this life.

'She wasn't a bad old cow,' said Archie, dismally. 'I looked at her records. She's one of the old faithfuls.'

Pember loaded a cartridge into the gun and visualised the exact spot on the cow's forehead where the captive bolt should enter to ensure instant death.

'Ministry of Agriculture – Disease Precautions – STRICTLY NO ENTRY'.

'It can't mean us, can it?' asked a perplexed Toby, reading the words aloud for the fourth time to Tiggy, who was standing beside him. He glanced over his shoulder at the coachload of impatient journalists, all less than fresh-faced after a two-hour tramp across a dreary building site in St Edwich. Even the insensitive Toby had sensed they had been less than impressed with his tour of muddy foundations, indifferent heaps of soil which he insisted was 'landscaping', and his enthusing about automated check-outs while they stood ankle-deep in mud, soaked by drizzle.

'It *can't* apply to us,' he repeated, looking at Tiggy for support.

'If it says keep out, then that is what it means,' she replied, unhelpfully.

Toby screwed up his face. 'They can't do this to me!' He glanced back at the bus, sensing the writers were sharpening their pens. 'I'm going in,' he declared.

'It looks official to me,' said Tiggy. 'It's a Ministry notice.'

He grabbed it, pulled it from the door and stuffed it into his jacket pocket. 'Bugger them!' he shouted, and turned back towards the coach, forcing a smile.

'Just checking they're ready for us,' he called to the journalists, and slid back the door of the barn.

'Mr Biddell . . . Mr Archie Biddell?' he shouted, voice faltering and sounding feeble in the huge void. He cleared his throat, nervously. 'I'm just visiting with a little party of chums, from the press. Are you there?' As his eyes readjusted, he gasped in disgust both at the sight of his brown suede shoes which had stepped into a river of animal excreta, and then at the spectacle of the anguished, prostrate cow.

'My God!' he cried, looking down at the dying beast. 'It's disgusting. Revolting. Argh! And my shoes!'

'Who the fuck are you?' demanded Archie. 'Can't you read? It says "Keep Out", and "Keep Out" usually means on the other side of the door.'

'Ah, but I'm from Applewhite's, the new superstore. We have a major deal with you as I'm sure you know. You are Mr Biddell, I presume?'

'And that gives you the right to march through disease precaution notices, does it?'

'Disease?' replied Toby. 'I didn't think there was any *disease*. You see, we've got a contract with you and we don't want any *disease*. I'm sure there's a clause somewhere . . .'

'We've got disease all right,' put in Michael.

'Well,' said Archie, 'I know nothing of this contract. But then, there are lots of deals around here I seem to know nothing about. Might I mention the name Marcus Hastings to you? Has he something to do with it?'

'You could,' said Toby, cautiously.

'You have a deal signed by Hastings in the name of the Biddell Estate?'

'Possibly,' said Toby.

Archie grabbed him by the lapels of his Simpson's blazer.

'Yes or no?'

'Yes.'

'Good,' said Archie, 'I'm pleased to hear it. That means this cow effectively belongs to you. What exactly would you like done with it?'

'We don't interfere with the farming operation at all,' replied Toby, plainly terrified. 'We are retailers. We just sign contracts with guarantees in them which insist on certain standards of animal welfare.'

'And certain levels of rock bottom prices. Prices at which no farmer can afford your so-called standards of animal welfare. You can write it all down on paper, that's the easy bit. But it's farmers who have to get on with it. And this is what farming really looks like.' Archie nodded in the direction of the cow. 'This is what life is really like one step away from those sanitised dives you call superstores.'

The door rumbled as it opened a little further. Standing silhouetted against the sky was Hopscotch's press party, all expecting a glimpse of a rural idyll.

'Come in,' said Archie. 'Come in, all of you, and welcome. The press, I understand. Perhaps we should introduce ourselves. My name is Archie Biddell, I'm the farmer here. This is Michael Pember, he's the vet. He's about to shoot this cow. It will make a lovely picture for your front pages.'

'Shoot it? Bastard!' shouted the woman with the pointed nose.

'Got to die sometime,' said Charles Danbury, unmoved.

'I'll never eat meat again!' vowed the matronly lady.

Tiggy said nothing.

'I'm sorry,' said Archie, 'but I think this is the perfect time for you to turn up, if I may say so. Now, friends from the press, I should get your notebooks out and listen carefully to what I have to say . . .'

'I am cancelling this press conference,' cried a panicking Toby.

'You can't,' said Archie, 'because it is *not* a press conference. Just a few chums, that's what you said.'

'Let's be off, everybody. Bus is leaving soon. Don't want to be back late to London. And – surprise, surprise! Applewhite's has laid on a marvellous dinner to celebrate . . . er . . . your viewing of the foundations. So, everyone, back on the bus, *please*.'

'No,' insisted the woman with the pointed nose.

'I'm not going either,' added the matronly lady. 'I think we all want to hear what this farmer has to say.'

'Tiggy!' Toby cried in despair. 'Tell the driver we're leaving in three minutes.'

'Tell him yourself,' she snapped. 'I want to hear what Mr Biddell has to say as well.' The women applauded as she pulled the final rug from under his feet, leaving him to slither into the mire. Toby's face paled till it was almost transparent.

The woman with the sharp nose patted her on the shoulder.

'Good girl,' she whispered.

'This cow,' said Archie, pointing at the beast which lay trembling at his feet, body covered in sweat, 'was once one of the finest animals on this farm. She has given the five best years of her life to providing milk and bearing calves. Before you leave here you are going to see her die. For if she does not die naturally in the next few minutes, the vet will shoot her. One way or another she cannot live. You might ask – or your readers might ask – why has this cow got into this condition? Before you blame me, I would refer you to Mr Hopscotch here and his highly successful supermarket chain. Mr Hopscotch makes huge profits for his company on the backs of cows like this. He screws the farmer down to the lowest possible price, so the farmer sits on everyone else and forces *their* price down as well. Some have to cut corners to stay in business. This cow has mad cow disease.'

There was a gasp as the implication of that sunk in. 'It is highly likely,' he continued, 'that once again it originated in the feed from a supplier who was forced to buy contaminated feed in order to stay in business.'

'Couldn't happen,' said Toby, instantly defending himself. 'All rubbish. There are so many regulations that infected feed could not have got into that animal's food chain.'

'We'll see who's right,' replied Archie. 'But alas, this cow will not be around to hear the answer. Do you want to shoot her, Mr Hopscotch, or are you content to have signed the death warrant already?'

'You will pay for this,' he said.

'No,' replied Archie, pointing at the cow. '*She* will pay.'

'Tiggy!' screamed a by now demented Hopscotch. 'Ring the police, the RSPCA . . . get me the press office . . . I want a full enquiry.' He stormed around the barn, fists clenched, veins in his forehead throbbing visibly.

'Toby,' replied Tiggy, calmly, 'I am not getting another thing for you, EVER! You care nothing for that cow, only yourself. You care nothing for me or for your son. You care about nothing but the bloody supermarket. So go and marry it, and don't pretend any longer that you're married to me. I'm not going to have a row with you here and now, because you're not worth it. You, Toby Hopscotch, are worth less than the cow shit on your shoes. Enjoy the fifteenth of July. It really is going to be a grand opening, isn't it? I'll think of you while I'm at sports day, when they fire the starting gun. Because it will remind me of you, and that cow, and the shot that will kill it. And I will thank God that I am miles and miles and miles away from you and your sordid supermarket. From now on, I am *out of your life.*'

With that, she ran for the door.

'This is going to make the front page,' sang the lady with the hooked nose.

'There'll be no more Applewhite's advertising in any of our food supplements,' added the matronly lady, shaking her head.

There was an ear-splitting crack then as Michael, impatient at seeing the cow suffer further, pressed the humane killer to

257

its head and fired. It fell back, instantly dead from the neat circular wound through which the captive bolt had punctured its maddened brain.

An hour later, Archie and Michael were back in The Peacock, Hopscotch's press party having finally piled back on to the bus. Toby himself was the last to leave after downing half a bottle of whisky to try and obliterate the catastrophic events of the afternoon.

'I think we can still salvage the situation, Chairman,' he repeated unconvincingly into his mobile phone, then sobbed when the line abruptly went dead. He looked around for Tiggy, but all that remained of her was a note. It said she had gone back to their cottage in Woodham Ford intending to ring her mother, ask her to get Georgie and bring him down on the next train. She had no plans to return home, ever. The coach pulled away.

'How's Eric?' asked Archie, sipping at his beer.

'Still pretty bad,' replied Polly. 'It's funny. He always seems worse in the evenings. He's not too bad in the mornings, but when he's had lunch he seems to go downhill. They're still doing tests but I think they're baffled.'

'Strange that,' remarked Michael. 'The cows always seem worse later in the day too, don't they? Coincidence, I suppose.'

'There's something I'd like to talk to both of you about,' she said, interrupting. 'It's Chuff.'

'To hell with him,' snapped Archie. 'I've got more important things on my mind.' Polly took a deep breath.

'I think he's going to kill you,' she said.

'*Kill me*!? Whatever for?'

'It's true, and I know how he's going to do it.' She turned to Michael. 'I think you'd better admit to what you know because I'm really worried.'

'It's all supposition, really,' he explained. 'Certainly not enough to go to the police with.' Archie stared in bewilderment as they batted the ball of conjecture between them.

258

'That's not true,' Polly intervened. 'I found things out last night that you don't know about yet.'

'*How* did you find them out?' asked Michael.

'From Chuff himself.'

'But he wasn't here last night. When I came back to the car for the humane killer, there was no Chuff. Someone said he hadn't been in all night.'

'That's because he was in an upstairs bedroom with me,' she admitted.

'With you! What do you mean – *with* you?' Michael asked.

'We had a cuddle, that was all. I had to. Do you think it was pleasant, having that filthy toerag pressing himself up against me?'

'You didn't . . .?' asked Michael.

'No, of course I didn't. But after what you turned up on that computer of his and then that Frater woman turning up, I had to find out what was going on. I gave him as much beer as I dared but that didn't loosen him up enough. So I had to try other methods.'

'Frater woman . . . in bed with Chuff! Can someone explain, please?' demanded Archie.

'I'll explain,' said Michael. 'Polly here was worried about some animal rights magazines she'd found in Chuff's house. I went to check them out and, sure, they were pretty nasty but no worse than a lot of those violent comics you can buy. Then I gave his computer the once-over because I knew he was into all that sort of thing, and the whole machine was stuffed with animal rights news from around the world . . . contacts with guerrilla groups . . . really unpleasant stuff. Some of it violent. But nothing conclusive you could take to the police. Then I found a message sent directly to Chuff from something called the CFFA.'

'The Campaign for the Freedom of Farm Animals,' explained Polly.

'They were requesting him to forward them any details he could get hold of about regular movements of animals from the Biddell Estate, convoys of lorries and so on.'

'So they can bomb them,' blurted Polly.

'I don't know anything about bombs,' said Michael. 'There was nothing about bombing on the screen.'

'But that's what they're planning,' she said. 'Chuff told me.'

'Told you what exactly?' asked Archie, now taking more seriously what he'd wanted to believe was all a fantasy.

'There's a manhole in the road outside. Chuff was measuring how far the manhole is from the front of The Peacock. Then he was going back to his computer to pass on the information to whoever. That's where they're going to put the bomb. The lorries from the farm have to come this way, and when they pass over it the bomb will be triggered.'

'How?' asked Michael.

'I didn't stay around Chuff long enough to find out.'

'There's more,' Michael told Archie. 'Part of the message on Chuff's screen included the name Amanda Frater.'

'Amanda! You think she's involved?'

'I think she might be running it,' Polly said.

'So do I, now,' said Michael, 'especially as she's been hanging around the village a lot lately. She was in the car park last night.'

'And in the pub,' added Polly.

'To be honest, the talk has been that she's spending so much time down here because she fancies you, Mr Biddell.'

'It could be that she's been seeing her father,' said Polly.

'She never used to come down much,' Michael put in. 'I don't see why her father's suddenly so high on her list of priorities.'

'He's getting higher on mine,' said Archie. 'And it's not out of affection.'

He thought for a moment. As he was about to speak, the door of the pub opened and Arthur Friend shuffled in.

'Muck on your boots,' said Michael to him.

'Been up to see the cows,' said Arthur in a sad voice.

'I'm sorry. I know Mr Archie said I was to stay away from the place till it was all sorted. But they're my friends, those cows. I can't just turn my back on 'em.' He swallowed hard and turned to Archie. 'I see there's a cow missing. Shot her?' Archie nodded. 'Damned shame. She was a good 'un, you know. Her grandmother was part of the herd in my day. Damned good old cow. Pity.'

'Get a pint for Mr Friend please, Polly,' said Archie.

'Any idea what this illness might be? Have you any clue, sir? Is it that mad cow disease again?' asked Arthur.

'Probably. There's tests to be done but we're pretty certain. It's not good news anyway.'

'Is there any cure?' he asked.

'Only the bullet. The final cure, so to speak,' replied Michael, quietly.

'What! Shoot 'em all? Like they did last time, and burn 'em? Oh, you can't, not again. It would be terrible. All those lovely cows. Not again.'

'I think it has to be faced that, one way or another, these cows are going to die,' Archie explained. 'It may be Mr Pember who deals the fatal blow, or it might come as a result of disease. But the harsh fact of the matter is that we had better start saying goodbye to that herd of cows, Arthur. Go and sit by the fire. I'll send you over another pint.'

He went, head bowed, to sit by the fire where the baron of beef was sizzling on the spit.

'He's a funny old boy,' said Polly. 'I watch him every time and the first thing he does when he comes in to the pub is to go and stand by the lump of beef. It's as if he's saying his prayers. He'll take this bad, will old Arthur, if anything happens to the cows.'

'Polly,' Archie pleaded. 'I want you to do one more thing for me. I think you've been very brave so far, and that what you have discovered may well save a lot of lives, here and elsewhere. Do you still have lines of communication to Chuff?' She nodded.

'Too close for comfort,' muttered Michael.

'Then make it clear to him that you have overheard a conversation in this pub to the effect that a convoy of lorries carrying cattle will be leaving the farm on Thursday night. That gives us three days to get organised. It will be going past the pub at precisely ten o'clock at night, tell him. A big delivery, mostly of animals for slaughter. They'll be fat bullocks, ready for killing, just as they would be if they were bound for the supermarket.

'And don't say anything about the cows. We'll keep that to ourselves for the moment. Just get the message across that this will be a consignment of healthy beef cattle. Tell him that, and let's hope he passes the message on. And if that bloody Frater girl appears in the village again, I want to know.'

The clock struck 7 as Chuff appeared through the door.

'Evenin',' he grunted.

Archie gave Polly a nod, and smiled encouragingly at her. She pulled a pint and went over to sit next to Chuff who had chosen the dominoes table.

'Shall I stay to make sure she's all right?' asked Michael.

'She's managed so far,' replied Archie. But seeing the deeply worried look on the vet's face, said, 'Yeah, you'd better stay. Never know what help she might need.'

Shortly after Archie left the pub, Arthur Friend rose unsteadily from his chair, placed his empty glass on the bar, courteously thanked Polly for the beer and shuffled towards the door. Michael shouted good night, but Arthur did not appear to hear. Worried, Michael watched him through the window as he made his way uncertainly to his bicycle which was lying against the wall. He usually used a chain to secure it, but Michael noticed that this time he had not bothered.

'He looks as though he's in a daze,' Michael remarked. When he got no response he looked round and found Polly had gone.

Arthur Friend pedalled uncertainly homewards, his course more erratic than usual. He abandoned his bicycle by the front gate rather than putting it safely in the shed, and for the first time in his life did not remove his boots before sitting by the fire. It was nearly out anyway. Only the slightest hint of dull orange showed amongst the grey embers. He could have revived it with sticks and newspaper, and normally would have done, but nothing mattered now except the cows. He was convinced they were going to die and could not bear the thought.

He fell into the chair and gazed sightlessly into the distance. He had failed the cows again, he thought. Despite what his father's notebook had said, irrespective of the medicines he had given them which he'd felt sure would guarantee their health, he had again betrayed the cows when they needed him most. Now he had to work out why and devise a remedy.

Despite his careful preparation, perhaps he had got the recipes wrong or muddled them somehow, he thought. He went over to the kitchen dresser where he kept his father's notebook when he was not carrying it with him. He lifted the dark, oak frame which contained a faded photograph of his dad taken while receiving a gold medal at the Royal Show, and reached for the notebook. He took it back to the chair and started to read it again, attending to every word, looking for any clues as to where he had gone wrong. He knew the book contained the secrets of animal health, his father had told him that. If there was any fault, thought Arthur, it was in his own application of the principles. He read the recipes once again, ticking off in his mind the ingredients that he had mixed from the cork-stoppered brown bottles his father had bequeathed him. 'One dram oil of rodian, 7 drops oil of thyme, 1 dram of corrosive sublimate, 12 grams of black sulphur, 5 drachms tincture of opium'.

He was forced to only one conclusion: if the mixture was not working, not safeguarding the health of the cows, then they were simply not getting enough of it. He was underdosing them, he decided. Having fixed upon that hypothesis, he took a less than scientific approach and made the evidence fit the conclusion he wished to draw. He admitted he had no real idea how much '1 dram' might be, or the precise amount to make '5 drachms' but started to believe his own guesswork and leaped from the chair like a man from whom a great burden had been lifted. He looked at the clock – just after 10. It was getting dark, but not too late if he took a torch.

Exhilarated, he removed stopper after stopper from his father's bottles and, using an empty milk bottle, started to mix more of the potion in double the quantities he had used so far. Acrid vapour crept into the air of the unventilated little kitchen; the wooden table top still bore the scars where drops from his previous attempts had burned the wood. He coughed as the fumes rose, his nose itched, his lips felt as if they were burning. Eventually he realised he would never be able to administer medicine as strong as this to any cow. So he added a little water, but then thought the dilution would only bring him back to where he had started, with medicine that was too weak.

His eye caught a tin of syrup on the kitchen shelf, and he recalled his father's old trick of making animal feed palatable by mixing into it thick, black, sweet molasses. Arthur remembered how, as a boy, he had stuck his finger into the drum of molasses every time he had walked past it in the corner of the old feed house. There was one old cow, he remembered, Blossom, who would never eat green kale. So his father had painstakingly dipped each stalk in molasses for a week till the cow developed an appetite for it. Arthur decided he would try the same trick. He grabbed the tin and prised it open with the end of a teaspoon, poured it into the foul-smelling mixture in the milk bottle, and stirred. He picked up the bottle and held it to the light. It looked no more appetising, but at least the acidic smell was masked. He thought it might do the trick. It was his only chance.

17

Tuesday morning, breakfast at the Manor, and the routine was unaltered; the bacon, the bad temper, Mrs Wilson pointlessly fanning out the mail, Sir Thomas reading out the grain prices.

'Drought in the central states of America,' was the first thing the old man said even before a good morning. He put down *The Times* and looked at Archie who was pacing the room.

'I hope that's sunk in, what I've just said? Drought in the central states of America. Did you hear?'

'What about it? I don't farm in the central states of America.'

'What about it! If there's a drought in America and the harvest is poor, world wheat prices will start to rise. So don't sign any forward contracts just yet. You could lose a small fortune.'

For the first time in four months, Archie had dressed again in army sweater and boots and was marching around the house with a confidence he had not felt since his regimental days.

'Thanks,' was all he said.

His father leaned across the table. 'You've still got Marcus Hastings on board, as a sort of non-executive director. He'll spot that sort of thing.'

'For a *non*-executive, he seems to have done a great deal that the bloody executives don't even know about! For example, I don't seem to remember his consulting me before signing some exclusive supply contract with this new superstore. Did you know anything about it?'

Sir Thomas looked sheepish. 'Rings a bit of a bell.'

'Well, it's going to ring a lot louder soon.'

'It's a damned good deal,' his father insisted. 'Anyway, you

265

were just back home. It was early days. I thought it might be one less thing for you to have to get your head round.'

'Good deal for whom, exactly?' asked Archie.

'Good deal for you, the estate, the people who work for us, the people who shop at Applewhite's, the shareholders . . . It's a good deal all round.'

'Is there not one group you have forgotten in that cosy little list?'

'Who?' replied Sir Thomas, bewildered.

'What about the animals? The ones we rear for them to kill and sell. Where do they stand in this profit and loss account? Or are they so far below the horizon that accountants don't reckon they're worth considering?'

'I have no idea what you mean. You really are strange sometimes, Archie. And why are you wearing those clothes? I thought the army was behind you.'

'One more battle to fight,' declared Archie, and marched across to the window from where he had a clear view of the cow shed. Less than a quarter of a mile separated the smug comfort of his father's lifestyle from the suffering of the herd.

'We've got mad cow disease again,' he announced, turning to face Sir Thomas. 'Nearly every cow's got it. The herd will have to be culled, the factory closed.'

His father dropped the newspaper.

'It's not possible!'

'It's true. I've seen it. The cows are mad. Do you want me to bring one up to the house to show you?'

'I'll ring Marcus,' said Sir Thomas.

'To do what, exactly?'

'To see if we're insured, of course.'

'Oh,' said Archie, 'so long as there's no financial loss, then that's all right, is it? Well, whatever Hastings says, I doubt there's cover from death by bombing.'

'Are you going mad, Archie? Bombs, mad cows . . . What the hell have bombs to do with anything? I don't trust a word you say. I'm going to get Hastings round here to sort this mess out.'

'He *made* this mess, Father. He built this heap of shit which is now about to explode in all our faces in more ways than one. He did the sneaky little deal with Applewhite's which forced Brian Frater to put God knows what into the feed. And he made us the perfect target for animal rights activists who are now in an ideal position to make one big bang and at the same time destroy the reputation of this estate and Applewhite's supermarket. All because of one sneaky little deal, signed and sealed by the greedy hand of Marcus Hastings. So by all means ring him, but I'm not certain he'll have anything of use to say.'

Sir Thomas gave him a look of deep bewilderment. 'Are you sure about this bomb? How could you possibly know?'

'It's a long story,' he replied. 'But let's just say that I'm as sure as I can be.'

'Then we must tell the police.'

'I have,' replied Archie, 'and I've told them what I plan to do. There will be a convoy of lorries leaving here on Thursday night at about ten o'clock, loaded with beef cattle intended for slaughter. We have reason to believe that when the first lorry passes The Peacock, there will be an explosion from a bomb placed down a drain.' He looked at his father whose face was now white, his expression fixed.

'What the hell is the point of that?' asked Sir Thomas. 'It's driving the cattle to their deaths. A waste of good animals. Nothing wrong with them. They'll all be killed.'

'Once mad cow disease is confirmed, as I am sure it will be, everything – cow, calf or beef animal – will be culled anyway. They're all going to die one way or the other.'

'We'll sue, of course, whoever is responsible.'

'Sue ourselves?' Archie suggested. 'That will make for a good court case.'

'We at Biddell's have always farmed in good faith,' his father argued.

'Good faith towards all except the animals. Ask the cows if you've kept faith with them.'

His father did not answer.

'And I shall be driving the first lorry to leave the farm on Thursday night, Father. I have decided that.'

'You will *not*,' Sir Thomas objected. 'If what you say is true, you could be killed.'

'I *shall* drive that first lorry,' Archie insisted. 'I think I know who is behind this, and if they're there on Thursday night, outside The Peacock, I want to be there too.'

'Then I shall come with you. And if it is the end of me, what will it matter?'

'You're an old man, Father,' said Archie, 'and this is no game. These people are deadly serious. I can't take responsibility for your life as well.'

'And what kind of responsibility is it,' asked his father, 'which makes you drive yourself and the cattle to certain death?'

'I have no intention of letting any cattle die by a saboteur's bomb. If they go, they go decently and humanely. Trust me,' pleaded Archie. 'For the first time in your life, trust me. I have no intention of letting down either you or the animals.'

The phone rang. He was already on his feet, pacing the room and planning his next move, so he reached it before Mrs Wilson, who came stumbling in from the kitchen with more toast. Archie pressed the receiver to his ear.

'Yes, good morning, Inspector,' he said. As he listened, his face stiffened and the blood drained from it.

'Thank you,' he said, his voice low. 'If there's anything we can do to help, I'm sure you will call. Sorry I can't oblige with Miss Frater's whereabouts, I've really no idea.' He quietly replaced the receiver and turned to his father.

'Brian Frater has been found dead. It looks like suicide.'

'Poor bugger,' replied Sir Thomas, quietly. 'Money troubles or women?'

'A particular woman, possibly,' replied Archie, thoughtfully.

'Do you think he was involved in this business? Was it *his* feed that was contaminated?'

'It's possible. The first thing the police surveillance team wanted was a list of feed suppliers. I had that faxed to them. He may have received a call already.'

'Must be guilty then,' replied Sir Thomas, dismissively, 'or why would he top himself?'

Ask Marcus Hastings, Archie was about to reply. But he did not think his father would understand.

The police could not contact Amanda Frater to tell her of her father's death. She did not answer the phone in her London flat and her mobile was switched off. This was because it was Tuesday morning and she was to be found in the upstairs room of The Social Chapter, fired by a new enthusiasm for action after her recent confrontation with Archie, and still unaware that her father had died. Conrad, unusually full of energy and enthusiasm, was the first to arrive. The creaking of expensive leather shoe heralded the arrival of Ernest shortly afterwards.

'It's Thursday night for definite,' said Conrad, eager to get the meeting started. 'We can blow the whole bloody lot sky high! I've had confirmation from that Chuff fellow. Apparently a barmaid with a big mouth told him the lot: where the lorries were leaving from, which way they'd go. He was a real find, that guy, for a prat.'

'Details?' snapped Amanda, being businesslike.

'Indeed, details are what we need,' added Ernest. 'My client has asked to be kept fully briefed on any operational matters. He wants to know exactly what he's paying for.'

Conrad rubbed his hands and started to sketch on a piece of paper in the middle of the table. 'There's a manhole cover right outside a pub called The Peacock . . .'

'Before you go any further,' said Amanda, 'don't forget I've met Chuff. He's as thick as pig shit. Can we be sure of what he's telling us?'

'Do you think I'm as thick as shit too, Amanda?' replied Conrad. 'Much as I trust and admire you,' he added, patronisingly, 'I thought I'd check it out for myself. I make quite a good double-glazing salesman, actually.'

'You would,' she muttered.

'People will say anything to get rid of me,' he continued. 'I spent some time talking to that fat landlord at The Peacock, Thwaite or something. He let me measure all his windows, and needless to say I had a good look out of all of them. All it took was five minutes to confirm that this bloke Chuff wasn't as stupid as he sounds. But just to be safe, I had the lads check it out last night.'

'Lads?' said Amanda.

'Yeah, lads. The ones who'll plant the bomb. I told you I had contacts in the right places. Really nice little phuffers these boys make. Bespoke, you could call them. They'll lift that manhole cover and sling it in the air like a kid's toy.'

'I don't understand the timing. How is it fired? Time switch?' she asked.

'Don't be so bloody daft. We don't want it going off without the lorry right over it, do we?'

'So?'

'So,' said Conrad, revelling in his own cleverness, 'just before you come round the bend as you're driving away from Biddell's farm, there's an uphill bit. Quite steep, yeah?' She nodded. 'Well, no lorry with a full load on it could possibly get up that hill without dropping down a gear or two.' Amanda nodded again. 'So, the lads measured how long it takes between that gear change and the time when the lorry drives over the manhole.'

'I don't see,' said Amanda.

'For Christ's sake, even a bloody kid could work this one out! You hear the lorry change gear – it's so bloody noisy you can hear it anywhere in that pub – and thirty-five seconds later it will be over the manhole.'

Amanda took all this in, the torrent of information causing muddy waters to stir and other thoughts to surface; of lorries changing gear, the squeal of brakes, animals bleating, Dover docks, Freddie . . .

'But how do you trigger the bomb?'

'Dead easy,' said Conrad. 'You sit in The Peacock with a thing that looks just like a mobile phone. Press the three numbers which are the detonating code and you've got the best fireworks display you've ever seen. You've got thirty-five seconds' warning because you can't help but hear the gear change. It gives you time to get the mobile phone out and dial the numbers without drawing attention to yourself. You couldn't very well sit there all night, fingers over the buttons, could you?'

Ernest leaned closer to her.

'You noticed he said "you sit in The Peacock". At our last meeting you did say you were going to press the button. You haven't wavered, have you?'

Amanda looked first at Conrad, then at Ernest. Conrad spoke first. In a quiet voice he said, '"I am in earnest. I will not equivocate. I will not excuse. I will not retreat a single inch and I will be heard."' It was the motto Freddie had used when conviction momentarily left him, the words of William Lloyd Garrison.

'I don't want anyone killed,' said Amanda. 'If animals have to die to save other animals, I can accept that. But no human beings.'

'None at all,' Conrad assured her. 'That pub's far enough back to suffer a few broken windows and no more. I dare say there might be one or two cut faces, but it will be a little something to remember us by, won't it?'

Amanda nodded.

'Of course,' added Conrad, 'I can't give any assurances about whoever drives the lorry. Sorry, but they'll have to take their chances like the animals.'

Amanda took in that piece of information and tried not to react. In her mind's eye she had visions of Freddie, dead on the road beneath the lorry, but instead of his face it was Archie's she saw. She blinked, shook her head to clear the thoughts and turned to

Conrad. 'I'm going to disappear, certainly till Thursday afternoon. I want some space. I'll probably check into a hotel some way away. Go and see Dad towards the end of Thursday. In the meantime, I don't want to talk to anyone, understand? How about the bomb? When is that going to be put in place?'

'There already,' said Conrad. 'The lads posed as Telecom workers.'

'Clever,' said Ernest.

'And where will you all be, on Thursday night?' asked Amanda.

'Oh,' said Conrad, grinning, 'I thought I might pop down to the country. Have a quiet drink in a little country pub. They say Woodham Ford's very pretty this time of year. Do you happen to know of a pub which might be laying on a bit of entertainment that night?'

Ernest was looking in his diary and shaking his head.

'Sadly I can't make it to the country on Thursday. Dinner, City chums. Ghastly but one's got to be there. I'm sure my client, your sponsor, will wish me to extend his best wishes.'

'Will we ever know who this sponsor is?' asked Amanda.

'I doubt you ever will,' replied Ernest, closing his leather brief case and making for the door. 'The very best of luck to you, Miss Frater. It has been a real pleasure doing business with you. Goodbye. I doubt we shall meet again, assuming all goes to plan.'

'Might see you, girl, on Thursday night,' added Conrad. She hated being called 'girl'. 'You will ring, won't you? I need to give you the code and confirm the final details.'

She rose from her seat with some difficulty, leg stiff and aching. Ernest shook her hand firmly and wished her the best of luck. Before she could sit down again and gain some relief, Conrad kissed her on the cheek. Closeness to him revolted her. As the two men went down the stairs, Amanda heard them greeting Marge, who was coming the other way.

'Oh, I do like that older one. Such a gentleman,' she said as she came through the door carrying a tray to convey empty coffee mugs back to the kitchen, a filthy rag tucked under her arm with which to wipe the tables.

'Given some thought to what we were saying the other day?' she asked.

'Sorry,' replied Amanda, 'loads of stuff on my mind. What were we talking about?'

'*We* weren't talking about anything,' said Marge. '*I* was telling you how I've seen sensible people like you come here, get silly ideas in their heads and wreck the rest of their lives. It happens so easily.'

'Yeah, so you said,' Amanda replied, indifferently.

'You're not going to take a blind bit of notice, are you?'

'Notice? Notice of what?'

'Wasting my breath,' sighed Marge, gathering empty mugs. 'I'll see you next Tuesday, I dare say. Might have got a bit of sense in your head by then.'

'Oh, no,' said Amanda, 'we're finished with the Tuesday meetings. Thanks, but you might say we've sorted out the problem we were working on.'

Marge shuffled back down the stairs, mugs clanking together, more chips being removed from the rims. Amanda sat alone and quietly seethed.

What right did *he* have, Archie Biddell, to call her father a crook, blame him for inflicting disease and suffering on the cows, when all the time it was the relentless economising of the Biddell Estate that had forced him into the financial corner which led to his actions? She could have happily spat in the Biddells' faces. Rage fuelled her bravado and convinced her that now was the time for them to be taught a lesson.

Yet, moments later, that conviction had evaporated. She had lived with this pendulum of emotion since her first visit to The Social Chapter, and it was no less violent now that she was here for the last time. She swung violently between deep loathing of Archie and all he stood for, towards what she was forced to admit to herself seemed like affection for him. He reminded her of Freddie;

the sparkle, the wit, the way his eyes creased when he smiled. It all suggested that, for the first time in ten years, she might be able to turn her back on the past and face a new future, one which was not haunted by the memory of her dead lover. Instead, she would have real, live Archie.

Then the pendulum swung again and she became disgusted with herself for even thinking of turning her back on Freddie. And she remembered Domino, and decided she hated Archie not only for the loss of that one calf but because of all of the others too. How many farm animals had suffered under generations of Biddells? She saw them all before her eyes; countless calves, just like Domino, stretching back for centuries and equally far into the future, all pleading for Amanda's help. Pain shot the length of her leg and she took a deep breath till it subsided. So, yes, she *would* press the button, she *would* be there on Thursday night. For *them*! She remembered another of Freddie's favourite quotations which had launched them both into a fevered defence of animals and their rights: 'With reasonable men I will reason, with humane men I will plead; but with tyrants I will give no quarter, nor waste arguments where they will certainly be lost.'

She could never forgive Archie Biddell for what happened to Domino. It was unreasonable to expect it of her.

The same afternoon, Arthur Friend was deciding what to wear. He was looking for something he would not be ashamed to be seen in standing at the sturdy oak door of the Manor. Arthur had never been up the tree-lined drive, never dared to knock, never thought that one day he might step inside. To a man as loyal to the Biddell family as Arthur Friend had been, and his father before him, the Manor was a palace, and servants did not knock on monarchs' doors.

If he cast his mind back, thought hard, he had the vaguest recollection of being taken there by his mother when he was barely five, and put amongst the other children from families who worked for the Biddells. It was a Christmas party, but he didn't fit in with the other children and had wandered off on his own and escaped from the servants' quarters. By opening doors and stepping carefully down corridors, he had found his way into the big entrance hall where a log fire blazed as brightly as any he had seen, and a Christmas tree stood so tall that to young Arthur it looked as if it reached all the way to heaven. He heard his mother calling for him, and the butler searching the rooms, but so transfixed was he by this glittering sight that he stood frozen to the spot.

'Lovely, isn't it?' said a deep voice behind him. Normally he would have flinched, but the shimmering Christmas tree had so captivated the boy that the only voices he could hear were the ones inside him saying this was the most wonderful thing he had ever seen.

'Where's your mother? Is she with you?' the voice said, and little Arthur looked round. It was Sir Hubert Biddell, Sir Thomas's father, although Arthur was too young to know it then.

'And what would you like for Christmas, young man?' asked the voice.

'If I could have anything in the world, I'd like a cow,' he said, boldly. 'I would prefer a Dairy Shorthorn if I could, 'cos them's bloody good milkers. My dad said so. And do you know what my dad says as well?'

'Tell me.'

'He says old man Biddell has the best herd o' bloody Shorthorns in the land.'

Sir Hubert smiled.

'Your father knows a thing or two about cows, clearly. He wouldn't be called Mr Friend, would he?'

'Yeah, that's right. Do you know him?'

'You could say so,' said Sir Hubert. 'I think I'll take you back to your mother now. She'll be worried. They said there was a boy lost. You haven't told me why you want a cow for Christmas, have you?'

'I don't know,' said young Arthur, 'there's just something about cows, ain't there?'

'There certainly is,' said Sir Hubert, smiling as he opened the door to the servants' parlour and handed the lad back to his cross mother. Arthur remembered getting a hiding for that. But it was worth it, for next day a brown paper parcel arrived. In it was a wooden model, Arthur's first cow.

And that was his only previous memory of going to the Manor. Now he was taking the bravest steps of his life down the drive. For he had not slept that night. Having given the sickly cows a double dose of his potion in the expectation of their making at least something of a recovery, he was desolate to find that by dawn they were as poorly as ever. He thought they even looked worse. His magic had not worked, his father's wisdom had proved to be false, there was nothing left in the world in which Arthur Friend might trust. Unwilling though he was to discard the instincts of a previous age, he was forced towards the inevitable conclusion that his medicine was worse than false, it was poison. It was then that he had taken a torch and for the first time thoroughly read the smudged labels on the medicine bottles as best he could. He had to admit that some did not contain what, in his initial excitement, he'd thought they did. He could now make out the words lead, copper and mercury. He remembered, years ago, a cow that died from licking lead pipes. Lead was poison, he knew that. But he could not let his father down, nor risk some kind of enquiry where his dad's old notebook and precious collection of bottles might be subjected to inspection by disrespectful detectives.

So he took the bottles to the bottom of the garden, pushed back the brambles and nettles and removed from the ground a weighty paving slab. Beneath the concrete block was the remains of the cottage's dried-up well. One by one, Arthur dropped the bottles down the deep well, counting as far as four before he heard them smash as they hit the bottom. Calmly, he replaced the block and went back into the house, where with tears in his eyes he picked up the oak-framed picture of his father.

'I'm sorry, Dad. I tried to be even half the stockman you were, but I let you down. And the cows too. I'm very sorry.'

He picked up the notebook, which until then had been the most precious thing in his life, and took it over to the fireplace. With a groan, he knelt before the grate, dropped the notebook into it and reached into his pocket for a match. 'I didn't mean no harm. I thought it was what you would have wanted, Dad.' He applied the match to the paper and watched till the last of it was burned through.

Sir Thomas was standing by the drawing-room window, bathed in afternoon sun, watching Arthur make his way slowly up the hill.

'There's some old chap coming up to the house. A bit of a tramp. Looks half dead to be honest.'

Archie walked across to the window.

'That's Arthur Friend,' he explained, irritated by his father's lack of recognition. 'He was your stockman for thirty years, actually, and his father before him. He's very upset about the cows.'

'Yes, the cows,' said Sir Thomas vaguely, and shuffled off, muttering, 'Friend? The name rings a bell.'

Arthur was out of breath, his heart pounding in his wheezing chest as he summoned the courage to raise the large brass knocker on the door. Archie beat him to it and opened the door at the same moment as Arthur reached out.

'Come in, Arthur. Nice to see you.'

He was taken by surprise. 'Oh, I won't come in, sir. Not my place. It was just a word I wanted.'

'I insist,' said Archie. 'The doorstep is no place for a conversation.'

Arthur stepped in and remembered to wipe his feet. He took a moment to look up and around. 'It was over there, sir, the Christmas tree,' he said, with a smile on his face. 'That's where it was. I remember.'

'Then it's some years since you were last here, Arthur. It's never been there in my time.'

'No, it's your grandfather's I'm talking about.'

'Come into the sitting room,' said Archie.

'I don't know if I . . .'

'Come on,' he insisted. 'Mrs Wilson will get us tea.'

'I couldn't have tea, not from Mrs Wilson. Wouldn't be proper, her to be serving me. I've always known my place.'

'Your place is as my guest, Arthur. Shall we say that she's serving me, and you just happen to be joining in? Will that make it easier for you?'

Arthur smiled. 'If you say so, sir.'

'Is it the cows you've come about?'

'Bless 'em, I'm afraid it is. It's what I heard last night . . . that they'll all have to be shot and burnt, like the last time?'

'There's no alternative,' said Archie. 'If they've got mad cow disease again, they'll have to go. It's the law now.'

Mrs Wilson appeared.

'Hello, Arthur. Don't see you up here too often. Dare say you'd like some tea? I was just making some for Sir Thomas. He's on the phone talking to Mr Hastings. Pretty worked up he was. He'll be ready for his tea.'

'Come through and sit down,' Archie said to Arthur.

He dropped into an armchair, so soft that he wondered if he would ever get out of it. His fingers felt the fineness of the red velvet upholstery.

'Is there anything to be done about the cows, sir? Can't we save 'em?'

'It's simply the law,' Archie replied. 'All hell will break loose if every cow isn't culled. You see, they can't risk another epidemic of mad cow disease, or another of the human version.' He dropped his voice. 'We all know how many died in that.'

'Very hard, sir, I understand that. But isn't there nothing that we can do?'

'Nothing, Arthur. There's still no cure because there's still no certainty where it comes from. Last time it was thought to be caused by infected feed. It may be so this time too. Unfortunately, the man who manufactures our feed is no longer around to tell us precisely what went into it. But I suspect the feed myself.'

'Yes, poor Mr Frater,' said Arthur. 'They're talking about it in the village. Said it was money troubles.' He paused respectfully and chose his next words very carefully.

'What if I were to tell you that I don't think it's mad cow disease?'

'I would ask you how you could possibly know? It's a job for the biologists now – examining brain tissue, and analysing it.'

'But they won't find anything if they do.'

'You don't know that,' replied Archie. 'Anyway, what's the point in speculating? The beasts have all got the symptoms of mad cow disease, they'll all have to be killed before the tests can be done. I'm as sad about it as you, Arthur, but there's no other way. The cows *will* have to die.'

'It's *not* mad cow disease,' he said, emphatically.

'Arthur, *please*.'

'I know it's not mad cow disease.' He took a deep breath and gathered his courage. 'Because what they're suffering from is due to what I have given them. I've been poisoning 'em. Not deliberate, of course. This is all my stupid fault, mucking about with my dad's old remedies, and his bottles and potions. I gave them all manner of stuff. Every day I went up to that barn and gave them something out of my dad's little book that I'd mixed up at home. He left a lot of stuff, you see, when he died. Boxes of various things. And I couldn't just throw them away, couldn't do it. So I gave 'em to the cows. Thought it would do 'em good.'

'But why?' asked Archie, in disbelief.

'Because they're lovely animals, sir, and I didn't want to see them go the same way as the last herd. I never trusted all these modern medicines and so I thought I'd give them something proper in their food, like m'old dad did. I went up every night, just after that miserable bugger Tomlinson had gone to the pub to drink himself silly instead of staying with his herd. Then I used to sprinkle stuff along the troughs. All manner of things there were. Powders and liquids my dad had stored away for years. I mixed 'em all up.

'I honestly thought they would do 'em good. I did, sir. But when they started to get sick, I doubled the dose and they just got worse. That's what made me decide it was me that was makin' 'em sickly. So don't have 'em shot, sir. It's not mad cow disease, I'm convinced.'

'Can you remember the names of the things you gave them?' asked Archie.

'There was extract of belladonna, I remember that. Nitrate of potash was another. There was acetate of lead, copper something, and mercury something else.'

'Lead, mercury . . .?' gasped Archie.

'Then there was some tree bark that came from Peru. I used to crumble that and give them it on Sunday, for a bit of a treat. They loved that. And of course there was that stuff called opium. Father always told me to be careful with that. There's lots I've given 'em. Didn't want them to go the same way as the others.'

Archie looked at Arthur, said nothing but merely smiled.

'I think that this is the sweetest thing I've ever heard, Arthur. It must have taken hours for you to sit down and dream up this tale. And I know why you're doing it. It's to save the cows. Bless you for that. But it's mad cow disease all right. Much as I would like to think the cows were high on home-made drugs, it just doesn't add up.'

'It's *not* mad cow disease,' Arthur insisted. 'There's no need for those beasts to die.'

'Can you prove it, that you gave the cows this mixture made to an old recipe?'

'I think I can, sir,' replied Arthur. Before Archie had time to quiz him any further, Sir Thomas burst angrily through the door and did not notice Arthur sunk deep into his chair.

'Bloody Hastings,' stormed Sir Thomas. 'Behaving very oddly. I think everyone's gone mad round here!'

'Father,' said Archie, 'may I introduce Mr Friend?' Arthur tried to get to his feet but the chair held him captive.

'How do you do?' said Sir Thomas, offhand. 'Seen you somewhere before, haven't I? Something to do with the cows, wasn't it?'

'That's right, sir. Presented me with a watch when I retired as head cowman.'

'Yes, of course,' said Sir Thomas. 'Anyway,' he turned back to Archie, 'I told Hastings about this mad cow business, and tried to ask him what the insurance position would be, and do you know, he didn't sound in the slightest bit interested? Kept saying over and over again that it would all be sorted out by Friday morning at the latest. Then he . . .'

Archie interrupted. 'He said what?'

'Said what? Who? What are you talking about?'

'What was it Hastings said, precisely?' asked Archie.

'He said it would all be sorted out by Friday morning at the latest.'

Archie turned to Arthur Friend.

'Excuse me, I'm going to have to go. Rather a lot on my plate at the moment. Lots happening over the next couple of days. Thanks for coming, and I think it's just marvellous how much you love those cows, I really do.'

His father left the room muttering that everyone on the estate was mad. Archie was about to follow him when Arthur held up one finger and said, quietly and with great determination, 'I can prove it. Prove those cows do not have mad cow disease, and that whatever is wrong with them is not due to anything in their feed. It wasn't what they ate, it was what I gave them. If I can *prove* it to you, sir, show you with your own two eyes, might you believe me and stop them from shooting those beasts?'

'Arthur, I *am* very busy.'

'It would take half an hour, sir, if we went in your truck. Just half an hour. Those cows have got to be worth that, haven't they?'

Archie had little choice other than to agree. He pulled Arthur out of his seat and Mrs Wilson, who was bringing a pot of tea and toasted teacakes, was surprised and somewhat put out to see the front door closing behind them.

'If you don't mind, sir, I'll give the directions,' shouted Arthur, trying to keep up with Archie as he strode down the front path to where one of the estate pick-ups was parked.

'Half an hour at the most,' cried Archie as the truck sped away from the Manor.

After fifteen minutes in which they had driven across unmown meadows, through decrepit oak gates which looked as though they had remained closed for years, and down lanes where no other vehicle was to be seen, Archie, who had been silent till now, turned to Arthur. 'Is this some kind of mystery tour? These are parts of the estate I don't think I've ever seen before. Where the bloody hell are we?'

Arthur smiled. 'Just follow my directions, if you'd be so good, sir.' The pick-up clattered down rutted tracks, bounced through ditches and along lanes so deserted that a strip of grass had grown down the middle, undisturbed by any vehicle. Archie thought he knew every inch of this estate, believed he had wandered every corner of it when he was a boy, but this was new to him. They forked right, as Arthur instructed, and the trees on either side of the track started to thicken till they were now in the middle of woodland.

'Lovely, isn't it, down here?' said Arthur.

'Bumpy, I'd say,' replied Archie, his head occasionally making contact with the roof of the cab as they bounced along the unmade tracks. 'Considering it's my estate, I have to admit to being completely lost.'

'You would be, because what people don't realise, and you've probably forgotten, is that down the middle of this old woodland runs a valley. If you look straight across, as you might if you were looking at it from the Manor, you'd never know it was there. It used to get a lot of visitors in foxhunting days, before they banned it. Now there's no reason to bother coming. A bit too far out of the way, really.'

'Arthur, this is a lovely ride out, and I am truly shamed by my ignorance of the estate, but what have we come to see?'

'Just a bit further, sir, you'll come out of the trees and there'll be a gate. Pull up there.'

The truck went over the final rut and had hardly come to a halt before Arthur opened the door and jumped out, overcome with excitement.

'Lovely bit of forest,' remarked Archie, casting his eye over ancient oaks and beech trees. Then he spotted in the distance an open area of grass, the vivid blues and yellows of wild flowers swaying to the breeze amongst tall, rough grass.

'You're right,' he said, 'it's like a secret world down here.'

'That's exactly why I chose it,' replied Arthur.

'For what, exactly?'

'You'll see, sir.' He started to make his way through the grass, stumbling occasionally as his foot hit a clump of tough, unyielding cocksfoot, or squelching where he came upon a damp and boggy bit.

'Lovely grass. There a little stream runs down the far side, keeps it sweet and watered.'

'Arthur, sorry but . . .' Archie was becoming impatient. 'It's all very pretty and I'm grateful to you for showing it to me, but . . .'

'Ssshh,' hissed Arthur. 'Don't move. Keep quiet. I mean, *please* keep quiet, sir.'

Arthur took ten paces forward to distance himself from Archie and cupped his hands round his mouth.

'Come on. Come here, my little beauty,' he shouted. Anxiously he looked to right and left, then behind him. 'She's somewhere here. I know she is. Come, come.' It was not a crude call, thought Archie, as a mother might summon a wayward child, but more of an invitation; for there was an unspoken element of 'come to me, it is safe, nothing will harm you' in the way Arthur formed the words. It was animal talk.

His eyes suddenly widened and he pointed to the far corner of the field, his extended finger shaking with excitement.

'Over there, sir. Look!'

'Can't see anything,' replied Archie, eyes straining to follow.

'You will. Just stand still. You'll frighten her if you're not careful. Only used to me, see?' Arthur gave a soft low whistle. 'Come to me, my lovely. Come to me.'

Archie's eyes were fixed on the far corner of the field where he saw something moving. At a distance it looked white or perhaps grey, possibly dappled; it was too far away to be certain. It could have been the beating wings of an owl, or a sheet of plastic, or a pigeon. Arthur called again. Slowly it approached and Archie could now see it was a four-legged animal, black and white, not grey at all. Soon, its bovine form became clear as Arthur willed it towards them.

'It's a calf,' cried Archie.

'Please,' hissed Arthur. 'If she sees two of us, she might take fright. Never seen two people together, she hasn't. Not since she were born, anyway.'

'What the hell is a calf doing down here all on its own?' whispered Archie. 'Why isn't it with the herd?'

'Come on, darling, come to your old dad,' murmured Arthur, and left Archie standing alone while he crept forward in carefully measured steps to meet it halfway. Then he stopped, the calf ten yards from him.

'She's got to take the final steps herself,' whispered Arthur. 'If I go towards her now, she'll run.'

The calf did not budge, her bulging eyes focussed first on Arthur. Then she spotted Archie and scampered a few steps backwards in fright. But she was as curious as she was timid, and slowly retraced her forward steps. And then she stopped, eyes wide and deep, anxious breaths emerging like gusts of wind from her nose.

Arthur took a bottle from his pocket and read the label – oil of cloves. He sprinkled a little of the contents on his hand and rubbed it well in. He held the anointed hand in front of the calf and together they started to walk slowly forward.

'Oil of cloves,' murmured Arthur. 'It's the only one of them recipes of my old dad's I still trust.'

'That cow's going to follow you. It's going to follow you!' declared Archie, when Arthur had finally brought the calf all the way to where he was standing. 'But it doesn't prove anything at all. It's just a nervous calf. Three or four months old, I'd guess. I can't see what point you're trying to make. What can I say, Arthur? I'm sorry, but I can't waste any more time.'

Archie turned towards the truck but Arthur grabbed him tightly by the arm and swung him round to face the calf.

'Beggin' your pardon sir, but you *have* to spend just another moment or two. Take a long, hard look at this calf and tell me if there's anything about her that might be familiar.'

Archie scanned the black and white calf. It was quite young. Its eyes bright, muzzle moist and its coat carried the glossy bloom of good health.

'Can't see anything wrong with it at all,' said Archie, perplexed.

'You're lookin' in the wrong place,' replied Arthur. 'Stand back a bit and tell me what you see.'

Archie stepped back, and half closed his eyes. Suddenly, with great excitement, he shouted, 'I'm seeing spots before my eyes. I really am!' The young cow frisked on hearing his raised voice. 'Domino!' he gasped. 'It's *Domino*, isn't it?'

Arthur beamed, and nodded.

'No doubt about it,' said Archie, as excited as if a long-lost relative had returned from the dead. 'Domino,' he cooed. 'Those spots, the dots along her neck and down her side . . . they're so unusual they couldn't belong to any other animal. It really *is* Domino.' He turned towards Arthur who was gently caressing Domino's face with one hand, while the other was being licked by the coarse tongue of the calf, now intent on tasting the oil of cloves.

285

'But Domino's dead. I saw her dead in the straw, the night Tomlinson died. Surely that was Domino? You said you thought it was, yourself.'

'Well, I may have to go to prison . . .' said Arthur, serious now.

'I doubt it,' Archie interrupted. 'But go on?'

'. . . but this was such a dear little calf, such an unusual one, and seeing the way your lady friend was so fond of it, I couldn't let it fall into the hands of that wicked man. I just couldn't bear the thought of another animal being cared for by *him*, especially not this one. So pretty she is, see? So I waited till he was in one of his drunken stews and just took her. That wasn't easy either. I had to get her into a sack, tie the end, and put the whole blinking lot on a wheelbarrow. Too heavy to carry. I put her in my shed overnight, came back first thing and milked some of the colostrum off her mother, and fed her like that from a bottle for several days. Every night I was up there, milking that cow, till she was strong enough to take milk from a bucket. Theft, I suppose it was.'

'You just took her?' Archie said, perplexed.

'I was terrified she would go the same way as all the others and it felt as if it was my duty to protect her. She deserved a bit of respect, that's all. And a proper chance in life.'

'But mad cow disease. I don't see what this proves about that?' Archie pressed.

'It proves that what those sick cows are suffering from is because of what I've given them, and not from what they've eaten. Because Domino here, and the rest of the cows, have all eaten the same. Truth is, you see, I used to take the odd bag of feed for this little darling when no one was looking. So she's had the same food as the rest of them, but none of them medicines of my old dad's.'

'Why not?' asked Archie.

'That's simple. Because she was out here in the open air, not locked up in that stinking barn with the other cows, and not with Tomlinson. I thought she was safe so I didn't give her anything. She's led what I call a proper life for a cow

286

with lots of fresh air and good grass. And she ain't mad, is she?'

'No, but I may be,' said Archie.

'As I tried to explain to you at the house, sir, I wanted only the best for your cows. Just what my old dad would have wanted. I always thought that the reason they caught the mad cow last time was because they needed something they weren't gettin' – like hungry kids used to get rickets in the old days from lack of proper food, understand?'

'But everything they eat is scientifically formulated,' Archie argued.

'I didn't believe in any of that,' replied Arthur. 'I believe the old ways, my dad's ways, were the best.' His voice cracked and he wiped the damp end of his nose on the sleeve of his overcoat. 'It was when I found his old medicine box that I started to mix up some of his recipes. I thought it would do the cows good. It was only last night, when the cows became more sickly and when I doubled the dose to try and make them better, that I realised I was wrong. Then I remembered Domino down here, and it all clicked. It wasn't medicine I was givin' 'em, it was *poison*.'

Arthur took a deep, trembling breath.

'And Domino?'

'I never gave her any dose of anything, 'cos she was here, safe, away from those vets and Tomlinson, as I said.'

'And if you stopped dosing the cows,' Archie's mind was in overdrive, 'as I hope you have, do you think they would recover?'

'I'm no vet,' replied Arthur, shaking his head.

'Right,' declared Archie. 'The first thing we have to do is get Domino examined to ensure she has no symptoms of any kind. That's the first step. Then we get the Ministry to remove the culling order and instead check for heavy metals, and then . . .'

'There's one more thing that I'm just a bit worried about,' added Arthur, quietly. 'It's Eric Thwaite, at The Peacock. I might have poisoned 'im as well.'

'What?' exploded Archie.

'You see,' Arthur explained, 'when we was kids, I remember my old Dad sometimes, in the long winter evenings, he used to put on what he called his firework display just to keep us amused. He used to get a little of the stuff out of those bottles of his, less than a half a teaspoon. And then he told us all to stand back from the fire and he chucked it over the hot coals. Lovely colours it made, really brightened up a drab winter night. Course, we loved it. All different colours he could make, all the colours of the rainbow; bright yellow if it was sodium something or other, green if there was any copper in it. The best of all was anything with magnesium because that gave a clear, bright light, as strong as daylight. He went on throwing the stuff on the fire as long as he dare, before mother came in from the kitchen and complained.'

'So?' asked Archie, impatiently.

'So, when I'd dosed the cows and found there was a bit of something left in the bottle, I waited till I got to the pub, stood by the fire and waited till no one was looking, and sprinkled it over the flames. A reminder of the old days, really. Brought it all back to me, just like being a kid again. Trouble is . . .' Arthur clenched his lips together and looked at Archie, '. . . I can't be certain none of the powder didn't fall on that blasted lump o' beef that was always roasting in front of the fire. Never worried, see? Never guessed it would do anybody any harm.'

'But no one else got ill Arthur. No customers at the Peacock, as far as I know – except Eric Thwaite!'

'I've worked that one out as well, sir. You see, it's Thwaite's own fault for being such a greedy bugger. That old sod was always cutting himself a slice, wasn't he, *from the outside*? Stuffing himself with it. Every day, sometimes twice. If anybody got a dose of them powders, it was him. I dare say he'll get over it if he stops eating the beef.'

'If it doesn't kill him first,' added Archie, 'which would, I suspect, leave you open to a charge of manslaughter. Add to that the damage you have caused to the herd, in particular the one cow we have had to shoot already, and if I had any sense my next step should be towards the telephone, and calling the police.'

Arthur's eyes became watery, his shoulders slumped, his head dropped.

'But I shall not, for the moment. I want you to do something for me first.' He noticed the dispirited look on Arthur's face, and reached out, grabbing Arthur by the shoulder and shaking him in a friendly way.

'Arthur, it was a mistake not a crime. A foolish mistake and a dangerous one. But you acted with the very best of intentions. If the cows recover, and Thwaite improves as well, there's no reason this should go any further.'

'I'm grateful, sir,' mumbled Arthur.

'Then you can show it. Do you think you can bring Domino up to the farm by Thursday afternoon?'

'Day after tomorrow? I don't see why not,' replied Arthur.

'As crimes go, yours may yet turn out to be insignificant compared with other atrocities taking place on this estate. I've got to go. Arthur, thank you.' Archie shook him by the hand. 'Is there any of your potion on the beef that's being cooked at The Peacock at the moment?'

'As it happens, I didn't have any left over last time. So no, there isn't, I'm pleased to say.'

'Then that's one less thing to sort out. Get into the truck and hold tight. I've got to move fast.'

Arthur patted Domino on the flank, then the nose, and she skittered off to the far side of the meadow. Archie watched her as she scampered away.

'That calf may yet save the lives of the herd. Thank you, Domino,' he murmured. Then he turned to Arthur. 'And thank *you*, too.'

Archie drove Arthur back to the village and then went as fast as he could back to the Manor. There he made three telephone calls. One was to Michael Pember, telling him to halt the slaughter of the cows. The second call was to the police, and was a direct result of something his father had said earlier that day, which had worried Archie deeply. Within the hour, the police had returned his call confirming his fears. It was then that he decided the Thursday night convoy of lorries would leave on time and drive past The Peacock at precisely 10 o'clock.

18

Until late on Thursday afternoon, Amanda had been in hiding, discreetly booked into a bed and breakfast on the opposite side of St Edwich to Woodham Ford, where she hoped she would neither be recognised nor remembered. Not wishing to be disturbed, she had discarded her mobile phone, and had not even bothered to use the pay-phone in the hall to check for messages on her answering machine in case the inquisitive landlady might suspect she was something other than the student of church architecture she was pretending to be. So as to arouse no suspicion, she had even read history books and reluctantly eaten bacon for breakfast despite seeing the *Biddell's Best Bacon Rashers* packet lying on the kitchen table. In between, she had thought a lot about Freddie. Once, in a heavy disguise of overcoat with turned-up collar and wearing spectacles which she hardly needed, she had hired a taxi and taken a ride through Woodham Ford and past The Peacock, to remind herself of the details.

At 3 o'clock she came out of hiding, her resolve undiminished. She went to the phone box in the market square and called Conrad on his mobile number, twice dropping the coins in her nervousness. She thought he sounded relaxed and somewhat smug, compared with the tightness of her own voice. She asked for the three-figure code she would have to dial to detonate the bomb. It was 7–6–2; the first three digits of Freddie's old telephone number. She shivered.

'I chose them 'specially,' said Conrad, 'so you wouldn't forget.'

'And where's the special phone? The one I have to use?'

'Get to The Peacock by nine,' he replied, 'and Chuff will bump into you accidentally in the car park. It's a small thing. He'll drop it into your pocket.'

'Is the convoy still going through at ten? No change of plan?' she asked, praying it had not been delayed, certain her nerve would not last much longer. Her leg twinged and she leaned against a corner of the phone box to take the weight off it.

'According to Chuff, it's all as planned,' replied Conrad.

'Ten o'clock, then,' she repeated. 'No change.' She said a hasty goodbye and the receiver was halfway to the hook when she heard Conrad's voice again and put it back to her ear.

'Before you go . . .' she noticed a lowering of his tone '. . . if I don't see you again, I want you to know that Freddie would have been proud of you. And I am too. You've got guts, Amanda, real guts. 'Bye, love.' And he blew her a kiss.

Amanda drove to Woodham Ford thinking she might have tea at her father's, arrive at The Peacock just before 9, rendezvous with Chuff, then take a window seat from where she could hear the approaching lorries. As she drove, she imagined the newspaper headlines; how the CFFA would claim responsibility for putting an end to the activities of one of the vilest farming families in Britain. They would say it was a huge victory, and while undeniably sad that animals had to die in the process, they were the real heroes who had died in a valiant cause. She decided not to issue the statement that night, straight after the bombing, but let the papers build up a head of speculation and then claim their attention. She had no more doubts about it now, it was the right thing to do. She gave a passing thought to Archie, how devastated he would be, the hurt it would undoubtedly cause him. But she knew she had to do it.

She turned into the yard at Frater's Mill and sensed straight away that something was wrong. There was only one car parked in the yard. No lorries. Not a sound, no movement, no bustle. The hoppers were closed, the grain elevators still. Power-cut, or something, she assumed, trying against all the evidence to imagine an innocent explanation. The door of the other car opened. She saw it was a young policeman. He adjusted his cap and walked towards her, his face grim.

'Miss Frater?' he asked as she wound down the window. She nodded.

'We tried as best we could to get hold of you, miss.'

The policeman did not spare her any of the details of her father's death. Brian Frater, only too well aware of the danger and the inevitable consequence of a fall, had deliberately scrambled high on to the top of his largest grain silo and taken one small step into the thousands of tons of grain. It could not have been an accident. Grain, the policeman explained, although solid, behaves like a liquid in large quantities and flows like water. Once Brian had set foot into it, there was no going back. He sank as deep as if he had drowned in an ocean.

Amanda showed no emotion. She looked at the policeman.

'It must have been an accident,' she insisted.

'I'm afraid there was a note,' replied the officer. 'It's at the police station.' He lowered his head. 'But he did send you all his love.'

She refused to bow to grief. Although every gut feeling urged her to collapse in deep despair, instead she thanked the policeman and asked him to help her across to the office. She said she had twisted her ankle.

With her arm across his shoulder, she walked slowly from her car to the office, dragging her left leg a little. The policeman made her tea and asked if there was anyone they could phone to come and sit with her. She declined, and since she appeared composed, sitting at her father's desk, the officer decided she was safe to be left alone.

As the police car left the yard, making the only sound in the silent mill, the fierce heat of shock blasted through the protective ice that Amanda had become so skilled at deploying to distance herself from the real world. But the frost she had first used to deflect the pain of Freddie's loss was insufficient to protect her from this one as well. Alone now, she screamed for her father and implored God to return him to her, throwing back her head, begging aloud, then flinging it forward till her brow was lying on the desk, fists beating against it in frustration, tears flooding across her father's letters. Her flailing hands grabbed anything that came within reach – the pen she had given him for a fiftieth birthday present, the pocket knife she remembered from childhood days. As she lifted her head and raised herself, she felt the pressure of his favourite cushion in her back. After a while, as her eyes began to clear and the weeping started to subside, she focussed on the notes from accountants, final demands from suppliers, threatening letters from the Revenue. Finally, with a shaking hand, she reached for a letter which was headed Biddell Estate, signed by Marcus Hastings, asking for further cuts in feed prices. Amanda guessed this mealy-mouthed letter had been the last straw.

The phone rang but she could not face a conversation. Instead, she switched on the answering machine and stiffened when she heard her dead father speaking, inviting callers to leave a message. She closed her eyes tightly, trying to stem a renewed flow of tears. There was a bleep, then a click, and a voice said, 'It's Archie Biddell. I was just calling to say how sorry I was. This is the only place I can think of to leave a message, Amanda . . .'

She reached for the phone, took a deep breath, collected herself and said, 'Archie, it's me. Sorry, but I couldn't face taking any calls for Dad.'

He expressed his sympathy, offered to do anything he could, made it clear that help would be given by the estate too if she requested it. This made her angry. She fingered the letter from Hastings, knowing that the estate had given no help at all when her father needed it most, only screwed him harder. And here was Archie Biddell offering all the help her father could have asked for, but too late.

She shook her head, trying to rid it of the thought that under different circumstances, had he not been a Biddell, then tonight she needed someone just like Archie, a reincarnation of Freddie into whose arms she could fall for comfort. *If* he had not been a Biddell. A reincarnation of Freddie . . . Her lover reborn . . . It was the first time such a thought had crossed her mind, the only occasion on which she had admitted to herself that he could be another Freddie. Unnerved, she tried to rid her mind's eye of a picture of Archie and replace it with one of her beloved Freddie. But Archie's image would not budge.

'Sorry, Archie. I've got something on tonight,' she replied.

As the church clock struck 9 and the early June dusk was beginning to fall, Archie and his father arrived at the barn. Six large animal transporters, each of which could carry a score of fat beef cattle, were assembled in a neat line; the tanks of Archie Biddell's army. Each lorry, except the first, had one driver up front in the cab while behind them the loading ramps were lowered and men were hauling bales of straw to litter the metal floors of the lorries and prevent cattle from slipping. Archie told them not to bother.

'No loads tonight, lads. Just a bit of straw in the first lorry. That's all. The rest will travel empty,' he shouted. The men looked at him as if he were mad.

'These men should be told the risk they're in,' insisted his father, nervously rubbing his hands. 'It's not fair to put them into any danger like this. They're innocent fellows.'

'If there were *real* danger I would not be asking them,' insisted Archie.

'Well, if there's no danger, there's no bomb,' replied Sir Thomas. 'Stands to reason! So why are we wasting our time when we could all be at home? This is pure fantasy.'

'I agreed you could come along, Father, and ride in the first lorry if you promised to let me get on with it and remain quiet. If you can't keep that promise you can get back in the car and someone will drive you home,' Archie said, sharply. The old man turned away, but he was neither pleased by the way he had been spoken to, nor convinced about anything that was happening.

'Usual run, sir, to the abattoir?' shouted one of the drivers, confused by having been told to drive an empty lorry. 'It's

295

just that the wife wants to know when I'll be back. Said I'd call her.'

'It will all be over just after ten,' replied Archie, confidently.

'Can't be going far then,' joked another of the drivers.

'Far enough,' he replied.

It was 9.05 and Amanda had been standing in the car park of The Peacock for ten minutes, waiting for Chuff. He was late. So as not to be conspicuous, she had dressed – appropriately given the death of her father – in black, and stood in the shadows behind the parked cars hoping the twilight would help her blend into the gloom. But passing cars were beginning to switch on headlights and for her to be suddenly revealed, standing self-consciously in a pub car park would have exactly the opposite effect from the concealment she desired. It was 9.07 and still no Chuff.

Archie glanced at his watch; the old army timepiece, rugged, accurate, an old friend, showed it was 9.15. Forty-five minutes to go. He had done the calculation scores of times in his head but repeated it once more to make sure. If the lorries left the farm at 9.50, he reasoned, they would be passing The Peacock as near to 10 o'clock as would make no difference. He nodded to himself, satisfied.

Arthur Friend, fresh straw falling from his boots as he moved, sidled across the yard. 'Any problem?' asked Archie.

'Good as gold, she was,' said Arthur, and winked.

'Loaded?' Arthur nodded. Archie looked at his watch again. 9.21.

Suddenly, the bright headlights of a car swung across the assembled lorries, highlighting the bemused faces of the drivers who were standing by their cabs, arms crossed, waiting for orders. The car came to a sharp halt, gravel flying from its rear wheels as it skidded. It was an agitated Michael Pember who emerged and sprinted across the yard without either switching off the engine or closing the car door behind him.

'War broken out?' enquired Archie, smiling. 'Are my troops needed elsewhere? Or have you brought peace in our time?'

'It could be, it just could be that the old boy's right. It could be heavy metal poisoning,' Michael gasped.

'Ah, then it may be a peace of sorts,' remarked Archie.

'I've got the results of the tests,' Michael continued. 'Preliminary results anyway. It's early for a full analysis but there are traces of some highly toxic heavy metals in those animals. They've been given some very dangerous stuff indeed. Whoever gave that to those cows had a very sick mind.'

Arthur Friend was within earshot.

'I don't think they were *given* that stuff,' said Archie. 'I've been thinking it over, ever since the idea of poisoning crossed my mind. It will never be proved one way or another, but I reckon there must be contamination of some kind. Might be some old paint or something the cows licked, or something somebody dumped in the field where they were grazing. You know what cows are for licking anything. Anyway, I went up to see them before I came here and they seem much better. Certainly not a hundred per cent yet, but on the mend, I'm sure. I don't think there'll need to be much of an investigation.' He saw out of the corner of his eye that Arthur had bowed his head, unable to meet his eye.

'Funny,' said Michael, 'but I looked at the cows earlier and I thought they looked better too. I think they'll certainly cancel the culling. But I still think there'll *have* to be some kind of investigation,' he insisted. 'You see, I've heard a rumour that Chuff's mother had high lead and mercury levels in her blood when she died. Chuff spoke to the doctor after the tests came back from the post-mortem. He was going on about it in the pub. Now, if she got the poisoning the same place the cows did, it could be in the water or the air. Something will have to be done. A full investigation's certain.'

Arthur give a slight, mournful shake of his head.

'Much of a beef eater, was she?' asked Archie, casually, trying not to arouse suspicion. 'Ever see her eating beef at The Peacock, for example?'

'Only what old Thwaite used to slip her under the counter,' Michael replied. 'But what's that got to do with anything?' Archie swiftly changed the subject.

'Do you know much about lead or mercury poisoning?'

'Cows usually get it from licking old lead pipes. Not certain about mercury. But the vapour's the most dangerous thing as far as humans are concerned.'

'Vapour?' asked Archie.

'Mercury and lead compounds give off vapour and when you breathe them in, that's when they start to do the damage. You get a slow build up, you see, and the symptoms just get worse over a period of time.'

'What about cows?

'Same, I guess,' replied Pember. 'But if the early analysis is to be believed, these cows had had far more than they could breathe. They must have been having the stuff by the spoonful.'

'How's Eric?' Archie asked, casually.

'Miserable as ever,' replied Michael, impatiently. 'But to hell with him. Are you going to send the lorries? Are you?'

'No. Not *send* . . . I'm going to lead them.'

'But you heard what Polly had to say, what they planned to do. It's suicide!'

'It would be murder then if I sent anyone else to do it, wouldn't it?' replied Archie. 'Anyway, too much of the dirty work has been done by other people round here. Time the Biddell family got their hands mucky for a change.

'Time to get on board,' he shouted across the yard, then turned to Arthur and said softly, 'You're in the back, of course.'

Arthur coughed nervously. 'Er, what about, you know . . .?'

'Put him in the back with you,' replied Archie, gesturing to a figure lurking in the shadows, who, on seeing Archie nod in his direction, joined Arthur in the back of the cattle lorry.

'Coming for the ride, Michael?' Archie asked. 'It might make a man of you.'

'Or mincemeat,' he replied, then jumped without hesitation into the cab.

'Michael, you'd better move that car of yours first before my lorries turn it into a crushed sardine tin,' said Archie, grinning broadly.

It was 9.30, and for a Thursday evening The Peacock was unusually quiet. Eric Thwaite was not on duty but lying down, recovering from a dizzy spell, although insisting he was feeling much better. Polly was there, pacing the empty bar, polishing the glasses for the umpteenth time, filling the dogs' water bowls at least three times an hour, watching the clock, wondering what was going to happen at 10 o'clock when the lorries came over the hill.

Amanda took a deep gulp of air and pushed open the door of The Peacock. Polly took a deep breath too when she saw her, knowing exactly why she was here but under firm instructions to do nothing unusual. Amanda looked around, hoping that in the corner might be Chuff with the vital detonator – the mobile phone lookalike on which she would dial 7–6–2. Time was running out.

'Good evening,' she said to Polly. 'May I ask if Chuff has been in?' She tried hard to convey indifference.

'Very sorry to hear about your father,' said Polly, purposely not replying to her question. 'We didn't see much of him. Kept himself to himself. But everyone in the village is very sad.'

'Just a tonic water please,' said Amanda, not responding to Polly's sympathy. 'Er, did you say if Chuff had been in or not?'

'Fire's lit, if you want to sit over there.'

Amanda, already sweating slightly, looked across at the fireplace; saw the baron of beef spinning slowly above the hot flames. She hated the sight of roasting meat. It disgusted her. Then she thought of the cows in the lorries. Wouldn't they feel pain, being burned alive?

'I'll sit near the window.' She took her glass of tonic water and walked over as best she could.

299

'You look as though you've had a nasty fall,' remarked Polly, noticing the severity of Amanda's limp.

'Old injury,' she replied. 'Playing me up these last few days. Don't know why.' She peered through the window and satisfied herself she could see the manhole, and, more importantly, the brow of the hill over which the lorries would come. She looked at her watch; it was 9.47 and there was still no sign of Chuff. He *will* be here, she told herself, arriving with the detonator just in time. Conrad would not have trusted him, she believed, if he had not been certain the lad was up to the job.

9.49. 'Off we go! Wagons roll! Army advance!' shouted Archie confidently across the yard of Home Farm. The drivers churned their diesel engines till they burst into life, filling the yard with noxious blue smoke and a raucous din that caused all the sleeping pigs to waken and grunt in a displeased chorus. 'Archie,' said Sir Thomas, 'if you don't want to go through with this . . .' Archie clenched the steering wheel of the lorry as tightly as he could.

'Shut up!' he barked through firmly clenched teeth, and taking one hand away from the steering wheel, released the hand brake and put the lorry into gear. He gave Michael a look as if to tell him that if he wanted to get out, this was the moment.

'Let's go,' shouted Michael with boyish enthusiasm, and fastened his seat belt – a redundant precaution under the circumstances. There was a fearsome sound of hissing as the air brakes of all the lorries were released, sending the nearby pigs into a further frenzy. Then they rolled forward, following Archie to Woodham Ford.

9.57. Amanda stood up, helpless. Soon she would be hearing the roar of the approaching lorries, the revving as they changed gear to tackle the hill. But still she had no detonator; no way to fire the bomb. Polly watched as, in near panic, crying out in agony as she banged her leg against the tables and chairs, Amanda searched the entire ground floor of The Peacock in case Chuff was asleep in a corner somewhere. There was no sign of him. She sat down again by the window and decided the plan must have changed. There'd be a different kind of bomb, perhaps. And Conrad had not been able to contact her to tell her! Yes, that was what must have happened, she convinced herself. Sighing deeply with relief, she realised she would not have to press the button after all – it would happen of its own accord.

A minute to go and the convoy came to the dip in the road, just about to change down to second gear to give them enough power to get to the brow of the hill. It was then downhill to The Peacock. Archie revved the engine loudly so there could be no mistake – the lorries were coming. 'Oh, my dear God, what are we doing?' muttered Sir Thomas. Michael remained pale but resolute. He looked at Archie who appeared unnervingly relaxed.

Amanda heard the distinctive roar of the approaching engines as they changed gear to tackle the hill. She closed her eyes, not certain what would happen, watching the headlights appear over the brow of the hill. Now it was all downhill towards The Peacock, she reckoned, and the manhole. Then, the church clock struck 10. Silence, apart from the approaching lorries. Amanda stood and looked out of the window, counting the chimes. By the third, still nothing. On the sixth stroke of the bell, she felt a hand on her shoulder, and turned.

'Please don't look so anxious,' said the elderly man standing next to her. 'We have both been made to look foolish tonight. I don't think there'll be anything to see out of that window.'

'Get off me,' she demanded, pushing his hand from her shoulder and turning again towards the window, watching first the manhole and then the wheels of the leading lorry. She counted another chime. It was the eighth, or perhaps the ninth. The lorry was now in full view, on the crest of the hill, its headlights beaming towards The Peacock, dazzling her briefly. She screwed up her eyes as she peered through the window. Then seeing Archie at the wheel of the leading lorry brought home to her for the first time that he was going to die and she was part of the killing.

'Stop him,' she screamed. 'Someone save him. He's driving the bloody lorry! Don't let him die.'

She stared through the window at the face behind the wheel, and for a moment she believed it to be Freddie. The images switched rapidly in her mind, first Freddie then Archie. They had become the same person, she loved them both.

She braced herself for an explosion as the final stroke of 10 chimed across the village. But there was none.

The elderly man took hold of her trembling body and eased her into a chair, away from the window. 'My name is Hastings,' he said. 'Marcus Hastings. You may not know this but I have been your rather foolish sponsor.'

From behind the bar emerged two police officers.

'I think we've met before, Miss Frater,' said the first. 'I was the officer who was waiting for you at your father's mill, to break the news. You might say I was doing two jobs at once. The other was keeping an eye on you.' The officer turned to Hastings.

The leading lorry came to a halt just short of the manhole. Archie switched off the engine and passed word down the line to the other drivers to cut theirs. The silence was sudden and stifling. He walked to the front of the lorry and with great precision stood astride the manhole cover. Then he shouted, 'Amanda! Amanda Frater. Come and look. I'm in your sights. Can you see?'

Inside The Peacock, she heard his shout echo around the quiet village. Lights were switched on, curtains pulled back, front doors opened as curiosity drew villagers away from their television screens.

'I am prepared to die with my animals, Amanda,' bellowed Archie. The policeman took her by the elbow and guided her to the door. The other officer clasped Hastings by the arm. 'Force won't be necessary,' he said, wiping his nose on his handkerchief. 'Just tell me where you would like me to go.'

Michael jumped down from the cab, panting like an excited dog.

'You've got some bottle,' he said to Archie, 'driving right up to it, and then standing over it like that.'

'I don't think so. Safest place in Woodham Ford tonight, right over that manhole.'

There was a pained noise from behind them. Sir Thomas was trying to get down the high step from the cab. Michael reached out to help him.

'Is that it?' asked the old man. 'Where's this bomb supposed to be? Will no one explain what the hell is going on?'

Marcus Hastings appeared first in the doorway of The Peacock, a policeman by his side.

'Somebody's got some sense round here at least. Marcus had the wits to get himself some police protection. Which is more than we bothered to do. Marcus!' he shouted. 'Good evening. Brave fellow for turning out. Well done!'

Archie leaned across to his father. 'When I explain exactly what's going on here, you will see that Marcus is possibly the least sensible person here tonight, or perhaps a close second to Amanda Frater.'

'Rubbish,' said his father.

Hastings came slowly across to where Archie and Sir Thomas were standing, leaning more heavily on his stick than usual. He looked Sir Thomas in the eye, as best he could.

'This is not the way I would have wanted any of this to turn out,' said Hastings.

'No one hurt, jolly good outcome as far as I can see,' replied Sir Thomas, bewildered.

'Not quite,' said Archie as he stared at Hastings. 'You will find it difficult to believe,' he said, turning to his father, 'but this whole bomb-planting charade has been funded by our erstwhile colleague Mr Hastings. Hasn't it?'

'You're crazy,' muttered Sir Thomas.

Hastings, head drooping, depending on the policeman for

support, nodded. 'It *is* true Thomas. He's right. But I had no idea they were planning bombs and things like that. All I ever wanted was a spot of disruption, for life to be made difficult. When the police, alerted by Archie, rang me last night and told me there was a plan to place bombs in the village, I tried to put a halt to it. This is all my fault.'

Sir Thomas, still unconvinced, said, 'This can't be anything to do with you, all this silliness. Tell me, Marcus. The truth.'

'It *was* me, Thomas. I did it out of love, not just for you but for this estate. I never thought you would retire. I thought the old days would go on forever with you and me in charge, making the estate into something even bigger and better. And then I heard your son planned to return home and take control, and I knew things would move on. I was afraid of being left behind.' He looked at Archie.

'Of course, I was a fool. It all went wrong and I shall pay twice for my mistakes. Once with my reputation, and secondly from my pocket. Sorry, Thomas, but I believed that what I was doing was right.'

Sir Thomas, dazed, leaned back against the body of the lorry, shaking his head slowly. 'What didn't work? What's Marcus on about? Is that policeman taking him home?'

Archie took a step closer to his father. 'Let me explain. When he first heard of your plans, he decided it was better to have no estate rather than one run by me. So he hired what he thought was a gang of animal rights saboteurs to do his dirty work for him. He was paying them, he believed, to set up an animal rights group, their first target being this estate.' He turned to face Hastings. 'Do you know how I realised this?' The old man shook his head.

'When Father rang to tell you about the culling of the cows, and you said, "It will all be sorted out by Friday morning." I thought that was a far from typical reaction. In the old days, you would have instantly brought in lawyers, vets, insurance assessors. Instead, you washed your hands of it because you knew the devastation planned for the night before would make it all irrelevant. By then, of course, I knew of the CFFA's plans for Thursday night. It didn't need Sherlock Holmes to put the two together.'

Sir Thomas's face hardened and he paled visibly. He sagged against the lorry till he came to rest on the step.

'Marcus, I don't know what to say,' he gasped.

'I did it out of love,' said Hastings, barely holding back tears. 'This was our place, we built it together. *He* would have destroyed it.' He gave Archie a glance of hatred.

'Strange thing is,' continued Archie, 'if you hadn't made that casual remark, I might never have connected you with the so-called Campaign for the Freedom of Farm Animals. But I've known about them for a little while. I was always curious as to why they should pick on this place. Now we know.' He paused before saying, 'Have you been in contact with the CFFA lately?'

'You know I've bloody well *tried*,' spat Hastings.

'But with little success, I guess,' replied Archie, 'because there *is* no CFFA, is there? There never was. The police confirmed that when I first alerted them. They checked every scrap of animal rights intelligence they had, but there was no CFFA. You were conned. It looked proper and convincing, with its magazine and Web page. But a kid can turn out that sort of thing on a computer. There were only six copies of the CFFA magazine, and three were sent to Chuff because they had the good fortune to stumble across him. They didn't really expect any response to their silly Web page, but when he contacted them they must have thought all their Christmases had come at once. How much did you pay them? Quarter of a million, was it? Isn't that a reasonable guess?'

Hastings did not deny it.

'Well, I would have thought a man of your skills would have chosen his investments more carefully and not signed cheques to someone called Ernest Manners whom you'd never met. A *con-man*, that's all he was.'

'You seem to know a great deal. I wonder how?' said Hastings.

'Shall we play a little game?' replied Archie. 'A school playground game? Shall we call it Tiggy Hopscotch? Does that name ring a bell?'

'Bloody woman,' said Hastings, under his breath.

'On the contrary,' replied Archie, 'she is the true victor tonight. She brought down her loathsome, greedy husband by shaming him at his moment of supposed triumph and put a stop to you by telling me every detail of her meetings with Ernest and Conrad. And, of course, Miss Amanda Frater.

'It appears Tiggy Hopscotch is the only one amongst you with sense to realise that there is no difference between the destructive ways of the so-called Campaign for the Freedom of Farm Animals, and the equally repulsive excesses of intensive animal farming. She worked out that the two weren't on opposite sides of the fence but, in fact, no better than each other. They both stink. That was why she came to see me, after her husband had made a complete fool of himself in front of the dying cow. Of course, she knew nothing about the bomb idea. I got that from Chuff.'

'I thought that lad was on our side,' muttered Hastings.

'Let's say I made him an offer he couldn't refuse. And leave it like that for the moment.'

'I thought I could trust Ernest and his friends,' said Hastings. 'They were recommended.'

'And I have no doubt they are at this very moment drinking your health in some foreign resort. You see, the police believe they left the country several days ago. That's why you couldn't get hold of them unless you had the mobile number they gave to Miss Frater.'

The policeman squeezed Hastings's arm and nudged him forward towards the open door of the police car. Sir Thomas, still sitting on the step of the cab, watched in disbelief as his old friend was led ignominiously away.

Michael started to walk towards the pub. His progress was halted by Polly rushing to meet him, arms outstretched.

'Michael, my Michael! My brave Michael!' She flung her arms tightly round him, pressed herself close against him, and hugged him fiercely.

'Not *brave*. Not as plucky as you,' he insisted, pushing her back a little so he could look into her eyes. 'If it hadn't been for you questioning Chuff . . . we'll say no more. But *that* was a courageous thing to do.'

'But, my darling Michael, none of that compares with what you just did, riding on that lorry, facing death like a hero.'

'I don't know about hero,' he said, bashfully. 'Anyway, before this gets out of hand, we'd better get Sir Thomas into the pub.'

'That's my Michael,' said Polly, beaming. 'Always putting others first.' And she gave him a brief kiss so brimming with love and affection that he almost fainted.

'Polly?' he asked, diffidently. 'Might we see a bit more of each other? And I don't mean across the bar. Perhaps we could go out for a meal, just you and me?'

She smiled. 'As long as it's not that place in St Edwich again.' And she burst into fits of laughter. It was too much of a temptation for Michael. He grabbed her again, pulled her towards him and gave her the deepest, most heartfelt kiss he had ever given a woman in his life.

'Polly,' he said. 'Don't laugh, but I think I love you.'

'I'm not laughing,' she replied, serious now. 'Because I think I love you, too.'

Amanda Frater appeared in the doorway of the pub, walked out of the shadows and into the pool of light spilled by the headlights of Archie's lorry. Stumbling, face creasing at every twinge of pain from her leg, she made her way very slowly towards him, her body trembling in the chilly night air but her head lifted defiantly high. The cab doors of each lorry opened and the drivers jumped down and formed a circle round Archie and Amanda. They thought they were owed an explanation too.

'Is there anything in you that wants to say sorry?' asked Archie when she was finally standing in front of him.

'All I'm sorry about is that my father is dead, because of you and your bloody estate. I'm sorry that Freddie . . .' her voice cracked as she spoke his name, '. . . that Freddie died under the wheels of a lorry full of farm animals. That's what I'm sorry about. *You* have never known what it is to lose someone you loved deeply.'

'Have I not?' replied Archie, ignoring the cruel remark. 'I have some news for you, Amanda,' he continued. 'There was no mad cow disease after all.'

'No disease?' she said, surprised.

'None. It was something else. The cows will recover completely.'

'So my father did not infect your cows with anything?'

'I apologise for suggesting that. It looks as though he didn't.'

'So why is he dead?' she shrieked. 'Why is *he* in a coffin and not you?'

'I am still here for one very simple reason. Because there was no Campaign for the Freedom of Farm Animals, and no bomb either. Ask Hastings over there.'

'Crap!' spat Amanda.

'It was all a con-trick to extract money from Hastings, cooked up between Ernest Manners and his mate Conrad. Ernest Manners was the mastermind. As soon as Hastings first made contact with him six months ago, he spotted what a misguided sucker he'd hooked, and how easy it would be to get money out of him. Hastings was so obsessed with pulling the rug from under my feet, his fixation blinded him to everything else. Obsession can do that, can't it, Amanda? Conrad was brought in to lend credibility because of his old working knowledge of animal rights, and you were the final piece in the jigsaw. You were their major piece of good luck. That and finding Chuff. You make a pretty pair, if I may say so. Without all that nonsense about the manhole and the bomb, Ernest and Conrad would never have got Hastings to sign the final, massive cheque. As far as your father was concerned . . .'

Amanda stopped him. 'It was that bloody letter from *your* estate, demanding cuts he could not make. *That's* what killed my father. Don't try and make excuses.'

'And who signed that letter?' asked Archie. 'Wasn't it Marcus

Hastings, your paymaster? Could it be that the cuts were not to keep the estate in profit, but to boost his own pocket *and* pay the fat bills the CFFA would be sending him? Think again about who is responsible for your father's death. You might also give some thought as to how much you, personally, were costing your father too.'

'I think we had better go,' suggested the police officer, walking slowly towards Amanda.

'Not quite yet,' insisted Archie. He turned to one of the drivers and said, 'Open up my lorry, Ted! The rear gates, please, and put the light on in there.' There was a rumble as the heavy tail gate fell to the ground.

'I want you to come and see, and look, and learn,' said Archie, reaching out a hand to her. She clasped it, part of her wishing she could hold it for ever, the rest of her resenting the fact she needed his help. She leaned heavily on him, followed him round to the rear of the lorry. There, haloed in a feeble glow, was a calf; a young black and white creature nestling in the golden straw, its wide eyes blinking. Holding it by a rope halter, stroking it, calming it, was Arthur, its best friend – its only *true* friend.

'Don't worry, my girl,' cooed Arthur, and the calf seemed to understand.

Amanda stared at the calf, and after a while she turned to Archie and said, 'Domino? It *is* Domino, isn't it?' She pushed his hand away from her and, unaided, walked slowly up the ramp of the lorry then, in tears, fell into the straw, wrapping her arms round Domino, sobbing. The calf, to Arthur's surprise, did not flinch. Instead she looked at Amanda, lying beside her, and sensing tasty, salty tears, started to lick her face.

'This is real freedom for farm animals,' said Archie. 'Domino *is* freedom. She needed no campaign to save her because she was born with loving attention, given a natural life under the care of someone who appreciates her true value, allowed to live according to natural rules and not those forced upon her by anyone else. In return, she will give us milk and calves; and all she asks in return is for someone to give her needs a second thought. That, Amanda, is what Domino wanted all along, a second thought. All she was going to get was your first thought, which was to blow her sky high. But you have achieved one thing. You have ensured that on this estate there will be no going back to the old ways where the needs of animals counted for nothing. That will be Domino's lasting effect on this farm. And I hope the sight of her has a lasting effect on you.'

After a pause, the policeman asked if Archie was finished. He nodded, shouted to the drivers that it was time to go home, and Amanda was led off the lorry.

Archie shouted one last thing.

'Would Freddie have been proud of you after tonight? Would he have thought a bomb-blasted Domino a fitting tribute?'

She turned, trembling, rage eclipsing distress, and shouted: 'How do you know about Freddie? How dare you even mention his name. Stop it! You know *nothing* about him!'

'Only what Tiggy Hopscotch told me, which is pretty much what you told her. Sorry, Amanda, but if this is what love drives you to, I think we can all count ourselves lucky you have lost the capacity ever to love again.'

Domino flinched and Arthur whispered soothing words to her as, from behind her in the lorry, a figure appeared. It was Chuff.

'Hey, Amanda,' he shouted, 'I'm sorry. But I had to tell 'em.'

'Useless bastard!' spat Amanda.

'He'd have been useless when you had finished with him, Amanda,' said Archie. '*Useless* after being an accomplice in your madcap little scheme. But I have no doubt the court will be lenient with him, when I tell them I've offered him a job on the estate, working with the cows. Arthur is going to teach him how to treat cows properly, aren't you Arthur?'

Arthur nodded.

'We need animal rights people on our side,' added Archie, 'not against us. All Chuff needs is a direction in life. The only steer you were going to give him was down into the pits.'

Chuff looked at Domino, then at Arthur. 'Can I stroke her?' he asked and pushed his hand forward towards her nose. The calf stiffened.

'Not like that!' insisted Arthur. 'Bring your hand up slowly, like *that*, give her time to think and focus. You've got a lot to learn, lad. But I'll teach you. I feel I owe you that, what with your mother dead and gone.' Arthur gave a guilty glance in Archie's direction.

The last thing Amanda heard before the police car drove away was the revving of lorry engines, the hissing of brakes, the grinding of rubber tyres on gravel. She put her hands to her ears. 'Freddie!' she screamed, so loudly that even placid Domino stirred.

In The Peacock, Sir Thomas was enjoying a large whisky, Polly was staring lovingly at Michael and he was enjoying himself more than he had ever dreamed possible. Archie came and pulled up a stool by the bar.

Down the stairs came Eric, wrapped in his dressing gown, and looking grumpy.

'What the hell's all the fuss about?' He looked out of the window and saw Domino being led by Arthur across the front lawn.

'One of your bloody cows is on my lawn, Mr Biddell,' he said indignantly.

'That's Domino,' said Archie, 'she's what you might call a touch special. She's earned a mouthful or two of grass tonight, even if it is from your lawn. Let's just call her a special guest and you can put the grass on my bill. How about that?'

'Do you know?' said Eric. 'I'm feeling a lot better. Haven't had one of those turns for days. I fancy a good slice of beef. Look at it there by the fire. Have you ever seen such a glorious piece of beef in your life? Magnificent! No one does a bit of beef like we do at The Peacock.'

And then he picked up the carving knife and steel and swished them with the flourish of a magician till the blade was fearsomely sharp. He slid it down the flank of the roasting beef, the smoothness of the meat causing the knife to squeal as he cut through it.

This time Archie did not flinch.

'And a bit for you, sir?' said Eric.

He smiled.

'Yes, I will. I think I can face it now. And make it a good slice too.'